PENGUIN BOOKS
A Breed of Women

Fiona Kidman was born in 1940 and grew up in North-
land, New Zealand. She worked first as a librarian and
later as a columnist and critic and as a writer for television and radio. She is married to Ian, has two grown-
up children and lives in Wellington. She currently works
as a freelance writer.

Fiona Kidman is the author of three collections of
verse, a collection of short stories (*Mrs Dixon and
Friend*) and four novels: *A Breed of Women* (1979),
Mandarin Summer (1981), *Paddy's Puzzle* (1983) and
The Book of Secrets (1987). Her work has been included
in a number of anthologies and she has been shortlisted
three times for the New Zealand Book Awards.

A BREED OF WOMEN

Fiona Kidman

PENGUIN BOOKS

Penguin Books (N.Z.) Ltd, 182–190 Wairau Road,
Auckland 10, New Zealand
Penguin Books Ltd, 27 Wrights Lane, London W8 5TZ
(Publishing & Editorial)
and Harmondsworth, Middlesex, England (Distribution & Warehouse)
Viking Penguin Inc., 40 West 23rd Street, New York,
New York 10010, U.S.A.
Penguin Books Australia Ltd, Ringwood, Victoria, Australia
Penguin Books Canada Limited, 2801 John Street, Markham,
Ontario, Canada L3R 1B4

First published by Harper and Row 1979
Published in Penguin Books 1988
Copyright © Fiona Kidman, 1979

Printed in Hong Kong

For my children Joanna and Giles

For generous encouragement and practical assistance in the preparation of this book, thanks are due to the following: Ian Kidman, Ray Richards, Joyce Laurenson, Leigh Minnett, Marilyn Misken, and the staff of the Reference Room at the General Assembly Library.

Grateful acknowledgement is also made to D. Davies & Co, for permission to quote from *The Twilight Time*.

The author is grateful for the assistance of the New Zealand Literary Fund, who provided a grant while she was writing this book.

1978

1978

1

Harriet woke that morning full of fantasies, because the sun was shining. It was an unexpected gift — the worst had been promised for the day, sleet, hail, southerly winds, yet here it was amazingly shining and bright. This is the day I stop drinking, she told herself, today I shall lose weight, be better understood by my lover and by my husband; today I shall undertake something new and significant in my life.

And then the wind turned, and the cold began again; there were deep blue shadows on the hills soon after noon, and it had to be acknowledged that it was indeed winter. She was sad. The summer had been so splendid, one of the best she had known in years, but somehow autumn had dissipated all its promise. It would have been good to resurrect something of the season, just to save some passing joy that one could look back on, and say that was the autumn of 1978. But it would not be so.

She felt absurdly naive and gauche all of a sudden; the day before, she had spoken to Michael on the phone, and he often made her feel like this. When they were in a restaurant together she would feel suddenly clumsy, as if she might make a mistake with the cutlery, or do something silly and embarrassing. She had never had trouble with her knives and forks before.

But then she had never had a young lover either. She was clever with older men. For years they had been grateful that a younger woman would take trouble over them and she had flattered them by her presence. Often she had told herself that she would never have a younger man — they were silly and immature. Now she was grateful and yearning and obsessed, and this had reduced her to a tender helplessness; she longed to ask him if she pleased him, but her pride stopped her.

Yesterday's phone call had again made her vulnerable and awkward. He had phoned her. It was good to be able to say that he had phoned, because it reinstated her. The truth was that she had rung him first, but he'd been busy; there were always people around him. He had asked if he could ring back in half an hour and when she had said yes, she had waited by the phone. It had rung on the half hour, for he was punctilious, courteous and totally reliable about the things he said he would do. It was just that now he said less often that he would do anything at all. She would tell whoever was interested that he had rung her to say goodbye, that he wouldn't be able to see her before he went abroad, and that she should take very good care of herself while he was away; it would be some months before he would be able to see her.

But she knew, she knew, that she had made the first move once again. Girls telephoned her son; it seemed that all the girls rang the boys nowadays and it was quite the teen, and pre-teen, thing. Her generation would never have done it.

She did, though. She rang Michael on absurb pretexts, and waited, sick, for his voice, passing through his firm's switchboard, through his secretary's cool and measured tones. She said 'Hullo, Michael, it's me, Harriet', and he would sound pleased, warm, but moderate, and she would find herself being sarcastic and cooler, indifferent and harsh. He rings me, she said, and I'm cruel to him, I don't know why. But she did know. It was because she had behaved like her teenage children, and rung him, and he had had to ring back, and she had thought of the summer, when he used to ring her on his own initiative. That was how she came to feel so silly.

This time had been different, though, because he really was going to be away all winter. She really had said goodbye to him, and there was no knowing whether she would see him again in the spring, or the summer to follow. He had said that she would, and

2

because he was reliable she believed him, but there was still the winter to get through on her own.

As she lay awake in the darkness on the night before the sun, her husband woke beside her and said, 'I'll always look after you'. She was at once cold with fear, and she lay there wondering what to say to him, certain that he must know something of the dark inner life she contained within herself. Had he heard her talking to Michael? Could someone have told him? She lay by his side, hands clenched in panic, certain that some frightening and committing conversation was about to ensue. But he rolled over and began to snore; whatever dream had awakened him seemed to have receded.

When the day dawned with cloudless skies and not a breath of wind, she was thankful and thought, this is a rebirth. I am about to begin again. When he returns I will be different, self-contained, able to cope as I have always done.

The cold struck, she poured a sherry and watched the sky grow dark.

Harriet could not remember when her awakening began, probably when she and her family started their migration from north to south.

The early years in the far north had been waking dreams, which sometimes turned to nightmare. She had been a wild impetuous child, clever and ungainly among children who were apparently just the opposite. Looking back, she guessed that many of those who had seemed stupid might have been quite bright; certainly they had a higher survival rate than she did. They were all friends with each other, whereas she was always an outsider. She spoke so much better than they did; her parents, particularly her father, were so correct in their use of words that she could not have failed to master the language of her teachers better than the others did. At the time, she was scornful of their disadvantages, and, for years after, she was ashamed at her arrogance. When she came top in spelling test after spelling test, answered every question and got all her English comprehension right, her teachers held the others' efforts up to ridicule. Justice outside the classroom was swift, non-violent, and, she realised later, more subtle than anything she could possibly have contrived. She was the target for well-placed taunts about her appearance, her lack of co-ordination and her accent, which sounded out of place and affected. The others had simply to imitate her voice and she would start to crumble.

She would try to say 'foine noight' to please them, and they would rock with delight. When she went home after school, she would be so confused that she would say, 'foine noight' to her parents, and they would laugh as hard. Her father would go around saying, 'Foine noight, did you know it was a foine noight tonoight, Mary?' to her mother, who would dutifully say, 'no, but it moight be a narce day termorrer', and her father would slap his side and keep repeating the joke all through their evening meal, until bedtime. Then he would change his tune, launching into a sharp broadside about how Harriet had the advantages of a good background and must not let the side down, and that she should always remember that she was of good British stock. Neither way could she win.

And when the kids were in full cry after her at school, all the pent-up misery and frustration that she dared not betray at home would come out, and in a few minutes she would be a screaming hysterical creature, wild-eyed and kicking. Then a teacher would be summoned, and the same teacher who had praised her earlier would drag her to the equipment shed and lock her in, 'to cool off'. There she would rage and shriek and shout imprecations at her tormentors, all of whom would stand outside, quietly murmuring and not answering back, so that she knew they were still there. Their timing was perfect, their behaviour beyond reproach — it was she who railed and cried.

When it was over, she would go back to the classroom, exhausted and dreary. For days she would try to hide that she knew the answers to questions, to be quiet and dull and not to do better than anyone else. But it was no good; in the end she would be unable to contain herself any longer and the answers would out, the arguments pour forth, fast and convincing.

By the time she was twelve, the teacher at the small school hated her as much as the children did. She knew more than he did — she defeated him again and again with her logic. He joined the subtle game of baiting her, telling her that if she did not behave herself, if she was arrogant, as her comments were now interpreted, she would be reported to her father. It was a time of terror.

In her last term at the school a relieving teacher came; the headmaster who normally taught the standard six children took another class. The new teacher greeted Harriet as though she were someone special, some rare being — not odd, not different, but someone whose company he could enjoy.

Together they would sit and talk — in the lunch hour, after school, while she was waiting for the bus — whenever they could. Yet at the same time he sensed her need to be private, not to make an exhibition of herself in front of the others. He would not draw her out in front of them, saving that for when they were alone. He lent her books, and they talked about them when she had read them, sometimes disagreeing, and each always recognising the point the other was making, weighing it up, casting it aside if it didn't work, reshaping it if it had merit. For a few weeks, Harriet was happier than she had ever been.

He was a tired, middle-aged man, who had once been handsome. There were whispers that he had gone up north to get away from some domestic trouble. At first the other pupils respected Harriet's new-found friendship and the quiet way in which she now handled the classroom situation, but when they realised that the teacher was ignoring them in favour of her, they began to torment her again. The girls took to haunting the conversations she and the teacher had, hanging round in cloakrooms and corridors, trying to overhear, or to catch the man's eye when he came out, for they all found him attractive.

Finally one afternoon, he said to her, exasperated, 'Harriet, where can we get away from this mob?'

After a moment's hesitation, she said, 'There's the equipment shed.' It would be good to go back to her old jail as a free agent.

'Right, let's get away from this crowd. I want you to read some

5

Shelley. I think he's important for you.'

Together they went to the equipment shed, and the afternoon sun poked gold fingers through the cobwebs in the window while he read aloud to her. For once she didn't hear the murmers of the kids outside, reminding her that they were there. She heard nothing at all but the words and his voice, until the headmaster opened the door.

The teacher left the district the following day and she never saw him again. The police came to the house and asked her questions. Her parents asked her questions, too — none of them made sense. Her mother took her aside and, in a strained faltering whisper, pointed to parts of her body and asked if the teacher had touched her there. The idea was so absurd that Harriet laughed wildly.

Her mother grasped the table for support, and tried to tell her how serious the situation was. She asked Harriet what they had talked about.

'The Epipsychidion,' Harriet told her.

The police and her mother and father held a consultation about it. Her father, who considered himself a well-educated man 'self-educated, you understand', hadn't heard of the subject. The policeman said it sounded remarkably like a fancy name for you-know-what.

The headmaster came to the house. They told him that the teacher had talked to her about her epipsychidion. The headmaster looked suitably distressed, and volunteered to look it up in the school's only dictionary.

Out of habit Harriet put up her hand to speak to him. Nobody took any notice of her at all.

Just as he was about to leave, she blurted out, 'Please, sir.' Everyone stood electrified, her mother pale at the revelation that was about to be made.

'Yes, Harriet?' said the headmaster.

'Please sir, it wasn't *my* epipsychidion,' said Harriet. 'It was Shelley's.'

The headmaster looked as though he wanted to strike her. She guessed she had probably embarrassed him by knowing too much

6

again. She was sent to her room, where she stood with her ear pressed against the door. There were mutters about 'no charges being laid', the headmaster said rather too loudly that 'the fellow would be got rid of', and Harriet knew she had done something dreadful to the man who'd made her so happy for the last three months. Something was said about it being a good idea for Harriet to be taught a few facts of life, and her mother said in a painful, careful way that she would see to the matter.

In bed that night, Harriet cried herself to sleep wondering how she could tell her friend how sorry she was if she had got him into trouble. She determined to learn the whole of *The Ancient Mariner* at the weekend as a surprise present for him. But he left, and she never had the chance.

A few days later, her mother discussed 'certain matters' with her, and when Harriet persisted with questions about things that didn't add up, she was told to 'go and watch the ducks and she would be sure to learn something'. As Harriet had long ago watched ducks, she was quite sure that the matter held no further interest for her. If that was all there was to sex, down in the mud full of droppings, she didn't want to know about it. Looking as if she wanted to cry at this stage, her mother reminded her that she would probably have to use the curious-looking bandages that were being kept in a drawer for her very soon now. Harriet asked how she should put them on; they seemed too short to wind around her, and wouldn't this mysterious issue of blood that was supposed to emerge slip down her legs? Her mother was too embarrassed to answer.

The school year was nearly over, and Harriet saw it out quietly. She responded neither in class nor outside it, and the kids soon gave up trying to draw her. It seemed that in some way they knew that anything they could do to her would be no worse than what had already happened. Harriet felt that they were sorry for something they had done, but if they were, she could not apply herself to working out what it was.

When the term ended, she and her parents moved to a remote valley further south, called Ohaka.

Harriet had been loading the trucks for an hour preparatory to

7

departure when she realised that something was wrong. Her dress was too short, and made of thin cotton and in the front was a tiny stain of blood.

She searched her hands for cuts, but there were none that she could see. Next she examined her legs, and with growing horror realised that the time had come; there was a small trickle of blood down the inside of her leg.

'Mary, Mary,' shouted her father. 'Up higher, put it on the top.'

'I'm trying, Gerald,' her mother replied, perched precariously on the edge of the truck's tray, and holding a chair above her head.

Harriet looked at her cautiously. To her astonishment she saw her mother, unable to wipe her face, suck a trail of mucus from her nose down to her top lip with her bottom one. Harriet had never seen her cry before. At least, that's what she thought her mother was doing, though the tears were being whipped away in the wind; only the tell-tale undignified dribble from her nose told Harriet that she really had been crying. With a dull ache for her mother she wondered whether the prospect of another change to another small, hard farm was more than she could bear.

It did not seem an auspicious moment to relay the information that she had just received admission to the sisterhood of women.

She knew that the bandages would have been packed, and she would have to extract them somehow. With everything now piled on the truck, it was hard to work out which case they might be in. A mental stocktaking added up to the possibility that they were with her mother's underwear, which was in one of the first boxes that had gone on the truck. There was no way that her father would agree to any unpacking — besides, what possible convincing explanation could she give?

When you had your periods, all sorts of taboos had to be observed, apparently. One should not go swimming, take a bath or run fast races — not that this was a problem for Harriet. A girl should certainly not let any male know that she was afflicted by this rare and passing malady.

'Mary,' shouted her father. 'The boys'll want a cuppa. Time to put the billy on.' He normally never spoke like this, but he used the colloquialisms to help the Maori workmen understand that they were about to receive the milk of human kindness.

Everyone trooped inside and the trucks were abandoned.

Gingerly Harriet started to climb up over the boxes. To get to the cases at the back, she had to stand on the chicken crate. It was made of thin plywood. Harriet studied it and decided that it would hold; after all, she was small for her age. If she balanced carefully with one foot on the crate and the other on her mother's sewing machine case, the latter would almost certainly balance out her weight.

While she was in this position, just as she had reached the precious suitcase containing her mother's underwear, her father emerged from the house.

'What in the hell d'you think you're doing?' he roared behind her. 'You stupid, thick-skulled, little cow,' he added, as she collapsed through the chicken crate with a shriek. A pullet flew straight out above her head, showering feathers on her, and the birds in the box set up a fearsome cackling. Looking down she saw that she had broken the leg of one of them.

When her father had killed the injured bird and boarded up the crate again, he turned on her and said venomously that it was about time she started to earn her meal ticket. There'd be plenty for her to do on the new farm, he'd see to that. There had been a time when he had thought she had possibilities, that she might go somewhere. After all, look at what he had done for her, leaving behind the old country, and all they held most dear and working themselves to the bone so that she could have a 'decent chance'. (As if, Harriet thought years later, he had analysed his sperm count years before and got on nodding terms with her years prior to her conception.)

And just look where it had got them all. A moron of a daughter who let dirty old men play around with her, a schizophrenic to boot if he could believe half of her reports. A girl, too, which was unjust when one considered that he'd put his life into building up a good farming background for a son. Now it seemed she was a bumbling sneak thief as well.

Harriet stood before this tirade without replying. She'd heard versions of several of the points before, but never delivered with quite such fury. At last he asked, 'What have you done to your leg?'

She looked down at the trickle of blood. 'Scratched it on the chicken crate, I think. When I fell through.'

Gerald Wallace turned away in disgust. 'Go and wash yourself at the tap,' he told her. 'We'll be ready to go soon.'

So it was that Harriet rode to the new farm with the outer edges of her vagina thoroughly packed with a wad of the *New Zealand Herald*.

The day they arrived, she was sitting squeezed up in the cab of the second truck with her mother. After they had been travelling for nearly three hours, the truck in front had slowed down and stopped. Gerald got out of it and came down the road to them. 'That's it, Mary,' he'd said, indicating a clump of bush.

'Where?' asked Harriet's mother, straining her eyes around the hot dry landscape.

'There,' he repeated, pointing. 'That's our boundary line. From here on it's our bit of country. We'll be at the house in a few minutes.'

'Thank you Gerald,' she said bowing her head.

The trucks rolled forward again, and Harriet watched, her eyes darting from her mother's face to the passing landscape. It occurred to her that her father had bought the farm without her mother seeing it. When the purchase had first been announced, it had seemed natural enough, the sort of thing fathers did. Now she was not so sure.

Clouds of dust rose round them. They seemed to be in a valley, a burnt-out bowl dried to a tinder by the bright North Auckland sun. The trees and scrub growing across what Gerald had described as their country looked as if they would pack up and leave if they could. Harriet was glad that she hadn't bothered her mother with other matters and hoped that her father had said nothing about the chicken crate episode. From her mother's distracted air, it seemed that her misdoings were quite the least important thing on her mind.

One last corner and they were at the farmhouse. Nobody had lived in it for some time and the burnt brown grass was up to the window sills. The trucks pulled up, and they all climbed out.

'Well,' said Mary feigning brightness, 'shall we go in?'

'You'll like it,' said Gerald, but even he looked uncertain.

The truck drivers hung back, sensing that this was not their moment. Gerald motioned for Mary to go in; Harriet decided that the invitation included her too.

The house consisted of four small rooms of the same size, each exactly square — the kitchen (a free-standing sink and a coal range), the lounge, as Gerald grandly called it (an open fireplace), her parents' bedroom and her bedroom. At the back was a lean-to containing a copper and a tin bath. They walked around, silently inspecting it.

In the room that was to be hers, Harriet stood and wondered why it seemed different to the others. She looked to the window and outside there was a plum tree, thick and leafy and laden with ripening plums, casting deep cool shadows into her room.

'Oh,' she exclaimed on an indrawn breath. 'Oh, thank you,' she said, inside herself.

She went through to her mother. Gerald had gone outside to supervise the unloading of the trucks. She touched Mary's arm.

'It's better than the last place, Mum.'

'Yes,' said Mary bleakly. 'It's better than the last place.'

'Don't you like it, Mum?'

'It's going to be a lot of work,' said Mary. 'Still, that's what life's all about.' She shook herself briskly. 'I'd better set to.'

'Come and look in my room,' Harriet said.

'It's just the same as mine, isn't it?'

'Just come and look' Harriet urged.

She took Mary in and showed her the plum tree. For a long moment Mary stood there looking at it. For the second time that day, Harriet saw the glint of tears in her mother's eyes.

'Mum ... would you like this room?'

'Oh my dear,' said Mary, 'I'm so glad. So glad for you.'

'I'll help with the work, Mum. Honest I will. I'm older now.'

'Yes, I know you will.'

11

'And I'll try not to make Dad mad at me. And I'll watch that I don't get a ... a colonial accent.'

'You're a good girl,' said Mary.

'Shall I hlep you now?'

'Why don't you go and have a look round?'

'But I really do want to help. And Dad'll think I'm being lazy again.'

That was one of the best and closest moments of the summer between Harriet and her mother. For the rest of the time, Mary was working hard, distracted or fretful when she did think about Harriet, raising her concerns about her possible loneliness, things which seemed impossibly silly in view of the world that was waiting outside.

Mary Wallace worried about her daughter that summer. Here she was, having left her old school without knowing a soul, and the whole summer holidays stretching before her. To Harriet, there seemed no point in explaining to her mother that she had shed the old place like a dirty dress, and that a whole summer on her own was the nicest thing she could imagine. Surely her mother could see that she had been unhappy right through primary.

Still, it was nice that her mother cared. It seemed possible that she had always been an ally, and Harriet simply hadn't noticed. It was odd, this new feeling between her and her mother. She guessed it was to do with the fact that she was now 'a little woman', as her mother put it. She searched diligently through the histories of Amy, Beth, Jo and Meg to see if they could shed any light on the situation, but there seemed to be an entire lack of information about the process by which they arrived at little womenhood.

Her father also seemed to like her considerably less than before, but perhaps she noticed him more.

The farm itself held some unexpected treasures. On that first day, Harriet made some bright and beautiful discoveries.

At first she didn't know where to begin, and for a moment she was engulfed by a blank dark terror that if she went away she would return to nothingness — the trucks would have gone away, her parents would have disappeared, and the house would have vanished, leaving the breeze rippling through a paddock of brown grass. She began to walk timidly down a track leading away from the house, through dusty lawsonianas. In front of it there was a gentle slope. At the bottom she found that she was on the floor of the valley, and it was quite different from the rest of the farm that she had seen so far.

The breeze did ripple through the grass, but what grass! Long and smooth like green silk, dotted with clover in flower, smelling strongly and sweetly, the scent of summer itself. Harriet dropped forward on her knees and spreadeagled out on the grass. Here was a scent, she thought, that she would never forget in all her life.

The sun, hovering on the brink of late afternoon, had become a friend again. The long dusty ride, the pain in her mother's face, her father's early morning anger had all gone away. This was her country all right.

She got to her feet, and started walking again. The flat plain was bounded by a river, dark with shadow, yet clear. Along its edge were thick trees, some native, as well as willows and poplars, hawthorns and wild roses. The hawthorns and roses were thick with flowers and she recognised honeysuckle among them too; its flowers were part of the patterns of fragrance around her.

Harriet was sure she would burst with joy. Only a short distance along the river bank, she came to a half-fallen poplar tree that had re-established its growth after it had fallen, so that it formed a verandah across the river. It was easy to climb up and along it, to a crook formed by a branch and the trunk, a naturally comfortable hollow for a small person to lie and look at the sky through the tangle of leaves and flowers above. There could be no more beautiful place in the world.

Time passed and Harriet had no idea how long she stayed there. At last, when whe realised that she was chilled, she climbed down from her perch. Before she left the river, she waded into it and washed, disposing of the shameful pieces of newspaper under a rock. The bleeding appeared to have almost stopped. She thought then that she would never need the bandages, and that it might spare her mother some worry if she didn't tell her about it at all. It didn't seem absolutely necessary for her to be like everyone else, and it was quite obvious that she was not going to have to endure her illness to the same extent that some women had done, if they needed such a wad of bandage when it happened to them.

When she got back to the house the trucks had gone, and she couldn't see anyone about. For a moment her panic returned; it was as if her vision had come true. In a few minutes, though, she heard voices calling, and realised guiltily that by now her parents would be out looking for her.

Her father sent her to bed early as a punishment for being out late, which was no great hardship, for the day had caught up with her and she was engulfed by the most profound exhaustion. She fell almost immediately into a heavy sleep and woke only when the sun, filtered by the plum tree, broke through her uncurtained window the following morning. A blackbird's singing streamed around her as he hung on the bough of the tree.

Was it a summer of waking or sleeping? It passed like dreams and rarely did the world outside intrude, from then until the beginning of school. Afterwards, when she was older, she sensed that the summer had been a time of wakefulness before the long sleep of conventional life began.

Christmas was always celebrated by her parents in a particularly traditional English manner, neither of them ever having accepted the notion of a colonial Christmas Day. The very idea of cold meat on Christmas was sacrilege. On Christmas Eve, a fire was lit, regardless of the summer heat, and the three of them sat in front of it to sing Christmas carols.

The same ritual was followed this year. The fireplace in 'the lounge' had not been used before, which presented some problems, for birds had been nesting in it since the departure of the previous owners of the farm. Smoke billowed back into the room within a few seconds of the paper being lit and the kindling flaring to light. They all staggered back coughing and gasping. Mary filled a pot of water from the kitchen, and threw it on the fire, which died to a hissing, spitting little flicker.

'Never mind, Dad,' said Harriet, 'we can sing carols without a fire.'

He stood contemplating the situation. 'No,' he decided. 'If we can't put ourselves out for Christmas, I don't reckon life's worth living. You shall have your Christmas, my girl,' he said magnanimously.

Soon he was perched on the roof with a pitchfork in hand. 'Watch out, here it comes,' he cried, and the nest came tumbling out of the sky.

At last the fire was lit, and they gathered around again. 'Right, one, two, three, go,' ordered Gerald. He gathered his reedy tenor together for 'The Holly and the Ivy,' and they dutifully followed him, then it was 'Good King Wenceslas,' and all the time the fire crackled and roared with a life of its own, and the room got hotter and hotter.

'When the snow lay round about, deep and crisp and even,' they carolled on. Harriet began to feel faint. She got up and went to the window. Outside it was still light. They had beaten tracks in the dry grass and it lay broken and untidy about the house. Why were they sitting here in this house, singing about the snow? It made everything seemed so unreal, — perhaps the Christmas story itself was all a myth.

The idea frightened her. Quickly she came back to the fire.

'What's the matter, Harriet?" asked Gerald.

'How do we know it's true, father?' she said, staring at the flames.

'Know what's true?'

'The Christmas story. How can we be sure that it's true?'

Gerald studied his daughter and said, 'It is true.'

'But who says it's true? There's nothing to prove it.'

'It's history. It's in the Bible.'

'But the Bible can't be proved to be truth,' said Harriet. 'The Bible is a collection of beautifully written literature, much of which was handed down by word of mouth amongst illiterate people, till

15

it was finally written down. There's no conclusive proof that it is absolutely accurate.'

Her father's face was terrible. 'Who told you that?'

She wrinkled her forehead. The words had come out so easily, that she must have got them from somewhere. 'I read it,' she said, remembering. 'It was in a book that my teacher gave me last term.' The teacher had not been mentioned since the night the police had called, months before.

Gerald sat very still. His voice was shaking when he spoke again. 'You will forget what you read in that book.'

'I can't forget what I read in books, father. How can I, if you want me to do well at school?'

'Then you will learn to recognise good from evil in your reading.'

'Is it evil?'

'Of course. Harriet, this has gone far enough. Believe me,' and his voice hardened, so that she shrank from it, 'It is the truth because I say it is.'

'Yes, father.' Why hadn't she thought of that? There was no more obvious reason for it to be the truth than that her father had said so. It removed whatever concern she had on the subject. She smiled and relaxed. The fire was dying, and the heat was more tolerable.

She felt as if she had been through the fire and come out the other side. How good it was not to have to wrestle with problems of the mind. There would always be someone to take care of such matters, while she, she would ... do what? Be like her mother? Have children? That meant being married. No, it was all too difficult. Probably she would just spend her life in the bough of a half-fallen poplar alone with the river and the sky, and some wild brown ducks she had seen down at the river. Yes, that would be it, and how beautiful it would be.

'We will have to see to her confirmation this year,' her father was saying to her mother.

In the morning there was cooking to do and preparations to make. Things were a little easier this year, for the farm had no stock. They had only managed to acquire a couple of house cows, and there would not be a sale until the middle of January. While there was much to do on the farm, and both her parents had been hard at work since their arrival mending broken fences and trying to get the cowshed into working order, at least it meant that they need not do any milking on Christmas morning; her father took care of the two cows they had.

Harriet and Mary had to finish plucking the fowl they were going to roast for the midday meal, and shell peas and peel potatoes, Mary all the time bemoaning the fact that they had had to have vegetables sent out from town instead of growing their own garden-fresh ones.

'Would you like to have dinner out under the plum tree?' asked Mary.

'Could we?'

'Why not? It would be fresher outside. We could carry the table out, and set it up outside. There's not a breath of wind today, nothing would be disturbed.'

'Wouldn't Dad be angry?'

Mary looked up, hot and flushed from the plum pudding. 'It'll be his Christmas present to me,' she said shortly. Harriet had never heard her mother refer to her father as 'him' before.

Between them, she and her mother carried the table out to the plum tree, then Mary went back inside while Harriet laid out the blue and white tablecloth that had been brought amongst her parents' best possessions from England. A thin edge of embroidery ran right around it, and in the middle were fat roses and violets, linked tightly together with immaculate tiny stitches. With the light of the tree lying dappled upon it, the cloth looked prettier and more sumptuous than she could ever remember before.

She carefully polished the worn knives and forks, also brought from England, on the edge of her skirt. The blades of the knives were so thin that they had great indentations along their cutting side, but Gerald had sharpened and re-sharpened them so often, spitting on his stone and grinding them hard in the shining globules, that they cut as clean as razors. Everything was set out, when Mary emerged again.

17

'Doesn't it look nice?' cried Harriet, surveying her handiwork. Sunflowers straggling through the long grass had burst into life near the house, the ancient memory of someone's garden. She had plucked three flowers and laid one beside each setting. Sun, and memories of snow on the ice-white of the table cloth — it must surely be the best of both worlds. There was a shine over it all.

Then she looked at her mother's face. Mary seemed to be suffering some sort of inner convulsion, unable to speak. Harriet put down the spoons she was still holding.

'What is it? What is it?' she repeated across a stillness. The birds, the cicadas, even the sound of the sun cracking the seeds and the pods in the trees, seemed to have stopped.

'Mother, what is it? Please tell me.'

Still her mother was silent. Then slowly she said, 'It's nothing to do with us, we wouldn't know any of them.' 'You're too young, I can't tell you on Christmas Day.'

Harriet ran to her mother's side. 'Please ... please, what is it?'

At last Mary said, 'You'll have to know sooner or later. It was on the radio. I can't keep it from you.'

'Mother, has someone died?' Through Harriet's mind raced the names of all the cousins, grandparents, aunts and uncles still alive in England. There were some cousins in New Zealand too, on her mother's side, but they didn't count. Only the ones in England really meant anything. Which one? Which one? Why was her mother's face so terrible?

'There has been a dreadful accident,' said her mother haltingly. 'At a place called Tangiwai, in the night, a train crossed a bridge, and the bridge broke, the water was high, the mountain flood had come down, a man came to flag the engine as it went by, the train didn't stop, the train carried right on down the line, they didn't see the sign.'

Her voice sounded as though she was intoning some ancient dirge. 'The man stood in the railroad tracks, it was too late, they couldn't turn back, and the train went down, the train went down.'

'What happened to the people?' said Harriet, although she already knew.

18

'They died, they were swept away. They're looking for the bodies. It was a great mountain flood, child, cold water, and the mountain swept away from its moorings.'

Through the sun Harriet saw the cold mountain waters flooding, foaming torrents and white pieces of mountain, and a train rearing high on its heels.

Hearing her mother chanting this liturgy, Harriet sensed some old, old tragedy in her mother that time would not heal, but yet she understood the nature of sorrow as if it were her own.

'Will it spoil Christmas?' asked Harriet.

Mary rounded on her. She did not speak. To her amazement, Harriet saw a strange half-smile on her face. She wondered if her mother was quite sane. 'It will not spoil the coming of the Holy Child,' said her mother. 'Come on in, we'll have a sherry.'

Harriet had never tasted sherry before. The bottle was produced only at Christmas and for her parents' birthdays, and one modest glass was taken by each.

Mary broke the seal on a new bottle. She poured the glittering liquid into two jamjars, brim to the top, and handed one to her daughter.

Harriet looked at it in alarm. 'Drink it,' ordered Mary. Harriet extended her tongue carefully into the glass. Sweet fire shot up into her mouth.

'To Christmas,' said her mother.

'To Christmas,' repeated Harriet, and drank quickly. The bottom of her stomach gave a strange painful lurch. It seemed that the bounty of default that had alighted on the Blessed Virgin would never be hers, for she told her mother that her illness was on for the second time in a month. Her mother said that she must now learn to protect her virginity, whatever that was, in deadly earnest.

At least the bandages were more accessible on this occasion.

The summer moved tranquilly onwards. Late in January, the hay was cut on the lower paddock where Harriet had knelt on the day they arrived at the farm. Stock was to be brought in.

Harriet was vaguely aware that her parents had made contact with the neighbouring farmers. Their holding was very large, and it seemed that they were rich, owning a large and handsome black Chevrolet. They seemed to know everyone in the district, judging by the vast numbers of people who made dusty tracks up to their gate during the holiday season. The gate was clearly visible from the Wallace's front window, and quite often people vomited over it when it when they were leaving. Harriet was sorry for them, assuming that there was some strange infectious disease at the house. She wondered if she ought to warn her mother, but her mother had clearly seen some of the visitors in action from time to time, and said nothing.

As there was some to-ing and fro-ing between her father and the men on the next farm, she guessed that the situation was under control. Their name was Collier, and a son worked on the farm with his father.

One of the main subjects for discussion during their visits and conversations appeared to be the hay. The people next door saw it as a desirable acquisition and were prepared to pay handsomely for it. Gerald was hardly likely to refuse; Harriet suspected as January wore on that they were already close to running out of money to send to the store for food. The Colliers had offered equipment and labour to help cut the hay, and the price would be deducted from the price they paid.

There was of course, nothing unreasonable in the cutting of the grass for hay, and she told herself quite sensibly that it was like having an unwanted haircut, a necessary evil from which there was no escape. And yet it was sacrilege.

Mary was up early on the day they began, and by the time Harriet came out for breakfast there was a large pile of scones already piled on the table, with a clean tea towel wrapped around them.

'You can start buttering,' said Mary.

Harriet sighed.

'And don't sigh at me like that,' snapped Mary. 'God knows, you've done little enough these holidays. For someone who was going to help me, you've done precious little. I don't know what's got into you.'

Harriet felt that she could well say the same of her mother, but wisely kept silent.

Mary eyed Harriet, and her face took on a curious expression, almost of disbelief. 'A bit of stuffing and a hide like a nigger. You'll be taken for a Maori if you don't keep out of the sun.'

She sounded so like Gerald that Harriet wondered what she'd done wrong. Glancing down at herself, the recent changes in her body acquired a fresh significance. The bumps under her frock gave her a sudden start of pleasure. Harriet Wallace's got tits, she said to herself cautiously, just like the kids back at school used to say when someone grew up a bit, only here there was no one to say it except her. Harriet Wallace's got tits, she repeated with glee. Tits and bums and cunts. Wow. Tits and a bum and a cunt, she corrected herself.

'The butter's in the cooler under the trees,' said Mary.

'Yes,' said Harriet. Tits and bums and what's a cunt? The soft little shell between her legs, she supposed. The hairy part, come to think of it. Funny, she hadn't noticed it till the other day. It was all part of the deal, though, she knew that. She'd squinted into the wash house more times than they knew when either of her parents was taking a bath. Hair was okay. She was okay.

'Are you going to do it, or shall I?' said Mary, in the sort of voice that meant that if she didn't nobody would speak to her for the rest of the day.

Tits and a bum and a cunt, sang Harriet's heart as she collected the butter and brought it inside and started slapping it onto the sweating scones.

'I expect you to help carry the billies down to the paddock today,' said Mary.

'Aw, gee, Mum ...'

"What's the matter with you? They won't bite you, you know.'

'Who won't?'

'The Collier's,' replied Mary.

'Who are they?'

21

'Oh, don't try to be thick. It doesn't suit you.'

'But I *don't* know who they are,' protested Harriet.

'The people that live across the road. The ones that are coming to do the hay. Haven't you seen the young fellow talking to Dad? Jim, his name is.'

'I must have been down the paddocks,' said Harriet.

'Well, that's where you'll be today,' said Mary. Coming on strong, Harriet thought. There didn't seem to be much room for negotiation.

At morning tea, she and Mary went down to the paddock. Jim was on a tractor drawing a large scythe behind him, cutting swathe after swathe of grass, the shiny soft stuff falling away like material cut from a bolt. Mary set out a cloth on the grass and they spread the food and the billy and tin mugs out on it, and signalled for the men to come over.

The tractor came to a halt, and Jim climbed down, and headed over towards them, followed by his father and Harriet's father.

Harriet supposed that Jim and his father were both very old. There seemed little difference between them — both were burnt with peeling noses, great thick brown arms and chests like barrels.

As they sat and ate and drank, little was said. Once Jim said. 'It'll be a good crop, Gerald.'

'I'm lucky,' said Gerald. 'It could have been bad.'

'Is there any cheap labour round here?' he added, too sharply.

The Colliers looked at him curiously. 'Isn't our labour good enough for you?' asked the father.

'That's not the point,' replied Gerald. 'I can't afford a lot, and I don't like charity. What about the Maoris? There must be a few round here.'

'You don't get 'em cheap. They come dearer than us,' said Jim.

'What he means is, you have to pay them,' his father put in.

'Well, that's better than charity. I know you've got work to do on your place.'

The two men got to their feet. 'Best be getting on with the job, seeing as how we've got that much to do,' said Jim.

'I didn't mean to offend you,' Gerald began, uncertainly.

'Look, you play it any way you like, mate,' said Jim. 'But don't go looking for cheap darkies if you've got any sense. The only ones I know round here I went to school with, and we sat in the same desks at school, and I reckon they don't come no cheaper than the rest of us.'

After the men had gone, Harriet said, 'Don't you like Maoris, Mum?'

'Of course I do' said Mary. 'It's just that they're different to us. They belong with the workers.'

'But what about us?' said Harriet.

'We're landowners,' said Mary.

'Did you and Daddy think you'd have a lot of people working for you when you came to New Zealand?'

'Oh, I expect we will. Some day. It didn't work out quite the way everyone thought when your Dad and I were a bit younger. The Depression, the war, you know. Things changed.'

'Would you have been landowners if you'd stayed in England?' asked Harriet.

Her mother flushed. 'Come on, help me carry the things back. We can rinse the cups in the river first.'

Down at the river they plunged the plates into the cool water. Crumbs of scone floated away. Suddenly there was a flurry through the water, and a lithe black shape streaked into the debris, scattering spray as its ugly black head broke the surface. Before Harriet could move or cry out, the eel had fastened itself into the side of her foot where she stood, ankle-deep in water. She kicked her foot high and for one moment the creature hung suspended above the water joined to her, then collapsed backwards, thrashing away.

As they walked back to the house, mother and daughter both shaken, Harriet thought, 'I will always dream of that shape. Always, as long as there is evil in hidden places, I will remember the eel. When I have nightmares, and black shapes walk abroad in the nights, I will see the eel.'

She did not return to the river for several days. When she finally went back, it was night. The sun had burned with a high fierce intensity all day, and there seemed to be no escape from it at the house. At night when it should have been cooler, a hot wind sprung from the north where her room faced, and the sleeping house was like an oven. Her face was burning, her skin felt so dry to the touch that she did not recognise her own body. Sleep was impossible.

She got up quietly and slipped into her dress. The door was unlocked. Even the Wallaces, who were regarded as strange by the local folk, knew that you did not lock doors in the country, that it was a sign of bad faith to the neighbours if they found a locked door. Outside she started to run, the river drawing her like a magnet. On and on Harriet ran, across the paddock stubbly with the mown grass lying in heaps waiting for the baler. Behind her stood the small house, huddled between the trees, the moon slanting across the roof. There was no other sign of human habitation; she might have been the only person alive, running across a moonscape bounded by bush.

The river talked gently under the fallen poplar tree, welcoming her back. She climbed up to the hollow and lay back in the wooden hammock.

With enormous concentration she turned her eyes to the stars. The whole experience of the night sky crowded down on her. Primeval forces were surely at work, an enormous voice spoke to her. It said, 'Come to me.' It was definitely the voice of God. Great exaltation filled her. It was just like Bernadette of Lourdes — not that she was a Catholic, only Anglo-Catholic. Her father said the Church here was low-caste. It only understood the simple pastoral things, but then one had to make the best of what one had. Well, she certainly had. A real mystical experience. For the moment, one could banish the eels in the water below.

Feeling much better, Harriet climbed out of her perch and made her way back to the house. Before she slipped inside she turned and took one last long look back over the paddocks and the moon.

Harriet woke the following morning to find Gerald shaking her roughly. Her first thought was that he had somehow discovered that she had been out of the house in the night.

'Wake up, you lazy little cow,' he said. 'Just get yourself out of that bed and do some work for a change.'

'Yes, of course,' said Harriet, scrambling out. 'Haven't I been doing enough?'

'Your mother's ill and we're bringing in the hay today. You'll have to cook for the men.'

He turned away with his back to her as she started to dress. There was suddenly an air of weariness and despondency about him.

'What is it, Dad? Is Mum very sick?'

'Sick enough.'

'Will she get better?'

'Of course. She just needs a rest.'

'Is it her head? She gets awfully bad heads sometimes.'

'I know. But it isn't her head this time. Now don't worry about it, just get on and help me out, eh?'

He turned to go out the door. 'Dad,' said Harriet. 'Is it my fault she's sick? Haven't I helped her enough?'

He turned back to her, his face full of pain. They studied each other across the room. She sensed some loss, some bewilderment, with himself, with her, she could not really tell. At last he said, 'I don't know whose fault it is, Harriet. I suppose it must be mine ... if it's anybody's.'

'I'll go and see her and ask her what to do,' said Harriet.

'No,' said Gerald quickly. 'No, on no account are you to see her.'

Frightened, Harriet hurried out to the kitchen. She desperately wanted to see her mother. Once she went to the door of her room. Inside she heard low moaning. She called out softly, 'Mum, Mum, shall I come in?'

'Go away,' her mother said.

'Don't you want me?' whispered Harriet, afraid that her father would come back and catch her.

'Not now, not now. Later.'

'Promise?'

'If you help your Dad. Promise.'

There seemed little for it but to start making scones. She faithfully followed what her mother had done a few days before, but doubled the quantities, for Gerald had told her that there would be twice as many men in the paddock today. Some more neighbours from up the road were coming to help.

The day was long and hot, and it seemed that hardly had she put one lot of tea and scones down in front of the men and got the dishes collected and back to the house than it was time to set off with the next lot. By afternoon tea, she was exhausted. She hardly noticed the men, so busy was she providing. As she cleared away the cups for the last time, Jim Collier said to her father, 'She'll make a good wife for someone.'

'Time enough for that,' said Gerald.

'She oughter be broken young,' replied Jim seriously.

Some of the men laughed. Her father didn't join in. 'You're married, are you?' he said rather stiffly.

After hesitating Jim said, 'She's gone off looking for a bigger dong. Reckon we'd better finish off them last bales before the dew starts, eh?'

The men got to their feet. Gerald hung back a minute. 'Harriet,' he said in a strained voice.

'Yes, father?'

'You've done well. Thank you.'

'That's all right, Dad.' She had never had such praise from him before.

'You can take a bit of time at the river if you want. I know you like it.'

'Shouldn't I be getting back to Mum?' she asked doubtfully.

'She wants a bit of a rest still.'

'Will I see her then?' said Harriet. She was beginning to thoroughly mistrust the whole situation. 'When we go back?'

'Yes. Yes, you'll see her. Just give her a bit more time. All right?'

'All right,' she agreed.

When he had gone and she'd gathered in the cups once more, she went down to the river. It had never seemed cooler or more inviting. For a long time she lay on the hollowed tree letting the sweet summer soak through her. After a time the noise of the machinery went away, and she peeked through the branches to see that the paddock was really empty. Out there, the once beautiful silk grass was now harsh stalks. Only here under the trees on the river bank, was it still rich and soft, luxurious and green, shot with the stars of flowers, and with the underside of each blade sleek as the river water. She wanted to lie close, close like the first day here, or closer, if that was possible.

Harriet slid her dress over her head. It was so tight against her chest that she had had to struggle with it for weeks past. When she had dropped her panties on the ground, she stretched herself in the grass. 'I am a lizard,' she thought, and pressed herself closer against the earth.

'Going to swim then, are you?' said a voice.

She shrieked and reared upwards on her knees. Jim stood in front of her.

'There's eels in the water,' she stammered.

'Never fancied them much myself. What you doing here in the nick, then?'

'The what?'

'The nick. Without your clothes.'

'I wanted to get cool.'

'That's an idea. Wouldn't mind getting cool myself.' He put his hands on the ends of the shirt tails hanging out of his dirty old pants.

'No, please don't,' Harriet whispered. 'Why did you come here?'

'Wanted to see what sort of a kid you were. Didn't expect quite such an eyeful.'

She reached for her dress. Jim put his foot on it.

'Please. Please let me put my dress on.'

'What's your hurry?'

'I just want to put it on.'

'Stand up.'

27

Her skin, pleasantly cool only a minute before, had turned to goose pimples. Slowly she got to her feet, with her arm across her chest, her other hand trying to cover her pubic area.

'I don't reckon you're shy. That's a lot of bullshit. You musta wanted it.'

She shook her head uncomprehendingly.

'Coming down here, and taking your clothes off. You wanted it.'

His clothes had funny bumps, she noticed. He lifted her hand away from her chest; she didn't seem to have the strength to resist. His lip curled.

'When did you stop growing?'

I don't think I have,' she said. 'I mean, I think I've only just started.'

'Oh, yes. How old are you?'

'Going on thirteen.'

His hand dropped away. 'Jesus,' he said softly under his breath. 'You sure you're not putting me on?' Harriet shook her head. 'Oh, Jesus,' he said again, under his breath.

'You don't want to say that,' said Harriet. 'My father says you should only say things like that if you're talking about the Bible, and the real Jesus.'

'Oh, but I am,' said Jim. He surveyed her with wonder, still holding onto her hand. 'What about Jesus wept? That's a whole sentence outa the Bible. I remember that from the parson what used to come round school. We all kept saying it for weeks after.'

'I suppose that's all right,' said Harriet.

Jim shook his head in slow wonder, then lifted her other hand away. 'I might as well get a good look, mightn't I?' He stroked her new pubic hairs with the top side of one finger, rather as if he were stroking the nose of an animal.

'Real Siamese pussycat,' he murmured. Somewhere round her pubic arch she felt a strange warm little quiver. Suddenly he twisted back the arm he was still holding. 'You little bitch, you're having me on. Aren't you?' She shook her head.

'You bloody are. You liked that didn't you? Eh?'

'It was just that it felt like...' she floundered for words. The

28

closest she could come was the night before up in the tree. 'It felt a bit like God,' she offered, at last.

He looked at her blankly. 'You're a queer one, aren't you?'

'Well it was like this, see, I was up here in this tree, this one alongside of us, last night ... you won't tell Dad, will you?' She took his silence for assent. 'Well, see, I reckon God spoke to me. It was good, it felt a bit like that.'

'I reckon I better give you a bit of a feel and leave it at that, eh,' he said uneasily.

'You're not going to feel bits of me, are you?' She wasn't sure why this seemed so important, but she knew it was necessary to check.

'Oh, no. None of that stuff. Here, like this.' He drew her hand onto one of his bumps. 'Go on, hold onto it. That's right.'

Through the cloth of his trousers the bump felt very strange.

'Jesus,' said Jim again. His hand dropped hers. 'I mean ... he wept. Put your clothes on, kid.'

'Thank you,' she said, starting to shiver violently.

'It's all right, I won't look,' he said.

'I wouldn't think looking'd make much difference now,' said Harriet.

'You don't want to be smart,' said Jim. 'That could get you into trouble. Being smart. It's not good for you. I mean, I could have got you, you know.'

'My father might have come down,' said Harriet, reprovingly, now that she was covered again.

'Nah. I knew he was seeing the doctor about your ma. Knew he'd be up at the house while Doc was there.'

'Is the doctor there?'

'Yeah, didn't you know?'

'Why? Did he tell you?'

'Haven't they told you nothing?'

'I've got to go,' said Harriet. Her mother had never had the doctor to the house in all her life.

She remembered the cups and plates and picked them up with awkward, hasty movements, trembling more violently than she had done when he touched her. Taking pity, he helped her gather up the things and shoved them into her arms. For a moment they stood looking at each other, then she turned, stumbling as she started across the paddock with her load.

'Remember,' he called to her. 'You just remember, fellas don't like girls that are smart.'

As she arrived at the house, a car was pulling away from the gate. There was a tired grey man at the wheel, wearing a collar and tie. She guessed it must be the doctor. She pushed the door of the kitchen open, and put down her load at the sink, then stalked towards the door of her mother's bedroom, determined to get to the bottom of this mystery.

At the door of the lounge she stopped. There were voices inside the bedroom. Neither Gerald nor Mary had heard her come in. The bedroom door slanted open. Gerald was sitting on the edge of the bed holding Mary's hand. Harriet could see that at least she was alive.

'You should have let him take you to the hospital,' said Gerald.

'There's no point,' Mary said. There was an edge of desolation in her voice.

'I want to know you're safe,' Gerald said.

'I am. I'm safe, it's only rest now that I need. All that's beyond saving is our baby. It's gone.'

'Yes, he's gone,' said Gerald.

'He. You never give up hope, do you?' As he bowed his head over her hand she touched his face. 'You mustn't hope for too much. The doctor said he didn't think there'd be another. My age ... I'm not a young girl any more.'

He groaned. 'Oh God, why did I bring you to this Godforsaken place?'

'Hush, you mustn't say that. God forsakes no one. Come on now, you brought in the hay today, and we've more money than we hoped for, and soon you'll be able to stock the farm and we'll have a good turnover before the winter. That's good fortune.'

'And you?'

'I'll survive.'

30

'If only ... oh, if only the child .... it was a boy, you know, the doctor told me.'

'I see.' Mary sighed. 'He shouldn't have told you that.'

'You knew, then?'

'Oh yes. What was the point of telling you?'

Gerald sat up straight on the bed. 'Well,' he said finally. 'We'll just have to make the best of what we've got, I suppose.' He got to his feet. Harriet froze against the wall.

Gerald emerged from the bedroom, and he and his daughter stood looking at each other. 'How long have you been there?' he demanded.

'I've just walked in this moment.'

'Oh, taken your time, haven't you,' he said gruffly, but with obvious relief.

'It was nice at the river bank.' The whole day swam before her eyes. She felt as if she was going to faint and for a moment the world shifted out of focus. She heard his voice again, saying, 'We'll just have to make the best of what we've got then, won't we?'

'I'll get the meal. I expect you'll be hungry,' she said, turning away.

'Don't you want to know how your mother is?' he asked.

'How is she?' she asked indifferently. Gerald looked at her with hatred.

'It was something to do with having a baby, wasn't it?' she added, as she began to peel potatoes.

'You have been listening round corners, you sly little bitch.'

'The men at the paddock all knew, didn't they?'

Gerald went very red. 'I had to tell them,' he muttered. 'I had to get an advance on the hay ... for the doctor.'

'Couldn't you have told me before you told the men? They've been talking in front of me all day'. The lie was deliciously powerful.

'I'm sorry, Harriet,' said her father uneasily.

For the first time in her life, she felt in command of a situation with him. There was an enormous temptation to press her advantage, but instinct warned her that it was only a slight one.

31

'Would you go and see your mother, please.'

'Oh, certainly,' said Harriet magnanimously, wiping her hands on her teatowel.

'It might be as well to say I told you she has the flu.'

'I'll watch out for infection.'

Another look of pure dislike passed over his face. Throwing discretion to the winds, she added, 'By the way, if you want me to skivvy for you, you'd better find a few bob towards clothing me properly before long. I don't like being looked at by some of the men round here.'

'Yes Harriet.' His shoulders slumped. For the moment she had him beaten, and that suited her.

In the night, she lay awake again. Sand seemed to have gathered under her lids. She realised she had hardly slept for two nights now, and it was hot again, she was aching and dry, parched and stiff from her labours. But so much seemed to have happened to her that sleep was still impossible. She thought of the experience by the river over and over again, with God and Jim all mixed up. She didn't even like Jim very much. One thing she reckoned on, and that was that she was a woman. The mechanics of the business were still to be worked out, but she was a woman all right, just like her mother was. Whatever strange act had brought her mother to this condition she was in now, she was capable of too.

She thought of her mother with pity and love. She was a wounded starfish cast up on an alien shore. She would never re-enter the sea, she was forever stranded on a barren, dusty beach where she had been tossed up by ugly wars called the Depression, the war, her father. Gasping and alone, she still allowed this act to be perpetrated upon her body, so that she might multiply and place upon the strange land males that would carry the seed and cover the country with Wallaces.

Well, now there was no hope. She, Harriet, was the one who held the power. But she must wait for the time to be right.

2

A few days later, Harriet started at her new school. Three years slid by, marked by few major events. Once again she was recognised as 'a bright child' and 'a difficult girl', but now there was a sense of purpose in what she did. In order to escape the farm, it was necessary to pass School Certificate. To survive in the company of other pupils, she had to be aggressive. They took her aggression as a sign of leadership, and often followed her in rebellion against teachers. She was what, in later terminology, would be known as a stirrer.

No teachers appeared to enlighten her on any of the real problems of the world, so she sought out as much as she could herself. While obediently learning where the wheatfields were in East Anglia (or were they oats, or did they graze cattle there? She hadn't the faintest idea in retrospect) she joined the library which opened in the small township where she travelled to school each day, and borrowed a copy of *Madame Bovary* in the original French, (it being banned in English) in the hope that she might discover the mysterious act that the kids called 'it'. 'It' remained a distressing problem to her, as, being established now as a leader, she could obviously not admit ignorance on the subject. She understood that one or two of the fifth formers did 'it', and she had once been invited to watch under the pine trees, but a vague suspicion that she was being tested made her airily dismissive. Her French was improved by the book, but the sum total of her knowledge certainly wasn't.

33

She managed to obtain some Micky Spillanes that were doing illicit rounds of the school, and propped them up inside her English grammar book. Spillane offered bare thighs, sighs aplenty, and plenty of talk about doing 'it' and having done 'it', though 'it' was never described.

When Harriet was in fifth form, a number of significant things happened. For one thing, her confirmation finally took place. It had been delayed for some years for a variety of reasons, including her father's lingering suspicion of the New Zealand clergy. The breakthrough was the arrival of an apparently high church vicar at the parish church.

Another problem had been the difficulty of providing a confirmation dress; an expense that the farm budget simply never took into account. However, at the same time that the new vicar arrived, some material turned up from England. It was a white slub linen, intended to be made into a tennis frock. As the aunt who had sent it had no idea how large Harriet was, or indeed whether or not she played tennis, there was considerably more material than was required for a tennis dress. Mary seized upon it eagerly, seeing in it the salvation of Harriet's immortal soul. As Harriet had also acquired what were generally conceded to be 'smashing tits' by now, and badly needed a brassière, Mary assured her that she would make her one of these objects as well. How she would achieve this feat of engineering skill Harriet could not imagine. However, she looked forward to the better presentation of her assets with considerable pleasure.

In the meantime, confirmation classes had to be attended after school at the Ohaka church. As they made her too late for the school bus, she had a long bicycle ride home across the hills, so the confirmation lessons were a labour of love.

The Anglican priest was fat and middle-aged with ash always spilled across his cassock. He liked to be called Father Dittmer, with all its high church suggestiveness, though theologically he often seemed confused to Harriet. He talked a lot about the apostolic chain, and became inordinately angry with Harriet when she asked him if he saw himself as a direct successor to St Peter. He was not a bishop, he said coldly, from which she deduced that he had had disappointments.

Towards the end of the indoctrination, the subject of confession arose.

'In the Church of England,' droned Father Dittmer as a fly settled on his bald patch, 'We have a different doctrine to that of the Roman Catholic Church. But, my little friends, we do not overlook the subject of confession. We recognise the right of the individual to do as his conscience dictates. We say some should, none must, all may.'

This struck Harriet as reasonable logic, the only identifiable piece of meat in the whole theological casserole. On the whole she had been profoundly disappointed in her own responses to the confirmation classes. Since her experience of God on the river bank during that summer, years before, she had sought some sort of recognition of God within herself. He seemed to have cheated her, having brought her thus far, and then having tantalisingly let her go.

She had welcomed the confirmation classes, and had at first paid them earnest attention. Her challenges to Father Dittmer had been made in all seriousness, for she genuinely wanted her confusions and doubts clarified. Her emerging cynicism was something that appalled her and she struggled to hide it from the other members of the class. Father Dittmer had obviously been warned about her, however, and took her questions as personal affronts. When he discussed the possibilities of confession, she felt that he fixed her with a particularly stern eye.

On a Saturday night two weeks before Harriet's confirmation, the Colliers held one of their frequent parties. As the Wallaces had no social life at all they had come to accept the odd invitation to go and have 'a few drinks', rarely staying long enough to witness the paralysis that afflicted those who stayed on for more than a few. A mixed bunch would turn up, and Harriet was invariably the youngest there. Little notice was taken of her, and as the conversation mostly concerned milk production, football, and how much beer could be consumed in the shortest possible time, she felt she had little contribution to make and kept silent.

Jim brought a succession of girls to these parties and by the time
Harriet was in the fifth form, one or two of them were girls who
had themselves been fifth formers when she was in the third form.
They always wore spindly high heels and a great deal of bright red
lipstick, and dyed their hair the same colour as Marilyn Monroe's.
Their cleavages were pushed up in the best possible imitations of
their heroine. Privately Harriet considered her own breasts to be in
considerably better shape, but the lack of a brassière made this a
rather unconvincing hypothesis. Once she had heard Jim mutter to
the girl with him that he 'couldn't wait for a bit'. Harriet supposed
that 'a bit' was 'it', which still hadn't been revealed to her. Jim
never appeared to notice that she existed and only nodded briefly
to her even when they met on the road and there wasn't another
soul in sight.

On this particular Saturday night, he didn't have a girl with him.
He'd played football all afternoon and was fired up and ready to
go. His balls were fairly popping, as he kept telling anyone who'd
listen, and he didn't mean a footie ball either.

'Lord love me, me own mother had better look out,' he said
more than once. His mother Doris, huge-handed and stocky, roared
with laughter and said, 'Jim Collier, you're not too big to clout yet,
I'll tell you that.'

When she heard that, Harriet's mother stood up and muttered
darkly to Gerald, who agreed they should leave. Really it was too
much, what one had to endure from the locals, said Gerald's
expression, but if one wanted to fit in, there was no help for it. One
simply had to put in an appearance at these things, and anyway it
was a break for Mary seeing a few other faces besides his own. He
knew the locals called him 'a right wallah' but it was rather
flattering; he enjoyed that. Sadly for Gerald, it was as close to being
a 'right wallah' as he'd ever get.

As they were about to leave, Jim suddenly said, 'Why doesn't
Harriet stay here? You always take Cinderella away before the ball
begins.'

There was a general clamour of agreement.

'Oh, I don't think ... ' Mary began.

'Harriet's studying,' said Gerald, with what might have been a hint of pride.

'Time she had a break, then,' said Doris. 'We'll look after her.'

Doris Collier had been good to Mary ever since that disastrous miscarriage. She had gone out of her way to be kind, sensing in Mary a frailty which she had never shared. In an odd way Doris understood that only some quite extraordinary sense of endurance kept Mary going from day to day in the cowshed and on the land and these traits had won more than passing respect for her.

Mary looked at Harriet, obviously hoping that she would come home, for to challenge Doris's promise to look after her would have seemed ungrateful, to say the least.

'Thank you,' said Harriet suddenly. 'I'd love to stay.'

'Good,' said Doris. 'Jim'll walk her home, won't you Jim?'

'Yeah', said her son stolidly, staring ahead and forgetting his talk about his balls. Faced by this suitably convincing demonstration by all concerned, Mary and Gerald could only nod mutely in agreement.

'Well, that's all right then,' said Mary. 'I wouldn't like her wandering round in the dark.'

Oh, if you only knew, thought Harriet. The nights by the river had become a part of her life. She had never again had anything but quiet night prowls after the first contact with God, and although she had been disappointed that it hadn't happened again, she was more than a little relieved that she had not been lumbered with a permanent Bernadette of Lourdes undertaking.

Probably just as well. Lately she'd begun thinking that 'it' had got something to do with the voice from the sky, though she failed to see the connection. Nowadays when she went for her walks at three or four o'clock in the morning, she contemplated the mysteries of 'it' more than she thought about God. When she considered the whole subject, Jim entered her thoughts more often than she supposed he really should.

After her parents had gone home she continued to sit quietly. The party started to liven up and old man Collier, who was getting a bit shaky these days, started up a few rounds of 'Mockingbird

Hill', after which Jim got them all singing 'Roll Me Over in the Clover'.

When they were all going strong, Harriet went over to him and said she wanted to go home.

'Bloody hell, kid,' said Jim, annoyed, 'Why didn't you go with your folks if you wanted to leave this soon? We're just starting to warm up.'

'It doesn't matter, then,' replied Harriet. 'I'll say goodnight to your mother.'

'Now wait a minute — I said I'd walk you home and walk you home I will. I don't go back on my word.'

Outside, the night was soft and fluttering. They walked along in silence. At last Harriet said, 'I'll be leaving here soon.'

'Go on, where you heading then?'

'I don't know yet,' said Harriet.

'Your folks'll miss you.'

'They don't know yet. You won't tell them will you?'

'What's it worth?' asked Jim automatically.

'I never told on you,' said Harriet.

Jim stopped in his tracks. He was quiet for a minute, then he said, 'You was supposed to forget that ever happened. I was in a bad way right then, what with being left high and dry like that by my missus. You got no right to go reminding a man he done things like that.'

'But I didn't forget, did I? And I have reminded you.'

'You're not trying to be smart, are you? Remember I told you, you don't want to be smart. From what I hear, you never listened to me. You gone and got smart with everybody round here.'

He paused, then added, 'You don't have a boyfriend, do you?'

'No-o,' Harriet admitted.

'Goes to show then, don't it,' Jim said triumphantly. 'I told you, blokes don't like smart-aleck sheilas.'

'I'll try and remember,' said Harriet humbly.

'Right, then we'd better get you home.'

'Only I want to do it again,' said Harriet.

Jim started walking. 'Oh, no you don't.'

Harriet pulled at his arm. 'But I do. Please, Jim. I wouldn't ... ' and she took a deep breath, preparing to maim the English language, 'I wouldn't never tell nobody.'

Jim stopped, obviously impressed. 'Say,' he said with awe, 'You really mean it, don't you?'

'I — I want to hold onto your ... dong again,' said Harriet desperately.

'Yeah, well ... er .. okay,' said Jim. 'Best lie down, then. Er — mind the cowshit.'

Harriet agreed doubtfully, and reminded him that the first time they hadn't lain down.

'You want a bit more than that, don't you?' said Jim.

'Oh yes, yes, please,' Harriet said hastily. The thought that she might not find out about 'it' was terrifying. God and 'it' were now on a collision course. Not only was she about to make a remarkable discovery, but she was also about to place herself in the position of having to confess.

At the moment, her position was rather uncomfortable. The paddock in which they found themselves was in the direct path taken by the Colliers' cows when they went to the cowshed each day, and the grass was thin over a crust of dried earth. The sharp little points dug into Harriet's back as Jim, on his knees, proceeded to push her down still further into the clay. She moaned as a nasty little edge dug into her kidneys. Taking this very well, Jim uttered an inarticulate cry and flung himself upon her, his mouth sucking hers like a limpet. For several minutes they ground their way through an exercise which seemed to involve Harriet in swallowing Jim's tongue. It felt like the largest tongue in the world, and she had a quick vision of the ox tongues her mother cooked and served cut up with salad for Sunday lunch. She often had to skin them when they had finished cooking. The skins were very thick, with a great furry grain over them. She had never thought that her tongue might be the same, but now she began to wonder — Jim's was obviously very similar to those she was used to handling.

'Ah,' sighed Jim, lifting his head at last. 'You're not such a bad kid after all.'

39

Fortified by this praise, Harriet tentatively felt around for the object she had been asked to hold the time before. It was positively mountainous through the cloth of Jim's trousers, and she was very impressed. When she had peeked through the bathroom window at her father, his had seemed a very tame, droopy little affair. She wondered how Jim managed to hide his splendid equipment.

He plunged his hand down the neck of her dress and clutched her nipple between his thumb and forefinger, rolling it round experimentally. The sensation was rather painful, in fact, the whole operation seemed more complicated and uncomfortable by the minute. With a profound sigh Jim collapsed on top of her so that she was ground into the crumbling earth, pierced from below and above.

'Ooo-wah,' wailed Harriet, unable to contain herself any longer. With a great effort Jim pulled back. In the moonlight, she could see that he was still bulging against his trousers.

'Ah, yes, you want it real bad, don't you kid?' said Jim hoarsely.

Harriet, not at all sure that she wanted 'it' any more, or whether in fact that might be all there was to 'it', could only mumble.

'You know I wouldn't hurt you, don't you?' he demanded.

Again Harriet could only mutter, feeling thoroughly bruised and mutilated. Jim apparently took this for a sign of assent.

'I couldn't touch you, you know that, don't you? Christ, I'd like to, but nah, I couldn't do it. You're too good a kid. Too good a kid. Muck up your life, I would, that's what I'd do to a smart kid like you. Old man'd shoot me.'

All this sounded suspiciously like a marriage proposal to Harriet, which was a great deal more than she had bargained for. Or was it? Were other mysterious elements involved? Had she done 'it'? She was pretty sure the answer was no, but it seemed embarrassing to ask. Crestfallen, she got to her feet, straightening her clothes as she did so.

'Come on,' said Jim, quite solicitously, it seemed. 'I better get you home.'

As they walked over the paddocks he said, 'I coulda got mad with you, you know. Not really fair, what you done to me.'

'I'm sorry,' she said penitently, her heart momentarily leaping at the thought that she might have accomplished her aim after all.

'You haven't been playing round with any of them fellas down at the high school, have you?'

'No,' said Harriet indignantly. 'Of course not.'

'That's all right then, that's what I thought.'

'Was your wife very pretty?' asked Harriet suddenly, not knowing why.

He was silent for a minute. 'Not that you'd notice, I guess. She went to that same damn high school, that's all. We was doing it from the time ...' He glanced sideways at her. 'Come to think of it, I guess since we was about your age. Put her up the duff first year out of school. Took our kid when we was both twenty and made off with this other fella.'

'Oh Jim, that's awful,' cried Harriet, genuinely moved.

'I dunno, kid,' said Jim, more thoughtful than she'd ever known him. 'I was awful mad at first, and I felt a right Charley, I can tell you, but you know, there's some things I dunno, an' I guess I won't ever be able to figure 'em out all that proper, but I reckon I don't blame her all that much. Some things we hadn't kinda worked on when we was fuckin' our way through high. See, that's why I couldn't a done it to you.'

'Married me?'

'Married you?' He was bewildered. 'You wouldn't want to marry the likes of me.'

Harriet was humiliated. Why had she ever said that? she wondered. One moment he was talking about marriage and the next he wasn't. The whole thing was impossibly mixed up.

They were nearly at her gate. Unexpectedly, Jim drew her close to the hedge. He put his hand on hers and pulled her to him, just gently kissing her face, the tip of her nose and her forehead, very carefully. No tongues, no bumps. He let go her hand and stroked the side of her face.

'You're a real sweet kid,' he said. 'I wish ...' He was silent. 'Thanks, kid,' he said finally, and than he was gone, loping through the shadows, as catlike as could be.

41

When she was in bed, Harriet wept, shaking, silent tears. So much of what had happened she didn't understand, so many questions were still unanswered, and so much emotion choked her up that it was almost more than she could bear. Why had he thanked her at the end? Had 'it' happened at last, and was there no more to 'it' than that? Should she have thought about marriage before they started the whole performance? And that bit about Jim's wife having a baby — well, of course, she knew that some girls started having babies before they got married, and you had to do whatever 'it' was first, but did that mean that if she had done 'it' she might have started a baby too? She hadn't thought about any of that before. There was so much to think about that it was terrifying.

One thing she did know, and that was that your periods stopped if you were going to have a baby. Everybody knew that. Even her mother had by now parted with this bit of information, and there'd been a big scare at school when one of the girls hadn't got her period for two weeks, and it seemed that she'd been up to something. Everyone had been scared stiff, and at every interval a covey would retreat to the school lavatories to make an inspection. One day her period came, and the girl cried all the rest of the day, which Harriet didn't understand either.

Anyway, Harriet's period came two days later, and she took its arrival as a sign that whatever the facts of the matter had been on the night Jim walked her home, she was loved by God, and she should thank him most sincerely.

The last confirmation class before the actual service took place on Thursday. Father Dittmer hurried them through their responses, which now came automatically, and he said that they were all now fully prepared as people who had come to the years of discretion, and he thought they should do very well as members of the church.

Then everyone filed out except Harriet, who now saw quite clearly that an act of contrition was required of her.

Father Dittmer was busily packing up his little suitcase of books when he saw that she was still sitting there.

'What is it, Harriet?' he asked testily. 'I have to be at the next church down the line at five o'clock.'

'I wanted to talk to you,' said Harriet.

'Oh dear,' said Father Dittmer. 'Oh dear, oh dear, oh dear. I suppose, young lady, that you are about to tell me that you are not going to be confirmed. I suppose you are now going to set about disclaiming God and all His mighty works. You will no doubt be on the verge of discrediting the holy apostolic chain to which we of the cloth subscribe, to prove to me that St Peter, St Paul and St Mark and St Luke and all the others did not tell the truth, that they were just scribes who wrote down folk tales on behalf of the illiterate peasants of the time, and that all the sciences and philosophies of our times have progressed beyond that of the first century AD, except for theology, and what was all right two thousand years ago will not do for you. Am I right?'

'I'd forgotten all that,' said Harriet.

'Ah!' Father Dittmer pounced. 'Then you admit that you have thought such things?'

'Yes, I suppose I did at one stage,' said Harriet.

'And were you not about to discourse on such matters now?'

'No. I came to confess.'

'Confess!'

'You said, Father, some should, none must, and all may.'

'Of course, of course,' he said, sitting down suddenly in the first pew. He took out his handkerchief and mopped his shiny dome. 'And in which category are you, my dear Harriet?'

She hesitated, about to choose the first edict, then said sweetly, 'The optional, Father.'

He shot her a reproachful glance but merely said, 'Then you had better kneel down, hadn't you, my dear girl?'

'Right here?' asked Harriet.

'Oh no. In the vestry, I think.' He led the way over the moth-eaten carpet and opened the creaking vestry door for her.

'Now,' he said sitting heavily on the high backed wood and

leather chair. 'Now, you shall confess, my dear girl.'

'Where shall I kneel?'

'Oh just here, just here in front of me,' said Father Dittmer. 'Near enough for me to place my hand upon your head ... for your comfort.'

Harriet knelt obediently.

'What was it you wanted to tell me, Harriet?'

'We-ell,' started Harriet cautiously, 'It's about this — boy I know.'

'Ah,' breathed Father Dittmer. 'A boy. I see. And what have you been doing with this boy?'

Harriet was silent.

'I see. Did you go ... all the way?' Father Dittmer leant forward anxiously.

Harriet looked up, perplexed. She hadn't bargained for this. In fact, the question seemed a downright insult, considering that she had come here to gain some enlightenment on physical as well as spiritual matters.

'I don't know, Father,' she said truthfully.

'Come, come, girl, you must know.'

'But I don't. I thought you might tell me.'

Father Dittmer gave a strangled gasp and half rose from his chair, then sank back again.

'Then ... where did he touch you?' he asked hoarsely.

'Pretty well everywhere,' said Harriet.

'There?' asked her confessor, suddenly stabbing a finger in the general direction of her vagina.

'Oh — sort of.'

He stretched out a trembling finger towards her chest. His finger had an overlong horny tobacco-stained nail, Harriet noticed, as it rested lightly on her breast.

'There?'

'Oh yes, yes,' she nodded, happy to be able to oblige him with something positive.

The nail hooked the corner of her blouse, pulling it aside.

'Underneath?'

Harriet felt mesmerised, unable to stop what was happening. She nodded, silent now.

'How?'

'He held — the bit on top,' she muttered desperately.

The nail descended on her nipple. To her amazement, she felt it go rigid. That hadn't happened with Jim. They both looked at this phenomenon in silence. Father Dittmer's hand dropped away.

'Did he — penetrate?' he asked. His voice sounded as though it came from ten thousand miles away, so loud was the roaring in her ears. Both her nipples were standing up like beacons, and there was a beat like the sea under her panties.

She looked at him and through him, trying to answer. She didn't recognise her own voice. 'Penetrate? I suppose so. He ... put his tongue inside my mouth.'

'And what else did he put inside?'

'Nothing.'

'Nothing at all?'

'No.'

'Not even his finger. Like ... this?' The wicked-looking fingernail was following down the line of her body.

'No. No,' she cried out, jumping to her feet, and cowering back. 'Nothing at all.'

The hand dropped. She and Father Dittmer looked at each other as across a great distance.

'I think we should kneel side by side in the church and pray,' he said at last.

They went back into the church, and knelt some distance apart in the front pew.

'We don't have a strict order for confession in the Church of England,' said Father Dittmer shakily.

'Can you not forgive me, then?' said Harriet.

'I can pray for you, said Father Dittmer, avoiding the question. 'And I think you should repeat the fifty-first psalm after me. I'm sure you'll find it a great comfort.' His normal voice was reasserting itself.

The late afternoon sun struck coloured light through the tiny stained-glass window as they knelt muttering one after the other. 'Wash me thoroughly from my wickedness, cleanse me from my sin ... I acknowledge my faults ... my sin is ever before me ...'

Harriet sneaked a glance at him from between tightly clasped hands. 'Against thee, thee only have I sinned, and done this evil in thy sight,' he murmured, and she saw a tear winkle its way down the side of his face.

'Against thee, thee only, have I sinned,' repeated Harriet, and slipped quietly from her place. He didn't seem to notice her going, his head didn't turn, as she hurried out into the sunlight.

Outside it seemed bright and clean and calm. An apple tree showered a profusion of petals over her, as she picked up her bike, leaning against it. A keen lemony fragrance came from the great cups of the magnolias in the trees by the church and the headstones stood upright as ever with their green-grey beards of lichen. Did it ever happen? she wondered. Then with a great burst of energy, she jumped on her bicycle and began pedalling furiously towards home.

The following week she was confirmed. Her tennis-cum-confirmation dress was finished, rucked and tucked with a multitude of pleats which swung fashionably wide around her calves. Her mother produced the brassiere she had made, and Harriet wept bitter tears in the night at the thought of having to wear it. It was an almost straight bandage-like affair that would hold her in, her mother said. Harriet determined to find work soon, if for no better reason than to earn the money to buy a suitable garment in which to clothe her troublesome breasts.

The confirmation service was attended by hordes of adolescents from all the outlying churches of the scattered parish. The amount of preparation which had gone into the affair hardly seemed worth it. All that catechism for this. One moment you were outside, the next moment inside, and all for some rote chanting that everybody could do. Did it place her above God, she wondered, knowing that the vicar had his weaknesses? She hoped not, it seemed a perilously high place to occupy, and one supposed that He must know every bit as much as she did, and more.

The bishop was a tired, gentle old man. He said something about 'Home is Heaven, and Heaven is Home' and begged them to remember it all the days of their lives, and she liked the man, because he truly seemed to believe it. In a moment of sudden and frightening clarity, it occured to her that she was not above God, not alongside, and still not inside like this kind man, but still an outsider.

Harriet glanced sideways at Father Dittmer, who had not directly acknowledged her presence, though he had shaken her parents warmly by the hand and said vaguely that of course he would be delighted to call at the farm someday for afternoon tea. She wondered if he knew that she was still locked outside — somehow, she guessed that he did.

As the words of the service flowed on, she thought of her tree and the voice of God. Years later, someone propounded theories to her about adolescent sexual-religio fantasising. Even at that moment, the tree was fading as a real symbol of anything more than a place to cool herself in the fast-approaching summer — the summer she already expected to be her last one at the farm.

For among the other things she found surprising at high school had been the realisation that she had friends. She had defended herself at primary school for so long that when she had tackled high school with her aggressive saunter, the following she accumulated in her wake had seemed unreal. Gradually some of these followers had demonstrated a loyalty for her which in the end she gratefully acknowledged to be friendship.

Among these was a girl called Wendy Dixon, whom Harriet had befriended because she was secretly in love with her elder brother Francis. Francis had little to do with the carnal interest of 'it' in Harriet's eyes, though she supposed that if she ever got to know him well enough, 'it' would probably be a pleasant part of their relationship. She thought that he was quite simply the most beautiful person in the whole world. He also seemed to be rather more intelligent than some of his contemporaries, though this was something that Harriet could only judge from afar. He would walk slightly stooped, contemplating some inner secret she could only guess at, but sometimes she suspected that some of the perplexities of her own life sat heavily upon him too. She longed to ask him, to see some sign in someone that she was not alone in all the things that puzzled and bewildered her.

When Wendy first made friendly advances to her, she accepted them with a secret glee that she was getting closer to the object of her interest — desire was too strong a word. Once Wendy invited her over to the house. It was a long journey on her bike, but she devoted a whole Saturday to it. Francis was not there. Harriet learned that he was working somewhere, up the farm and that he wouldn't be back till after the evening milking. As Harriet had to be home for milking herself, there was no possible hope of waiting for him.

As the year wore on, Francis seemed quieter, even more remote. She knew that he was aware of her, for sometimes, idling by the places where she expected to find him in the school grounds, they would meet. His heavy-lidded dark brown eyes would flicker wide for a moment, then he would raise his cap gravely and pass on. Whatever was troubling him, Harriet was not told.

At the end of the year Francis left not only school but the district as well. Wendy told Harriet that her parents were angry, and seemed reluctant to discuss the matter. If it occurred to her that Harriet was unduly interested in Francis's fate, she gave no indication of it. Harriet had felt unenthusiastic about resuming the friendship the following year, but it seemed that something was expected of her from Wendy and indeed, Harriet herself had come to warm to the attention which her opinions, and frequent dissensions with the staff, attracted.

Throughout that year Harriet's loyal coterie grew. There was a certain recklessness and daring in her actions, there was so much she knew that no one else did, there were so many things that she didn't know at all. There seemed to be no halfway house. She suspected that people like Wendy had some basic information she lacked. By the same token, no-one had her flair for setting up arguments to which teachers had no answers.

There were times when she had sailed perilously close to the wind, but few pupils were dismissed from the high school. Erratic though her behaviour at Ohaka District High might be, it was the behaviour of an eccentric who would certainly get School Certificate, and as there were all too few such shining lights in the ranks, her survival was assured. Certainly she was dismissed from class and from the school council which she had had the audacity to treat as a democracy, and for three weeks one teacher had followed her around the playground, entreating her to apologise for her dissent in history class, so that she could be reinstated 'without any more fuss', and naturally, although the teacher didn't say so, without loss of face on her part. Harriet had finally said that she was sorry if she had caused the teacher any embarrass-ment, and regretted very much making her unhappy. The teacher had reported back to the head, and to Harriet's chagrin, she discovered that she had been interpreted as having delivered an apology for questioning the teacher's judgment, which was not what she had meant at all.

So, as the year after confirmation drew to a close, Harriet's tree became a refuge for dreaming about the fulfilment of unrealised longings, and as good a place as any to study.

At school, Harriet, Wendy and a handful of other girls would congregate in the lunch hour to discuss their futures. Wendy planned to go to Teachers' Training College if she got the magic piece of paper, though apparently there was some unspecified family difficulty owing to Francis's departure the previous year. Marie Walker entertained the same wistful hope, though her chances seemed incredibly slim. Ailsa Wilson's parents hoped that she too would become a teacher, not knowing at this stage that Ailsa was having a baby and planned to marry the father, a nineteen-year-old farmer's son. This occupied a considerable amount of the conversation, as Ailsa couldn't get married until the January when she turned sixteen, and thought it prudent to stay at school and out of range of her mother's observation for as long as she could, seeing she couldn't marry straight away. While secretly horrified by Ailsa's condition, Harriet was nevertheless grateful for having learned a little basic biology, through listening to the discussions of the other girls who assumed knowledge on her part and who discussed the whole business with fascinated regularity. Ailsa's sex life was now blissfully active, there being no concern on her part any more as to whether she got pregnant or not, and she was always ready to give a dissertation on her lover's prowess. Apparently it improved daily, though Ailsa thought her condition might have a lot to do with her supreme enjoyment, and she gazed contentedly on a future of child-bearing. She was deliciously graphic about the size of the father to-be's penis and how difficult it was to get it in on occasion, and from this Harriet was able to do some rough diagrammatic equations. While they didn't answer all her questions, these conversations gave her what she considered a working knowledge of the forbidden fruit and what she should probably try to avoid, seeing little future in Ailsa's rosy pictures.

Her own future was still very uncertain. One day she discussed it with her mother.

'I'm not staying on the farm, Mum, and that's that,' Harriet said.

'I didn't expect you would,' Mary replied quietly.

'Didn't you?'

'Not really. I wish you could, but we can't give you a very good life here. We can't afford to pay you if you stay on the farm. We could go on keeping you if you helped, though.'

'Helped? Do what you do?' Harriet thought of her mother's daily toiling with fence strainers, encroaching gorse and cows in all weathers.

'Or you could go back to school for another year,' said Mary quickly.

'A lot of good that would do me,' said Harriet scornfully. 'A sixth form of one. Great stuff. And who'd teach me? They've never had a sixth form at that place.'

'Do you want to go teaching, then?' said Mary.

'Me, teach? Good God, no.'

Mary blanched slightly at the blasphemy.

'Sorry,' Harriet muttered.

Mary wrinkled her forehead. 'You could go dental nursing,

they've got a hostel you could go to, but the head said you were too intelligent for that.'

'The head! You've been talking to that old idiot,' Harriet asked.

'Well ... I wanted to know what your chances were.'

'I don't want to stay on the farm, and I don't want to go teaching, and I'm damn sure I'm not going to go dental nursing. Bzzz, bzzz, bzzz, no thank you.'

'You can't have everything you want in life,' said Mary rather acidly.

Harriet looked at her mother. 'Some people can.'

Mary looked back at her daughter strangely. 'Yes, some people can if they try hard enough, and ...' she tailed away.

'If they're selfish enough?' said Harriet instinctively. Silence fell between them.

Finally Mary said, 'First you have to decide what you want.'

The girls at school were equally incredulous when she announced that she had no intention of going teaching. Wendy and Marie, who both desperately wanted to go, treated her as if she was a weird specimen that they had viewed under a microscope in biology lesson.

'What'll you do then?' Mary asked. 'You can't leave home if you don't go teaching.'

'You mightn't. I will,' said Harriet, though secretly she was beginning to wonder how she'd manage it herself. 'Anyway, would you go teaching if you didn't want to leave home?'

Wendy sat back on her heels, suddenly blushing scarlet. 'I'll be awful trying to teach physical education. And music.'

'You're scared, aren't you?' said Harriet.

'And you're hard as nails,' said Wendy.

'Why, because you don't want to face up to the fact that you'll probably be a lousy teacher?'

'Do you really think I'm that stupid?' said Wendy.

'No,' said Harriet, who hadn't really thought about it before, but could suddenly see Wendy much more clearly than she had ever done. 'I reckon you should paint and draw all the time. It's what you like doing best of all.'

'But I can't go away to do that. I'd starve.'

'Why can't you? Lots of people in Europe do. Anybody whose talented over there gets taught to do what they're good at properly, and they get famous ... and rich too.'

Wendy's temporary interest vanished. 'This isn't Europe,' she said shortly. 'It's New Zealand. You do what you can.'

'Even if you know you'll hate it?'

Wendy got up and walked away.

'You're pretty hard on her, really,' said Ailsa, momentarily distracted from her own concerns.

'It'll be pretty hard on the kids she teaches, too,' said Harriet.

'My, aren't we public-spirited?'

'I shouldn't let it worry you, your kid'll probably be too dumb to care,' said Harriet, nodding in the direction of Ailsa's waistline, and stalked off.

In the end, the headmaster and the history teacher came out to the farm to see the Wallaces, when the Teachers' Training College selection panel visited the school.

The teachers told the Wallaces that Harriet was wasting her life. She had no future outside of teaching, they had endured Harriet, they had coaxed her through high school for three years, they had given of their time to her because she was clever, it seemed, so that she might have a good future. What was it all for? What sort of gratitude was this? Had they been wasting their time?

'Yes,' said Harriet when the tirade finally came to an end, 'As far as I'm concerned, you've been wasting your time all right. You started wasting it thirty years ago when someone persuaded you that going teaching was a good thing to do. You never taught me one single thing I couldn't have found out for myself, except how to pass an exam.'

'Which you haven't passed yet,' the headmaster pointed out, his eyes glittering.

'No, but I probably will, and I need to, so that's why I've put up with school this long.'

'You're arrogant,' said the head.

'I expect so,' agreed Harriet.

'Why do you need School Certificate?' asked the history teacher.

'I mightn't need it, but then again, I might, to do what I want to do. I can't afford to gamble on not getting it.'

'And what do you want to do?'

'Be famous,' said Harriet levelly.

'Immature,' said the headmaster to her parents. 'She needs all the help she can get. I suggest you send her back to us for another year.'

'To knock into shape?' asked Harriet as she walked out. At the door she stopped and said, 'It's a bit late for that now, don't you think? After all, you've tried this long and failed.'

She did pass her exam. It wasn't the best mark in the school, Wendy did much better and Marie quite convincingly, while Harriet just squeezed through.

Mary wrote to her cousin Alice Harrison who lived in Weyville, a prosperous and growing town south of Ohaka. Alice had lived there since her immigration and subsequent marriage more than twenty-five years before. Both her children were grown up and she was a widow. She agreed to take Harriet.

She wrote that there were plenty of jobs going in Weyville, and she was sure she would know somebody who would know somebody who could get Harriet a job. It was a pity she didn't have better marks in School Certificate, but there you were, she'd been lucky with her children, both smart, and Mary hadn't had much luck, had she, so she was happy to do what she could for Harriet. At least she could learn to type at night school, and she might work up to something better than the process line at one of the factories if she put her mind to it. Not, Alice said, that she would put up with any nonsense. She'd never had any from her own two children and she certainly wasn't going to take any from Harriet, especially after she'd seen the report that Mary had sent to show prospective employers. She could tell that Mary hadn't been firm enough with the girl, but she supposed with all her troubles, what else could you expect. At least she had time now, and she would see to it that Harriet didn't go off the straight and narrow. So it was decided.

On the day before Harriet left, Ailsa was married in a great smother of white tulle and net that clouded the issue of her bulging stomach. At the wedding dance, Harriet waited for Jim to dance with her, but she only had him in a change partners waltz, and he kept smiling idiotically over her head at the school dental nurse, who had stayed on in the district at the end of the term.

'Do you know her?' Harriet asked, as all other conversation seemed to fail.

'Know her?' said Jim, with a huge complacent smile. 'You'll be dancing at *our* wedding in May, soon as the cows're dry.'

Harriet decided against telling him that she was going away the following morning; nor did she say that she wouldn't be back for his wedding.

On her last morning she got up and dressed and had breakfast with her parents for the last time.

Her father gave her an austere glance, and she knew he was looking at her lipstick. 'Don't come running to me when you get yourself into trouble, then' he said, and continued to eat.

Mary had nothing at all to say. Her hands were permanently thickened and red from washing up at the shed, Harriet noticed. When they had eaten, she followed Harriet into her bedroom and helped tie down her suitcase, a battered relic dating from her own immigration to New Zealand. When it was done, she went to the window and stood looking out.

'You'll miss the plums this year,' she said.

'Yes, another week and they would have been ripe.'

'Just too soon.'

Harriet looked at her mother and longed to put her arms around her and stroke her hair, once brown and thick like hers, now straggling and drawn back into a bun. But the Wallaces weren't that sort of family.

'Things always ripen in time,' said Harriet, not knowing what else to say.

Mary nodded. 'But if the season goes wrong, then you lose them. That's the way it is.'

Later the three of them stood together on the side of the road, awkward now that the time for parting had come, wishing to postpone it and at the same time willing it to be over. Before long a cloud of dust heralded the bus, which came trundling towards them. They shuffled together, touching, not touching, not knowing how to behave. The bus stopped, Harriet bought her ticket from the driver, the door slammed and they moved off. Down the long road she turned back to look and wave for a last time to the couple standing unusually close together, both smaller and somehow frailer than she had ever noticed. As she turned, a hawk spiralled from the river paddock. In the morning sun it looked as she imagined an eagle might. A great cloud of sparrows rose underneath it and then around it; they were attacking the larger bird. Almost like insects, they blotted out the world for an instant, then as the hawk rose high above them, they collapsed down towards the earth, and the big solitary bird, feathers gleaming, lifted higher and higher.

It seemed to have taken only a moment, but when the sky cleared of the sparrows, Harriet was out of sight of the farm, and her parents and Ohaka was dropping behind her.

3

At first Alice Harrison, seemed to be as formidable as her letter. Harriet barely knew her, for she had come to New Zealand many years before the Wallaces had done, and was considerable older than Mary. She had met Mary and Gerald off the boat from England and, in their first years before they moved to the north, some sort of contact had been maintained between them as the Wallaces had straggled from one run-down farm to another. There had been one or two visits south during Harriet's early childhood, but the trip to Weyville had finally proved too costly. Besides, they had little in common except family ties, though sometimes Harriet had detected a wistful note in her mother's voice when she spoke of cousin Alice. Alice's name was usually introduced into the conversation after talk of 'home'. There was no longer any point in going 'home', and there was no point in going to see cousin Alice. There was no longer any point in going anywhere, it seemed, just staying on in Ohaka.

Thus Harriet's image of her second cousin was very vague indeed, though she still had a rough mental picture of her outward appearance at least.

She had spent a lot of the school holidays wishing that she could think of some dashing way to leave home, having made so many brave statements about her future. It seemed a bit ignominious to be docilely trotting off to her elderly cousin's home for an unspecified job and the possibility of a typing class at night school, armed with a second-rate School Certificate. But when it boiled down, there wasn't much else she could do. There had been wild moments when she had even wished that she was joining Wendy and Marie at Teachers' Training College. The feeling would pass quickly when she considered the implications, but obviously there was little she could say to anyone on the subject of her departure, while the Ohaka community sat back with pride and considered their latest candidates for success. She was quite definitely not one of them.

The bus to Weyville trundled south till they reached Auckland, where after midday the driver announced they would stop for half an hour.

Harriet started to push her way through the crowd to the counter, to collect grey buns and muddy tea. The crowd was very thick, and the food looked unappetising. It occurred to her that she really wasn't very hungry — besides, she had a whole thirty minutes to spend in Auckland. She must be mad wasting her time on lunch.

Auckland! She'd never been there, or not that she could remember. It was a mild overcast day, the humid midsummer sky sitting low on the city.

Outside the bus depot, Harriet looked up and down the street. She walked a little way along, and to her left was a long wide street with more people in it than she had ever seen before. Not far away on her right lay the wharves. With a lifting heart she turned, and walked down towards the sea.

The port was full of boats, large and small, but few people seemed to be about. She leaned on a railing and stared down into the listless water. Then, quite suddenly, an edge of cloud lifted, and the sun came out. All the sea shone and twinkled at her, and the boats seemed to rock more easily at their moorings. A ship was drawing out to sea, and for the first time Harriet noticed that crowds of people were standing together on the dock, waving, cheering, crying, hanging onto streamers. They were some distance away from her, which was why she had not seen them immediately. The ship was tall and white and proud and its decks were lined with people, hundreds and hundreds of them it seemed, and they clutched their streamer ends, some of them as if their lives depended on it, and when the streamers broke they hung onto the remaining ends as if they were the last things left in life. Their faces, laughing a moment before, broke into weeping like those on the shore. The ship uttered a long wailing note, as if taking up the moment's grief.

Harriet had stood transfixed throughout the scene, which seemed to have lasted only a few moments. As quickly as it had lifted, the shutter of cloud fell again, and the sea resumed its sullen look. A woman walked towards her, her face set in harsh white lines.

'Excuse me,' said Harriet.

The woman looked at her and through her.

'Where is the ship going?' asked Harriet.

In a long sigh, the woman replied, 'It's going to the other side of the world.' She walked on.

Harriet turned away, wondering with a sudden quick fear just how long she really had been standing there.

Crowds of people were now coming towards her from the dock. As she hurried back to the bus depot, they seemed to engulf her on every side. She started to run, tripping and falling amongst them.

When she had freed herself from the throng, she ran up the street, her breath sobbing in her chest. The depot had a deserted air. A man wearing a khaki coat with NZR initialled on the pocket was sauntering around.

Harriet raced over to him and grabbed his arm.

'The bus to Weyville,' she gasped. 'Where is it?'

The man rolled a fat cigarette with the tip of his tongue from the centre of his mouth to the side. He poked a finger in the direction of the nearest corner. 'Reckon that's its back end,' he said.

So it was. The bus was just vanishing.

'I've missed it, then.'

'Looks like it, miss.'

'My luggage, will it still be on it?'

'No reason to take it off.'

Harriet's heart somersaulted. A fine start this was to life with

58

cousin Alice, her luggage turning up, and no sign of her. She only had a rough idea of what Alice looked like, but her letter had hardly been an encouraging testimony to the gentleness of her spirit. She looked around wildly. Across the road was a taxi rank, and a taxi had just cruised up to it. She had read about people hailing taxis in emergencies, and this seemed a crucial moment in which to take command of her life.

Within seconds she had slammed the door of the taxi behind her, and was perched on the edge of the front seat beside the driver. 'Follow that bus, please,' she ordered.

'Which bus?' said the driver, for it had now disappeared.

'The bus to Weyville,' said Harriet. 'Mind you,' she added lamely, 'I don't quite know where it would be, because I don't know the way to Weyville.'

The taxi driver almost appeared to be in the habit of pulling up at bus stops just after buses had left, because he seemed quite unconcerned.

'Right,' he said, as they eased into gear, and picked up speed, 'No trouble.' He glanced at his watch. Should pick it up round Newmarket.'

'You think so?' Harriet was overwhelmed by the possibility that her crazy reaction might pay off.

'Sure thing. Depends of course on whether it gets the lights and we don't or the other way round. First way it'll take longer, or we might miss it altogether; second way, we might pick it up at the top of Khyber Pass.'

Faced with such a gamble, Harriet had second thoughts. She reached for the purse in her pocket, knowing exactly how much was in it.

'And that is,' Harriet said woefully, 'we might catch it provided we don't go more than two pound ten's worth.'

'Oh dear,' said the driver, 'Now there's a thing, isn't it. Are you sure you really want to catch this bus?'

'I have to,' she said desparately. 'You see, I'm going to live with cousin Alice.' Her voice trailed away; there was too much to explain to this stranger upon whom she was suddenly so reliant.

'Tell you what,' he said, after a sideways look at her. 'Two quid's worth and the rest's on me.'

'You mean it?'

'Got a couple daughters myself, haven't I? Now go on, kid, watch out for that bus. We'll catch it.'

That was how Harriet came to ride into Weyville on a Road Services bus, some hours later, to face cousin Alice and the big wide world with exactly ten shillings in her purse.

Cousin Alice stood at the Weyville bus station, waiting for her protegée. As soon as Harriet saw her she recognised her, a tall spare woman with beautiful white hair drawn back into a bun on the back of her head, not a tight bun, but a big soft one, surrounded by expensive waving. Alice Harrison had been a beauty, there was no doubt about that. Her eyes were blue, as near to forget-me-not blue as it was possible to get, and pleasantly bright; soft, rather than piercing, or so it might seem to the casual observer. Her skin was aged of course, for she was in her sixties, yet fine and immaculate like bone china; and her hands reminded Harriet of an iris that had been pressed between the covers of a book, with faintly vlue veins pressing against the translucent petal. Her nails were painted a soft pink. She wore a tailored linen suit, nipped into a waist that was still amazingly small.

As the bus drew in, Harriet was overwhelmed with relief that she had managed to catch the bus again. To have disappointed this elegant lady at their very first encounter of any consequence was unthinkable. Her second reaction was to feel totally ashamed of her own gracelessness. She caught a glimpse of her reflection in the driver's rear vision mirror as she stood in the queue of people waiting to get out of the bus. Her cotton dress was baggy and ill-fitting over the home-made bra which she hadn't worn from confirmation day until now, but which she had put on that morning in a rush of loyalty towards Mary. Her brown hair was shaggy and rough and badly needed cutting. The eyes in the mirror stared back at her, brown flecked with green, in a sunburnt face. Not bad eyes, she thought, but I look like a heathen.

The queue shuffled forward, and the moment had come. Cousin

Alice was straining forward, searching each face. Her eyes lighted on Harriet and travelled over her. Harriet's heart sank. Obviously she was looking for a different sort of person. Alice's eyes returned to her when all other possibilities had been exhausted.

Hand extended, she moved forward. 'My dear Harriet, how like your father you've grown. No wonder I didn't recognise you.'

Was this the lady who had written such a strong letter to her mother? The disciplinarian? The mother of two successful children, who wasn't going to be put out by a girl with a poor pass in School Certificate, and who believed what they said about her on her report? The blue eyes appraised Harriet from head to foot. Later that night Harriet wondered if the reference to her father was a studied insult. Of course the relationship between Alice and her parents had lapsed when Gerald had failed to be successful.

Alice said, 'My dear, you must be starving.'

Harriet's suitcase was stored away in the back of Alice's Morris Minor and in a few minutes they were driving through the streets of Weyville towards what Harriet realised with a pang she must now regard as home. In the late afternoon, a few people meandered down what she took to be the main street. It was very wide, and lined with shops, a mixture of small old frontfaces and large expanses of glass. Milk bars stood on a couple of corners, and outside loitered boys and girls, the boys with drainpipe trousers and slicked-back hair, the girls wearing wide circular skirts halfway down their calves and a great deal of makeup.

'I'm afraid we have a rough element here,' sighed cousin Alice as they drove past, and Harriet was aware that she gave her a sidelong glance. 'Still,' she continued, 'there are some nice young people here. Of course, a great deal will depend on the sort of job we can get you.'

'Yes, Alice,' said Harriet meekly. Cousin Alice shot her a very sharp look indeed. Harriet didn't know what she had done to offend, but she felt the woman stiffening beside her. Little else was said on the rest of the drive, except for her cousin pointing out some of the streets, and a park which bounded the edge of a small sulky lake.

61

However, Alice seemed to regard it as one of the town's beauty spots and described it as a nice place for a walk on a summer evening after work. Warming a little, she also said she was very lucky that she and her husband had bought property near it all those years before, as of course now it made her place quite valuable. What value meant when you were perfectly happy where you were and never intended to shift, she had no idea, she said, though she supposed that her children would do quite nicely out of it one of these days. Not that she intended to die soon enough for them to make any plans about the sale of the property. Of course she wasn't mean in her treatment of them; she didn't want to be one of those well-off parents who actively encouraged their children to wish their death upon them, by sitting on all the money and not handing any out. Still, she was careful, one needn't go throwing money around, and Harriet's board would go into one of several trust funds she had. It all added up you know.

And on this note she lapsed once more into silence, leaving Harriet to contemplate the job that would be of such assistance in subsidising the future of the younger Harrisons.

The car pulled up at Alice's house. It was a tidy brick bungalow, half-hidden behind well-trimmed shrubs. At the gate was an arch of hedgeway, apparently shaped by a topiarist, who had provided some elaborate angles for them to walk under. A monkey puzzle tree stood on the front lawn. Several perfectly aligned gardens were full of marigolds and summer roses, dahlias and lobelia borders. It was more colourful than any garden Harriet had ever been in; farmers' gardens, if they existed, were almost invariable a wild tangle of free-standing self-sown seeds sprung from long-ago attempts at establishment when the farms had been opened up; that's how it was up north, at any rate. At the same time, there was something formidable about the regularity of this one.

'Well, what do you think of it?' asked Alice, watching her.

'It's awfully pretty,' said Harriet. 'It must be a lot of work. Do you have a gardener?'

'Good heavens, no,' said Alice briskly. 'Does your father have someone in to milk his cows?'

'No, but that's different, that's his work,' said Harriet.

'Quite so, and the garden is mine. We shall plant the asters out at the weekend.' From which Harriet divined that gardening had become a joint project in which she was involved. Things didn't change much, wherever you were.

Inside, the house was like the garden, well-appointed and immaculate. Harriet's bedroom was at the back of the house, a rather dark room, away from the sun, but carpeted and with a soft fat eiderdown on the bed. It was quite the nicest room she had ever occupied. But she thought of the plum tree at Ohaka, and suddenly she was sitting in the tidy room, crying. The whole weight of the day pressed down on her. She felt alone and totally inadequate. Right now Mary and Gerald would be putting the last of the cows down to the river paddock, and Mary would sluice the yard down until he came back, then she'd go up to the house and start preparing a meal, just for the two of them. And Harriet knew that they would sit in silence, having nothing new to add to the day except her going, and that was a subtraction, an absence that they could never fill. She thought of the time when Mary had lost the baby, and she wondered how many other children had escaped her mother's womb, and wished for the first time that her mother could have had another child to take away the pain of losing her.

Somewhere she suspected that there were other things besides poverty, work and the isolation of her life for which she would come to resent her parents; that they held concepts, motivations and deep-rooted prejudices that she did not share, and that in time she would evolve a set of values of her own which were in conflict with theirs. She knew that all was not right with their world, and yet now she felt so sick with longing for them that she was physically nauseated. What acts of comfort could they perform for each other, she wondered; what might somehow ease their hurt, their loss? What fumblings in the old oak bed would be repeated tonight to hold them together against the loneliness outside? What was it all about, what was the whole purpose of their lives that they went on enduring and suffering and losing and were finally left alone on the arid farm? None of it made sense.

63

Harriet was aware that someone had come into the room, and knew that it must be Alice. She turned her face away from her, towards the window which faced a high wooden pailing fence.

'It's natural to be upset when you leave home. You haven't been away before, have you?' said Alice.

Harriet shook her head.

'You'll feel better when you've had something to eat. Why don't you wash you hands and face, and come into the dining room? I left a meal prepared when I went to get you — I was sure you'd be needing something.'

Harriet realised that she hadn't eaten since early that morning, and even then it hadn't been much. She nodded gratefully. 'Thank you, Alice,' she murmured.

Alice paused at the door. 'I think that's something we should talk about,' she said, turning back. Intuitively, Harriet knew that whatever had disturbed Alice in the car had happened again.

'I notice you call me Alice.'

The girl studied her cousin's face with care. 'What should I call you?'

'You're a great deal younger than I am. It seems a little ... shall we say — impertinent.'

'You are my cousin,' said Harriet, and repeated, 'What should I call you?'

'It's true you're my cousin, second cousin to be accurate. But I really think ... to have a child, a child,' she emphasised, 'call me by my Christian name, is really ... not good form. A lot of my friends visit here. They would find it ... most odd.'

'Will I call you Mrs Harrison, then?'

'Oh dear, no. No, my friends would find that most peculiar too, if I explained that you were a relative, as of course I shall have to.'

Harriet started to feel mildly exasperated, but it seemed a poor time to let it show. She said, as reasonably as she could, 'Then I'm sorry, but I can't see what I should call you. You'll have to help me.'

Apparently this was the opening Alice had been waiting for. She said sweetly, 'I think Aunt Alice would be best, don't you?'

Silently she withdrew from the room, leaving Harriet seething.

Ten shillings, that was all she had, just ten shillings, and somehow she had a feeling that ten shillings would not buy her a bed in any of Weyville's hotels. At least she was beginning to feel like herself again.

After she had washed, she went out and joined Alice at the table. A meal of cold meat and salad had been prepared and Harriet grasped her knife and fork eagerly.

'Gently, dear,' said Alice with mild reproval. She bowed her head and murmured with seemingly endless emphasis, 'For what we are about to receive may the Lord make us truly thankful.' She raised her head, and observed Harriet, whose eyes were fixed straight ahead. 'You don't give thanks, I see.'

'Not till I know what I'm giving thanks for,' said Harriet. 'And then I like to say it to peoples' faces.'

Alice made no comment, and Harriet started her meal. As she ate, she felt herself recovering completely. The history teacher's face flashed in front of her. It was possible that Alice was made of sterner stuff than the history teacher, but on the whole, although a cursory examination of the situation didn't make it immediately apparent, she herself held most of the cards.

Putting her knife and fork together on the plate, she said deliberately, 'Thank you, Alice. That was very nice. I was very hungry.'

The forget-me-not eyes looked as if they'd been left in the frost overnight. 'I thought we'd discussed the subject of my name,' said Alice.

'You made a suggestion, I've considered it. Now I'll tell you what I think of your suggestion.

Alice looked as if she was about to fling Harriet straight out into the street on the spot. 'Please go on. I'm fascinated.'

'Thank you. Well ... the point is, you are my cousin, as I said before. Only my second cousin, I know, yes, you've reminded me of that. So I should prefer to address you correctly. I'll call you Mrs Harrison if you like, I'll call you Cousin Alice at all times if you like, or I shall address you as Alice in private and by no name at all in the company of your friends if you like. Or I shall simply leave here tonight. I have money. I know you didn't expect my parents to provide me with any money, but they have. I'll find a room in Weyville for the night and leave for Auckland in the morning. There should be work there for me. After all, what's the difference between a factory in Weyville and a factory in Auckland?'

'You couldn't do that,' said Alice.

'Yes, I could. Easier than I could call you my aunt when you don't happen to by my aunt. I might be a child by your standards, but I'm not a baby.'

You may be excused,' said Alice coldly.

In her room Harriet sat shivering. Trust her to make such a total idiot of herself, she thought. As if she had enough money to get herself from here into the middle of Weyville, let alone to Auckland. She couldn't do a thing except shiver in this neat, unlovely room. But there was no way she was going to go home. However bitterly she might have missed her parents a short time before, however attractive Ohaka might seem from this distance, there was no going back. She'd laid herself on the line. Is this going to be the story of my life? she wondered. Always sticking my neck out, taking chances, not weighing up the outcome of things.

There was a tentative knock on the door, Harriet didn't reply. Slowly the door opened, and her cousin's voice said, 'It's ... Cousin Alice. May I come in?'

She came in, and sat down beside Harriet. For some minutes neither said anything, then they turned to each other at the same instant. 'I'm sorry,' they said together.

A faint awkward smile crossed Alice's face. 'I suppose we'd better try and get to know each other a little better, hadn't we?' Harried nodded.

Taking a deep breath, Alice continued, 'I'll help you find a job. You'll need to have a little attention paid to your appearance, if you don't mind my saying so. I expect a little help round the place, not much, no more than I expected from my own family when they were your age, the dishes, the garden, that sort of thing ... your board will be a lot less than you'd get anywhere else, you know. Apart from that, I won't interfere in your life, provided you don't interfere in mine. Do you understand?'

'Not entirely,' said Harriet.

'You're not my child, but I've got a responsibility for you, and I've got a position in this town. Whether you approve of that or not is of no great interest to me, providing you do nothing to bring my position into disgrace. I don't want any scandals round here. Do you understand now?'

'I think so.'

'You're a great deal cleverer than I'd expected,' said Alice. 'I apologise if I treated you ... less than civilly. Now tell me, what do you want out of life?'

'I want ... began Harriet, and stopped. What did she want? 'I want to do well. I want to do better than my parents.'

It was a betrayal, a sellout to this woman; still, it had to be said. And it was the truth. Again, Alice measured her with a long look, re-evaluating, re-estimating.

'That's up to you. If you mean that, I think we should get on very well. In the meantime, shall we say three months' trial for both of us? Do you consider that fair?'

'Yes. Extremely fair. If I were you, I'd have sent me packing tonight.'

'I know. That's why I find you so much more interesting than I had anticipated.' A real smile crossed her face for the first time. 'Don't consider the battle won on the strength of one victory.'

'How could I?' said Harriet. 'I'm not at all sure that I have, anyway. Only a splendid tactician could turn a retreat to such advantage.'

If that remark nonplussed Alice, she didn't show it. 'I think you should get some rest ... Cousin Harriet. We're going to be busy tomorrow.'

The upshot of this was that Harriet, somewhat better groomed, with her thick brown hair layered into the back of her neck, a fresh new linen skirt and light print blouse covering a properly constructed brassière, took to the job circuit, a day or so later.

Finding a job proved no easy task. Weyville had its own problems. While the surrounding forests were beginning to provide some employment, particularly for young men, it was limited. Most young people who displayed any ability at all had been smartly shipped off to Auckland or Wellington to find better jobs, or to go teaching, particularly if they were girls. Harriet quickly realised that her fury about Ohaka's policy of doing exactly the same thing was rather futile; Weyville simply did it on a much larger scale.

What was worse, she also realised that Alice knew this and that she held very little hope for her prospects, long-or short-term. Alice might be curious, perhaps even bewildered, by some conflicting aspects of Harriet's personality, but basically she still saw her as an indifferent scholar from a whistle-stop North Auckland farming village, whom she had taken off Mary's hands out of the goodness of her heart, so that she could find some employment, however menial. To underrate Alice's knowledge of the local scene was unrealistic, as she had been through job placement for her own children years before, not long after the war. They had proved no particular problem for her, because they were clever and diligent, and Alice and Ted, her late husband, had sunk the appropriate amounts of money into seeing that they were justly rewarded with a place in the academic sun. Alice thanked her God (a very important figure in her life) that she'd never been placed in the position of some parents, and felt that it would break her up if she'd ever had to try and place a child of hers in Weyville. Of course, as Harriet wasn't hers, she felt a certain challenge in trying to find her a position, without the emotional trauma that would have attended the matter if Harriet had been her own child. Harriet discovered this by surreptitiously listening to equally surreptitious telephone calls, to people who 'Ted used to know' and who might be able to help.

Alice's general view of Harriet seemed fairly depressing, and within a couple of days, despite the confidence that her new appearance now engendered, Harriet felt herself slowly slipping. It had never occurred to her that she wasn't good. Of course, she was going to be very good. Not good at anything specific, just good — the question of her ultimate goodness was never in doubt. But serious doubts were forming in her own mind, and she was beginning to see very little reason to challenge Alice's view of her.

To make matters more difficult, the previous year's school leavers who had stayed on in Weyville already had the available jobs.

Finally, when things were starting to seem fairly desperate, and Alice was going around with a distracted expression, the phone rang. The caller was a friend of hers who had gone back to work in a local department store when her children had left home. Elsie had rung to pass on a bit of gossip. Julie, who worked on the haberdashery counter, was having a baby. And she wasn't married, either. An awful tragedy for her mother, but there you were, and now wasn't that the end?

Alice agreed, and they commiserated over Julie's mother for some minutes. Then, with a gleam in her eye, Alice pounced.

'Who is going to take Julie's place?' she asked.

It seemed that Elsie hadn't thought about that, and supposed that they could really get by without a replacement. After all, Julie hadn't done much work round the place, and now all she could think about was weddings. The little hussy was actually thinking about getting married in white, could you believe it?

Within half an hour Alice and Harriet were being interviewed by the store manager. With considerable deference to Alice, whom Harriet guessed had probably been a very good customer for many years, he said he could really see no reason why Harriet shouldn't start the following day. Mr Stubbs looked remarkably like his name, being short and thickset, was tufty gingery hair round his coarse-skinned face yet with oddly tiny white soft hands. He blew his nose, mopped his face with a handkerchief and said that the sooner this other girl got on her way the better. Not that he could exactly sack her, but he wouldn't encourage her to stay any longer than a week or so. It would not hurt her and Harriet to be on the counter together for the time being, either. Julie mightn't be much use, but at least she knew where the buttons and hooks and eyes were and what size was kept in what drawer, and what with having her School Certificate and all, Harriet was certainly a better sort of girl than some they employed.

Alice asked if it would be possible for Harriet to leave fifteen minutes earlier on Thursday nights so that she could go to her typing class at night school.

Mr Stubbs' eyes narrowed, 'Doesn't Harriet intend to stay?' he asked.

'Oh, yes,' Alice assured him hurriedly, 'But Harriet could find it useful to have a bit of typing, you know. And,' she added with a flash of inspiration, 'she is the sort of girl who might work herself up in your organisation. After all, you do have quite a large office staff, don't you?'

Mr Stubbs scratched the back of his thick neck, causing an explosive-looking pimple to start suppurating. He flinched at the pain of it, but finally agreed that this was quite a laudable ambition. However, he would have to take two shillings a week off Harriet's pay.

'What would the total be, then?' faltered Harriet, feeling that after such an enormous concession she should be grateful for anything that came her way.

'Three pounds eighteen clear.' His look challenged her to take it or leave it.

'Thank you,' whispered Harriet.

Alice was very cheerful that evening, and roasted a chicken for dinner. It was a good meal, and Harriet felt her spirits lifting. At least she was employed. In a week's time she would have three pounds eighteen of her very own, and the week after that, and the week after that. It didn't do to dwell too long on the fact that the point of her adventure was so far contained in a job on a department store haberdashery counter, only vacated by its previous incumbent because of an unfortunate condition. The world wasn't exactly shouting out for her talents, but it was a start.

Julie turned out to be a sallow girl with permed blonde hair. She seemed indifferent to Harriet's presence, but considerably more methodical than Harriet had anticipated from the comments she had heard. Hooks and eyes, buttons and thread came in a variety of weights and sizes and it was no good trying to fool customers who were their own home dressmakers that they wanted anything but what they specifically asked for. If you did eyebrows would be raised in long-suffering supplication and fingers would be drummed on the counter.

The weather in Weyville was hot and oppressive day after day. By midday, the shop was like an oven. The customers were almost all old, or mothers of querulous children, sweltering in prams or held in harness by leather reins. After the lunch break, Harriet felt as though she were suffocating. The whole weight of her loneliness had started to bear down on her afresh. It was an exhausting process.

Julie was staying on for another fortnight, but they had hardly exchanged a dozen words that did not deal with the shapes and sizes of domes and buttons or the ever-present heat. Whatever was going on in her mind, and it was obvious that there was a great deal, she didn't seem prepared to share it.

When closing time came on the second Tuesday that Harriet was at the shop, Julie followed her into the cloakroom.

'You want to walk along with me?' said Julie.

Harriet looked up in surprise. 'Yes, please,' she said, trying to conceal her eagerness. She didn't find her pale pregnant workmate particularly appealing, but being with anybody in the world was better than being alone.

The two girls walked along in silence. Harriet hadn't asked where they were going, but it seemed to be in the general direction of Alice's house. Perhaps Julie lived near there. She hadn't thought to ask, and it wouldn't have meant much anyway.

Near the lake that Alice had pointed out on the first day was a milk bar. Harriet had noticed it as she walked home, and, again, as on the first day, she had seen a group of young people gathered around it. She had been too shy to look up as she passed, but there had been a whistle or two. The atmosphere made her very nervous.

'Coming in?' said Julie.

'You mean ... into the milk bar?'

71

'Why not? Don't you like milk bars?'

'I've never been in one,' admitted Harriet.

'What?' Julie looked at her as if she was some strange curiosity. 'Wait till I tell the kids!'

'No, please don't,' begged Harriet. 'No, honestly, I won't come in if you do.'

Julie shrugged. 'Suit yourself.'

As they walked in, the whistles became deafening. They drowned out the jukebox in the corner, which seemed to be fairly jumping off the floor with 'Blue Suede Shoes.'

Harriet knew something must be expected of her. She forced herself to look around. There were about a dozen boys in the room and six or seven girls. A couple had been jiving in the corner. As Harriet looked around they stopped; the whistles died down.

The boys wore stovepipe trousers, and their hair was slicked back with grease. Some of the girls wore the huge circular skirts she had noticed before, others were in tight skirts that showed their bottoms. In spite of the warmth of the evening, most of them were wearing cardigans back to front, buttoned down their backs, with sleeves pushed back to their elbows.

'Hi, everyone,' said Julie. 'This is Harriet.'

'G'day, Harriet. What're you having?' asked one of the boys, at last.

'Er ... a milkshake, please," said Harriet, wondering if she was meant to pay for it. 'Chocolate.'

'Choc-o-late for the little lady,' said the boy, with a nasal imitation of what Harriet imagined was meant to be an American accent. She started scrabbling round in her purse.

'I'll pay for it,' she said anxiously.

'Oh, Ay'll pay for it, will Ay? Say, Julie, where'd you pick up this twanky doll from? She suck a plum for lunch?'

The kids had pimples and spots, and she noticed that none of them was particularly good-looking. She felt as she had in the old days at school, and yet she'd had a chance to stop it being like that. Only a year before, she'd made a stand for herself. It hadn't won her any friends amongst authority, but she supposed that this lot didn't stand for authority, except maybe that of the group. That's the way it had been at school, the last years, and things had been all right then. She took a deep breath.

'I'm not a twanky doll,' said Harriet firmly. 'I come from up north because there was no work up where I lived. My family are English, but I'm not, I'm a Kiwi. I can't help sounding like I do, there weren't that many people living near us for me to talk to besides my parents, so it's hardly any wonder if I talk more like them than anyone else. So either you like it or you lump it.'

The kids were listening intently.

'And if you don't like it, okay, then I have been eating plums, but if you stand too close I might just spit the stones in your face.'

The boy who'd offered her the milkshake grinned.

'All right, Twanky Doll. Wanta jive?'

The atmosphere had turned all right. He said 'Twanky Doll' in a friendly sort of way that suggested that if she wanted to stay it was as good a name for her as any, nothing malicious intended. She smiled back.

'I can't jive, but I don't mind if you teach me.'

'Well, what d'you know!' The boy let out a whoop and a holler and grabbed her hand. 'Come on, baby, let's go. Hey, feed the machine, we got learning to do here this day.'

'You going to dance with Noddy, then?' asked one of the girls. Harriet glanced at Julie and back to the other girl.

'Not if you don't want me to. I only want to learn the dance.'

The girl lifted her shoulder and let it fall with a flounce. 'Nobody's stopping you doing that.'

The money in the jukebox fell into the slot with a jangle and the beat started. It was 'Blueberry Hill'. Harriet felt the music in her head, her thighs, right down to her feet. Noddy took her hand, his feet slid apart, knees bending. He jerked her towards him and she half fell.

'Not like that, Twanky Doll, lean back, that's right, like you was fighting me, good, good, fight baby, fight, rock that's right, that's right ... follow me feet, beautiful ...' He let go her hand, she lurched into space and he caught her, as it seemed she must surely

73

fall headlong into the seat beside them. 'And around you go when I let go, twirl baby, again like this, and around, come on Larry an' Jill, come along with us ... let her see ...'

Another couple got up and joined them. The rhythm inside her started to make sense as she followed Jill. 'More, more' shouted Noddy. 'Stay with it, Twanky Doll, you're coming on great ...'

'You were my thrill ... on blueberry hill ...

She was exhilarated, she was flying, she was suddenly dying, as Noddy whipped her body horizontal to the floor and flung her like a dart as far as she would go back through his legs. He pulled her back up as the record ended. 'Well, how about that,' he said, shaking his head in wonder. 'For a beginner, that wasn't bad.

'Well, gee, thanks,' retorted Harriet. 'I guess you're coming along quite good yourself.'

The others laughed and Noddy shook his head again, this time in admiration. Harriet wondered if he got his name from the number of times he waggled his head.

The proprietor of the milk bar had been watching more and more uneasily.

'What say we have one mo' dance?' suggested Noddy. 'Really shape up.'

'You kids made enough noise for one day,' yelled the proprietor.

'Ah, get knotted,' Noddy called back.

'I reckon I'd better be getting on, anyway,' said Harriet. 'The cousin I live with won't like it much if I'm late for dinner.'

'Yeah, come on,' said Julie, 'I gotta be on my way too. See you, guys.'

Everyone called back, including the girls, and Noddy called, 'Come again, Twanky Doll.'

Outside, the air was still thick, but a slight breeze was stirring some life into the evening. At the lake, Julie stopped.

'You have to go home yet?'

'I guess not for a little while. But soon.'

Julie flopped wearily down onto the grass, and Harriet followed. 'You did real good in there,' said Julie.

'Thanks. Are they milk bar cowboys?' It was an expression

Harriet had heard and read in the papers up north. She thought they were supposed to have motor bikes as well, but couldn't remember seeing any round the milk bar.

'Milk bar cowboys? Oh if you like. If you wanta put a label on them.'

The remark surprised Harriet. Perhaps there was more to Julie than met the eye.

'I don't believe in putting labels on anybody,' she said.

'Well, there you are. Didn't think you would. Didn't seem the sort.'

'How can you tell what sort I am?'

Julie picked a piece of grass, stretched it expertly between her thumbs, and blew. A piercing whistle split the air. Both girls giggled as a duck flew up from reeds at the waterside, letting out a startled and indignant trail of noise.

'I dunno that I can tell anything any more. I've never been much of a picker at things, for that matter. Took to you, though. See I've always had a big fat label stuck on me.'

'You have?'

'Yeah. No-hoper. They're not disappointed now, are they.'

Harriet took it that she meant the baby, which Julie hadn't mentioned to her before.

'You'll feel okay when you get married,' she said.

'Married?' Julie laughed shortly. 'You gotta be kidding.'

'But ... Cousin Alice said...'

'Yeah, yeah, I know, Cousin Alice and old Elsie and my old woman and the whole darn town, they all said wah, wah, look at Julie Simmons, got herself up the duff, and I'll bet she gets herself married in white and a veil and all, she's just got the cheek to.'

'They said ... you said...'

Julie was quiet. Then she dropped her head forward on her knees and started to shake without sobbing, or even seeming to be crying outwardly at all.

'Yeah,' she said in a very low voice. 'I did say it, too. But it's no good, you know. I had to say something ... like I couldn't just say, yeah well, I'm going off to the home to have a baby and I don't know whose it is for sure or nothing, could I? Not while I was still here.'

Harriet sat very still. She remembered Ailsa prattling on. This seemed very different. Come to think of it, Ailsa seemed very unreal, like a litttle girl playing out fairy stories. Only for her, it seemed to have been all right. There were fairy stories after all, and she would live happily ever after. She looked at Julie's bleak face, and supposed that she was about to be admitted to some sphere of the adult world which she hadn't seriously anticipated until now.

'See, I got a boyfriend, well, we got on all right,' Julie was saying. 'Alf his name was. Not much of a name, like one of them jokes, eh, but he was a good sort. He wouldn't set the world on fire, but he was okay.'

'Was he one of the crowd at the milk bar?' asked Harriet.

'Nah, not really. He used to come in sometimes, but he was older, see. That lot's all the kids I went round with at school, most of 'em anyway, give or take a couple that come for the forestry. Mind you, that's what Alf came here for, come up from Wellington, 'cause he likes the outdoors. Anyway, he went home over Christmas. I was mad as hell because I was looking forward to a good time then, but he said his family was kinda close. So-o I was on the loose, see. And so was Noddy.'

'Noddy!'

'Yeah. Nance, the girl that didn't want you to dance with him, she got sick and couldn't go out for a bit either. Well one night I was just mucking round the fairground ... they have a fair here at Christmas, pity you missed it, it was great ... and I run into Noddy. Well ... I dunno, you kind of get used to it and I was missing not having a bit, so, you know ... he had his brother's car, and we come down here.'

'Right here?'

'Yeah. Everyone comes down here to have it off. I tell you it's something terrible in the moonlight, if it's a bright night. A whole row of cars and a bare bum going for the record in every one of them. He was okay too, but I couldn't go anywhere with Noddy. You know, not for a big deal.'

76

'So you think the baby's his?'

'Dunno. No ... that's not true I know darn well it is.'

'You told him?'

'Don't be nuts. I haven't told anyone. Not anyone in the whole world. Not till you.'

'Why me?'

'Got to tell someone, don't I? I mean, the whole thing's driving me nuts. See, I told Alf, but he was too cunning. He was real careful about when we done it, and he reckons it's a thousand to one it could be his unless I got my dates mixed up.'

'What d'you mean?'

'Mean? Well, rhythm, you know.'

'No.'

'Honest?' As Harriet was obviously telling the truth, Julie elaborated. 'You must know. You know ... not having it off in the middle of the month. Alf was real good about that. He looked after me like that. That's what he said to me too when I told him, he said, 'I looked after you, Ju—Ju, that's what he used to call me — and you done this to me. Anyway, he's buggered off now, I don't know where he is.'

The lake stirred under chill little breezes. Harriet shivered.

'Are you going to tell him, then?'

There was a long silence. 'No,' said Julie at last. 'No, they might try and make him do something about it.'

'You mean, get married?'

Julie nodded.

'You wouldn't have to,' said Harriet.

Julie looked at her sideways. 'Of course I would. You know that.'

There was such a simple inevitable logic about the way she said it that Harriet believed her.

'Would it matter so much?'

The other girl stared out onto the ugly manmade stretch of water. Her face had a sparseness that Harriet had not noticed before, a kind of paring back of flesh to the essentials. Harriet had an odd sensation that Julie was, if not beautiful, at least fine, and that sitting here with her was good and that she wouldn't forget it.

'Yes, it would matter,' Julie said. 'I'm thinking about the kid, see. Someone'll take it in that can afford to look after it, and who'll really want to look after it properly, as much ... as much as I could, if I could.' She started to cry hard, sobbing and shaking and snuffling, the fine spare look dissolving puffily into her sodden handkerchief. 'Jesus, Harriet, I won't even get to see what it looks like, they don't even let you see it, but I will. Honest, I'll fool them. No matter how much it hurts I'm not going to give in, I'm going to have a look at it before they take it away. They're not going to fill me up with dope so as I can't see anything. I want to see my baby, wouldn't you want to see your baby?'

'Yes, oh yes,' said Harriet fervently. 'Couldn't you keep it? D'you have to give it away?'

Julie got to her feet, still trying to mop up her face. There was an air of finality about her.

'No,' she replied shortly. 'Don't you understand what I've been saying? I got to do what's best for it. That doesn't count keeping it. I love it too much. Always wanted a baby, all the time Mum didn't want me, I used to think, well, some day I'll have my own baby, and then I won't have to worry about anyone loving me because the baby'll love me. Of course I knew I'd have to have a husband. Maybe I should have thought more about that part. Anyway, I've got my little baby inside of me, and I'm not going to be rotten to it.'

They walked along in silence. There didn't seem much for Harriet to say. At Cousin Alice's gate, they stopped.

'Well ...' Harriet began awkwardly.

'I'm finishing up at the shop tomorrow,' said Julie. 'Told old Stubbs to make up my pay for me. Should have seen how relieved he was; almost made me laugh. I'll be around for a couple more weeks till there's a vacancy in the home up in Auckland. You want to go round with me?'

Harriet looked at her questioningly.

'Well, go on, don't look like that. You worried about your reputation?'

'Of course not. I don't have one.'

'You might if you stick round with me. Well ... seems to me you don't have that many friends.'

'I don't have any.'

'Didn't think so. The kids liked you. You could stick around with them after I've gone. Think about it anyway. There's a party Saturday night.'

Inside the house, Cousin Alice said, 'Who was that girl you were with?'

Harriet told her. Cousin Alice pursed her lips and said, 'I thought as much. When does she finish at the shop?'

'Tomorrow,' said Harriet.

'Just as well. I wouldn't like you to be seen walking home with her too often.'

'She introduced me to some of her friends on the way home. They seemed nice.'

'Did you go into that milk bar?' said Cousin Alice sharply.

'No,' said Harriet, quickly. 'Of course not.'

'That's all right, then.'

'But she did ask me to go out with her on Saturday night.'

'She didn't! The cheek! Where to?'

'Oh ... the pictures.'

'Really,' said Cousin Alice. 'You told here what to do with herself, I hope.'

'I thought I might quite like to go.'

'You what?'

'Well I don't know anybody, do I?' Harriet said defensively.

Alice looked shrewd. 'So she's not getting married, eh?'

'How should I know?'

'Because she wouldn't have you in tow if she was.'

'She hasn't got me in tow. I like her, that's all.'

Alice shook her head. 'You won't be going anywhere with that one. Not from this house.'

Harriet could see that she was deadly serious. It didn't even seem worth an argument. She wondered what to tell Julie the next day, and settled for the truth. Julie didn't seem at all surprised; in fact, she behaved very much as if this was entirely as she had expected,

79

and Harriet was relieved that she had told her. She felt that Julie would have seen through any lies.

That evening, when Harriet would dearly have liked to walk home with Julie, Cousin Alice was waiting in her little Morris Minor outside the shop. She had 'just been passing by' and thought Harriet might like a lift home. Julie hung back.

'Could you drop Julie off, too?' asked Harriet as boldly as she could, thinking that things had gone far enough, and after all it had been Julie's last day at the shop.

Cousin Alice was obviously nonplussed, but her immaculate manners came to the fore. 'Certainly,' she said smoothly, opening the back door.

Julie hesitated a moment, then tossing her head defiantly she got into the car. 'Drop me off at the corner milk bar, please, Mrs. Harrison,' she said, as she settled herself.

And that was really that, for the time being anyway. The next day being pay day, Harriet bought herself a tight pointy brassière, turned her cardigan back to front, pushing it up to the elbows, put a deposit on a tight skirt on store discount, and started training her hair into a pony tail.

If Cousin Alice noticed, she said nothing, but she 'just passed by' the store more frequently. The risk of meeting her was great enough to make Harriet avoid the milk bar. On the days that Cousin Alice didn't pick her up, walking past was something of an ordeal. Julie vanished within a week or two, as she had intimated to Harriet she would. On the day before she was due to leave, Harriet had been walking home. Julie had ducked out of the milk bar to say goodbye, but when the two girls stood in the middle of the street, there didn't seem much to say. They looked at each other awkwardly and Harriet said, 'Good luck'. It seemed limp and inadequate, and from where she stood the whole situation looked decidedly unlucky.

From time to time, in the weeks that followed one of the milk bar crowd would call out, 'Hullo, Twanky Doll' as she passed. At first the greeting seemed friendly, but before long she detected a mocking note.

Easter came and went, and with it a small triumph for Alice.

An ex-boarding school pupils' reunion dance was held in the town, so that when the top brass returned to pay their respects to their parents, they were able to mix in seemly company. Cousin Alice's own children had once belonged to such a group, and her contacts were still good enough for her to organise an invitation for Harriet.

Harriet suspected that Alice had said that poor little Harriet was so far away from her parents that she couldn't get home for Easter. The thought of going home at Easter had loomed in Harriet's mind but her finances were still precarious. They had been so severely hobbled, as her feet had been, by the purchase of a pair of stiletto-heeled shoes, that a trip home seemed more and more difficult. By the time her mother had written and offered her the fare home, the buses were fully booked and there was no retreat from Weyville. Faraway Ohaka had never seemed more beautiful or tantalising, and the thought of the effort it must have cost her mother to find the fare quite desolated her. Yet, a small warning bell sounded inside her head, telling her that if she were to go back to Ohaka now she might never return to Weyville — and Weyville, limited though it was, still held vague promise of things to come.

So as Easter approached, Harriet and Alice found themselves companionably sewing and hemming some green chiffon stuff to be set over paper-stiff taffeta, Alice delighting in Harriet's response to her instructions.

The dance was surprisingly successful from the point of view of Harriet's social conquests. The accent which had dogged her for so long proved an advantage. She danced well, despite the fact that Noddy's lesson in the milk bar had been her only contact with rock and roll. Music gave her feet wings, and dancing seemed as natural as breathing. The mothers of the young elite were enchanted, and told Cousin Alice, who was watching in the wings adorned in pale grey crepe, that her relative was delightful, and what a pleasure it must be for them both to be living together. Alice smiled benignly and nodded her head, eyeing Harriet with brand-new approval.

Unfortunately, Harriet found the company itself intolerably

boring, as it was composed of aspiring and perspiring under-graduates, student teachers, and a trainee Presbyterian minister whose assumptions about God she made the mistake of challenging. He was a dark man with a long upper lip and a great deal of Brylcreem on his hair, and he managed to hold himself away from Harriet's crotch in a way that clearly stated that he was doing his social duty and no more.

After they had danced, an uneasy little knot gathered at one end of the room, and Harriet presumed from the sidelong glances in her direction that her conduct was being discussed.

However, the moment soon passed, for supper was approaching. Cousin Alice took her aside and said in a gentle reproving tone, 'Harriet, dear, you're doing beautifully, but don't be intelligent will you? There's a good girl.'

'Of course not,' said Harriet, understandingly.

The rest of the dance went well.

The following week, Cousin Alice was able to say with much satisfaction that the dance had paid off well; one of her friends had said that when Harriet had learned typing for six months, there might be a place for her in her husband's office.

Harriet's heart sank at this. There was a small matter which she had over-looked discussing with Cousin Alice. She and typing didn't seem to get on very well, so much so that she had feigned a headache twice in the past month and sat outside during the class. Worse, and much more dire in its implications, during the week after the dance she hadn't gone at all.

On the Thursday night, instead of going on to the College and her typing class, she had suddenly balked in front of the milk bar. Music streamed out of the milkbar. The pale Weyville day was drawing to a close, lit by the neon interior of the shop. The jukebox shone with its row of numbers lit up, and cigarettes moved and glowed in circles in peoples' hands, or just marked stars in the air. Like the weight of sorrow, loneliness overwhelmed Harriet. She could never return to Ohaka and she was not a part of Weyville that made any kind of sense. She would never belong to the boarding school set, or to this crowd, who, with equal assurance, ran their own secret society. There was no halfway house, and she was alone.

Yet she had briefly been admitted, and perhaps they would have her back. Tentatively, almost furtively, she went in, and without looking left or right, she walked up to the counter to ask for a Coke. She paid for it, took a straw and stood sipping it, eyes downcast. The place had gone quiet, she was being watched.

'Well, hi, Twanky Doll,' said a voice at her elbow. It was Noddy. 'We thought you was never coming back.'

'I'm just passing by,' Harriet said nervously.

'You're always passing by,' said Noddy, 'only difference is, this time you've stopped. That's real friendly. What say you come and say hi to some of the others?'

Nance was the only one who didn't seem especially pleased to see her. Nance's hair was now a sight to behold. It had been teased up and up to the highest, biggest bouffant that Harriet could imagine. Her own hair, which still wasn't long enough for anything but a scraped-back unbecoming knot, seemed shabby by comparison. She couldn't take her eyes off Nance's hair.

'Something wrong?' inquired Nance.

Harriet shook her head dumbly.

'You'd think so.'

'Your hair looks fabulous, Nance,' Harriet offered at last.

Nance was obviously pleased, and relented. 'Want a cig?'

'Er, I don't, thanks,' said Harriet.

It had occurred to her that she probably should take a cigarette if she was to make her mark on the world, but the idea of beginning here was somewhat intimidating.

'Ah, not to worry,' said Noddy. 'You'll get round to it. You still the rock'n'roll queen?'

'Me?' Harriet was flattered. 'I've only ever danced once. Oh, and last week, but that was different.' She told them about the dance, and the careful young man who had held himself away from her so discreetly. This pleased them enormously, as she had guessed it

A BREED OF WOMEN

would, although she was not quite sure why, as she still had some private information charts of her own to fill in. They all knew the young man she was talking about, because he'd been at primary school with some of them.

They were so delighted that they suggested she should join them 'for a bit of fun'.

'When?' she asked cautiously, knowing with a sinking feeling even before they answered her that the answer was, 'Now'. Her knees shook so violently under the chrome table that she felt it must start to wobble and betray her, but she knew that she would go.

The 'fun' turned out to be visiting the local camping ground, where there were still a few holidaymakers from the Easter break.

The game was to shine torches on the canvas tents and to catch couples doing 'interesting things'. They caught quite a few people, although there was never any time to study 'interesting things' because, as the strong torch beam hit the wall of the tent, there would be a flurry of activity. Whatever was happening stopped, a tent flap was thrown open and shouts of abuse were hurled into the night.

After half a dozen tents had had these attentions bestowed on them, Noddy said, 'Right, that's it. One more, and then they'll send out for the cops.'

So they did one more which looked like a good one. The shadows were excitingly graphic and as the people inside jumped to their feet, curses burst forth from the tent. Noddy and Nance shouted in unison, 'A one, a two, a sing' and they all broke into 'Silhouette, silhouette on the shade, oh ah, two silhouettes on the shade', then Noddy started the car and they all jumped in and headed back towards town. They passed a police car at a point where the road narrowed, and by the time the police came into the milk bar ten minutes later, everybody was sitting inside with milkshakes.

Nobody batted an eyelid. Burping onions after his evening meal, the middle-aged policeman asked them what they'd been up to.

'Up to?' Noddy said innocently. He looked around. 'We're up to having a quiet drink with our friends. What's with you, dad?'

'The camping ground,' said the policeman.

'Yeah, the camping ground, dad. What about the camping ground?'

'You know.'

'There been some trouble up that way?'

The policeman simply glared.

'I'm sorry if there's been any trouble, Noddy said regretfully.

'You lot've been up to the camping ground tonight,' stated the policeman.

'We have?'

'You have.'

'No law against going up to the camping ground.'

'You've been making trouble.'

'Us making trouble? Look here, not one of us people has touched another human being tonight. We haven't even spoken to anyone. Was anybody hurt in this trouble you're talking about?'

The man in blue sighed. 'I almost wish they had been,' he said softly.

'That's no way for a policeman to talk,' Noddy said piously.

'And you know why? Because then I could take you in.'

He stalked out. There were quiet smiles among the crowd.

Harriet glanced at the watch on Noddy's wrist. 'Oh my goodness, I was due home nearly half an hour ago,' she said.

'Say teacher kept you in late,' suggested Nance.

'I'll have to,' said Harriet grimly.

'Come back,' they called as she left, even Nance.

Small wonder then, that Harriet's heart sank when Cousin Alice mentioned a job that might expose her lack of typing skills.

She determined to do better and to make up for time lost the previous week. When the next typing class came round, she attacked the machine with tremendous energy, tat,tat,tat,sat,sat, tit,sat,tat,tits,sit,tits,sit.

85

The instructor looked at her work and sighed.

'Have you ever thought of going in for anything else?' he asked.

Harriet considered telling Cousin Alice that she would never make a typist, but Cousin Alice was already talking about Harriet's forthcoming job with such enthusiasm that Harriet didn't have the heart to say anything.

She didn't have the heart to go back to typing again the following week, either. Instead, she found herself sitting in the milk bar. She regarded this as inevitable, after the last time she had been there.

Noddy smiled when he saw her.

'We've been waiting for you,' he said.

'I suppose you have,' she said, and again she was not surprised by her reply.

'We've got someone here to meet you,' said Noddy.

Behind the counter of the milk bar, a young man was stripping electrical wires down behind the fridge. He had sandy hair and a face that was smooth, if rather red, as if he liked the open air but it didn't like him. He had large pale blue eyes that protruded slightly, and a small neat mouth. She supposed he was handsome in a way, though exactly how she couldn't decide. Certainly he was older than the rest of the crowd.

'This is Sydney, someone said. 'Sydney, meet Harriet.'

Sydney ducked his bottom teeth in front of his top ones in a curious little gesture of greeting. 'Hi, he said. The kids told me there was someone new in town, but I never guessed she'd look as good as you.'

Sydney's presence was oddly disconcerting. He was an electrician who serviced equipment in the shop, and that was how they'd got to know him, they said. Of course he was older, as she had thought. He'd done his time, which it appeared meant he'd served his apprenticeship, not been to jail.

When he'd finished the job, he brought a milkshake over and sat down with them.

'So tell me about yourself, Harriet,' he said.

She blushed and hung her head. He was much older and more

86

sophisticated than anyone she had so far encountered. Of course there was Jim, there was always Jim to remember, but he was different. Sydney was obviously a man of the world. And there had been Francis, and her heart turned over, wondering where he was, and what had happened to him, and if she could ever fall in love with anyone else in the world. She looked at Sydney. Perhaps it would be possible to fall in love with him. But then he was so old, he was probably tied up with a girl. He was sure to be in love with someone.

There were short coarse red brown hairs on the backs of his hands and along the tops of his fingers.

What could she tell him that didn't sound childish and banal? She lifted her head, helplessly looking for something to say.

'Do you come here often?' she said at last. The words sounded so awful and so foolish that if she could have escaped immediately she would have. But Sydney was wedged in firmly beside her.

'No,' he said gravely, as though her question were perfectly normal. 'Only when I've a job to do. Don't you think that perhaps now I've met you I could find more jobs to do here?'

Harriet met Nance's approving gaze. She nodded sagely. Bob jeered, meaning it was a good idea, and wasn't love grand.

Noddy said tenderly, 'She's not one of us, you know. Not really.'

Harriet gave him a protesting look at this apparent betrayal, but Noddy's wisely wobbling head was telling here, this is my way of assuring Sydney that he won't have to spend all his time with us if he takes you on. It was an act of such exquisite concern and consideration that Harriet felt her insides melting with love towards them all, towards Sydney. She hoped he felt her soft and loving feelings coming through.

Apparently he did.

'Shall I play you a record?' he asked.

'Please.'

He got up, went over to the jukebox and slid a coin into the slot. He knew exactly what he was going to play for her. As the disc settled onto the pad, he sat down beside her again, and this time he picked up her hand and held it in his lap. 'You'll like this.'

Elvis started to sing 'Love Me Tender'.

Now all of her melted, the voice dissolved round her like marshmallow held in her mouth and sliding down her throat. She throbbed, she was spellbound, the voice was molten gold. She noticed that her free hand was wet, and saw it was with her own tears. This was a dream world and she was part of it. She had been admitted, songs were being played for her, she had friends, and, it seemed, she was in love.

When the song was over, it was time for her to go again. 'Next Thursday?' whispered Sydney against her ear.

She nodded, as if hypnotised. Her world was loving her and she loved it back. 'I'd run you home, but I've got another job to go on to,' Sydney said. 'I'll be better organised next week.'

Outside in the crisp dark, more than the cold hit Harriet. Certain inescapable facts had to be faced.

For a start, there was no way she was going to typing the following week, which meant that she would have missed three nights out of four. She could only type things about sitting on tits, and Cousin Alice seemed to think that she was almost ready to go on to higher things.

There was no way that she would be able to learn to do better than that by the time the job became vacant, and what she would do was a question with such frightening ramifications that she quailed. Even if she were to give up Sydney after the following week (and she had already come to think of him as somebody valuable) she still wouldn't be able to type in time to take the job. The May holidays were almost there, with only one more typing lesson left before the end of term, and on that night she was committed to Sydney. It was disturbing, and yet somehow comforting, because it was abundantly clear that her misdemeanours would catch up with her whether she went to that last typing lesson or not; it would not be a miraculous cure-all for her past failures, so meeting Sydney wouldn't make all that much difference.

But that brought up a new and even more devastating problem. If the May holidays were only one typing session away, she would have no excuse to go out on Thursday nights for two whole weeks. The situation was oppressive. There was no other single solitary excuse for staying out late in Weyville.

'I'm thinking too far ahead,' she told herself sternly. 'I must concentrate on next Thursday night. One thing at a time.' And, suddenly buoyant, she went in to face Cousin Alice.

Her relative looked at her approvingly. 'I'm glad to see you looking so happy, my dear. I can see you're ready for that job. I must have a talk to your typing teacher about your speed before the end of term.'

Harriet reached over and kissed Cousin Alice swiftly on the cheek, something she had never done before. 'Don't do that. I want it to be a surprise for you,' she said, and Cousin Alice's face shone with pleasurable anticipation.

The following Thursday dragged endlessly. She couldn't find zips that were the right colour for people, she gave wrong change, and when Mr. Stubbs heard a customer complaining, he sharply rebuked her. His words brought home to her the desirability of change, and reminded her that a change might be more disastrous than the way things were. It was a nagging discomfort. Something she would face tomorrow. Though that wasn't far away.

At last it was time to go. It was almost dark as she walked down the street to the milk bar. A quiet wind was stealing through Weyville, scattering lolly papers in the air. A newspaper wrapped itself around a lamp post, and as she rounded the last corner before the milk bar, it caught her, sending chill little shudders through her like a premonition of something she was about to lose forever. She put her head down and hurried on.

Outside the milk bar, an electrician's van was parked, and sitting at the wheel was Sydney. As she approached, he leaned over and opened the door. 'Hullo, there,' he said softly. 'Ready?'

'Aren't we going inside?' she asked, with a stab of panic.

'They told me you didn't have much time on Thursday nights. They gave us blessings and said they wouldn't keep you all to themselves when we haven't got much time together.'

Harriet got in uncertainly, not sure whether to shut the door or not. Sydney leaned across her and pulled it shut, his arm leaning heavily against her breast as he did so.

'Where are we going?' she asked, fearfully, now that this adventure had begun.

'To my place,' he said cheerfully, as he started the van.

'You have a place of your own?'

'Not my own. My parents' place. I live with my parents.'

'Oh.' A great flood of relief passed over Harriet. She was going to meet Sydney's parents. It occurred to her that she didn't know his surname.

'Merrott,' he told her. Sydney Merrott — it seemed a safe reliable name, even one that you could live with. Mrs. Sydney Merrott. Taking her home to meet his parents. Already. And he had a steady job. Handsome in a sort of way, too. Not that she'd want to get married straightaway of course. All sorts of things would have to be planned, and they'd need to know each other a bit better.

At least she wouldn't have to worry so much about a better job; she could just stick this one out. Being Mrs. Sydney Merrott and an electrician's wife would take up so much of her time that she wouldn't need to get involved in anything else much.

Now she found it easy to talk. As they drove through the empty streets of Weyville, she told him about the bad day she'd had, and how she wasn't too keen on selling haberdashery. She supposed his mother must come into the shop, and he said he supposed she must, and Harriet said wouldn't it be funny if they'd already met, and Sydney said, yes, wouldn't it be funny and did his curious little act of ducking his bottom teeth over his top ones as he looked at her out of the corner of his eye. That didn't seem to matter very much because she felt so beautiful and happy. Already she was planning how she would tell Cousin Alice about Sydney, because if he was taking her round to his parents' place so early in the piece, she would certainly have to invite him to Cousin Alice's. Maybe that was quite a good thing because sooner or later she would have to take him to Ohaka, and he might never have met people like her parents before; not that she was ashamed of them, but Cousin

90

Alice was Weyville. He would understand that she came from a mixed background and might even find it quite quaint and see his new wife as somebody rather exotic.

They pulled into the driveway of a wooden bungalow. It was difficult to see in the dark, but by the lights of the van Harriet discerned that Sydney might be quite impressed by Cousin Alice's house. There seemed to be nothing wrong with the Merrotts' house, but Cousin Alice's looked better established. This house had the slightly raw look of a place that had been built recently, but it seemed prosperous enough. Maybe the Merrots hadn't been rich for very long.

One outside light was on. Harriet thought this curious, and supposed that the family must all be on the other side of the house. On the whole, though, the place had a strangely bleak and uninhabited air.

She became conscious that Sydney was nervous. Perhaps after all she didn't come up to standard. She watched him take the key out of his pocket in an idly detached way, and the truth hit her. Silently he let her in, and turned on a light, shutting the door behind them.

'Your parents aren't here, are they?' she said, matter-of-factly.

'No.'

'Why did you tell me you were taking me to meet them?' she asked.

'Hey, wait a minute,' said Sydney. 'I never told you that.'

'You said you were taking me to your parents' place.'

'That's right. I didn't say they were here.'

The simple truth of this statement was irrefutable. 'When will they be home?' she asked.

'In two weeks.'

'You mean they're away for two weeks?'

'That's what I said. Bit of luck, isn't it?',

'Can I sit down?' she said, at last.

'We'd better get on with it if you're short on time,' said Sydney, and now there was no doubt that he was nervous.

So this is what it comes down to, thought Harriet, as she

followed him silently to his bedroom. *I am now about to be introduced to the great mysteries of life.* After wondering all this time , she hadn't even had time to anticipate the event — or even to decide whether she particularly wanted to find out what 'it' was right now.

Sydney's room was very neat. Twin beds were made up just in Cousin Alice's style with bright bedspreads and matching curtains. There was very little to indicate Sydney's interests in life except for a guitar standing in one corner.

'Do you play that?' asked Harriet, running her finger across the strings and making them twang.

Sydney shrugged. 'Used to. Nearest my mother ever got me to learning music.' He pulled off his shirt.

'How old are you?' she asked.

He looked faintly exasperated. 'You ask a lot of questions, don't you?'

'I just wondered,' said Harriet.

'Twenty-three. Are you going to take your things off?' He seemed much more in command of the situation now that he was shedding his clothes. He abandoned his socks quite briskly.

Reduced to his underpants, he observed her standing motionless. 'You're a cool one, aren't you? Look, do you want me to do it for you, and all that stuff?'

She thought of Jim and standing naked before him. It seemed to have happened a hundred years ago. She remembered his gentle finger stroking her where the hair had started to grow; now it was a wild bush.

She wondered if Sydney would be as gentle. Something told her that he might not be, for he was beginning to look decidedly impatient.

'It's all right,' she said. 'I can do it myself.' Quickly she took off her clothes, until she was down to her brassière and panties. Sydney still had his underpants on. 'Shall I go first?' she inquired, noting that his bump was most pronounced. She sat down on the bed and watched him, pleasantly fascinated that she was about to see what the thing actually looked like uncovered.

'God, you're cool,' said Sydney again, with some agitation. He pulled his underpants down, and Harriet gave a startled cry. The revelation of this very large piece of apparatus pointing at her like a witch doctor's bone was quite terrifying.

'Ah, you want it, eh,' said Sydney, pleased. 'Come on, get them off.' Obediently she took off the rest of her clothes. What did she do now?

Muttering a series of ahs and ohs, which she took as an indication that he was pleased, Sydney sprang on her and threw her backwards onto the bed. Remembering her previous effort with Jim, she settled herself back while he rolled onto her.

As it was quite obvious that he expected her to know what to do next, she felt somewhat embarrassed at the prospect of asking him. She really had no idea what was expected.

'Come on, get 'em up,' said Sydney. He was crouching intently between her legs. Harriet put her arms around his neck, as she couldn't think what else to put up.

'You do want to do this, don't you?' said Sydney.

'Oh yes,' she said fervently.

'You don't seem all that keen. You going to make me work for it? Here, let's see if we can work you over a bit.' He fastened his mouth on hers, grinding away with determined licking and snorting. His skin felt very sweaty against the palms of her hands.

Suddenly he grabbed her under the knees and pulled them up into the air. This seemed an extraordinary posture to Harriet, who began to laugh.

Sydney froze. 'What's so bloody funny?' he snapped.

'Nothing. I'm sorry, I was just ... thinking.'

'Just thinking, were you? Don't you like me?'

'Oh yes, I do,' Harriet assured him.

'You looked me over enough — didn't you fancy what you saw? Never had a girl look at me like that. It's bad manners to look at a bloke the way you looked at me.

'Oh, damn,' he suddenly groaned. He levered himself up on his hands and knees, and they both inspected the splendid penis he had been sporting a few moments earlier. It hung limp and shrivelled,

93

like a fleshy little carrot that had been kept too long. Harriet
wanted to laugh again, but she had the nasty feeling that Sydney
might hit her.

'Will it come back?' she asked, now genuinely interested.

'You could help,' said Sydney.

'Could I?'

He shook his head in wonder. 'Christ, you're not frigid, are you?'

'It's not very warm in here,' Harriet admitted.

'I don't know whether you're putting me on, or what. I've never
met one like you before.'

Harriet toyed with the idea of confessing all, but before she
could say anything, he got to his feet and said huffily , 'I'll do it
myself.'

'Will you? What will you do?'

'Are you going to watch?'

'Shouldn't I?'

'You've got no feelings at all have you,' he said. 'I'm going to the
bathroom to do it.'

At the door, he turned and said, 'Don't try any funny tricks, will
you 'I'm not going this far without getting it up. No going off on
me, just because my hard's gone. It'll come back, you know.'

'Of course not,' said Harriet. She was beginning to feel quite
sorry for him. It seemed that even if she didn't know what to do, he
wasn't much better off than she was. Curiosity was getting the
better of her, and the wish that he had correctly guessed to dress
and get out as quickly as possible was fading. She pulled an
eiderdown from the end of the bed and lay there in a small cocoon.
Nestling against its feathery warmth, she felt almost luxurious.
Taking her clothes off had always been a pleasure, disastrous as the
consequences could apparently be.

Soon Sydney returned, holding his penis carefully in one hand.
It seemed respectably large again, though somewhat softer than the
first time it had come in contact with her legs.

He climbed under the eiderdown, and pressed himself over her
again. He continued to hold his penis and said softly under his
breath, 'Grow, grow.' Interested in this process, Harriet put her

hand on it. Immediately it sprang to life.

'Aah,' sighed Sydney, 'I knew you were all right. Let's get it up before we have any more problems, eh?

Following the previous course of action Harriet raised her knees as far as they would go. This seemed to please Sydney considerably, for his penis started probing her with great enthusiasm.

'Christ, you're tight,' he said with perspiring admiration.

Then the pain started. She had never been hurt there before, and now he seemed to be raining blows into her. Her body started to shake in anguish.

'I — can't get — into you,' Sydney panted. 'Ah, there we go. We're away,' and her body seemed to disintegrate in a great spasm of pain, so searing, so terrifying that she screamed aloud, again and again.

'Wowee, I knew you were great, whoo, you like it, don't you?' Sydney shouted. 'Yah, that's right, writhe, I love it, God that's beautiful, keep it up baby, that's great stuff.

Is this what it's always like? moaned Harriet to herself. Does this pain happen every time? Is this what sex is? Why does he keep moving in and out like that? I thought he just put it inside me. Perhaps he's doing something else to me — *am* I having sex? When's he going to stop?

Finally Sydney did stop, after a lunge that seemed to go right up to her breastbone. He lay on top of her, panting and exhausted. 'Worth it, eh?' he said when he had recovered a little. Harriet whimpered in reply. He pulled himself out of her, and for an instant her body exploded with quite a different sensation. She supposed it must be the relief of being unpinned from the bed, but years later she recalled that feeling, and thought with a kind of wonder that that miraculous little orgasm had saved her from instant retreat to a nunnery. Certainly she regarded Sydney with a tender and more forgiving glance than she would have thought possible moments before.

As they disentangled themselves, Sydney looked down at the bed. It was covered with blood.

95

'Kerist,' he yelled. 'Why in the hell didn't you tell me you had your period?'

'I didn't know I had it,' Harriet said, as startled as he.

He looked at it furiously, then disappeared, coming back in a moment with a damp towel. He started dabbing at the blood on the bed, but the stain seemed to spread more widely.

Harriet had started putting on her clothes. 'I'm sorry,' she said.

'So you bloody well ought to be. Haven't you been watching your dates? You must have known it was due.'

'They don't always come right on the day. If you know so much, you ought to know that,' Harriet pointed out acidly.

He pulled on his clothes, and stood staring morosely at the bed. 'Oh, for goodness sake,' said Harriet, beginning to feel cross with him. If you wash it, it'll be dry long before your parents come back.'

'Yeah, I know,' said Sydney. 'But I'm picking up my girlfriend when she finishes work tomorrow night. I won't have it fixed by then.'

'Girlfriend?'

'Fiancèe.'

'You're engaged to her?'

'Yep. Getting married at the end of the year. I've got a section, nearly saved up for the deposit on the house. We're going to have ranch sliders and things like that so it'll cost a bit. Still, I reckon I can get it together by the end of the year. Not bad, eh?'

'No. Not bad,' said Harriet numbly.

'Still, it's not going to help her seeing that, is it?'

'Take it to the dry cleaners in the morning and tell them it's a rush job,' said Harriet.

'I can't, wailed Sydney. 'She works in the dry cleaners.'

'Oh, that's really too bad, then. For goodness sake! Change the covers over on the beds and put the eiderdown over the spare one.'

'Hey, that's good. That's a swell idea. Thanks, Harriet.'

'Glad to help. D'you mind if I go home now?'

'No, sure I don't.' His spirits had recovered quite remarkably, and her crime seemed forgiven.

As they drove past the milk bar, Harriet felt the cold despair of loneliness descend again. They'd know, they must have known, that Sydney was engaged to be married. They'd set her up with him. There was no way back to the milk bar. She had been betrayed.

'Please don't stop outside my gate,' said Harriet, as they approached Cousin Alice's house. Sydney parked the van a couple of doors up the street.

'Next Thursday?' he asked.

'Night school's finished for the term. I can't get out. Unless of course you like to call on Cousin Alice and ask her if I can go out with you!

'Oh, come on now! Jeez, I can see why the kids call you Twanky Doll. You're putting on the dog a bit, aren't you?'

'I think I'd better be going in,' said Harriet.

'Well, look, Harriet, you know I can't do that. What would your — what would Mrs. Harrison think of me, with a fiancee and all that?'

'Quite,' she said coldly.

'So if you knew I couldn't, what did you want to say a thing like that for?'

'I really had better go in.'

'Hey.' He suddenly caught her arm fiercely. 'You won't tell them about you know what?'

'What?'

'You know.'

'I don't.'

'Oh, Ker-ist! Me not being able to get a hardie, you know. I mean, I did in the end, didn't I?'

'I won't tell, Harriet promised wearily. 'Now, please ... I'm late.'

Another thought struck Sydney. 'That blood. You weren't a virgin, were you?'

Harriet hung her head. 'Oh, Ker-ist,' he said. 'You shouldn't have let me do that to you.'

'I thought men were supposed to know all those things.'

'Yeah, well, I never ... you know, with one before. I just didn't think. You know, you stuck round with those kids.'

The last part was an accusation. She said nothing.

'I didn't hurt you or anything, did I?'

The pain was solid, from sore heart to aching genitals. Harriet climbed out of the van without another word. If there was any point in what had happened, she couldn't see it.

As she walked up to Cousin Alice's front gate, Sydney cruised beside the footpath, the door of the van swinging open. He was calling out, anxious little noises asking for reassurance. She turned into the driveway and didn't look back.

In the night she wondered again if that was what 'it' was really all about. She wondered if she had really, at long last, done 'it', and if so whether she might ever expect more from 'it' than she had had tonight. For a moment she recalled the strange pleasure right at the end of the act, but the memory was swallowed up in a great black hole of grief and loss. And there were Ailsa and Julie to consider. If indeed, all the correct steps had been taken to fulfil the act of sex, then there was pregnancy to consider.

Fortunately, and capriciously, her period arrived in full flood the next morning while she and Mr Stubbs were setting out a new and tantalising assortment of the latest in safety-pins. At lunch time, on an inspiration, she retired to the public library to find a book which would set her mind at rest once and for all.

At the library, for the first time, she met Leonie.

1978

4

Leonie and Hamish had survived. Sometimes Leonie would pretend that if she were someone different, someone she recognised from long ago, all would go on for Hamish as it did now, but she knew that this was not true.

She had to wake with care every morning, to remember who she was and where she was. This sense of displacement took one permanent form. When she was a child there had been a room, a tatty ugly room with frayed curtains, the hems down, and rotted patches where water had seeped through. They had yellow roses on them. They had been the first things she saw each morning.

It was merely by accident that years later when she and Hamish lived in a company house in America, their bedroom had had curtains with yellow roses. They conceived Brent in that room and brought him home there. How could she explain to anyone that Brent was the first creature she had ever had to herself, whom she could love passionately and possessively and by whom she could be loved in return, without question or fear? The bad old life that still haunted her, the life of which Hamish knew almost nothing, would go away. The child was everything and Hamish could come and go, light years away in his world of business and deals, politics and intrigues, and she and the baby would grow together in a boundless mutual fascination.

Every morning she woke to the curtains with yellow roses, and thought for a second of the old room. The curtains seemed symbolic of how she had overcome that other world, and now had

101

this one. Nothing could take it away or destroy it, for she had arrived from some other place and was safe.

It shattered her to leave that house in America. When they moved to England, their bedroom curtains did not have yellow roses. They had been easy enough to replace, though Hamish had thought her absurd, but as their next child was on the way, he regarded her desire for them as a whim.

The curtains belonged to them now. When they left England they replaced the company curtains and took the yellow rose ones to the Middle East. They were unsuitable, but Leonie insisted on having them. By then Hamish had come to accept that his wife, who was doing so well at so many things, felt some private unreasoning terror connected with the curtains. It roused in him some unnamed fear of his own, so it was better to let the curtains go up and come down from house to house.

It was done then, each time they moved, quietly, without comment. Life proceeded, there seemed no problems. Over sixteen years, Leonie became the asset that took people like Hamish to the top.

Finally, when they were living in Australia, the curtains wore out and the material became unavailable. Leonie convinced herself one day that she had given them the value of a superstition. It all seemed like a silly game and with relief, she agreed to an alternative. For a time, it was a valid choice; she seemed to forget that she was afraid to wake up in the mornings — that is, until they came back to New Zealand.

On the evening she made the phone call, she had started to drink between eight and nine in the evening. Laurence, her younger son, was closeted in his room doing homework. Brent had been on the phone most of the evening. She wondered whether to demand the phone from him so that she, too, could ring friends. However, since their return to New Zealand, there were few people that she knew well enough to ring in the evening. She had wined and dined what seemed an inexhaustible number of business people, mainly colleagues of Hamish's. The women had talked about husbands being away on business. She had felt an empathy with one or two, as if they might quietly conceal some private anguish, some hollow in their existence, as she did. They might have carried their loss privately and well-packed, from country to country and continent to continent, as she had done, but she wasn't sure. And even if she had been sure the acknowledgment that mutual recognition could well be the threat that might topple them — topple her, too, for that matter. She had no right to ring. Nor did she know whose husbands were away; she might ring and the husband would be home, and the private horror tucked out of sight for a few days. They might be having a company dinner party, and they could be embarrassed by her call, at her having caught them at a private revelry to which the Coglans were not invited.

And that left almost no-one to telephone, except perhaps Harriet. Perish the thought. Harriet was a link with the past. A difficult, prickly, sometime feminist who seemed to have had some sort of extraordinary success. Harriet might be doing anything — addressing a rally, launching her latest book, or appearing on television. Almost certainly the last, for that was her job. Not to mention fighting with her husband. Or making up with him — both facets of Harriet's relationships sounded equally terrifying.

Perhaps she would ring Harriet tomorrow. In the meantime, there was television. There was a current affairs programme on, and Harriet was on it. She decided to have a drink.

She was onto her fourth gin when she rang Todd Davis.

In Toronto it would be 5 a.m. Todd answered so quickly that the time of day or night hadn't occurred to her.

His voice was sleepy and husky. She remembered that there was a phone beside the bed.

'Hullo, it's you. Where are you?'

'What time is it?'

'You are in Wellington, then? Really?'

'I'm sorry. I didn't mean to wake you. I'll hang up.'

'What? Don't be crazy. What's the matter?'

'Nothing. Nothing.' She started to weep. 'Is there someone in bed with you?'

'No. Of course not.'

103

'There could be. You don't have to be alone.'

'No, that's true.'

'We agreed that it was over. I expect you to take other women to bed.'

'I know. I do. But there isn't anyone here now.'

'It was stupid of me. What is the time? You didn't say.'

'Five o'clock in the morning.'

'I suppose it must be. Is it going to be a good day?'

'I haven't looked yet. But I think it might be. It's spring, you know.'

She was quiet.

'Are you just unhappy? he asked. 'Is that why you rang me?'

'The winter's just starting here,' she replied hopelessly. 'Good-bye.'

'Don't hang up. Leonie. I want ...'

'Yes?'

'Are you all right?'

She put the phone down. Why had he asked such silly questions? She had no idea whether she was all right. She had no idea whether anything had ever been wrong.

'Why did you ring Todd Davis last night?' asked Brent the following morning.

Leonie put down the lunch packet with care.

'I didn't ring Todd Davis,' she answered. And inside her head, she was saying to herself, I did, I did, I did.

'You rang him last night,' said Brent. 'It was a person-to-person. I heard you put it in.'

'No. You're mistaken. I rang Mr Hicks, to cancel the paper when we go away next weekend.'

'Laurence heard you, too, didn't you.'

Laurence raised his eyes covertly from fried egg. She handed him his orange drink.

'I can't remember,' he said.

'Yes, you can,' said Brent. 'You said, that's Todd Davis that used to work in Dad's lab. That's who she's ringing, that's what you said.'

'I must have have made a mistake,' said Laurence. 'Like Mum said. Is my lunch ready?' he asked Leonie, as he swallowed the last of his breakfast.

She handed it to him silently.

'See ya.' The door slammed behind him.

'He did hear you.' The boy stood there looking at her, waiting.

'You've got no right to listen to my telephone conversations, she said at last.

'I didn't. I just heard you putting it through.'

'I don't listen to yours,' she said, aggressive and self-righteous now. 'What business is it of yours who I talk to?'

'Why did you ring him?'

'Please don't tell Dad when he comes home.'

Brent smiled, a secret pleased smile, having won an admission from her. 'Would he be angry?'

'Possibly. A toll call to Toronto costs a lot of money. I was being lazy. Todd Davis wrote to me to get some information, and I simply hadn't got round to answering his letter, so I rang him up. Dad would be cross with me for spending all that money.'

'What sort of information?'

'Oh ... he was thinking of emigrating here.' By what wild flight of fancy have I uttered such nonsense? she wondered.

'He wanted to know whether it was a good idea or not.'

'He could have asked Dad. He used to work for him.'

Leonie wondered how much longer she could stand the interrogation without screaming at her son. It was too much. She had to hold on, there would be no way back once it was done. 'Dad didn't like him much. I think he thought it was better to ask me.' Getting in deeper. Damn. A bad line that. Why should she like Todd Davis better than Hamish? Why should Todd Davis trust her to like him if her husband didn't?

Brent shrugged and turned away. 'I'd better be getting off. I'll be late for assembly.'

She wanted to yell at him. He couldn't do that now, so casually abandon her without committing himself. Learning the power game. Hamish was a good teacher; both these boys of hers were quick. 'Then is it between us?' she asked.

'Eh? Oh yeah. Of course.'

'What about Laurence?'

'He'll be okay.'

'How can you be sure? I don't want to discuss it with him any more.'

'Easy.' Brent was filling his bag with books, and his lunch, taking apples from the sideboard. 'He doesn't like Dad.'

'Brent.' She stood still, shocked. 'How do you know?'

'He doesn't have to like him does he?'

'I don't know. Do you?'

'Better than Laurence. Yes, I guess he's okay. I reckon he gives us a pretty neat time. None of the kids have got as many things as we have.'

'And that's important?'

'Don't you like things?'

'You can get by without them. I haven't always had things.'

'Sure you haven't, but you never talk about when you didn't. Dad hasn't always had things either, but he talks about when he was a kid and didn't.

'Maybe Dad had a happier time than I did. It . . . it doesn't always have to do with things.

'Yeah. Maybe.'

'Anyway, it's an awful reason to say you like Dad.'

'Tell me the other ones when you've got an hour to spare. Bye.'

At the door he turned and smiled. 'It'll show up on the phone bill, you know,' he said, and then he shut the door behind him, and she heard his feet, running up the path.

Dully she started cleaning the kitchen. Was it good luck to have a dishmaster, a wastemaster, a juice extractor? She repacked steaks methodically in a freezer tray, and put them away, then took them out again, removing two, replacing one, red, lonely and decidedly alive-looking. She shuddered. Perhaps it was contemplating eating her.

The boys would have their steaks in front of the rumpus room telly. Again.

A BREED OF WOMEN

Her head was burning. She walked to the window and leaned her forehead against the cold pane of glass. The chill seemed like an extra ache. Obviously the pain was behind her eyes, heavy tears. They wouldn't fall, she knew that; they had never fallen when she most wanted them to, not even in the old room long ago. Harriet would cry now, she was sure. In rage and fury and frustration.

She wished she could get Harriet off her shoulder. The wretched woman seemed to have no intention of leaving her this morning. Well, she had decided to ring her today, hadn't she? Perhaps she might even tell Harriet what had happened last night, and this morning. She could make it sound like a joke.

She might tell her, or again she might not. It was almost Harriet's fault, what had happened. Or so it seemed. She dialled Harriet's number.

107

5

The friendship between Harriet and Leonie developed quickly from the time of their first meeting in the library. Harriet was searching the shelves for a book that might help her solve some of the problems that faced her, and finally lit upon one that seemed to promise some enlightenment. Its author was Van der Velde, and it was called *Ideal Marriage*.

She sat down on the edge of the chair, gingerly, because she was still hurting. The combination of her period and the encounter with Sydney the night before had left her tender and uncomfortable.

Quickly she rifled through the pages. There seemed to be a lot about sex, but it was all for the ideal situation, and that of course meant being married for a start. She wondered if there was any point in pursuing the matter and decided to look up the index. She was just hunting under 'V' for virginity when she noticed someone standing in front of her.

A girl was watching her curiously. Caught staring by Harriet, she looked embarrassed, shrugged and then said ruefully, 'It doesn't help much, really.' Harriet blushed scarlet and attempted to cover the book with her hand. The girl sat down beside her and Harriet tried to decide whether to turn and flee, leaving the book behind, or whether she should put it back on the shelf.

'I tried that one but it didn't make me much wiser. Perhaps it's because I wasn't married,' she said with a flicker of a smile.'

'How did you know?' Harriet blurted.

'Just guessed, really.' But that's the reason I went looking at it.'

She paused. 'I'll bet no-one's ever told you anything.'

'My mother told me to look at the ducks,' said Harriet miserably.

The other girl hesitated a little more. It was as if she was weighing something up. Harriet was suddenly afraid that she would go away, but the girl seemed to have made up her mind.

'You're lucky,' she said. 'I don't have a mother. The orphanage I was in told me only married people could have babies.'

'Well, I do know that's not true,' Harriet said.

'It's a start.'

'Two girls I know are having babies. I guess one of them's had hers by now.' It occurred to her that none of her mother's letters had mentioned Ailsa.

'One of them'd be Julie Simmons, I suppose.'

'How d'you know?' said Harriet, startled.

'I knew you worked with her. Well I could hardly miss, could I? I work in the shop across the road.'

'Do you? Which one?'

'Bookshop. It's not a bad job. I was lucky to get it, I can tell you. Orphanage kids don't get first in the queue with the good jobs. Oh, they say you do, and of course, if you're smart, that's different. I mean really smart. If you're going to make it to university or something people move heaven and earth, it suits them to look good. But if you're just middling smart like me,' she added, matter-of-factly 'Then there's no kudos, you see. What about you?'

'I thought I was okay,' said Harriet, shrugging. 'I seemed to do all right at school, but they wanted me to do a whole lot of things I didn't want to, so I kicked up.'

'You like what you're doing now?'

'You've got to be joking.'

The girl looked her over and Harriet returned her gaze with determination. The situation seemed to be slipping out of her control. This girl who seemed to be taking charge of her was tall and rather too thin. Her hair was black and straight, she had wide very green eyes and a nose covered with freckles. She was altogether pretty, with an oddly fragile air one also suspected of hiding steel. She was wearing a creamy open-necked blouse, revealing a very long white neck. The blouse was tucked into a wide cinch belt, such as people had started to wear recently, and her skirt was very full, flowing around her as she got to her feet.

'I'm Leonie Tregear,' she said. 'Feel like a walk?'

They left the book lying on the table and walked out into the street.

'I'll bet you haven't had anything to eat today,' said Leonie.

'No. How did you know that?'

'You could always tell kids at the home who hadn't had anything to eat. I'll get us some pies.'

She disappeared into a shop, and reappeared a minute later bearing a couple of brown paper bags.

'Now, come along, we've only got half an hour till lunch hour's done. There's a seat down by the war memorial. Keep your finger's crossed there's no one there.'

The seats were empty, so they sat down under a hunk of concrete which had a lot about the glorious dead etched all over it. Harriet, suddenly faint with hunger, devoured the pie almost in a mouthful.

'Here,' said Leonie, handing her the other bag.

'That's yours.'

'I've eaten. I got it for you.'

'Why?'

'Because I knew you'd be hungry,' Leonie explained patiently. 'If I hadn't got two bags, you wouldn't have eaten by yourself.'

As Harriet ate the second pie more slowly, they started to talk.

'Someone get you last night?'

'Yes.'

'The first time's awful. At least, I haven't met anyone who didn't think it was.'

'I thought it was supposed to be nice. Ailsa ... that's one of the girls that's having a baby, I went to school with her up north, she kept saying it was so great.'

'Yes,' agreed Leonie grimly, 'That's what they tell you when they've got a man and they want to keep him.'

'Perhaps it gets better,' said Harriet hopefully.

110

'Could be. I've only tried it once, and it hurt like hell.'

'You do seem to know a bit more about it than I do,' said Harriet.

'Well, I had a few mates at the orphanage, you know. I still see them sometimes. At least they told me more than the books.'

'I'm not sure I did it,' said Harriet. 'I'm certainly hurting most awfully.'

'You still bleeding?'

'Don't know, can't tell. I've got my period. It came this morning.'

'Bloody hell, you're not haemorrhaging are you?'

'I don't know. D'you think I might be?'

'Probably not. Were you bleeding when you got up?'

'No, it just started this morning when Mr Stubbs and I were putting out the safety pins. The other bleeding had stopped when I got home, after Sydney ...' She stopped ashamed.

'Sydney, eh? That sounds like his style, he tried it with me too. It was his mate Neville that got me.'

Suddenly Leonie started to laugh. Harriet couldn't see the source of her amusement.

'It is funny, isn't it? God, how they take us for a ride. But what the hell, we're both okay, neither of us is pregnant and we might help each other to keep out of harm's way.'

'Why do you want to be friends with me?' asked Harriet, curiously.

The other girl looked defensive for the first time, even a trifle sullen.

'Suit yourself. I can take it or leave it.'

'No ... no, please, I'm sorry. It's just that I'm — well, I'm pretty lonely, you probably guessed that, and I feel ... you see, there was a crowd of kids that sort of arranged for me to go with Sydney. I think they must have known what was going to happen to me. I guess I don't feel too good about the whole deal here.'

'Don't blame you,' said Leonie, relaxing. 'Sorry I snapped. It's just that where I come from, sometimes people don't want to know you.'

'But that's awful. How can people be like that?

111

'Easy. Would you take me to your place? You stay with Mrs Harrison, don't you. No, hang on, I'm not asking you to, I'm asking if you would. Like if we got to be friends, and you thought, gosh, wouldn't it be nice if Leonie came round Saturday afternoon, I'll phone her up, what would she think? Would she let you do it?'

'I don't know.'

'There you are, you see.'

'Now, wait a minute,' said Harriet. 'Stop jumping down my throat. You asked me. All right, stop thinking I might be going to offend you. I said I don't know and I don't. She wouldn't let me have Julie Simmons round.'

'Can't say I blame her.'

'Now, who's making judgments? You don't even know Julie Simmons. All right, so she threw me in with Noddy's lot down there at the milk bar, but she thought it'd be company for me, and it was the only sort she knew. It's not her fault what happened to me, it was her way of being kind. So I don't know about you, but if Julie had been going to stay on in town I might have sorted it out with Cousin Alice, but she wasn't going to and I've got plenty of troubles with my board as it is, so it didn't seem worth the trouble. If I got to know you and we really got on, well, I guess she'd have to decide whether she could put up with my friends or put me out. I can't keep living like this.'

Leonie had listened to this carefully. She seemed to be looking at Harriet with more than a little respect.

'Sorry,' she said. 'I wouldn't have stuck up for Julie Simmons like that. I guess you haven't got any side.'

Harriet asked her if she still lived in the orphanage. Leonie said she had got out nearly a year before, leaving school the day she turned fifteen. The orphanage had been out in the country, and she too had gone to a district high school, with little distinction and less happiness. If the inmates were not making great progress at school they were urged to try and find a job as soon as practicable. Because Weyville was the nearest sizeable town, it was usually the first place where work was sought, though Leonie said a lot of the boys got farm work in the area and stayed on at the orphanage after they left school. In her case that had not been possible and she had had to come in and get board in town. She was still under welfare and hoped to be out of it by the time she was seventeen so she could have some say about where she lived.

Harriet asked her where she had lived before, but Leonie simply looked bleak and turned her head away. Harriet never discovered the answer, though from time to time over the next two years she added together pieces of information that suggested that Leonie had been sent from place to place for a long time, possibly by relatives. Social welfare had only picked her up when a school teacher had noticed that the people she lived with had injured her. Whatever the circumstances had been, Leonie never fully discussed them with Harriet. There seemed to be a deep-seated horror under the surface of Leonie's life. Nor did Harriet ever find out whether she was a true orphan or not.

When Leonie left school, she had been given an unpleasant and boring assembly job in a factory, and she had made sure she got fired in a very short space of time. This had caused the welfare people great displeasure and she had been placed in a waitressing job at the forestry canteen. There she had met the merry band of local electricians, her downfall with Sydney's mate had occurred, and she had decided to take a stand on her own behalf.

She enjoyed reading and had often retreated to the library during lunch hour. She had befriended the librarian there, a shy elderly man who had found books for her.

One day, she had gone to the library crying and he had asked her what was wrong. She'd told him about the job in the canteen, and he'd been shocked. He found her a job in the local bookshop. It was a good shop, and he felt she might get some interest out of life working there. It seemed to have more than worked out and Leonie said she was very happy.

When Harriet heard this, she found herself launching into the story of how she was expected to go into an office in a week or two and start work as a typist. She confessed how all her predicaments of the moment seem to stem from this one frightful basic cause.

Leonie listened thoughtfully. Then she said 'Mr Whitwell, that's

113

the librarian, is looking for somebody now. Have you got School Cert?'

'Yes.'

'You read?'

Harriet admitted that she hadn't done much reading since her arrival in Weyville, but told her about all the books she had tried to get her hands on when she was at school at Ohaka.

'Then that settles, it, it'd solve everything for you. Surely your cousin couldn't mind you doing that?

'Of course not, she wouldn't believe it was true. But what about you?'

'I tell you, it's no good. I haven't got any more qualifications than I had before. Mr Whitwell talked to them about me, and they'd have taken me, only the chairman of the library committee's got a real bee in his bonnet about getting someone to qualify in library school. Nobody from Weyville ever has, and he feels its downgrading the library at a national level, so it has to be someone with School Certificate who'd be eligible to do their Library Certificate.

'That means I'd have to swot?'

'Do you mind?' Leonie looked at her keenly.

Harriet thought that she really didn't have much choice, all things considered. The beginnings of 'the big plan' even seemed to emerge from this totally unexpected encounter.

'I hadn't thought about swotting,' said Harriet, as honestly as she could, 'But I can't see why I shouldn't.'

'I think you should come and see Mr Whitwell. I'll take you.

It occurred to Harriet when she faced Mr Whitwell that she couldn't have been a very prepossessing sight. In the morning she had dressed badly, she knew she was deathly pale, pie crumbs were sticking to her dress. Yet he liked her, she knew it right away.

When she had to admit she had no references, he said that he was quite happy to accept Leonie's recommendation. Provided she could promise him that she would turn up armed with her School Certificate to show to the committee, he could see no reason why she shouldn't start on Monday week. He rang the committee chairman who approved the appointment, filled in an application form for her to join the next library school course, and a short while later the girls emerged from the library with Harriet appointed to the position.

'Thank you, thank you,' Harriet burbled to this amazingly generous girl who had not only found her a job but who was a character referee as well; this girl who had been prepared to do this thing even at the expense of her own heart's desire. She was quite extraordinary, and Harriet's heart sang.

'I have a best friend,' she said, laughing out loud.

'Of course, of course,' Leonie sang back, swinging around a lamp post. 'And up See-de-nee's backside. With a lamp post.'

'And up Evil Neeville's, too.'

'Down with men.'

'Young men. I like Mr Whitwell.'

'Of course. Of course, we like Mr Whitwell,' Leonie said joyfully, 'but he's not *men*.

'My father's men, though,'

'Stamp him out, stamp him out!'

The girls weren't the only ones dancing. A blast of music suddenly blared forth from the top of the street, and a truck lumbered towards them with a loud hailer atop it. 'We're gonna rock around the clock tonight, we gonna rock, rock, rock till broad daylight,' yelled the music. The truck came close and they saw a huge placard bearing the words 'ROCK 'N' ROLL JAMBOREE'. Three staggering white creatures stumbled around on the tray of the truck, apparently in time to the music. They were Noddy and Nance and another girl that Harriet didn't know. She remembered that she hadn't seen them the previous evening because Sydney had picked her up outside the milk bar.

'Whatever do you think they're doing?' Harriet asked.

'Didn't you know they were going in for the rock 'n' roll marathon? They're trying to win a hundred pounds for dancing the longest. I guess they must be taking them down to the Town Hall so everyone can watch them.'

'They look awful,' said Harriet.

115

'I've heard they've been going for two days. They're the last ones left in.'

The truck crawled past them. None of the contestants looked at Harriet. Nance's feet seemed to be all bound up, and Noddy's head looked as if it was the only part of him moving; nothing unusual about that. They looked for all the world like sleepwalkers.

But I have sleepwalked too, thought Harriet and now I'm awakening again. Here in Weyville, there is hope, there are dreams, but one wakes to dream. Awakening and dreaming — again she wondered where one left off and the other began. Who are the sleepers? Who are the dreamers? Nobody knows.

Just as they were parting, Leonie turned to Harriet, and her face lit up. 'I've got a best friend now,' she said.

It was a touchstone for each of them, something to hold onto. For both of them it was the first time.

It was three o'clock when she went back to haberdashery. Cousin Alice was standing with Mr Stubbs, her expression decidedly unpleasant. Harriet eyed her cautiously. Cousin Alice didn't blink.

Harriet decided to take up her place behind the counter. 'Hullo, Cousin Alice. You didn't tell me you wanted anything. I could have brought what you needed home for you.'

'I certainly didn't want to come here,' said Cousin Alice, in a voice of pure chipped ice. 'Mr Stubbs rang me.'

'Were you concerned about me? That's awfully nice of you,' said Harriet warmly. You have a spirit still, a voice inside her whispered.

'Harriet, are you being flippant with us?' said Cousin Alice.

'Well no, not really. I was just thinking how nice it was that Mr Stubbs was worried about me when I felt so awfully ill. I didn't like to tell him this morning, but really it was very understanding of him to notice.'

'Ill?' said Cousin Alice uncertainly. 'Then why didn't you come home?'

'Oh I was on my way home but I got caught up. Some business cropped up and I'm afraid it took rather longer than I expected. Once I was in the fresh air I felt better, so I decided to come back to work after all. But Mr Stubbs, I'm terribly sorry, I'm finishing up here and starting another job. Would you like to take a week's notice or shall I finish up today, seeing it's Friday?'

'Harriet,' said Cousin Alice, 'you don't have another job to go to. Mr Stubbs tells me that you are quite useless. Even Julie Simmons sold haberdashery better than you do. He planned to dismiss you instantly unless you had some suitable explanation about your absence this afternoon. But this story about being ill, if it's true, Mr Stubbs might reconsider.' She turned her cornflower eyes on Mr Stubbs, reminding him that she had been a customer for many years.

'But Cousin Alice, I've already told Mr Stubbs. I have a new job to go to.'

'No, you *don't* have a job to go to,' said Cousin Alice, in a voice that might have passed for patient if Harriet hadn't known her better. 'I checked up with your night school teacher after Mr Stubbs had phoned me, and ...' Her voice trailed away and they stood looking at each other. 'It's true, isn't it, Harriet?'

'I don't like typing.'

'Not teaching, not typing, not selling haberdashery. Which, as it turns out, you're not even capable of doing properly. A little job like selling haberdashery. Could it be that you can't actually do anything, Harriet?'

'Not anything. Some things.'

'You won't be starting work in the office. You've shamed me in the town where I've lived for the best part of a lifetime. None of my family has ever made me ashamed before, yet you've done it simply through your inability to sell haberdashery. I am certainly not going to allow you to embarrass me any further by having you go to work in an office owned by an old and respected friend.'

All of this issued from Cousin Alice in a quietly controlled stream. For the one or two customers of Weyville who wandered through the shop they might have been discussing what they would

117

have for dinner that night. In spite of herself, Harriet began to tremble.

'Are you saying you want me to leave?'

'It might be better if you spent a little time with your parents.'

Harriet looked at her in astonishment. 'I'm sorry, Cousin Alice, I meant, did you want me to leave your place? I've got no intention of leaving Weyville.'

It was Cousin Alice's turn to look bewildered, and she started to betray her agitation. Her chin trembled as she said, 'You wouldn't stay here in Weyville and humiliate me. I wouldn't allow it.'

'And you can't stop it, either,' said Harriet. 'You don't own Weyville, Cousin Alice, and despite everything you've said, I do happen to have a job to go to, and I'm going to start it on Monday week.'

'Where?' hissed Cousin Alice. 'Down at the forestry canteen, where all the little sluts from the corner milk bar go for work? Oh, don't worry, that's something else I've found out about you. A job, indeed. I mightn't own Weyville, young lady, but I own enough of it to make a difference to you. Do you know I've got shares in that mill?'

Harriet sighed. 'Don't you think this is all getting a bit public, Cousin Alice?' And indeed they had acquired some surreptitious listeners. 'I start work as a library assistant for the borough council, and I'm studying for my New Zealand Library Certificate. It's a two-year course and the papers were filled in for me to do it this afternoon. Now, if you don't mind, I want to be sick.'

And she was. Right there in the middle of haberdashery, with a mortified Mr Stubbs mopping the boil on the back of his neck, Harriet threw up a neat pie-shaped and pie-coloured little plop of vomit.

All in all it wasn't such a bad exit from the haberdashery counter. She didn't even feel remorse. And at least no one had called her a liar.

From that point, Harriet felt that she was living a double life in many ways.

For a long time after the episode in the shop, there was strain between Harriet and Cousin Alice, yet Cousin Alice had no reason to complain. In fact, in the week between jobs, Harriet had caught her on the telephone to her friend with the office job, thanking him fulsomely for having considered Harriet, but explaining that she did have a better job to go to. Of course considering Harriet's ability this was to be expected, she said, now that she was on her feet.

Cousin Alice bought her a neat grey tailored suit in good worsted material, which fitted very trimly round the waist and gave her a rather severe and, Harriet hoped, intellectual look. A headache persisted through the following week, and the doctor she visited referred her to an optician who said she must wear spectacles. Again Aunt Alice came to the rescue, though Harriet said firmly that as the glasses were essential, she would accept her cousin's offer to pay for them on the condition that she repaid them out of her wages over a period of time.

This transformation in Harriet's status certainly gave her all the outward trappings of respectability. Her hair was almost long enough to scrape back into a French roll, and she managed a quite passable one, even if it did wisp out of place a bit. Far from making

119

her look like Nance, it gave her an air of austerity which was quite formidable. Both she and Cousin Alice knew that, given time, things would be well between them again.

As for the job, it really was love at first sight. The first morning she walked in, it was like coming home. Mr Whitwell proved to be a somewhat stricter employer than his outward appearance suggested, but with four young women in his charge, Harriet supposed it was his way of surviving. Every morning from nine when they arrived till ten when the library opened, the girls were required to sort the books back into alphabetical order on the shelves, dust them, stand spine even to spine right along the shelves, and put the books that had been returned the previous day back in their right places. There was a certain amount of pressure on them at this stage, and though they were tempted to talk because this was the only quiet part of the day, Mr Whitwell discouraged it. The other girls were pleasant enough, all recruits from the local high school and all grateful they had such a good job in Weyville. One was married, the other two, slightly younger, had worked there for some time; they were all older than Harriet. She felt in them a certain deference, however. It was she who would make the grade, who would qualify, as none of them had done or attempted to do. Grace, the married woman, admitted that she felt slightly resentful towards Harriet. None of the other girls had been particularly encouraged to take her certificate, so Harriet was moving straight into a rather special situation. Still, she liked Harriet, and didn't really see much point in resenting her. It wasn't Harriet's fault that the others had missed out.

The other part of Harriet's double life she shared with Leonie. Their intention to rid themselves of men didn't last long, and social life in Weyville being what it was, things were bound to get complicated.

Cousin Alice didn't demur when Leonie was brought home to visit. Harriet had sketched in a few essentials about her, and told her that Leonie came from the nearby orphanage. As Leonie had had an important role to play in Harriet's getting her job (though of course Cousin Alice was spared a number of the details) it was decided that she had 'risen above things' and as such, she was given the red carpet treatment.

One evening, Harriet emerged from work and found Leonie waiting for her.

'Guess what?'

'What?'

'I've been asked to the Rugby Ball. His name's Chas Campion. Captain of the Rovers.'

'Lucky you, is he nice?'

'Delish. But d'you know what else?'

'Go on. I know you're going to tell me anyway.'

'Of course I am. It's about you.'

'Hurry up, then. Don't keep me in suspense.'

'Just because it's about yourself. You're an egotist. Oh, all right then. His mate hasn't got a partner. He wanted to know if I had a friend.'

'Honest?'

'Of course. Well, are you coming?'

'What do you think? Yes, yes, yes, please.'

'You don't even know what he looks like.'

'Do you?'

'Haven't a clue.'

They both started to giggle.

It was a turning point, though. Cousin Alice's late husband had been a keen rugby man, and rugby players were decent chaps. She wholeheartedly approved this direction in Harriet's social life, because, little talent though there was in Weyville, she was now about to meet the cream of it.

Decked in the green chiffon once again, Harriet awaited the arrival of Leonie, Chas and the as yet unseen partner, Dick.

'I think you should pop your white cardy in the car with you,' said Cousin Alice anxiously. 'It could get chilly.'

Harriet obediently took out her white cardigan, and viewed herself yet again in the bedroom mirror as she did so. Her hair had been set for the occasion and stood in a polite and tidy row of curls across her head. She had bought herself a padded bra, though she wasn't quite sure that that was necessary, as her breasts had rather a pleasant contour without it. With long white gloves above her elbows and the green swirling skirt which she and Cousin Alice had overlaid with an extra layer of nylon net, she was the complete ball-goer.

While she was thus surveying herself, the doorbell rang, and she froze. What if she didn't like him?

Chas was as Leonie had described him, quite lovely to look at and very physical. The Rovers were the top team in the town and Chas was the top of the team; there was no denying that he was a great catch. He was a young farmer too, working on his father's farm a little way out of town. If Harriet had stopped to think about it, she would have realised that he and Leonie would not have been compatible in any real sense. Leonie still had visions of some of the unhappy victims of the farmer's exploitation, who would come wearily back to the orphanage in the evenings. Still, she obviously had none of this on her mind at the moment. She was sparkling, and Harriet felt tremendously warm and glad for her friend. This was her night.

Dick, on the other hand, was almost mute with shyness, and about half the size of Chas.

'This is Dick,' said Chas. 'Our wing three-quarter, that's why he's a little runt. We don't have big chaps out on the wing, you should see him run, wow, he sure flies.'

Dick blushed fiery red at this praise, and everyone sidled round, not knowing where to look next.

'Well, better get going, eh?' said Chas, used to taking charge.

Leonie and Chas got in the front of the little Standard Ten, with Dick and Harriet in the back. They were all squashed up together, but the car was really something — Chas's very own, as Dick whispered in awe to Harriet. Harriet nodded in appreciation of such affluence. She and Chas didn't seem to come from the same sort of farm.

As the car moved through Weyville to the Gala ballroom, Dick muttered to her, 'I don't go to many balls.'

'That's all right,' said Harriet.

'I — I mean, I hope you weren't expecting someone different!'

'I wasn't expecting anyone. I mean, I didn't know what to expect, so I didn't. And I've never been to a ball in my life, so you'll have to teach me everything. Do you mind?'

His relief was exquisite. 'Oh, that's terrific.'

'What are you two whispering about back there?' said Chas.

'I was just telling Harriet that I hadn't been to many balls, and I was just going to tell her that you made me come to this one.'

'You idiot.' Chas sounded annoyed.

'B-b-but it doesn't matter,' protested Dick, 'B-b-because she doesn't go to balls either.'

'What about you Leonie? Don't tell me *you* don't go to balls.'

But Leonie just turned towards him, smiling in the dim light from the street lights. 'Not in Weyville,' she murmured.

'Didn't think I'd seen you around.' said Chas. 'Ah well, we'll make a right old night of it.'

Before they left the car, they performed a strange ritual. Chas went round to the boot of the car while the others stood waiting, then surreptitiously whipped it open and, glancing up and down the street, produced numerous bottles of beer, a bottle of whisky, and a bottle of Pimms.

'Didn't forget you girls,' he said proudly, flashing the label at them for an instant. Then he opened his suit coat and put the whisky and Pimms in the inside pockets. Dick did the same with a couple of bottles of beer.

'Your turn, girls,' said Chas.

Harriet and Leonie looked sideways at each other.

'You'll have to tell Harriet what to do,' said Leonie.

'Well ... you, you stick them down round your ... the bottles ... you know you put them in your um, girdle round your, mm, well, round your girdle anyway, because they can't see them under your skirts. It's all right, we won't look.'

The boys turned their backs while Leonie and Harriet, dazed, tucked as many bottles as they could between their girdles and panties.

'Finished?' asked Chas, 'Coming, ready or not.'

He inspected them carefully. 'Mmm. not bad, remember to keep your hands under them, we don't want any slipping out, do we?'

'Why did we have to do that?' Harriet asked Leonie, as they were stowing away the ubiquitous white cardigans in the cloakroom, and putting on another layer of bright red lipstick. They had taken the bottles out and put them in a corner while they attended to their hair and makeup.

'I don't think you're allowed to take drink into balls,' said Leonie.

'You're cool, aren't you?'

'Had to learn.'

Outside, Chas took the beer from them, and said, 'The only time I ever enjoy warm beer.' He took a deep sniff at one of the bottles, exhaling with clownish pleasure, to loud cheers from the men around.

For most of the evening Harriet and Dick watched the others and talked. He was no dancer, but when it was absolutely necessary they shuffled around together. A large crowd of footballers from the same team sat round in an alcove that had been created with lumps of timber draped with wilting punga ferns.

'We went out and collected those this morning,' Dick said proudly. He opened another bottle of beer, and offered her some. She had already drunk two glasses of it, the Pimms having long gone. Her head was beginning to ache, but she accepted another glass. The noise, the smoke and the whole atmosphere were getting to her. A woman fell drunkenly across her. The band struck up the supper waltz, and she and Dick shuffled off once more.

In the supper room, long trestles were spread with chicken and saveloys, tomato sauce, pavlovas and trifles, interspersed with dishes of savoury eggs and sandwiches.

'A good spread,' said Dick, eyeing the tables with approval. 'Come on, tuck in, old thing.'

Her stomach churned. Since the episode in haberdashery, she was beginning to think that she must have a weak stomach. She and Dick seemed to be at the head of the queue, the result of their inept trot around the dance floor.

Dick turned to her. 'Thanks awfully for coming with me,' he said. At that instant the doors burst open and hordes of dancers flocked around the tables, engulfing them. Wave after wave pushed forward, there were hundreds of people straining to get at the food. It looked as if it was the end of wartime rationing, although everyone looked exceptionally well-fed.

Dick looked dejected. 'Come on,' urged Harriet, 'I know you want something to eat.'

'But you don't, do you?'

'Not awfully, but why don't I go and sit out on the dance floor where it's quiet? When you've got some food, you can bring it through. Go on,' she said encouragingly, as he seemed to hang back, 'If you get me a piece of chicken, I'll have some of that.'

His pleasure was evident, and he disappeared into the throng, ploughing his way towards the paper plates. Harriet slipped out onto the dance floor. The room was still thick and heavy, but at least it was quiet. The chairs stood at angles like disjointed limbs, abandoned and neglected and the pungas had given up any pretence of being decorative. Only one or two people floated past Harriet and they seemed ambivalent nebulous figures, disconnected, though one man made his presence known rather loudly in a far corner by being sick.

A man sat down beside her but she didn't turn around.

'Dick left you on your own?' he said.

She turned around. The man was sitting close to her, smiling, protective. 'I've been watching you all evening,' he told her.

'I asked him to leave me, he's getting some supper. I guess he'll be through soon.'

'He's a nice guy.'

'I know, you don't need to tell me that.'

'You his girl? I didn't know old Dick had a girl.'

'No. Chas jacked it up. You know Chas?'

'Of course I know Chas. He's our captain.'

'So you're a Rover too?'

'That's right. Why did you think I've been watching you and Dick?'

125

'I thought you might have enjoyed looking at me,' Harriet said, not at all surprised at herself for saying so. Nothing seemed very surprising any more.

'Yes ... well ...' He looked at his hands. 'There was that, too.'

Over on the band platform the band was starting to come back in. The leader was picking away at a guitar.

'Wait here for me ... you, what's your name?'

'Harriet.'

'Okay, Harriet. You wait here for me, eh?'

'What if Dick comes back?'

'Still wait, he won't mind.'

'Who shall I ask for if I have to come looking for you?'

'Denny Rei.'

Denny went over to the band, and spoke to them briefly. They seemed to laugh at him, or with him, or maybe at her, it was hard to tell, but they all looked over her way. Then they started to play, and he came back to her, asking her to dance.

They danced as if they had always been dancing together, and the band played 'Twilight Time'. 'Heavenly shades of night are falling', they sang and he hummed in her ear, 'deep in the dark your kiss will thrill me, its twi ... light time.'

Her feet were light, and her head had cleared and there didn't seem to be anyone else there at all, but when they stopped there was a round of applause and she saw people everywhere. Standing amongst them was Dick, clutching a plate of chicken.

She let go of Denny and hurried over to him.

'I'm sorry. Please forgive me, it was terribly rude.'

'I'm glad you had a good partner. You're really a very good dancer, aren't you?'

'I don't know. Maybe. I've hardly ever danced before, but when I do it's like I forget myself. It's beautiful, like flying.'

'Denny's a nice bloke. Plays good scrum half too.'

'Hasn't he got a partner?'

'Never know with Denny, he's the sort that could get away with coming on his own. I couldn't.' He stared round unhappily. To please him, Harriet took the piece of chicken he'd been clutching.

126

'Tell you what,' said Dick, inspired, 'Now everyone's out of the supper room, it'll be empty. We could go back in there.'

'All right,' she agreed, and followed him once more into the other room. It looked as if dreadful carnage had taken place being littered with chicken bones and squashed oozing pavlova remains. A decorated pig's head grinned obscenely from the middle of a table and in a corner of the room lay a pile of broken glass.

They sat down. Dick watched her with concern. He really was a very nice boy Harriet decided, not as plain as she had thought at first. His complexion was poor and he had too much Brylcreem in his fair curly hair, but apart from that, he was someone you could really like.

'I'm sorry,' she said. 'Honestly, Dick, I didn't mean to embarrass you.'

'It's not that,' said Dick. 'It's just that Denny's — Denny.'

'What about it?'

'He liked you and you liked him. I could see it.'

'Well, I'm not going to walk out on you.'

'I wouldn't blame you if you did. But don't you see, you're a nice girl and if Denny ... oh, I dunno. What's the use?'

'You mean because he's a Maori?'

'He's a good joker, I told you. But he goes out after what he wants.'

'But that's not what you meant.'

'Look, Harriet, I don't care what he is, it's just that if you got tied up with him, I reckon you could be in a lot of trouble.'

'That's stupid,' cried Harriet. 'All I did was dance with him. You are jealous, aren't you? You're a miserable little sod. You sit around making stupid talk all evening when everyone else is dancing, then you throw a shitty at me when I get the only decent partner I've had all night.'

Dick looked as if he could cry. 'I-I-I think y-you're a b-bit drunk,' he said.

Her head was spinning. She kept trying to sit up straight but great black wells kept getting in front of her eyes.

'Dick, you're not stupid,' she mumbled.

She didn't remember getting into the fresh air, but when her head started to clear she was propped against the Standard Ten while Dick unlocked the door. He shovelled her into it, and they drove off in silence. When he stopped at the lake, she could feel herself coming to life again very quickly.

'So that's what happens is it? I know why people come down here. Believe me, I've been told about you lot. No, thanks.' She tried to open the door but Dick grabbed her wrist in a tight grip, his hands much stronger than she had expected.

'Stop it, Harriet. I'm not going to hurt you.'

'I'd rather walk.'

'I'm not going to touch you. I just want you to sit here with me for a while. Chas lent me the car to take you home, but it's too early for you to go home to that cousin, or aunt, or whatever she is, of yours, just yet. Especially when you're not feeling yourself. Come on, let's just sit here till you're feeling better. I won't even talk to you if you'd rather not.'

'Please, I'd like you to talk to me,' she said. There didn't seem to be any point in saying she was sorry any more.

So they sat and he talked about his dreams. He told her what it was like to want to leave Weyville, and how he'd dreamed of becoming an engineer, but it would have meant going away to university and his parents didn't have the money so he'd taken out a boilermaker's apprenticeship. Nothing ever seemed to fulfil him. He was twenty-five, he told her. She was shocked because he seemed so young, but he was a man. Playing football with the Rovers was the only thing that had kept him sane. He'd at least liked to have had a car, but he'd just kept on helping out with the family finances year after year; there was a great horde of younger brothers and sisters to look after.

People like Chas helped him out by jacking up dates like this for him. He was from the wrong side of the Weyville tracks, but he was a good footballer and the jokers liked him for that. He didn't know how many blind dates they'd jacked up for him over the years and always kept hoping that one of them would turn out right for him, someone plain and homely who wouldn't ask too much. He'd been disappointed when she turned out to be a smasher tonight; he'd known that she wouldn't like him.

'But I do like you,' protested Harriet. It was true too. She felt warm and secure with Dick, not afraid. The possibility that one might actually be friends with a male occurred to her for the first time.

He explained seriously that she had everything going for her — looks, a good job by Weyville standards and she talked 'nice'. That was why he'd been upset when she saw him looking at Denny like that.

'I'll probably never see him again,' Harriet assured him, but neither of them believed it.

When he dropped her off at home, he said, 'If you need someone any time, I'll be around.'

That was when the double life began. Denny waited for her outside work a few days later. He led her to a battered pick-up truck, not expecting her to protest. As they climbed in, there was a feeling of inevitability between them.

Dark fell early in Weyville these deep winter nights. The frost had hardened across the plateau town as the lights flickered on. Lake water slapped with a dead empty sound outside the pick-up as they parked. Dark pressed deeper in.

Dark his face as he kissed her, deep his hand finding her. He lifted her body with its melting cunt across his, her buttocks resting on the seat, her legs tucked up against his shoulders. There was no pain at all this time, as he pulled her onto him. This miracle made her gasp with pleasure, and she felt herself like floating as she moved, pulling herself onto the strong shaft inside her.

Suddenly he was clawing at her thighs, trying to push her away as a great tide engulfed her. Bewildered she lay against his chest, feeling their sobbing breaths.

'Girlie,' he whispered, 'Do you always come like that? How can I be careful for you when you keep on coming at me like that?'

She shook her head uncomprehendingly.

'I shot inside you,' he whispered. 'I'm sorry, I couldn't keep it back no more.'

129

She understood him now. 'Please do it again.'

'But I told you ...'

'There'll be so much up there now a bit more won't make much difference, will it?'

So he laid her across the seat, and this time it was slower and more gentle. Still she heard herself calling his name, listening to it as if someone else was crying out in the still cold dark.

When they had finished he said, worried, 'They say if you have a mi-mi it'll wash it out. You know, pee.'

She hesitated, and he said, 'It's all right, you can do it on the ground here by the cab door. I'll hold it open so no one can see if they come.'

Harriet squatted on the ground beside the truck. They could dimly see each other as she streamed, hot and pungent, making the crisp grass crackle as her water hit.

'We'll have to get some Frenchies, eh?' he said when she was back in the truck.

She nodded.

'That's if you're going to keep on with me.' He laughed, knowing that he didn't need an answer.

Leonie and Harriet met for lunch as usual the following day at the tearooms. There was quiet between them. Since the night of the ball and Harriet's sudden departure, they seemed to have been living in two private little worlds. Harriet had gathered that Chas, although an attractive-looking catch and one of the most popular young men in Weyville, was domineering and expected his own way. Leonie liked him well enough to want to go out with him again, but the evening had ended with a tussle and a fit of sulks on Chas's part. A lot of it wouldn't have happened, Leonie seemed to imply, if Harriet and Dick hadn't been away so long with the car and they could have gone home before Chas became unmanageably drunk. Harriet's version of what Dick had done for her and why seemed to satisfy her, however. Denny's name was not mentioned.

Now Leonie looked at Harriet shrewdly across the gingham tablecloth. Harriet was fiddling with an egg sandwich.

'Your eyes look a bit heavy, kid,' she said.

'I didn't sleep very well last night.'

'Something on your mind?'

'I — went out with Denny Rei last night.'

'Ah,' said Leonie softly. 'And he fucked you.'

Harriet nodded.

'God, why did you let him? If anyone found out — are you okay?'

'Of course I'm okay,' said Harriet sharply. 'Why shouldn't I be?'

'Well,' said Leonie. 'Okay, then. It's a bit different from the first time, is it?'

'It was beautiful,' said Harriet. 'It was the most beautiful thing I've ever done. Nobody ever told me it was lovely.'

Leonie closed her eyes. 'Oh Christ, Harriet, what are you doing?'

'I love him. Don't you see? I want him inside me, right now. This minute. I'm seeing him tonight. Anything as nice as that can't be wrong, Leonie.'

'Black babies,' spat Leonie at her across the table, like an obscenity.

'That's prejudiced.'

'Sure, it's prejudiced. You'll have to learn to live with it if you keep on like that.'

Leonie got up and walked out of the tearoom. After a moment Harriet, filled with weeping, followed her out into the street. Already Leonie was striding away, rounding into the next block. Harriet started to run, calling her. Leonie slowed down only imperceptibly as she caught her up, her face stone.

'Why? Why, Leonie?' said Harriet, pulling at her elbow.

Leonie stopped in the middle of the street. 'How could you? Don't you know what you're doing to yourself?'

'Do you feel that strongly against him?'

Leonie shook her head in wonder. 'I don't have anything against *him*, you silly bitch. I've got something for *you*. You're the first real friend I've ever had in my life, don't you understand that?'

'It's the same for me,' said Harriet.

'Then don't you care that I'm scared silly for you? You go with him, you get pregnant, you've had it, you give away everything. Weyville won't wear it, and you've got a future in Weyville. God knows, it's a hard place to have a future in, but you're making it. Oh yes, I know, you think I'm up myself because I got you that job, well sure I'm proud I did, but I haven't done any of the work that you're putting into it. Don't worry, I hear plenty about you in the bookshop. People like you — that new girl at the library, they say, she's great. I talk to Mr Whitwell, he hasn't forgotten me, but you're the one that's tops. She'll make it, that one, that's what he says, you put me onto something first class there. She's got a good mind, can sense books, I'll put her on buying soon; that's what Mr Whitwell says. God, we know at the shop, no assistant at the library's ever been allowed to buy a book. He does all the buying, always has. But you ... you've been there six months and you're whizzing to the top. Where do you think you'd stand in Weyville if you dropped that lot on yourself?'

'He said he'd look after me,' said Harriet, hanging her head. 'He said he'd get things so nothing'd happen to me. Honestly Leonie, he was really upset last night because ... he hadn't taken care of me properly. It'll be all right, nothing'll happen, you see.'

Leonie impulsively slipped her arm through Harriet's.

'Oh, Harriet,' she said softly, 'You are a mess, aren't you? What am I going to do with you?'

She and Harriet had reached the seat under the war memorial, where they had sat on the day of their first meeting. They sat down together. Harriet started to cry in great anguished sobs. Leonie, who was not a weeper, sat observing, saying nothing.

Finally she said, 'All right, all right, that's enough of that. I guess we're just going to have to see you through it if that's the way it is.'

'Dick said he'd always be around if things got tricky.'

'You mean about Denny?' As Harriet nodded, Leonie said, 'Wow, you really have moved things along, haven't you? All right then, just promise me that we'll keep it between ourselves. When you've got it out of your system, it won't have done any harm.'

Harriet snuffled into her handkerchief, wiping her eyes.

'Hey?' said Leonie.

'Yes?'

'Is it really nice?'

'Yep.'

'Lucky old you. I'm tempted to try it again.'

Eventually she did, without such good luck. Despite numerous conscientious efforts, Leonie seemed doomed to failure in this department.

The football club became the centre of both girls' lives. Every Saturday saw them bundled up in heavy coats on the sidelines, cheering themselves hoarse for the Rovers, and in the evenings they would go on to a party, almost invariably at an old house where three of the boys, including Denny, lived together. Dick took to calling at Cousin Alice's house often enough for it to appear that he and Harriet were keeping company.

He was not really suitable from Cousin Alice's point of view, but she seemed to sense in Harriet a lack of any great interest, and on the odd occasion that she had queried her about the seriousness of the relationship, Harriet's light-hearted answers reassured her. The ball season was nearly over; Dick only called once as if he were taking her out. Having deposited her in Denny's pick-up, he then carried on to the latest of Chas's unsuitable arrangements. Chas was not a permanent fixture in Leonie's life and her boyfriends varied, but they were always Rovers.

So the winter lengthened into spring, and the double life continued. It was almost a triple life, for Harriet had another secret inner life developing which only she and Mr Whitwell knew about it. They both loved poetry, and Mr Whitwell would take her aside almost daily to air a new book, a new poem, or even a line he had discovered; she rewarded him with similar gifts. She was reminded of the long-ago teacher who had read to her in the school shed. Every now and then, she wondered why she and Mr Whitwell had to make such a secret of it, and the thought must have occurred to Mr Whitwell too. He said as much one day, when he had called her into his office on the pretext of going over one of her papers to go off to library school, and then flourished a book of Robert Graves under her nose. 'Read "Star Talk", my dear. Go on, go on, read it, it's all about the stars, and goodness knows you've got enough of those in your eyes these days.'

Her eyes scanned the page, and she laughed with the pleasure of the poem. 'Aloud, aloud,' cried Mr Whitwell.

'Are you awake, Gemelli / This frosty night?' Harriet read.

'Ah yes,' cried Mr Whitwell. 'We'll be awake till reveille / Which is Sunrise, say the Gemelli. Tell me, Harriet, have you ever watched the sunrise?'

'Only through my windows before I went to the cows, up home,' said Harriet, 'But I've often seen the stars. Only I never knew their names until you showed me this.' And she told him about the nights when she had wandered by the river bank in dead of night, back at Ohaka. He nodded.

'Yes, yes, I can see you doing that.'

Pleased, he handed her another book, 'I've only just discovered this one. *Collected Poems*. They've been out since 1953, never even heard of the woman till now, but she seemed to be like you.'

She turned the book over. Charlotte Mews. The pages fell open, and as her eyes lit on a page, she exclaimed sharply.

'Sensual, yes, I knew you'd like it, I knew you wouldn't prove me false. It's for you. Yes, you must take it, I insist. It's never been my pleasure to give a book of poetry to anyone before, let alone such a very young lady. Oh,' he sighed, 'But I should have liked to. It's our secret, of course?'

'Yes,' she said.

He looked away, embarrassed. 'You understand, your pleasure is my indulgence. I should dislike anyone to think it more. People have strange ideas about people who like poetry.'

'I do know what it's like,' Harriet assured him. She toyed with the idea of telling him about the teacher, but it seemed inappropriate. 'So you think I'm sensual?'

'You're a brazen lass, that's what you are. I should have you turned out of my office.'

'But you trust me enough to answer me.'

'Mmm. Yes, I do.' He began pacing round. 'A bad thing, a body and a mind, Harriet. They don't go together. A curse more damaging for poets and those who would follow them than for most. They, poor deveils, have to follow the flesh and the brain. It should not be allowed to happen. It's a cruel God, one who invites partisans, to afflict mortals in such a way.'

'If there is a God.'

'And you think that there may not be?'

'Until someone proves that there is.'

'Aren't you afraid of the fact that nobody ever has proved that?'

'Some would say that they have.'

'True.'

'So you doubt, too?'

'Harriet I'm too old to be certain of anything now. Three years to a pension. I love my books, I love my work, I might have done greater things but my life didn't allow for conflicts...' he paused. 'Yes, the conflicts. I know the problems, Harriet ... why should I have anybody come in and ask me to spell out what I believe? Once I would have said there is no God, now I can only say that some may know God, and others may not. You must make up your own mind, neither be deceived by charlatans nor fail to choose the truth, even if it's unfashionable. Now go, I want the returns on last week's issues by midday. You're wasting my time.'

When Christmas came, Harriet wrote and told her mother she would be arriving in Ohaka on 23 December. She left Weyville on 22 December.

Denny was waiting for her at the Auckland bus stop. He'd brought a curtain ring for her to wear on her finger, and they set off in search of a hotel. They tried three private hotels before they came to one that would take them. At each place, the eyes at reception had flicked from Harriet to Denny, then shuttered down, with the formula reply, 'Sorry, booked out.'

The fourth place was run by a derelict old creature with thick bandaged legs.

'Four pounds in advance,' she said, scarcely looking at either of them. She put the money in a dirty apron pocket and wandered off, saying through a sticky wet fag caught on her lip, 'Room six, third on your left down the corridor.'

Harriet shivered as they went down the dank passage. A dining room was on one side and it looked as if it hadn't been used for years. A few tables covered with stuck-on plastic stood fly-specked and ugly, waiting for diners who never came. Or if they did, they probably risked food poisoning, Harriet thought grimly. On the other side, as they continued, was a row of open lavatories, not proper ones either. Judging by the smell, they had to be emptied every day, or should have been, and hadn't.

Their room was just about as unprepossessing as the rest of the hotel. Wallpaper curled off the walls, the furniture was utilitarian and beaten up, the bed cover stained. Harriet collapsed on it, worn out. The bed crackled.

'What on earth is it?' she exclaimed.

They lifted the covers, feeling around, and discovered the source of the noise. Under the bottom sheet was a layer of newspaper.

Harriet pulled it out. 'What sort of place is this?' she demanded.

Denny rubbed his chin. 'I reckon it's a quickie joint,' he said.

'You mean a place where prostitutes take their men?'

'Something like that.'

'We can't stay here, then.'

'Doesn't look like we'll find anywhere else much, does it?' he said reasonably.

She sighed, agreeing.

'You want me to put you on the bus for Ohaka?'

'I can't go home today, you know they're not expecting me. Somebody'd guess something was up. Besides,' she said, crumpling, 'I wanted to sleep all night with you.'

'Let's have another look.'

They turned the bed back. Miraculously, the linen was crisp and snowy white. It appeared that at least it was laundered regularly, perhaps something that even prostitutes and their men had standards about, heaven knew. Denny pushed up the creaky window. Outside oak trees pushed green against the building, a branch even springing its leaves through the open window. Pale gold light fell in a bar across the room. Denny looked at her, asking her to say yes.

136

'It'll do,' said Harriet.

For the first time she was able to show him all her body, and they were able to do things to each other that hadn't been possible before. He ate her cunt with her legs around his neck till she came, and then, holding back on her, he begged her, 'Blow me, girlie, please,' and showed her how to fellate him. Limp and exhausted, hours later, they went to sleep in each other's arms.

Harriet woke before him the next morning. She realised she was frantic with hunger as they hadn't had a meal the night before.

She raised herself on one elbow, wondering whether she should wake him. The morning light was filtering green through the leaves, they had left the window open all night. It threw his dark face into relief. She supposed that his appearance was unusual for a Maori. His face was thin, almost hollow-cheeked, and his nose aquiline and proud, the forehead very high, so that his hair seemed to be on the point of receding. Only his skin, stretched tight on his face, told anything of what, or who he truly was. It was so dark that around his mouth it was almost blue-black. She touched his mouth with her finger; he stirred in his sleep and settled back against her again.

She wondered how they would spend the day until it was time for her to leave on the bus for Ohaka. He was travelling on up to Kaikohe where he came from. There had been talk of him driving to Ohaka, which was scarcely out of his way, but she knew that as her bus passed the farm she would have to join it somehow, and if she missed the connection she was in trouble. The effort didn't seem justified. Denny had accepted without comment or query that he would not be welcome at Ohaka, just as he had accepted the need for Dick to play the role of her suitor in Weyville. There was a tacit understanding between them that this was the order of things.

Perhaps they would talk. What about? She and Denny seemed to have talked about everything and nothing. Would he like the poetry she loved? Did he read? And what about him? There seemed to be nothing that she did not know about him, and then there was virtually nothing at all. Only the week before had she found out where he lived, and that he was going home to his

137

family for Christmas, just as she was. They'd talked about football, and whether Dick or Chas, or one or other of the rest of them had been beaten by the whistle, or the ref, about which record to play next, about how many pigs' trotters to take back to the flat with them when the party got hungry, about whether her period had come all right. All that, but not much else, thinking back.

Of course she knew that he worked at the mill office, as a clerk in the accounts department. He'd always been good at figures, they fascinated him. She wondered why, for she herself could never understand them. Perhaps he could explain them to her. He'd told her once with pride that an office manager had suggested he should go for his accountancy exams. Maybe he would one day. One day? What was one day, and what did it need to make him reach out for that goal? He was twenty-three, how did he plan to spend the rest of his life? She knew, too, that he had wandered south looking for work, and ended up in Weyville, answering an advertisement in an Auckland paper. Why had he left home? For the same reasons as she had, or because of some different wanderlust? They could be like each other, but again, maybe they were nothing like each other at all.

So where did they begin? Maybe it was all between their bodies. She shifted restlessly. It couldn't be like that, it couldn't. The movement half awoke him. At her breast, like a child, he caught her nipple in his mouth and began suckling her. She felt him hardening against her leg. Before he entered, once more he said, lazily releasing her nipple, 'Will you let me do that when you're full of milk, eh? Will you let me share with our babies?'

And as they coupled, she thought, 'Am I too late? Are we already committed? Is there no turning back?'

They wandered round Auckland hand in hand all morning, after finding a place to eat breakfast. The boarding house had repelled them both once they ventured out of the room, and Harriet felt doubtful that breakfast was part of the service, anyway. A greasy cooking smell came from somewhere in the building, but then she supposed that the proprietress must eat. She didn't even dare look in the dining room.

138

With Harriet's suitcase safely deposited at the bus depot, they found a cafe that served a handsome breakfast. Full of double helpings of bacon and eggs and chips, toast and coffee, the day seemed to hold promise again.

Denny asked her to help him buy presents for 'the little fellas at home'. She would have liked to buy presents for her parents in Auckland too, but that wasn't possible if she were not to give away her secret.

There seemed to be a hundred people for whom Denny had to buy presents. At least she got to look around in the shops, though not much at the places she would really have liked to spend time in. Mostly it was toy shops; nobody in Kaikohe seemed to need pretty clothes from the dress shops.

By eleven o'clock she was tired out, and her hand hung heavy in Denny's. He looked at her, worried. 'You all right?'

'Just tired.'

'We'll have a cuppa, all right?'

They found an Adams Bruce shop, smelling top-heavy with chocolate and ice cream. It was packed out with families as tired as they were, all of whom had been doing their Christmas shopping. When Harriet and Denny had fought their way through to a table, he sat her down, without sitting down himself.

'I want to get something. Don't you go away now.'

'Where are you going?' she asked in a panic, having a sudden vision of him disappearing into the crowd and not coming back without her having a chance to say goodbye.

'Hopping back to a shop. I want to get something. You get us some tea and stuff, okay?'

She nodded and watched his back disappear through the throng. Goodbye? Was that what she really wanted? Perhaps they were coming closer together, but she felt adrift on an alien sea, not knowing where to head for the shore. Denny got what he wanted. Dick had said that. Was she really what Denny wanted, and if so, was he what she wanted too?

Harriet felt around in her purse for the little box which held the present she had bought for him. The cufflinks had cost her twenty-five and six at the main jewellers in Weyville. The jeweller had helped her choose them with care, saying with a wink as they went through the trays together, 'My word, young Dick'll be getting ideas above his station.'

That had comforted her considerably. Obviously Cousin Alice was talking around, and putting a good face on things as far as Dick was concerned, fully believing the lie. The crowd had stuck close together that year. It was amazing, when one thought about it, that word hadn't filtered back to Cousin Alice.

Now that the time had come to give Denny his Christmas present, she was shy, wondering whether he'd like the cufflinks, whether the paua shell in them might seem too ostentatious or too much catering for the fact that he was a Maori. Maybe she shouldn't have even bought him anything at all; he'd be sure to be embarrassed, particularly if he hadn't bought her anything, and there was no sign that he had.

Denny arrived as tea and cakes were brought to the table, She was frantically counting out change from her purse, having a horrible feeling that she would arrive in Ohaka penniless. How on earth was she going to get to the Ohaka post office to draw some money without her parents finding out? With a bit of luck she'd be able to slip into the big post office at the bottom of Queen Street before the bus went.

Denny put a pound down on the table, and pushed her money back towards her.

"Not much of a housekeeper, are you?" he said, sitting down. 'Have to teach you not to spend all my money.'

She felt faint. 'That's my money I was counting, not yours.'

'No, but it will be mine some day, eh?'

He put a huge balloony paper bag down on the table between them.

'What is it?'

'Go on, open it and see.'

She opened the bag carefully. Inside was a white Breton straw hat. 'For me?' she asked.

He nodded. 'Put it on, girlie. Happy Christmas.'

140

So she put the hat on, there in the middle of the Adams Bruce place, with people staring at her.

'You like it?'

'It's — it's lovely, only I can't see myself in it. Do you like it on me?'

'You look like a lady,'

'Is that why you bought it?'

'A bit.'

'Who'd you buy if for, you or me?' she said, laughing at him a little.

'Me,' he said complacently, without a trace of remorse.

She opened her purse and got out the little box. 'These are for you. Happy Christmas to you too, Denny.'

He stared at the contents for a long time. 'You got these for me?'

'Are they all right? You wear lovely shirts when we go out.' Her voice sounded high-pitched and anxious.

'They're beautiful, the most beautiful present I ever had. Here's the rest of yours.'

'Oh no, Denny, not more presents,' she cried as he put another box on the table.

'That one's really for you,' he said, watching her intently.

Inside the box there was another box, a musical box covered with blue velvet and gold wrought birds. The interior was lined with blue velvet too, and as she lifted the lid, the box started a reedy rendition of 'The Blue Danube'.

They both stared at it, entranced. A waitress came over and said, 'Excuse me, but if you don't mind there's a whole queue what's waiting to get in here, and would you mind picking up the paper on account of our litter bins are all full up.'

So they made their way to the bus, due to leave at noon, Harriet completely forgetting to go to the post office. Even if she had remembered time was running short. Denny made her look at herself in shop windows in the white Breton, and she had to admit it did look good framing her pale and rather weary-looking face.

She loved him, she loved him, nothing could ever part them. The morning's doubts fell away — how could she ever have thought not to love him? She would love him forever and have his children and lie by his side every night for the rest of her life.

At the bus stop she clung to him, wordlessly trying to convey this to him, until the bus driver was ready to leave, and said that whichever one of them was coming with him had better get aboard. Leaving him there on the footpath was like leaving part of herself.

At Ohaka, Gerald and Mary were both out waiting for the bus, though it was right in the middle of milking time. She guessed they must have milked early.

Mary clutched her with such fierceness that she felt she would break, and Gerald seemed gruffly pleased to see her. Nothing seemed to have changed on the farm, nor had her parents.

Possibly they had grown quieter than before, and goodness only knew, that had been quiet enough. It was almost as if her absence had imposed on them a habit of silence. She had taken away their need to converse, and they went about their chores wrapped in their private inner selves. She felt that they seemed to have difficulty re-establishing familiar conversational habits. However, she knew that she rekindled all the warmth and love that lay dormant in Mary, that her mother would have taken her in her arms if she had known how, but that it was not possible. Gerald was obviously pleased with the progress she was making, and claimed a good part of the credit by assuming responsibility for her decision not to go to Training College. She would, he said, show those teachers a thing or two. He always knew his daughter had it in her. If this was so it was a revelation to Harriet, but she didn't say so.

There wasn't much news in Ohaka. Harriet had wondered if she might see Jim, but it seemed that he was taking a season off the farm, and labouring in the South Island. The Wallaces suspected that he was looking for a wife. His last prospect had fallen through, to everyone's dismay, and he was on the market again, though nobody seemed very keen. They supposed that he was getting a bit old for most of the local girls. She visited Ailsa, and inspected the baby, which was suitably fat and doing all the right things.

Ailsa looked older and rather tired. She was frankly envious of

Harriet's appearance, and said how lucky she was being a working girl, but then some people never knew when they were lucky. There was a tinge of frank resentment in her voice, which Harriet thought a little unfair, as Ailsa had been so elated about her own successes only a year before.

After Ailsa, there were Wendy Dixon and Marie Walker to telephone. Marie was enjoying Training College and felt she'd make a good teacher. Wendy thought it was all right, but was vaguely dissatisfied. She thought she might travel in a year or so — how did Harriet feel about going with her? To England of course, but maybe they'd go up through India and the Middle East.

Harriet said she'd think about it. It all depended on her own studies, and it would take them a while to save, so she suggested that they should just keep it in the back of their minds for a bit. Privately she thought that if she went anywhere it would be with Leonie, but on the other hand, would she ever go anywhere without Denny? Nevertheless, she repeated the conversation to Gerald and Mary and they were impressed with the idea and said it was something to work for. They didn't know if they'd ever get back to the Old Dart, though the price of butter fat was up that year. Things had been a bit easier, but their unit was too small to ever make them a fortune, however much prices rose.

When she telephoned them, Wendy and Marie had both asked her to visit, but the trip to Ailsa's had depressed her, and the depression seemed to be getting worse. She felt herself tense and brittle as the days wore on, and now that they had settled back to something like the old days, she could see that Gerald was more overbearing than before, and harder on her mother. Harriet, on the other hand, had become less tolerant and ready to accept his absolute authority, and the situation flared suddenly into a quarrel between them.

It was resolved after she had wept and said she was sorry. The old order didn't really change. She was furious at herself for having cried in front of him, and the thought that she could return to Weyville in a few days became increasingly attractive. The only thing that made her pleased to stay on on the farm was the fact that

143

she'd spared her mother a bit of milking, but she hated doing it so much that she hated herself.

One day she went down to the old poplar tree. There had been a flash flood down the river during the winter which had swept branches downstream, covering the poplar with flotsam which made it impossible to sit in.

She sat on the edge of the river. There was a flick in the water and an eel slithered away. She shuddered. It was time to leave.

Coming home was to have been a cleansing for her, a putting of her house in order from the events of the past year, but it wasn't really possible. Perhaps if her period had come on time it would have been better. One didn't need to look far to know that this was the real problem. She and Denny hadn't taken precautions during their night in Auckland; or rather they had the first time they'd made love, but neither of them had anticipated the demands they would make on each other, and they'd simply given up.

Terror that she might be pregnant was building up inside her. There was no way that she wanted to be forced into decisions she wasn't ready to take. Some of the doubts and fears of the morning in Auckland returned.

The weather turned humid. Mary wanted to talk to her, but a barrier was building up between them. It had always been there, of course, but now it was an almost tangible wall, so real that Harriet felt as if she could touch it, and woke from a dream one night crying because the wall was crumbling and falling on her.

A day or so before she was due to leave, her period came. With it some of the tension was dissipated, the bloated discomfort she had been feeling melted away, and her sense of relief lightened the atmosphere all round. But it was too late to be of much help. She was due back at the library at the beginning of the second week of January, and the time had come for her to leave again. Her leaving was in itself a new strain to be borne by them all, until the bus collected her from the roadside on the Saturday morning.

Cousin Alice was pleased to see her back. The house had been lonely without her, she said.

She rang Leonie, who was elated at her return. It was arranged that they should meet that night and go to the lake front fair, which had only another couple of nights to run.

The girls linked arms as they wandered past the candy floss caravan and the shouting hawkers.

'It's been terrible without you,' said Leonie. She had been back to the orphanage for Christmas Day.

Harriet told her about Wendy's proposal that they should go overseas together.

'Would you go?' asked Leonie sharply.

'I wouldn't mind,' said Harriet. 'But not with her. I wondered what you thought about us going together in a year or so.'

'Did you?'

'You know I wouldn't want to go with anyone else.'

'It'd be marvellous. Oh yes, Harriet, Let's go.'

'There's only one thing.' said Harriet. 'I think Denny might want to marry me.'

Leonie stopped, pulling them both to a halt. The expression Harriet remembered from the first time she had told Leonie about Denny was close to the surface.

'You'd be a fool,' said Leonie bitterly. 'After all we've tried to do!'

'You mean our crowd, the football club and everyone?'

'Who do you think I mean?'

'It looks to me as if everyone was doing just the opposite; trying to get us together.'

'Maybe,' said Leonie, beginning to walk again. 'Maybe they were, I don't know. Only I wasn't and Dick wasn't. You're wilful, Harriet, d'you know that?'

'I could be. I don't see what that's got to do with it.'

'You want to be with him because it would put people's backs up.'

'That's not true.'

'Isn't it?'

'I don't know, I don't know.'

'Oh for God's sake, don't start crying. I've got no patience with it. Chas and Denny said they'd meet us here tonight. I should have

145

said I didn't know where you were.'

'Denny's back?'

'Three days ago. He's been ringing me every day. I kept saying I didn't know when you'd be back, but he rang the library yesterday and found out you were starting again on Monday.'

And as she spoke, Denny and Chas appeared at the other end of the fairground, waving out to them.

'Back with Chas,' said Leonie impatiently.

'Back with Chas?'

'Oh fuck Chas,' said Leonie impatiently.

'Have you?'

'Of course. But I tell you, Harriet, it's not worth the candle. I don't know what you see in it.'

Later, as dusk was descending, Harriet and Denny rode the ferris wheel together. At the very top of the arc it stopped, so that people at the bottom could get aboard. They were hung suspended over Weyville, the lights coming on in the ugly flat little town. Away over to their right, they could see the pine plantations, and beyond that again, the hills, blue smudges on the sky.

'Look over there, Denny,' said Harriet pointing.

'Nice, eh?'

'Where would you like to go?'

He looked surprised. 'Same place as you, I expect. Back to our little bed like we had in Auckland.'

'I don't mean that. I mean go. End up. No, not end up, one shouldn't end anywhere, but find some place to go, as far as possible.'

'Hey, you carry on a bit, don't you? You're raving, woman. I'll start rocking this boat if you keep on.' And he jiggled the seat so that they swayed at the top of the machine, pitching perilously. She screamed and hung onto him.

'That's better,' he said, his arm around her. The ferris wheel started to move forward slowly, then picked up speed. Music was piped shrilly up to them, Bing Crosby singing, 'True Love'...

There is no escape, Harriet's mind whirled, except if I stand up in this swirling crate and leap out into space. Maybe I would fly into space, and soar on and on and on — like some great bird. Or will I fall from this great height like a sparrow, crashing earthwards?

The year crept forward, summer lapsed into autumn again, and then it was time for the long winter season. The football boots were brought out, the first party of the year took place, the old crowd re-formed.

For a few months, Harriet and Denny had seen less of each other. Without the cohesion of the group, seeing each other was not so easy. Leonie and Harriet had taken to going to dances together on Saturday nights without partners, and although Denny almost always turned up and took her home, the permanence of the relationship seemed to be fading. Chas had been busy on the farm, Dick was rarely around. At Easter Denny had gone north, and Harriet had refused to go to Ohaka and meet him in Auckland en route.

Instead she stayed in Weyville, and went to the out-of-towners' dance. Later, she went to the lake front with the theological student of the year before. He made love to her very inexpertly on the back seat of the car, and afterwards prayed that God might forgive them both, then proposed to her.

As she had shown him how to remove himself from her vagina before he ejaculated, she assured him that this would not be necessary. He seemed at once profoundly grateful that she should have thus delivered him, and righteously angry that she knew such a technique.

Cousin Alice seemed well pleased with her, although she asked her rather quietly at breakfast the next morning if it was true that she had been seen around town with a Maori boy from the mill on a number of occasions. Someone had mentioned it to her at the dance the night before.

'Quite possible, Cousin Alice,' said Harriet, buttering toast. 'There is a Maori boy called Denny Rei in the Rovers' team. The other boys think a lot of him.'

'But what are you doing with him?'

'If they accept him as a friend, what sort of person would I be if I

147

snubbed him? I always walk downtown with him if we run into each other.'

Cousin Alice looked reflective. Despite the worthiness of the football team (and some of the lads from very nice families who played with the team), there were obvious difficulties. Her forbearance with the now absent Dick had seemed quite enough to handle. However, Harriet was able to conduct herself graciously in a variety of company, she noted, and her exemplary behaviour of the night before was a very hopeful sign indeed. She scarcely had cause to complain, particularly in view of Harriet's departure with the theological student.

Harriet smiled inwardly. How disappointed Cousin Alice would have been. But then, she herself was also disappointed. She had actually hoped that the theological student might have provided her with a little divine guidance in certain areas too. There was the hope in the back of her mind that sex might be as delightful with him as it was with Denny. It would solve a lot of problems if the excellence of the act was proven to be universal. As her encounter with the student had been so disastrous, she felt an urgent need for Denny's return.

As the team reassembled, so did the order of things. Dick reappeared, Leonie started going steady with a boy called Selwyn, the team's lock, and Denny and Harriet began to see each other again almost daily.

At the same time, she and Leonie were laying more positive plans for their trip overseas. Harriet was in to her second year of library training, doing cataloguing, which she didn't find nearly as interesting as her first year of essays and research into such diverse areas as library architecture and children's books. Never the less it went well, and she was now Mr Whitwell's deputy. Harriet had become a popular figure with Weyville's reading public, for she knew books better than any assistant the library had ever had, and would keep aside the right book for the right person. It was a busy and convivial place, and Harriet guessed that the number of approving comments from the library patrons probably swamped less flattering utterances that might have come Cousin Alice's way.

Perhaps she had even created a mystery round herself. Maybe people really did give her the benefit of the doubt, the people who had seen her round with Denny, or going into the flat on party nights.

Whatever the facts of the matter, Cousin Alice didn't comment adversely on much that she did, and she and Harriet were what amounted to friends.

With the end of her library course in about eight months, Harriet looked forward to a substantial pay rise, in addition to the one she had had when she became deputy. She might even be able to go abroad in about a year. Leonie was not as well paid, but she'd been working and saving for longer than Harriet, and thought she might be able to scrape up enough to go by then as well. Together they had gone to see a travel agent to start planning bookings.

Neither of them had mentioned this to Selwyn or Denny. Leonie's feelings towards Selwyn were ambivalent. She liked him because he was good company, he liked being seen around with her, and didn't ask very much. Although Harriet liked being with Denny regularly again and also enjoyed being part of the crowd, the doubts of the summer and the cooling of their relationship in the few months that followed were hardening into a resolution. Denny would have to go.

She hadn't made up her mind when to tell him this, and was still turning it over in her mind when Cousin Alice announced that she'd like to go to a wedding in Gisborne, and thought that Leonie would like to spend the weekend with Harriet. She was quite happy to leave the two girls in the house alone if they thought they would be all right.

Having their agreement and assurances that all would be well, she set off on Friday morning. That night the girls slept together in Cousin Alice's big double bed, as there was only one bed in Harriet's room.

They hadn't meant to sleep together, but Harriet had sat on the edge of the bed for so long, shivering in her nightie while they talked, that in the end it seemed silly to sit out in the cold.

'For God's sake, cover yourself up, Harriet,' said Leonie, opening the bedclothes so she could get in.

They talked on and on, about the places they would go to, how they would go to Greece, and join grape harvests in France, what clothes they would need, whether they would have enough money, and what they would do if they didn't.

Eventually Harriet said, 'Shall we put the light out?'

'Yes, it's stupid to go out in the cold again now that we're so warm.'

'I've been thinking,' said Harriet when they were settled. 'It's Denny. I'm going to have to break with him soon if we're going to go away. He just takes it for granted that I'll go on being there.'

'Mm, not like Selwyn, thank goodness. He knows marriage is the last thing on my mind. Still, I think you're right. You and he have had some good times haven't you? It can't go on forever.'

'It could,' said Harriet 'but that's just the thing, I don't want to. I don't even know how much he wants it. If only we could have talked...'

'*If* you had, but you never have.'

'Not really. Sometimes ... oh, I don't know. I think if we could maybe learn ...'

'But you're not sure that you believe that, are you?'

'No.'

'Isn't it just that you're two people who like fucking, and if you ever stop liking it, there won't be much going for you?'

'Does it really look like that to you?'

'I guess so. But what can I say? You think I'm prejudiced. God, that *I* should be, of all people. That's the trouble, if it were Chas or Dick or anyone like that, you could say you're just not suited for each other. It's Denny being what he is makes it so hard.'

Harriet groped for her hand. 'Thanks,' she whispered. 'It's just telling him. I wondered if I might do it tomorrow night ... you know, if you go out with Selwyn, we could maybe talk here, I could make him some tea and tell him.'

Harriet could feel Leonie's stillness. 'I expect you'd want him to stay the night.'

'I didn't mean that ...'

'No, I know you didn't,' said Leonie briskly. 'It's all right. Probably be better though, wouldn't it? I mean if I didn't come back. Doesn't put a time limit on you.'

'Might persuade him it's a better idea to come round here than spend the evening with the boys.'

'Tricky cow, aren't you? I'll keep out of it then. That's if you really, honest to God, cross your heart and hope to die promise me that you're going to do it.'

Harriet laughed. 'You know that's the worst sort of promise to ask me to keep.'

'You will though, won't you?'

'Yes, I will.'

'I could hug you.'

The dark blanketed their quiet breathing.

'At least I should kiss you goodnight,' said Leonie at last. Her hand groped for Harriet's. As they touched she flung herself into Harriet's arms, her mouth seeking hers. They kissed in the gentle night, Leonie's passion holding her to Harriet as if she could never let her go. Harriet felt her own deep cave pulsing as if she was waiting for Denny, and against her Leonie's nipples were hardening.

Leonie jerked herself out of Harriet's arms, and threw herself away to the other side of the bed.

'Is that what it feels like to want somebody?' she cried in a strangled voice.

'Yes,' whispered Harriet. 'That's what it feels like.'

'Forgive me, please say you forgive me.'

'It's all right,' said Harriet, 'It's all right, Leonie. We only kissed each other goodnight.'

'You don't want to go sleep in the other bed?'

'No. I'll stay with you all night. Come on, give me your hand.'

'I love you, Harriet,' said Leonie. 'I've never had a friend before.'

'I never had a sister, but then neither did you.'

'Yes. Yes, I think I did, sometime. I hardly remember. It doesn't matter. I've got you.'

They dropped off to sleep, exhausted, lying on either side of the bed with only their hands clasped. When Harriet awoke, Leonie was already up and showering. Harriet went out into the kitchen and the kettle was just on the boil as she came out of the bathroom, fully dressed.

Neither of them mentioned the night before. There had been a frost in the night, and it lay in gleaming wedges across Cousin Alice's lawn, sculpturing the monkey puzzle trees to brilliant and fanciful shapes. They sat, eating breakfast, talking again about the trip. *'On the Road'* had just become available in New Zealand, and they were full of its force. There seemed never to have been a book like it before, and they saw their journey across the world as some sort of similar adventure. Somewhere on a Mediterranean shore, in time to come, they would sit sunburned and sandalled, and thank Kerouac.

Later they went to football, and Harriet returned with Denny. While she cooked him sausages and chips, he went around the house admiring things and picking them up. She found herself jumping as he picked up Cousin Alice's Royal Doulton plates. It was hard to remember that he hadn't been here before. It was all such familiar territory to her that it had not occurred to her that he might be fascinated with where she lived.

'Someday you'll have a house like this,' he said. 'All these beautiful things, I'll get them for you. You wait and see.'

'How do you propose to do that, Mr Moneybags?' she asked as she put the food down in front of him.

'I get what I want,' he said, smiling.

'I've heard that one before, too.'

'You want me, don't you?'

Faced with this inescapable question, Harriet looked down at her hands.

'Time for us to settle things, isn't it girlie?' he said.

She thought that it would be easier to talk to him in the dark. She did try to talk to him while he had his meal, but he didn't seem to notice, or if he did, he pretended not to. She could eat nothing.

When he had finished they washed up, and she suggested they

should sit and listen to the radio for awhile. Request programmes were on, she reminded him, although it was so long since she had spent a Saturday night at home that she had almost forgotten.

'You want us to be just like any old married couple on a Saturday night?'

'Perhaps we'll never be an old married couple at all,' she said sharply.

'Come on, girlie,' he said, leading her by the hand. 'I know where that big double bed is. I went and had a look. D'you know it's eight months since you and I slept next to each other all night? You think I haven't been counting?'

'I've had enough of this,' he went on as they undressed. 'You've got to tell all these fellas where you and I stand. I know they won't like it, but they'll get used to it. You think my people will be crazy about you for a daughter-in-law? Maybe you do. Lots of pakehas do, they think they're a big white catch. Well, I tell you, girlie, you're some catch all right, and you're what I want for my own, but not for the colour of your skin. I'll have a bit of explaining to do to the family, they had a girl or two lined up for me up home. I went back at Easter and I thought to myself, perhaps I should decide for them, and I went through a bit of hell for them too, and for you. And I come hurrying back here to be with you, because there was no way I wanted it to be anyone but you. I looked round me in the church in Kaikohe, and the girls all had white hats on, and I thought about you in your white hat that I bought for you to wear at Christmas, and I thought, yeah, okay Denny. You told me I bought that hat for myself, and I did too. I bought it for my woman to be in church with me, the one I picked.'

Harriet gazed at him in fear. Fear for him or herself, it was hard to tell. She only knew that he was saying all the things that should have been said long ago. Why had he waited so long? Perhaps it was not too late.

Her mind turned to Leonie lying in the dark beside her. 'I love you Harriet,' she'd said. Maybe there was some way that she and Leonie loved each other that excluded Denny, or any men. Perhaps somewhere, far away, they would discover what it was.

153

'I love you.' He'd never said that. Just, 'I want you.' Did they mean the same thing?

She reached for the light above her head. 'Don't turn it out,' he said harshly. 'I want to watch us do it.'

'I've got things to talk to you about too,' she said.

'They can wait,' he said, rising on her.

This was how Cousin Alice, who had been prevented from getting to the wedding by a car breakdown, and who had spent hours in a small town waiting for repairs, walked in and found them in her bed.

In the morning, before she and Denny headed north in the pick-up, Harriet called on Mr Whitwell at his home and then visited Leonie.

At Mr Whitwell's house, a plain, ageless woman answered her knock. She led Harriet down to a threadbare room, lined with books from ceiling to floor, where Mr Whitwell was sitting reading a book about the Carthaginians. He introduced the woman as his sister. At another time, Harriet might have paused to reflect that this was the first intimation she had ever had of Mr Whitwell's domestic arrangements. As it was, she was so barely able to return an audible greeting that Mr Whitwell, noting her distress, asked his sister to leave.

When she told him what had happened the previous evening, he shook his head slowly from side to side. 'Ah yes, Harriet,' he sighed, placing his long slender fingers together, 'yes, the conflict of body and mind. Here,' and he rose to his feet, and went to one of the bookshelves. He scrabbled round for a moment, and produced a book. 'Take it. Frost. Put down by some of the critics, but never mind that, revered by others. Read 'The Road Not Taken'.

'I shall be telling this with a sigh / Somewhere ages and ages hence: / Two roads diverged in a wood . . . and his voice broke. 'Take the thing and get out of my sight.' He pushed the book into her hands, and opened the door. She saw that he was convulsed with silent shaking tears. 'Get out. I'd have helped you, you fool,' he said, his voice rising. As she went down the passage, he shouted after her, 'I wouldn't have cared whether he was black, green or pink. Fool!'

And the door slammed behind her.

Harriet had rung Leonie and warned her of her arrival, and the fact that she was leaving town and why. The woman who answered the door told Harriet that Leonie was ill and had asked that she be left to sleep, as it was Sunday morning. Harriet pushed past her.

Leonie was lying with her face to the wall.

'Leonie. Please,' said Harriet. 'Please speak to me.'

The other girl rolled over in the bed, turning a stony face on her. 'I don't want you in here.'

'There's nothing I could do,' said Harriet.

'We could go away, you and me,' said Leonie. 'That was what we were going to do.' Her voice, hard as it was, held a hint of pleading.

'We haven't enough money. You might get the welfare back on you.'

'Excuses.' Leonie's mask fell.

'Have you been crying?'

'I don't cry.'

'I wish I was like you, then,' said Harriet.

'But you're not, are you?' said Leonie. 'Now please leave me alone.'

'Is that all you've got to say to me?'

Leonie rolled back towards the wall, her fingers white round the edge of the blanket. After a few moments, Harriet left without either of them speaking again.

Denny and Harriet drove out of Weyville, past Cousin Alice's house, and headed north. There was no movement behind the lace curtains. They had said their goodbyes, quiet and polite on Cousin Alice's part, but as implacable as she'd been when she had telephoned the Wallaces to tell them their daughter would be coming back the following day.

At Ohaka, Denny went in with her and met Gerald and Mary. He promised to return on the Thursday with the arrangements made.

On the Thursday afternoon, he, Harriet, Gerald and Mary went to the church together. The spring was coming earlier here in the north than down in Weyville. Little had changed since the year of

155

Harriet's confirmation, except that the lichen on the graves had grown a little longer. A faint wind stirred the grasses and blew a shower of petals from an early flowering tree, the same one where she had leaned her bicycle years ago when she was a girl. A girl? Now it seemed she was a woman.

That was what Father Dittmer said. As though in a trance Harriet heard him say, 'We are gathered together here in the sight of God, and in the face of this congregation ...' He faltered, his eyes resting on Gerald and Mary, the whole congregation, 'to join together this man and this woman ...' and she knew that the woman must be her. She had graduated to fullblown adult status. She would follow the responses through, there was no turning back. 'I, Harriet Wallace, take thee, Dennis Matiu Rei ...' She hadn't known his full name till that morning. 'I pronounce that they be man and wife together ...' Catching her eye in a fleeting glance, she thought she could feel him saying, 'And who wouldn't have known it.'

When they emerged from the church she knew that she was now Mrs Rei.

Nobody had discussed what would happen next. Very little of any substance had been discussed since Harriet's return the previous Sunday. During the week she had sat dully in her bedroom, while her equally uncommunicative mother had sat in the kitchen, or dragged herself to do what had to be done round the place. On the Wednesday she had gone through Harriet's suitcase, mended, and ironed her clothes and repacked them. When she spoke her voice had been monotonous, seemingly without emotion. Harriet hadn't offered to help, nor had she been asked to.

Gerald spoke to give orders and to tell them what arrangements had been made. They didn't sound like arrangements — more like military drill. The night before the wedding Harriet had caught him alone.

'Dad,' she'd said, and then, hesitantly, as he didn't reply, 'Father.'

He'd turned towards her with fierce contempt in his face. 'Bitch,'

156

he said, and walked away. And she'd started crying. Oh, she always cried in front of him, he was the master of her tears.

Now, as they stood outside the church, he said stiffly, 'I think your mother and I will be getting back to the farm, Harriet. We don't want to be late with the cows coming in and all.'

It was a dismissal. Not that Harriet altogether blamed him for that. If they returned to the house, sleeping arrangements might have to be made for them, and even Harriet, dazed as she was, could see that this would be a quite impossible dilemma for them all.

They shook hands all round. Harriet ached to have her mother hold her, but already Gerald had shepherded her away, and she saw them drive off, a cloud of dust following them up the metalled road towards the farm.

Denny and Harriet climbed into the pick-up and he said, 'Where to, now?'

'I don't know,' said Harriet. 'Do you?'

'We could go to Kaikohe, but it's a long drive.'

'To your parents?' She recalled what he had said about them possibly having reservations about her too.

'We'll leave it for today, I think. I rang a mate of mine in Auckland and he said he could jack up a job for me to tide us over till something else turns up. I reckon he might put us up for a couple of nights while we have a look around. What d'you say?'

So they headed for Auckland and arrived late, when the diamond sky was alight.

7

The marriage of Harriet and Denny lasted fifteen months. It might have lasted longer, but a number of factors contributed to its collapse.

They had difficulty finding accommodation. After the episode at the hotel the Christmas before, this hardly came as a surprise to either of them. Harriet assumed that it wouldn't have surprised Cousin Alice or her parents either, but then, like everything else, no one had discussed anything like that with her. In fact, Denny's race had not been mentioned by anyone. This seemed quite extraordinary, when Harriet considered it, as she did more and more often during the following months.

She sometimes wondered if she had imagined their wedding, people having said so little at the time. It even passed through her mind sometimes that her own inertia had led to all this. After all, she had simply followed a series of tacit assumptions that she would adopt a certain course of action.

Denny's friend put them up on a creaky sofa in his three-roomed Auckland flat for a week. Neither of them slept, and Denny was bad-tempered and tired out with his job at the freezing works at Otahuhu.

Harriet looked at flats, agreed to take one or two rather pleasant ones, and then found there had 'been some sort of misunderstanding' when she turned up with Denny. It was finally agreed that she should take what she could get without Denny showing up. The place she took near Parnell wasn't marvellous, because the owners wouldn't risk letting you have the really nice ones without looking you over as a couple, but it wasn't too bad either. It was furnished, but without linen. Gerald had pushed a ten pound note into her hand before they left for the church, so she bought a pair of blankets, and Denny had enough money over from his pay for a pair of sheets.

They seemed to need a lot of other little things. A lot of towels, for instance, because Denny needed a bath every day. He came home clean, but the smell of the meatworks seemed impregnated into his skin within a week or two. She would have liked a bath every day too, but there wasn't enough hot water unless they shared it. That was something she couldn't get used to because she'd never had to share anything in her life. Spoilt, some might call it. Looking back over her life, she couldn't quite see that it was so. But she supposed that's what people would call it. Denny did.

In bed at night Harriet would feel her stomach heaving at Denny's smell, and often she would turn her head away while he made love to her. He, offended, rolled sullenly over to the other side of the bed and sank into a weary sleep.

She did think of going to see Wendy and Marie at Training College, but the idea was unattractive. She represented failure, they success. Later she thought that everything was her fault for being so negative. She could have tried harder. If guilt were to be the price, she would pay it in full.

The decision that she should take a job was made after Denny came home one evening and found her with a pile of library books. At least reading seemed a sensible refuge, and coming back to books, she had been spellbound all day. When he came in, exhausted as usual, dinner was not ready and she hadn't even shopped.

He was grim and angry when they went out to find somewhere to eat. After their meal, he told her, 'If you want to play fancy games, you'd better help me pay for them.'

She took a job the next day in a Queen Street milk bar. Let the punishment fit the crime, she thought.

Every night after that they both came home tired, and there was

159

little to talk about. They could have talked about something, she thought later. If they'd really wanted it to be good, they could have told each other what they had been doing and about the customers that came into the shop, and about the men that Denny worked with.

They could have made something, but they didn't. She could feel herself getting thin and ugly. She didn't think she'd ever really been pretty, but she had had something, she knew that. Shiny eyes, shiny hair, good skin, and a nice shape. All the shine was going, and the shape wasn't what it had been, and it was getting worse all the time because her shoulders fell forward every time she sat down.

In the evenings Denny would sit reading the *Herald*. She knew he was looking for jobs, but the paper would be a day old by the time he read it, and two days old by the time that he could go out after the job. His resentment was deepening into permanent lines on his face.

Then without telling her he took a couple of days off, coming back to the house after she'd left for work and changing into his good clothes. A few days before Christmas he got a job in an office in town and would start after the Christmas break.

The atmosphere lightened. The job wasn't as well-paid as the one he'd had at the mill, but he was working with figures, and there were prospects. You could work your way up if you were good. He'd told the people to ring the mill when he couldn't produce a reference, and that had been better than a piece of paper. The manager of the mill did mention that he'd skipped off rather suddenly, but as the cause had apparently been family trouble, there was no reason to hold that against him. The new boss was obviously impressed, and he'd got the job right away.

He suggested that they go up to Kaikohe for Christmas. Harriet said that she only had two days off over Christmas because they'd be open right through the holiday break, it being a milk bar. Shove the job, he said, she could get another one when she came back; she was good enough to get any job she wanted.

Kaikohe was good for both of them. She'd been shy of the Reis at first, and they of her, but Denny was their prodigal son, and as far as Harriet could make out, there were fewer tensions about her arrival than she had expected. If anyone felt less than happy about her, it was certainly not allowed to show.

'What d'you think of my skinny little pakeha?' Denny said, prodding her, there in front of them, and laughing with them all when she blushed. The drive north through familiar countryside, and the sun and the companionship between her and Denny which had been missing for so many months had put colour back in her cheeks. The night before they left, she had washed her hair and brushed it, sitting up in bed beside him, and he had taken a hand too, brushing it for her. It was long round her shoulders now, and in the morning she tied it back from her face with a ribbon. She felt more like herself than she had since she left Weyville.

At midnight on Christmas Eve they all went to church, and for the first time she saw Denny among his own people. For a fleeting instant she had felt like an observer, like someone at the pictures, her own old religious judgements hesitating at this participation. However, it was not real participation; she was playing a part in a play that was real for everyone else. Then Denny slipped his hand into hers as they knelt, and she was happy just to be part of them.

In the morning they went to church again, and she wore her Breton straw for him. Standing beside him, while he sang in Maori, like the rest of them, she thought, 'He said he wanted me. Now he has me.'

Presents and Christmas dinner followed. Harriet had trouble with the Reis' food which was fattier and richer than she was used to. When she seemed not to be eating, Denny whispered to her, 'Hey, what's wrong with you? My mother'll think you don't like her if you don't eat her food.'

The food was a continuing problem during her stay in Kaikohe, not helped by the fact that her plate was piled high at every meal. Denny's mother said, 'We'll put some meat on her bones for you, Denny.'

She developed a technique of dawdling over her food, and then when everyone else was finished, rushing to help clean up, so that

161

her own food could be scraped in with the other scraps. She knew that the deception hadn't fooled Denny's mother, but she kept her own counsel. It seemed to work with Denny, and for the moment that was what mattered.

Several times they drove to the sea, usually accompanied by a crowd from the family, and they dug for pipis and collected mussels from the rocks. These were happy times for them all, and Harriet could feel the glow of the north creeping back into her body, as well as her remembered love for Denny.

The day before they were due to return, he took her by herself over to the Hokianga. This was old ground indeed, going back to the days before Ohaka. She showed him the school where she had been in so much trouble when she was a girl, and he was astonished, wondering that they had been brought up so close to each other without even knowing it. The place where she had lived had gone, replaced by a shiny new house. Things seemed to be prospering round those parts.

Along the coast, in the grass near the sand dunes that went down to meet the sea, they made love in the midday sun. High midsummer sun beat down on their stripped bodies.

'Denny, I'm going to have a baby,' she said afterwards.

'When?' he asked, his face alight.

'I don't know. I'll have to work it out won't I?'

'Why didn't you say ... Hey, wait till we get back and tell everyone.'

'We can't do that,' said Harriet. 'We just started it.'

He looked at her. 'Don't be silly, woman, you can't tell that soon.'

'I can,' she said, Maybe being back in the old place had done it, but whatever it was, her body knew.

Years later, other women told her that they, too, had known the moment of conception, though mostly they admitted that it was a retrospective thing. Men never believed it.

But she knew, she knew her body had been open to receive. Sand and sea and sun, a child, they went together.

The next day they travelled south again, passing through Ohaka without stopping, as on the way up. Denny had become edgy overnight. They'd been happy up north, happier than either would have thought possible a month before, but she thought he knew as well as she did that it was because of the support of his family. Group support — it was a bit like the days of the football club.

It was a sobering thought that they might always have to rely on other people for their comfort. Harriet suspected that he was thinking this, too. There might be little common ground between them, but she had never doubted his sensitivity or powers of deduction. He was smart in a different way to her, but he could work out the same things when he wanted to.

Well, there would be the baby, and that would make more people, Harriet thought. She didn't say it, because the baby hadn't been mentioned again; obviously Denny thought she had been sunstruck to say what she had. Possibly she had been, too, she wondered, not sure whether she herself believed what she had said.

For all that, she went back to her old job. It didn't seem worth taking on something new if she wasn't going to be at it for very long. The milk bar hadn't been very pleased with her, taking off like that just before Christmas when they needed staff, but she was as good as anyone they'd had, and good staff were hard to come by. Denny wasn't happy about her going back. She guessed it didn't fit his new image, but she told him it was just for a few weeks until she could find something else. In a way she meant it too.

Two or three weeks later, they both began to take her pregnancy seriously. At the end of February it was confirmed by a doctor.

Every February day in the milk bar was virtually unbearable. Her feet swelled regularly, and she was limping so badly by the end of work that she could hardly make it home. She'd started to feel sick too, and what with the heat, it was all bad. In the weekends all Denny's shirts had to be washed and ironed; he had a fresh one every day, now that he was in a city office.

Things were starting to drag back to the pattern they had followed before Christmas, until he told her one night to get the hell out of her job because he couldn't stick it any more.

She asked whether she could give two weeks' notice, when she'd have enough money for the baby's things. The weather was taking a cooler turn, and she managed to see out the two weeks. When she stopped work, she hardly got out of bed for a week except to get Denny his meals and do the washing.

The doctor prescribed pills for her nausea but told her morning sickness was all part of being pregnant. It was impossible to convince him that she was sick all the time.

After Easter Denny's parents arrived unexpectedly on the doorstep, saying they had come to stay for a couple of weeks. Denny and Harriet moved into the sitting-room, and his parents took over their bed.

Having them to stay was much less satisfactory than going to see them. If they didn't go out, it meant that they and Harriet sat in the flat all day with little to say to each other. Denny's parents tried hard to make themselves scarce, and Harriet could see that her mother-in-law knew she wasn't well and was concerned, but they couldn't just stay out all day in Auckland with nowhere to go.

The visit ended abruptly after about ten days, when Denny brought home some mutton birds for her to cook for his parents. The smell destroyed her. The thick oil stench was like nothing she'd ever experienced before. All night she vomited, sitting on the floor of the toilet, crying between bouts, too weak to stagger in and out to the sitting-room.

Denny's mother came in and knelt on the floor beside her, rubbing her back to make the vomiting easier, bringing her boiled water to drink when she was reduced to bile, and washing her face.

'I think you ought to get the doctor,' she said to Denny. 'I reckon this girl might lose her baby.'

Towards morning the doctor came. She'd be all right, he said, if she had total rest. He could put her in hospital but it was pretty crowded in there, and it was not really necessary if she was sensible. After he'd gone, Harriet heard Denny talking to his parents in the bedroom. His mother's voice was calm and flowing. It was difficult to catch her words, but Denny's voice carried clearly. He thought they should stay and care for Harriet. It was lucky they were there, and they need not go home for a while longer.

His mother explained gently that what she wanted was no strain, and her own comfy bed to sleep in at nights. They'd be pushing off, because that was what Harriet really needed. Denny wasn't to be angry with her. She was a brave girl, but not too strong. He'd have to do for himself a bit; it wouldn't hurt him now that he had a fancy sitting-down job.

When they had gone, he looked at her bitterly and said, 'You sent them away. You sent my parents away.'

She turned her face from him. He was making her cry, just as her father had always done. There was no answer for his anger.

She started to recover, and the doctor kept a closer check on her, giving her special diets, and iron injections because she was anaemic. Gradually she began to cope again. Her stomach was huge by late May, and she was only halfway there. The days seemed long but she had taken to reading again, careful now not to neglect Denny's meals, and she was painfully teaching herself to knit. The serials on radio were quite good, too.

One evening Denny came in and said that some of the chaps at work were in a football team, and he'd like something to do besides just go to work, come home, go to work. He thought he'd join up with them.

That was the beginning of the end — if one didn't count the end as having started at the beginning. Several times she asked him if she could go and watch the game and once he said yes, the other times he said it was too cold for her to be out watching. The time she did go, it was to a field a bit like the ones at Weyville where you could park the cars near enough to the sidelines to see what was going on without getting out. Denny suggested she'd be more comfortable sitting in the pick-up.

He was still splendidly fit and played a good game. Seeing him like a panther amongst the scrum she felt the old pride and something of the old longing. For months she had been unable to bear him to touch her sexually. She was sure that this was wrong, and with great embarrassment had asked her doctor about it.

'Sex?' he'd boomed back at her. 'Perfectly natural. Not too close to when the baby's due, that's all.'

So she'd tried, and it was hopeless. Denny, rejected and frustrated, left her alone. She said she'd ask her doctor what was the matter, which was a lie because she had already asked him. A few days later she told Denny that the doctor said it might be best to leave it alone for a while because of the way the baby was lying.

At the end of the game when he came back from the showers, some of the men he'd been playing with followed him to their cars. 'See you at the club room, Denny,' they called.

'Are we going out?' she asked with momentary elation.

'I thought I'd have a few at the club rooms,' he said.

'Not me?'

'I don't know that they have birds at their rooms the same as the Rovers.'

Thinking back, she guessed he meant wives. The wives never got much of a look in, even in Weyville. They were a forgotten race, people of whom you occasionally thought if one of the married boys started playing up a bit.

Saturday nights it started, then it was Friday nights as well. Harriet wrote to her mother and told her when the baby was due and gave her her phone number. There was no reply to the letter, as to all the others she'd sent.

In early September, she guessed he'd been with a woman a couple of times. He moved onto the sofa for good, and she enjoyed the luxury of the whole bed to herself. Once there were telltale lipstick marks on the shirt when she washed it, but she didn't mention them.

The phone rang one evening when Denny was in the bath.

'I'll get it,' he called.

'Don't be silly, you're in the bath,' she called back and picked up the phone. There was a hesitation at the other end when she answered.

'Is Mr. Rei there, please?' said a girl's voice after a moment.

'He's in the bath. Can I give him a message?'

There was another pause, then the girl replied, 'Could you tell him Gloria from the office rang.? I forgot to give him a message today from ... from Mr. Peters.' Mr. Peters was the boss, Harriet knew.

'Well, I could pass it on to him if you like,' said Harriet.

'Oh, not to worry ... it's probably not important. I expect it can wait till the morning.'

She gave Denny Gloria's message. Later in the evening he said he had some gear in the pick-up that he was supposed to drop off for one of the boys from the office, and he wouldn't be long. At one o'clock he still hadn't returned, nor was he home when she woke in the morning. She phoned the office at mid-morning and spoke to him.

'I'm sorry,' he said. 'The boys were having a few drinks and I got talking, bit boozed. Fell asleep on the sofa.'

That night she asked as she put his dinner in front of him, 'What did Gloria think about the hotel in Symonds Street?'

She thought he might strike her, but his hand dropped away to his side as quickly as he'd raised it.

Instead he sat down beside her, fingering the knitting she'd been labouring over. 'What's the matter with us girlie?' he said dully.

'It'll be all right,' she said, and put her arms round him. He dropped his head on her swollen stomach, and she cradled him, soothing him. 'It'll pass, everything'll be all right.'

He caught her hand and held it. 'I do bad things for you. I was going to do good things for you. What say we go up home and live near Mum and Dad and the kids, somewhere up the Hokianga, after the baby's come?'

'You know you wouldn't really want that,' she said. 'You want to get on, you always have.'

'It doesn't matter,' he said, 'You and me getting on's more important than that. Why don't we just get up and go now?'

The prospect was enticing. Perhaps it could work. But it was now into October and the baby was due in less than a fortnight. She'd been so sick and she was booked into National Women's Hospital. For the baby's sake perhaps they had better stay where they were. It was only two more weeks, and they'd be able to travel pretty soon after that. It was something to look forward to, something to keep them going.

The baby didn't come on time, though. It was, said Denny at first, 'keeping Maori time'. When the second week came with no sign of the child, things started to be strained between them again. The phone rang several times, and the caller simply hung up if Harriet answered. When Denny answered he sounded curt and businesslike, as if the calls were from the office. Gloria, Harriet supposed.

The doctor decided to put Harriet into hospital.

On an impulse, Harriet scrawled a note to her mother, telling her she was being admitted. She had resolved not to communicate with her parents again, but at the last moment she weakened. She posted the letter at the posting-box on their street, near the flat, before Denny drove her to the hospital.

Outside the hospital, she said to him, 'Denny, I don't want to go in. I don't want to have a baby.'

To be so totally helpless, so out of control, was terrifying. She was committed to this situation. Nothing could take the baby away except the act of birth itself.

Inside the hospital, women cried and screamed and whimpered and begged for their shots. Harriet did not know what shots they meant. It didn't seem to do much good because the women in white mostly ignored their entreaties. They shaved Harriet's pubic hairs with cold soapy water and they talked over her about other women as if they were cattle. It was hard to believe that they shared the same genital patterns as Harriet and the other women in labour. Harriet felt sure they must belong to a third sex. Perhaps, with the doctors, they were eunuchs. Whatever it was, they were united against sweating, heaving, grunting women in childbirth. Doctors came around, two or three of them together, laughing and chatting about their golf handicaps. One of them had a hangover. He put his finger up Harriet's rectum and the pain was so appalling that she started to cry. The doctor raised his eyebrows at the nurse and said, 'Another sniveller. Give her a shot if she's awkward.' He looked at her card and tossed her a contemptuous look. Harriet heard him say 'Another little black bastard,' as he walked away. They thought she was not listening. She didn't get her shot. A woman died of a haemorrhage in the night. The nurses were embarrassed, but the patients were given to understand it had been the woman's own fault.

Two days later, Mary Wallace tried to telephone her daughter while her husband was cleaning out the shed after morning milking. The phone kept ringing and ringing when tolls put her through and eventually they said it was no good trying any more. It was too early for Denny to be at work, so she decided he must be at the hospital.

Gerald Wallace came in from the shed as his wife was plonking her old pudding-basin hat on her head and putting a pile of things in a large canvas carry-all that they'd brought from England. Mary faced him defiantly. He just said, 'I'll carry your bag to the bus,' and waited with her to flag it down as it passed the farm.

Mary sat with her daughter through the long and savage labour, for as long as the staff at the hospital would allow her to. She rubbed Harriet's back at the point where the strain imposed by being half-suspended with her legs in stirrups was most intolerable. She and Harriet were allowed to see the little cream-caramel coloured boy briefly before a nurse took him away. The doctor suddenly seemed nicer and more concerned.

Denny never saw his son. When he checked in the hospital the next morning, three days after leaving Harriet there, the baby had given up its struggle for oxygen. Mary had tried to find her son-in-law all through the night before, but all her enquiries had met with blank walls of silence. A protective wall, she thought grimly, when she tried to reach him through his office.

Sitting on the paper-white bedspread beside her that day, he took her chalky face in his hands and said, 'What I've done to you, girlie.'

'To each other, Denny, to each other,' she said, returning his look.

'Will you ever come back to me?' he said.

'I don't know. I'll need some time to think.'

169

Ohaka was sliding into summer when she returned. The river banks had never been more beautiful. The Wallaces watched their daughter when she went down to the water, covertly, fearing for her safety. There seemed to be little to fear, however. She sat quietly, spoke little but sensibly enough. She did not say very much about the previous year and what it had meant to her.

The Colliers called in from time to time, Jim coming too. He was a heavy man now, fast fading into middle age, but he was good and gentle to her, understanding what she'd been through without it having to be talked about. He still hadn't married, and it almost seemed as if he was going off the idea.

Shortly before Christmas, Harriet wrote to Cousin Alice, and on receiving a reply a few days later, she told her parents that she would be returning to Weyville at the New Year.

The Wallaces told her that they had obtained evidence for a quick divorce. It wasn't an ideal Christmas present, but it was the best they could do. They understood if she didn't want to use it, but it was there if she did.

Harriet sat on the river bank for a long time the day before she went away. The eels seemed to have increased in recent years, sliding across the rocks in ever greater numbers, and the wild duck population had decreased.

It was her last summer there. The following year Gerald Wallace injured his back beyond repair as far as farmwork was concerned, and the farm was sold.

For years afterwards, she would wake in the night from deepest sleep, wondering whether she had dreamt her first marriage. Often it would take several moments of consciousness to work out whether or not it had really happened. When her children woke crying in the nights too, she would wonder which child it was, as she groped her way through the house. When she put the night light on, she would start in terror, because she did not recognise the child, but saw instead some other one.

She was returning to the world of Harriet Wallace. For many years, no one knew that she had ever been married. There were rumours, of course, but they were so nebulous and she seemed so self-sufficient that nobody dared to ask. Many years later, a reporter interviewing her after the publication of a book, threw in a question. He'd gleaned some chance information and checked it out. She answered truthfully, for it didn't seem to matter then, that she had been married in her teens, and yes, her name had been Mrs Rei, and yes, her husband had been a Maori.

'Why did it break up?' the reporter asked.

'There were a lot of pressures on us in those days,' she'd answer.

The story was published and she became a kind of martyr. She was expected to become part of various movements, to make declarations about having been a 1950s victim of discrimination against people who had Maori partners in marriage and relate it to the present. Editors who had previously rejected some manuscripts of hers with Maori emphasis as being 'not truly ethnic' now discovered implications they had overlooked before. She withdrew all these manuscripts.

Nobody ever asked her what the pressures were that she had mentioned. She supposed it was partly true that they existed because she was a pakeha and Denny was a Maori. But the main thing was that they were two people who'd got married for the wrong reasons, and who didn't get on. Denny and Harriet. Harriet and Denny. Always too late, just too late.

It seemed the saddest thing that nobody, nobody at all, ever saw them as anything but a Maori and a pakeha, rather than a couple. Until people like her and Denny could be real instead of peepshows, no statement of hers seemed to bear any relevance to what they were talking about.

Perhaps it went deeper and was even worse than that if people were going to insist on seeing things in terms of race. She was the culprit because she had rejected a Maori. Nothing could change that; only she knew that she had been rejected by a man. Her rejection as a woman was less significant than his rejection as a Maori. She had understood and accepted rejection as a woman since birth, but her oppression counted as nothing. Because he was a Maori. And that, in the end, was worse for Denny than it was for her. If only her critics could see that they were making allowances for him. If he had been a typical white male of the 1950s, they might have condescended to view her oppression with compassion. Because he was a Maori, they made allowances. She had to be the one who was wrong and ugly.

No wonder the hatreds spread. Denny would come back to haunt her in the 1970s on new battlefields. He would serve to remind her that in the scale of oppression, it would be women whose claims were the largest, and who were the last to be considered.

She returned to Weyville on New Years Eve. She and Cousin Alice sat talking into the night, for the first, last, and only time, about Denny. Cousin Alice talked to her about her marriage, too. She said that Ted had been a good man, but living by his rule book had been hard sometimes. She was set in her ways now, there was not much she could do to change what she was, or what she had learned to be for him. Yet there were times, she said, when things puzzled her, she was uncertain of her ground. It seemed to keep shifting. What had happened to Harriet had filled her with grief. If the old rules held good, she shouldn't have felt as she did. She should have gone on believing that Harriet had got what she deserved, still felt the self-righteous anger that had filled her on the night that she had caught Denny and Harriet together. But she didn't feel these things, and she was confused. Some of the blame must rest with her. Out in the world beyond Weyville, she thought there might be change in the air for women, at least for those who were strong. It was too late for it to mean much to her, but she hoped good things were about to happen, and she hoped that Harriet had strength to be part of them.

When midnight struck, it was 1960. The 1950s were over. Harriet was about to pick up the threads of her life again. As they were on their way to bed, Cousin Alice remembered to tell Harriet that Leonie Tregear had left town nearly a year before.

1978

8

There was a message for Harriet at the studio one day, saying that a Mrs Leonie Coglan had called and left her number.

Harriet was late for makeup, and she was not particularly interested in people who left messages without giving details. She resolved to phone at the end of the day, but by that time her interview schedule had been messed up by an incompetent cameraman, then by a difficult subject who was nervous and had to be fed large amounts of coffee before being sufficiently relaxed to give a coherent performance. She was called away to check the editing of some work she'd done the day before, and by the time it was all over, she had forgotten.

The following day there was another message from Mrs. Coglan. Harriet sighed. She expected that it was a member of the public who wanted to praise her too fulsomely, or abuse her to the point of obscenity. Still, there was always the chance that it could be a lead on a story.

'Did she say if it was business?' she asked the girl in the office.

'She said she knew you personally,' was the reply.

'Oh nonsense,' said Harriet irritably. 'In that case, she's a nutter. The only Leonie I've ever known ...' She stopped. Impossible? Of course it was.

She sat at her desk thinking. Leonie Tregear? After all these years? Nearly twenty since she had last seen her. And it was unlikely that she would get in touch with her. Not the Leonie she knew. Only of course she didn't know her now. She wondered what she'd be like. If it was her.

175

When the office girl had gone out for lunch, she dialled the number.

The voice that answered was tentative, fragile.

'Mrs Coglan?'

'Speaking.'

'Harriet Wallace. You called me.'

'Harriet. I'm afraid you must think it an awful cheek. I saw you on television. I suppose you get all sorts of remnants from your past cropping up.'

Leonie apologising? It seemed preposterous. 'It really is you? Leonie Tregear?'

'Yes. It's been a long time, hasn't it?'

'Over twenty years. I was trying to work it out before I rang ... supposing it was you. Where have you been all this time?'

'Oh — all over. I mean around the world, dozens of places, we've only just come back to New Zealand to live. It's rather strange after sixteen years abroad.'

'You've — good heavens, then you did go away?'

'Oh yes,' said the woman at the other end, rather too brightly. 'And you, I suppose you must have travelled a great deal?'

'Afraid not, Leonie. I've never even made it across the Tasman; you were always the adventurer at heart.'

Again there was a careful brittle note. 'My husband's work's taken us to a great many places. He's in oil, you see.'

Harriet thought she did begin to see. The upshot was that she visited Leonie for coffee one morning a week or two later on the way to the studio.

Like her voice, Leonie was fragile, and much more beautiful than when she had been a girl, in a cultivated international sort of way. Her hair was superbly cut and styled, her makeup flawless on a skin that had long ago lost its freckles, and her clothes, so obviously casual morning coffee gear, were so expensive that Harriet was moved to think that the young Taylor children (hers and Max's) could be fed for a month on what they alone might have cost.

Leonie's home exuded wealth, good taste. Was it simply to show it off? Harriet wondered later. It seemed unlikely, for surely there must be many women among the oil clique who would find it attractive. But then, possibly they all had homes like this, so it wouldn't make any particular impression. Then she thought that it could be retaliation for that early betrayal.

But if there was any reflection on the past, it was not mentioned. Leonie did say that she'd heard before she and Hamish left New Zealand that Harriet had returned to the library in Weyville. Presumably she knew why, if she'd taken the trouble to find out that much.

Harriet hazarded a guess at some sort of loneliness, but that too was hard to pin down, and Leonie was determinedly elusive. She talked about her children, about Hamish's job, the places they'd visited. Harriet, for her part, took up her story from the time she met Max, and told her about the children.

'There must be so much more to your life, though,' sighed Leonie, a trifle theatrically, 'You seem to have made so much of it.'

'Perhaps life made me,' said Harriet in what she hoped was a cryptic manner, but that too came out stagey, and wrong.

It had been the end of the coffee break, anyway. They'd said all there was to be said, and left it at that. When Harriet left, she determined to avoid seeing Leonie again, although there had been a vague murmur about dinner.

After that, Leonie rang her twice, with tentative invitations which Harriet managed to dodge. Instead they had some desultory conversation about what Harriet was doing, discovered with some surprise that they both still enjoyed books, and Leonie had asked Harriet what people in New Zealand were reading these days. But that was as far as it went.

Harriet eventually accepted an invitation to lunch in a moment of weakness. She did not really want to see Leonie again; their last meeting had been a disaster, stilted and uneasy. They had avoided political confrontation and talk about money, and worst of all, they had pretended to have no past in common, although their shared past was the reason for their renewed contact. If in an odd unguarded moment they did recognise and recall the time they had spent together, their memory had been carefully veneered. Despite all this, suddenly Harriet was talking, in a great torrent of confession, talking as she had not done in years. She was talking as she had done long ago in a street in Weyville. She told Leonie about Michael, about the phone calls, about his youth, and his beauty, and her love for him, and how it was slipping away. There was nothing she could do to hold on to him.

Harriet had met Michael at a book launching party. She went to a great many of these functions, since she had left Weyville and moved to Wellington. At first she had been a minor talent, then she had moved into television which made her a highly public figure. Whether her talent for writing poetry was minor or not, she was sought after by a great many people.

Afterwards, she had no idea what book had been launched. However, she remembered when the party had taken place — late in October. The chill, light air that signified a Wellington spring evening still lingered over the concrete canyons of The Terrace.

It was Harriet's almost invariable habit to arrive at parties unescorted. Her husband Max Taylor was a draughtsman with the Ministry of Works who did not share her interests. They had three children and, as they both said, they had a happy family life. That was their common meeting ground — they had no need to make public appearances. Harriet still called herself Harriet Wallace, as she had done since the end of her first marriage, and particularly since she had begun to write, so that Max was not embarrassed by her activities and he was hardly ever asked if he was Harriet Wallace's husband. That they went their separate ways in public life seemed to need no explanation to anyone else or to each other. Or so they said.

Because rumours circulated about her 'reputation', Harriet made a point of entertaining her male friends at the most improbable times of day or night whenever she was away from home. A reputation like that, as she explained to Max, was worth money. And he, loyal and patient with her flamboyant excesses, had agreed that this was so. Sending out for breakfast champagne in her room and summoning some man of her acquaintance to share it with her at eight o'clock had made her reputation much easier to handle. The men always came running. And well they might too, she thought with a glimmer of satisfaction, catching a look at herself in the mirror above the bar. Her dark hair was beautifully cut into a long free swinging bob to her shoulders, her wide eyes were as tawny and clear as they had ever been. To be sure, there were signs of wear and tear on the skin beneath her eyes. And yes, she was overweight, but she wouldn't even be without that — it was a sign of maturity. She had reached the point where her plain and rather conventional clothing had a significance of its own.

She specialised in current affairs programmes with a bias towards the arts, but she was known as a writer, a minor one, of course, with a big name and thus she was expected to take a particular interest in book topics. Which, to be fair, she did. And damn well too, she thought grimly, surveying the all too familiar scene with distaste.

She scanned the room for the last time to make sure that she had not missed anybody who might be a valuable contact. She was just deciding against an aspiring politician when she noticed a very tall man standing in a far corner. He stood a good head above any other man in the room, and across the room he challenged her. Or did she challenge him?

As it turned out, they had already met three months before. He remembered, but she had forgotten. It seemed unbelievable, but it was so. He had been determined, this time, to make her see him.

179

Really see him, not just look through him with her cool stare, analysing his profile for a television shot.

He was the editor of a large international magazine based in Auckland, which was trying to establish itself in New Zealand. The market was wide open for an intelligent women's magazine. He had come out from England for eighteen months to see if he could establish it with an all New Zealand staff. He'd already been in the country for six months. His name was Michael Young.

'You're from Canterbury?' he guessed, after they had made themselves known to each other.

'No. Why on earth should you say that?'

'Then you've lived in New Zealand since you were, oh let me see, five or six years of age, about the time you were starting school?'

'I've lived here all my life.'

'Hawke's Bay?'

'Is it my accent?'

'Yass,' he said in the pleasantly light and cultivated English voice that she at once despised, admired, and classified. 'I find I can't place it at all.'

'I've never been out of New Zealand in my life. I'm not the daughter of a founding father, in fact I'm really nothing at all.'

'Oh come on, Harriet, he said, with a blend of old-fashioned reticence at such familiarity and a touch of arrogance, as if she were in fact the serving wench class which she was caricaturing for him. 'You're certainly something. I know a great deal about you.'

'Everything and nothing. I'm a first generation New Zealander. My father has delusions of grandeur and the feudal estate was a small stretch of barren land with only one rather excellent stand of growth beside a river, where he ran the absolute minimum of cows on which to make an economic unit.'

'Past tense?'

'They live in a pensioner flat in a town called Whangerei.'

'Why are you trying to make yourself sound so insignificant?'

'Because,' she said, 'I have so consistently to wage war against those who believe they're significant. And are almost invariably wrong.'

'I'm suitably humbled,' he said, bowing his head.

'Oh no, you're not.'

'No,' he said, inclining his head again. 'But I wish I was.'

'It doesn't matter,' she found herself replying. 'You may be as arrogant as you wish.'

'You must never like me,' he said, quite gravely, she felt. 'I'm dissolute by nature, and I intend to be dissolute all my life. Look at me, I'm thirty-five and I intend to be very rich by the time I'm forty, and live in Paris and keep a French mistress.'

'Look at me,' she replied, 'I'm thirty-nine and going to seed and my reputation is a mixed bag of inferior glory and manufacturered stories about myself, and by the time I'm forty I'll probably be starting to think about becoming a grandmother. That is to say, with respect to nature and the law, there would be no obstacle to my becoming a grandmother.'

'A telling saga. Do you mind?'

'I should mind if my daughter made me one. For her sake,' she added, more than a little defensively.

'I'm sure I would, too. I'll be nearer to fifty than forty when my daughter faces me with such uncomfortable prospects,' he said. 'But that's a long time away.'

Somehow it seemed as if fifty was, for him, considerably further away than the four years that divided them.

'You have children, then?'

'Oh yes.'

'How many? And how old?'

'A son and a daughter. My son is three. 'He hesitated perceptibly. 'And my daughter is just — a month old. Now shall we have dinner?'

As they stood talking, neither noticed that the rest of the party was quietly melting away. They were the only two people left in the room, except for waiters trying to tidy away glasses and ash-trays.

'I don't know.' She looked round distractedly, suddenly thinking that she ought to retreat. The man was quite unbearably attractive. His mouth was full and sweetly drooping, almost childlike in its appeal that she should please him. And she wanted to do whatever he suggested.

How old was his newborn child? A month, he had said. Old memories came back, of herself, long ago in childbirth. Of loss. Of betrayal. What did this man mean asking her to bed with him? But of course this was a nonsense, for she who had always known how to handle any situation. There was no need for her to bed with him.

'Why do you want me to have dinner with you?' she asked weakly. She prayed he would be honest.

'I'd like to hear about your work, and maybe we could talk a little business together.'

She sagged inwardly. It was a sane approach, yet she wished that it had been otherwise.

'I have to go home,' she heard herself say dully. 'The children ... I didn't leave them anything for ... my husband's working late...'

'You become more admirable by the moment. I find it quite extraordinary that anyone who looks like you, and does the number of things for which you're so famous, could also be such a totally nice human being.'

'Don't be sarcastic.'

'I'm not. Truly.' And so intensely and beautifully did he look at her that she was tempted to believe him. 'Of course you must go home.'

Her heart sank. It seemed that he was not going to persuade her, or convince her of his honourable intentions, or do any of the things that might have made her stay with him.

He is afraid too, she knew quickly and instinctively. He knows that if I stay, we shall become lovers tonight.

'May I walk you to your car?' he asked.

'Please.' Her knees were trembling.

In his hand was a little notebook and a pen. 'You'll let me have your phone number so I can ring you next time I'm in Wellington, though, won't you?'

'Of course.' He wrote it down carefully.

'May I ring you at any time, or are some times better than others?'

It was as if they had already moved into some private pact. There seemed to be no turning back.

'People are always ringing me. All sorts of people, nobody minds.'

As he continued to stand looking at her, she added faintly, 'But maybe ... the mornings would be best.'

'Of course. Now shall I take you to your car?'

'Please,' she said again, and together they walked through the muzak-laden air and into a lift that stood open, as if expecting them.

Outside, dark had fallen, and high above, between the buildings, the small hard light of stars could be seen. Beside the car, he inclined his head gravely towards her and kissed her lightly on the mouth. 'I look forward to seeing you again,' he said. Then he was gone.

I will never see him again, she thought despairingly to herself. She drove home in a frightened vague way, almost as if she were drunk. Somewhere along the way she missed a turn-off, and she kept driving for a long time, without noticing that she was on the wrong road, driving slowly and cautiously, crawling her way up the roads, continually checking her speedo to make sure that she was doing a regulation fifty kilometres an hour. Slowing at an intersection, she glanced up, and saw to her horror that the sign above her head read 'Makara' the way to the coast, maybe twenty-five, thirty kilometres away. She stopped the car and pulled to the side of the road.

For a long time she sat there trying to orient herself, not so much in place, but inside her. It had now become evident to her where she was, and she knew that when she started the car again, she would drive home sensibly and alertly, knowing exactly the route to follow. What so terrified her was her sense of misdirection.

After all these years, the thing that she had most feared seemed to have happened to her. And across a crowded room at that. She tried telling herself sternly that it was an extraordinary upsurge of physical attraction after a long hard winter, the old story of the sap rising. He had all the hallmarks of the kind of person she had come

183

to despise most thoroughly in recent years, dining well in New Zealand, dressed out in an immaculate accent, and manners that no Antipodean could possibly hope to emulate. There was no reason to believe that he had any talent whatsoever, and every reason to suspect that he had a great deal of money.

She was quite sure that she loathed him, and hoped that she would not hear from him again.

But of course she did. The children had just left for school one morning a few weeks later. Max, tired from working late again, had crept out of the house like a grey shadow, giving her a hug as he went.

A great deal had to be done at speed. She was due at the television studio at ten to front a programme which would feature a visiting overseas author, an American whom she had met and instantly detested the previous evening. Their interview was occupying her mind when the phone rang. It was Michael Young calling her person-to-person from Auckland. He'd be in town the following day — could they have lunch together? He had business to talk with her. Really, it was business, he'd like to leave it till her saw her. Of course it was possible for her to have lunch with him.

'That was a brilliant interview you did last night,' he said when they met at the restaurant.

'You saw it?' she said, pleased.

'Of course. I always watch you.'

'Oh rubbish, of course you don't.'

'Mm-hmm. I do so. You must know that I'd watch you.'

'More or less since you met me?' It sounded silly when she'd said it, but it had come out without her meaning it to.

'More, of course. And I read your books.'

She blushed. 'Excesses.'

'Wallace tells all. I never thought to find you a shy person. You're incredibly much nicer than I expected.'

'You mustn't believe it's me telling all. My poems are ... um, personal expressions of universal experience. Well, they're meant to be.'

'How many times have you told that lie?'

184

'Did you have a good flight?'

'Beautiful. It's a beautiful country.'

'Have you seen much of it?'

'Not as much as I'd like to. I need a suitable guide, otherwise I shall simply return to England like a tourist book. It's not like me, I like to see places properly, but this job ... He sighed.

'It's not going well?'

'We haven't started the magazine, if that's what you mean.'

'And will you?'

'With a lot of luck, and a lot of help in the right places.'

'So that's what the business is? You want me to get it off the ground? I don't have a lot of say in what I do, you know.'

'What? Oh ... a programme, well, of course that'd be marvellous. If you can do it.'

'Wasn't that what you had in mind?'

His face lit up. 'I thought you were being super-cautious. I suppose people always take you out to lunch to see what you can do for them.'

'I have one or two friends,' she said drily.

He laughed. 'I'm sure you have a great many. I'm sorry, I said it was business and it is. Listen,' and his face was alight with eagerness, 'We've got a good format. The idea is that we carry the best of our hardline basic formula and relevant material through into a New Zealand magazine, but that we cover the local scene with local material. For instance, New Zealand design, New Zealand books, New Zealand art, particularly New Zealand issues and New Zealand politics. That's where you come in. I want you to do a political column.'

'Me?'

'Why not?'

'Michael, you don't know very much about me.'

'Of course I do. I'd watched you in action long before I met you. I had every intention of getting in touch with you. Meeting you that night was a bonus that made it all so much easier, finding out that you really were the right person, instead of groping round in the dark, hoping that you might turn out to be who I was looking for, but dreading that you might be a bitch at the same time.'

'No, you really don't understand,' she said, taking a long drink of her wine. 'I'd be completely knocked down by the pundits here, I stand for nothing in political science terms in this country. I'm barely educated, for a start.'

'Oh nonsense. What does it matter what you did your degree in, or whether it was first or third class? People who get good degrees often never progress past that point. It's all a matter of progression from particular points that matter.'

She burst out laughing. He looked slightly offended.

'I'm sorry,' she said. 'It's just I never got a degree ... when I say I'm uneducated, really I am. I scraped through School Certificate, a very minor qualification I assure you by today's standards, in a small North Auckland high school. I did even less well than I expected to. You really must forgive me. I get angry with other people for trying to con the system, like that man I was crucifying last night, but I suppose in a way I have no right to, nobody's conned the system to get what I want and where I am more than I have.

He regarded her strangely. 'The true New Zealand do-it-yourself Kiwi Kathie.'

'If you like, though I don't like the political inference.'

'I suspected you mightn't.'

'Besides, if you know my political sympathies, then you must realise that I sail very close to the wind in my work. Media people aren't supposed to have political opinions. Or if we do, we're supposed to have learnt to worship the great god objectivity.'

'Difficult for such a subjective person?'

She paused. 'Possibly.'

He sat for longer than he should have without speaking. She concentrated on her food which she had hardly touched, and drank more wine.

They both looked up at the same time, and he held her eyes. 'I don't know ... I don't know,' he said finally. 'Harriet, I wish I hadn't met you.'

'Before you offered me this job, or at all?' She was throwing all pride and sense to the winds, yet everything they both said seemed inevitable. She saw that his finely curling fair hair was already grey round the temples.

'I couldn't have borne the thought of not meeting you at all,' he said. 'Does that answer you properly?'

'Yes.'

'And you?'

'I work hard at being married,' she said in a stifled pleading voice.

'I know, I know. I can tell.'

They ate in silence again, though the food was beginning to make Harriet feel ill.

'About the job, then?'

'It would compromise my position in television.'

'Not if you could be objective. I think it's possible. Do you like the idea at all?'

'Very much.'

'Well, then?'

'I'll have to talk to people, you know, the ones I work with, see how they feel about things. If I can get a go-ahead without losing my job ... I mean after all, it's possible that the magazine might not keep going, then where would I be?'

'True enough. And fair too. I can't ask for more than that. Can you talk to them by next week?'

'I could try. It depends on whether all the right ones are around. They come and go on assignments so much, one can never be sure ... why next week?'

'I'll be back here this time next week. I've got a big meeting, mostly financial, and the head of our organisation will be over from Britain. If I knew where you stood, that would be a big help. I'll have appointments all day, perhaps if I could make you the last person I saw before I caught the plane. After all, I can't really drink till the end of a day like that.'

'You mean, we'll have a drink then?'

'Right. And you'll tell me what you've decided.'

But the following week, he was looking drained with exhaustion.

187

The figures for the meeting were not shaping well, and a lot of things he'd been planning on finalising were still unresolved. Harriet had little to offer in the way of comfort. She had had little support from the corporation. Besides, her own confidence was uncertain. Numerous people had pointed out the quality of other columnists in the field. She would have to be very good indeed to make any sort of dent on the following that more experienced political observers held. Of course there was no doubt that she'd be read, on the strength of her name alone, but if she crashed they felt it would be a bad crash. Harriet had to tell Michael that, while she was happy to work up some good publicity for him in a number of media areas, as far as her own participation was concerned she'd have to wait till the magazine was under way and reconsider the gamble.

The thought of saying this to him had been depressing her all week. She knew it was absolutely true, yet she so longed to please him that the thought of turning him down was almost unbearable. When she saw him, drooping and fatigued, in the bar where they had arranged to meet, her heart sank.

Yet, it was almost as if he had known what she was going to say. He shrugged and said in his most drawling voice, 'My dear, it's been a beast of a day, I've got an awful headache. Let's get out of this crummy little place.'

She felt that she had satisfactorily been put in her place. After all, it was she who had suggested the bar that they meet in, and his disapproval signified that she had poor taste. It was an adequate snub from a person like him. She ought to resent it, she knew, and found it impossible.

'I'll take you to the airport, then. Perhaps we could have a drink there.'

'Thank you, thank you,' he said languidly, and then started cursing as he tried to curl himself into the Mini. 'These cars were made for pygmies,' he snapped, his knees almost touching his chin.

On the way to the airport, he asked where they were going.

'To the airport. I thought we agreed to go there.'

'I loathe the airport,' he said, almost petulantly. 'What am I supposed to do there for an hour?'

'We were going to have a drink, I thought.'

'I cannot abide that second-rate barn,' he said, and would have thrown himself back in his seat if it had been physically possible. Instead, he gave a convulsive and somewhat ridiculous little lurch. 'One forgets that there is no decent place where one can have a drink in this Godforsaken country.'

They drove in silence towards the airport, along Cobham Drive. Harriet thought that he seemed so detestable that forgetting him would be a pleasure.

'I'm awfully nervous,' he said miserably.

'What about? Will your — your chief roast you?' she said, emphasising the chief.

He ignored the sarcasm. 'You.'

She glanced sideways at him.

The sea by the road was indelible blue, and the sun very bright and gold as late afternoon drew in. The colour seemed to be caught up on him somehow. He was more beautiful than she had been seeing him in her mind's eye all these weeks past.

On an impulse, at the turnoff to the airport, she turned left instead of right.

'Where are you going?' he said in real surprise.

'You're quite right. It's a very uncivilised watering hole out there,' she said. 'And I don't really want to drink and make small talk. I thought you might like to sit and look at the sea.'

'I would,' he said. 'Very much indeed.'

They drove in silence for several minutes, past the wharf where Japanese shipping boats were tied for refuelling. Three Japanese men were sitting cross-legged on the side of the road, wearing huge coolie hats. The sight was so sudden and startling that Harriet felt transported out of herself, and out of location, and she felt that Michael was experiencing the same feeling. Neither of them spoke, until she had pulled in to a small bay, a short way along the sea coast. In the late day, the waves were capped with fire, and as they danced and glittered, she felt a great peace.

'It must be as I imagine the Mediterranean to be,' she said at last.

'It is,' he said. 'Or like Greece. Haven't you been there?'

'I've never been out of New Zealand,' she said.

'Really?'

'Really. You're shocked?'

'Surprised. You constantly surprise me. You seemed more — international.'

'Perhaps it's only a comparative thing, while you're here in New Zealand, I mean. After all, the only advantage not having travelled gives me as a New Zealander is that I don't talk about my overseas experience.'

'True. And it had me fooled. I thought you did it standing on your head.'

Almost alongside them, the ferry bound for Picton loomed up, seeming to come straight towards the car. It veered off and slid away across the water.

'That's my overseas experience,' said Harriet, and laughed bitterly. 'I'm sorry, my favourite joke. It starts to fall a bit flat when you've made it as often as I have. Still, it's true. A few trips to the South Island is as far as I've ever been.'

'You mind? But of course you do, or you wouldn't talk like that.'

'Yes, I mind. But I settled for being married and kids and ... oh, a lot of other things.'

'And it satisfies you?'

'I comfort myself with the thought that someone has to stay here and record what is going on here. Who can do that better than someone who's stayed here and been part of it, all her life? Some day I'll do it properly. Or so I tell myself.'

'A rather glum rationalisation?'

'I fear so.' She sighed. 'And yet ... it doesn't always seem to matter so much. Less at some times than others.'

'Now?'

She looked down to her hands folded in her lap. Cars were passing them constantly, people on their way home from work, or others just picking up some sunshine at the end of the day. 'I could go now,' she told herself inside, 'I could stop this thing that's happening. Or I could take a chance and travel another dimension.'

When he did kiss her, the cars passing and honking didn't matter, and the absurd schoolgirlishness of the situation didn't matter either, as she might have thought they would. Looking back afterwards, it seemed silly and rash, and daring because it could have been embarrassing to them both. Only it wasn't, and she didn't want to stop kissing him.

At last they drew apart, and he said quietly that perhaps they should think about going to the airport for that drink; they agreed that the airport bar wasn't such a bad place after all.

They sat together in the deserted bar, a converted hangar, barely disguised in its ugliness under gaudy lamps and some big blown-up pictures of old aeroplanes. He told her about places he had been to, about his father's recent death, how bad it was to be away when something happened that really mattered, how he had gone tearing across the world to be at the funeral, only to get there in time to see the coffin being lowered, in an old grey churchyard. 'A long way to go across the world to see a box going into a hole in the earth,' he said. And then he'd come back a day or so later, there being little for him to do and everything to come back to, especially with his child due in a few weeks. Harriet started, remembering the child which had made her leave him so hastily on their first meeting. It must now be some months old, she reflected. And however his personal life was re-ordering itself, he had still come to find her again. She suspected now, that the proposed political column would never eventuate. Possibly he didn't believe it either.

They talked about books. She found him better-read than she had expected; he had read some of the women writers who she much admired. This surprised her greatly, though on reflection, it was not as unlikely as it seemed, for if he was good at his job he would have done some sort of market research into women's tastes and ideas. He had read Drabble, Lessing, Mortimer, all people she liked.

'The trouble is, they do write about such miserable marriages,' he said.

'Why not?' she said. 'Don't most people have them?'

'I don't know,' he said, in what seemed like genuine astonishment. 'Do they?'

'Most of the people I know do.'

'Do you?' he asked.

'I said most people,' she said uneasily.

'I've never thought about it,' he said. She didn't know whether to believe him or not, yet he seemed so direct and straightforward, that she almost did.

A drunk at another table came over and interrupted their conversation. It was someone she knew slightly, who wanted to criticise her performance on a recent programme. Failing to penetrate her well-rehearsed defences, he asked if he could sit with them, preparing to insinuate himself into the conversation and looking for his companion, an equally drunk businessman, to applaud his effrontery.

Michael asked him to leave. The man's eyes flicked from one to the other. Harriet sat very still, holding him steady on a faltering eye. He smirked, and got to his feet again. 'So good to see you again, Harriet,' he said, stumbling a little as he returned to the other table.

'Bastard,' said Michael under his breath.

'He's harmless,' said Harriet.

'He was being insulting. Couldn't you see that?'

'Of course I could, but does it matter?'

Beside her, she could feel an enormous suppressed energy, some vibrant quality which matched her own. She suddenly remembered that long ago up the Hokianga, she had divined water. Her father had told her that a man would come to decide where a new well should go. When she had asked how the man would do this, he had explained, cutting a piece of green branch with a fork in it, and shown her how to hold it by each prong while walking over the ground. When the man held it, he had told her, the stick would point down when he came to the place where water would be found. She had done as he had said, walking backwards and forwards over the ground, a small child intent on the thought of water beneath the earth. And then in her hands, the stick had started to turn. At first she had been frightened, about to drop it, then in extraordinary fascination she had tried to fight it, to wrestle the living thing in her hands, but it would not be stopped.

Now, sitting beside Michael, she felt the same strange pulling. It was almost as if energy was being transferred from one to the other. The fibres seemed to be drawing, and like the green stick, she was fighting it, and feeling joy and satisfaction that it could not be stopped.

The voice on the intercom announced the departure of his flight for Auckland.

'I have time to walk you back to your car,' he said.

'Oh no, you'll miss your plane.'

'I don't think so. If I was on a losing streak, there would have been a lot of things I would have missed these past months, wouldn't there?'

It was one of the last flights of the day out of Wellington, and the travellers bound for Auckland were already emptying out of the terminal in the opposite direction, as they walked through the echoing high-domed building. Harriet and Michael made little sounds to each other, about seeing each other early the following year when he would be down again in Wellington — loving small exchanges, as if they were indeed already lovers. In the last few minutes between them they parted as lovers might do — careless, close, holding each other till the last possible moment. When he left her she sat in the car waiting to see him out of sight, but at the entrance to the building he turned and stood stock still, looking at her in the car. She waved, panicking suddenly, because it seemed essential then that he catch the plane, that he mustn't stay. Enough had already passed between them. Then she was longing for him to stay a second longer, so that she could see him in his fine beauty.

She drove home exulted, light-headed, and so happy that she was sure it must show.

It seemed that it did, and this condition lasted all through the summer. Her friends noticed that she was beautiful and seemed younger. She began to lose weight. The sun was intermittent, yet she stayed in it enough to get brown and berry-like, her skin ripening each day until she was like the girl who had roamed summer fields at Ohaka long ago.

In the long holiday the family travelled north for the annual visit to the Wallaces in their Whangarei flat. Mary was nearly blind now, worn and cowed with years of Gerald's fretting, but she touched Harriet's face, and held it saying 'You're happy?'

Harriet had told her that she was indeed happy. As she and Mary had grown older, things which had been difficult before had relaxed between them. They never spoke much in words, but over the years the two women had come to understand each other. Mary knew better than to ask her daughter what made her happy; Harriet knew Mary was aware that her happiness extended to some area beyond her success, her public life, or Max and the children. She guessed that it gave Mary some quiet satisfaction, although it was difficult to analyse why, for the more disastrous areas of Harriet's life had caused Mary such distress in the past that it seemed hardly likely that she might be pleased by any new gambles. Possibly, Harriet thought, it was because she had come to understand happiness as an end in itself. She, Harriet, had done so too.

Without expectation, without hope, but in a certain quiet knowledge that he would come to her, Harriet was living out the summer, until Michael returned.

The family moved on up north beyond Whangarei to stay at a long curving yellow beach, where the sun beat down each day with a steady white heat. They ate sand with their mussel fritters and blackberry pies, made from fat and unbelievably swollen berries collected by dusty paths, lived in bathing suits and swam daily, sometimes hourly, in a sea as original in its clarity as a beginning. The children roamed for miles, returning exhausted and golden to be with Max and Harriet when they were tired. None of them was really a child any more, except Emma, who seemed more childlike than childish; yet during that holiday they were her children again. Genevieve spent time away from the others, talking to boys who ranged themselves around as near to her as they could, but none of it seemed to matter. She was still Harriet's baby, her first — well, not quite her first, but that too was another matter that had no place in this summer — and she saw her with love and pride, a young splendid creature whom she and Max had made together. In the rare times when they would be sure that they were alone, they made love, she through a dreamy haze, his face a blur as if the sun had come between them.

When they went home the family said that it was the best holiday they had ever had, and implicit in their pleasure was gratitude that Harriet had created an ambience of harmony around them.

Michael rang her early in February to say that he would be down at the end of the month. It was the first time she had heard from him for over two months, but it didn't seem as if she had been waiting, nor did she feel that she had time to wait until he came to her. There was work to be done, there was more sun, and there was more of the certain joy of knowing that he would come. She didn't want to relinquish any of it through hurry or impatience.

On the day he rang through, her status among her friends changed slightly. She went to a party that evening and a woman friend said to her, 'You must be in love. You can't look like that all the time without there being someone.'

And Harriet, a little drunk and longing to share her secret, had said, 'Yes. Yes, of course I'm in love.'

The next day Lynley and Joan rang and said in effect, 'Welcome to the club.' They were pleased that Harriet had strayed at last. Of course her rapport with men, particularly older men, was widely known, but women, like men, had never been able to place her in a context in which any of these relationships had the sort of validity they understood.

At first Harriet thought to try and explain that her love for Michael was still an affair only of the heart, but explanations seemed pointless. So she accepted their phone calls, but did not enlighten them any further than was necessary. His name was Michael and he lived in Auckland, she said. The women tapped away at her marriage. Had anything happened between herself and Max, had she always been unhappy and kept it hidden from them? She had no answers, only those inside her.

This seemed very odd to her, for over the years she had been seen with so many men, had cultivated her free-wheeling image and proven them all wrong time and again. To be the centre now of curious and respectful attention seemed very strange indeed.

Possibly this changed, charged atmosphere finally created tension within her. She began to await Michael's coming; the days took on the colours of reality once more, and she counted them one by one.

Leonie studied Harriet across the table. The lunchtime crowd had ebbed away, and the restaurant was quiet. She lit a cigarette, and fine blue smoke rose lazily above them.

'Well! she said to Harriet. 'And did he come to you?'

Harriet looked back to Leonie. One could say that there was no turning back, that she had committed herself. But it needn't be so. There was still time to withdraw, to make some polite noise to cover her tracks. Perhaps this was the point to which she had been leading Leonie, in order to help her, only she had gone a little too far.

But she knew that this was not true. Leonie was firmly a part of her life, even if the time she occupied had been brief.

When Harriet returned to Weyville, there was little outward evidence of change in the time she had been away.

Leonie's departure had been a blow when she first heard about it, but in a way she also saw it as a blessing. There would have been the difficulty of re-establishing the friendship if she had still lived there, or worse still, having to live with her hostility. As it was, Harriet was spared both these difficulties, and Leonie's absence made it easier to resume the role of Harriet Wallace. Many people had speculated about her and Denny's disappearance the same weekend, and she knew without being told that the old football crowd assumed that she had gone away to have a baby on the quiet, and that Denny had been suitably chastised. That their marriage had never been revealed soon became obvious too. Leonie had never told anyone, nor had Cousin Alice, or Mr Whitwell, and they were the only people who knew, so that with Leonie's going there was no need to pretend to anyone.

Mr Whitwell's disappearance was a different matter, and she bitterly regretted his absence. He had been sent to jail for incest with his sister. What had become of the quiet plain sister nobody knew, as Mr Whitwell was considered the villain of the piece. He had been suitably dealt with, as far as the residents of Weyville were concerned. His house stood shut up and neglected. It was said that he planned to come back when he got out of jail, but it was hard to imagine how a man could have such a cheek. Nobody really believed he would return. They were right, for he never did come back, and whenever Harriet thought of him, she hoped that he and his sister had found some peace to settle down together with their books.

He had been replaced at the library by a tight-lipped spinster called Amy Mullins, who, it was reported, ran a tidy ship. Certainly, some sages remarked, she had cleaned up the shelves of some of its less desirable literature. Miss Mullins took Harriet back on her staff somewhat grudgingly. Her record wasn't very good, as she had gone away without notice, (a recurring problem of Harriet's employers, if Miss Mullins only knew it) but one had to take into consideration her marks from library school. Having gone through herself, and having a profound respect for all opinions emanating from this august body, Miss Mullins could hardly overlook the very favourable view they held of Harriet's work. Heaven only knew, it was difficult to find a girl in Weyville who knew how to catalogue a book. Harriet would have to re-do the year she hadn't completed, but since Mrs Harrison had explained that Harriet had been called away by family trouble, there didn't seem to be any real objection. The really black mark against her was implicit. That ogre Mr Whitwell had written a very good report on her. Harriet knew that Miss Mullins would therefore keep a close eye on her for any signs of frivolity or immorality.

When Harriet had collected her first pay, she went out in the lunch hour trying to find a good linen skirt that would fit her, as her waistline still hadn't settled down to its former size, and she had few summer clothes suitable for the library. Armed with several parcels, and considerably lighter in pocket than she had intended, she was turning down the main street when a woman pushing a pram hailed her. She was a blonde, rather tubby person in her twenties, and it took Harriet a few minutes to register who she was. It was Julie Simmons, now married to Dick. She'd come back to town about the same time that Harriet had left after 'bumming around down south' and getting thoroughly fed up with the life. She and Dick had met the first week she was back; he had still been mourning Harriet's absence, according to Julie.

'He had a real shine for you', she said mischievously. 'Not that he ever thought you'd take him.'

They'd hit it off like wildfire, and been married more than a year. She glowed with a lovely warm self-confidence.

'You ought to come and see me and Dick sometime,' she said. Harriet thanked her, knowing that she probably wouldn't go. In a way she was sorry about that, because seeing someone like Julie who'd been through the mill, so happy, was a kind of revitalising energy source that Harriet now badly needed. But it was too close, too raw. It was hard to know how much Julie might know about her, or think she knew, but of all people in the town now, Dick was the one most likely to have gone fossicking into what had happened to her. That was a risk she wasn't prepared to face. She told Julie how happy she was for them both, and that was the truth. She said that when she was settled she'd give her a ring perhaps, which was rather less than the truth. The encounter had clarified one thing for her, though, and that was that she would never return to the old crowd. In a way it was like severing the last link.

Later that month, Wendy Dixon, with whom she'd been at school in Ohaka, wrote suggesting that they go to England that year. Again, Harriet had no way of knowing how much Wendy knew of the past two years, but she guessed people like the Colliers had talked a bit in Ohaka. And why not? They were part of a closely-knit community, and they would hardly be to blame if they did talk among themselves. Harriet wrote back, warmly thanking Wendy for her kindness in thinking of her again, and said that in a year's time she would certainly go, but at the moment she had no money and she hadn't completed her library training. Wendy replied almost immediately, saying that she really wished that Harriet could go with her but that she was very restless. Harriet wouldn't be surprised to know that she wasn't all that keen on teaching, so she felt she couldn't wait any longer now that she'd served out her bond. She hoped Harriet would eventually go, but she was off on the very next ship she could find.

Harriet thought of the ship she had seen leaving Auckland on

199

her first trip to Weyville, and how it had made her miss the bus. To be sure, she'd missed every bus that was going in the end, she thought grimly, still prone to fits of black despair. She was overwhelmed with longing to be on a ship going somewhere, anywhere. But instead, Weyville had to be faced; sometimes it seemed a daunting prospect.

One of the good things about it was how well she and Cousin Alice got on together now. Cousin Alice's own little wells of quiet unhappiness had grown deeper in Harriet's absence. Both her successful children had taken themselves overseas, both more or less permanently. Her daughter had come back to stay before departing for an indeterminate stay abroad, and her son had visited her several times before taking up a position as an engineer in the Middle East. The prospects of promotion were so good that it was unlikely that New Zealand would ever have much to offer him. Cousin Alice wrote to them zealously every Sunday, but although she heard from them both occasionally, it was obviously she who made the effort to keep in touch. It was to be several years before Harriet met either of Cousin Alice's children, and, Cousin Alice never met some of her grandchildren.

Harriet's return had filled an enormous gap in Cousin Alice's life, and they lived together like any two sensible adults.

The year passed quietly with Harriet studying hard and passing her exams without difficulty. At the end of the course she was required to go to Wellington for a six week block course before she could be finally awarded her Certificate. She looked forward to this with mounting anticipation. It was a step further than she had ever gone before, and the thought of a new place excited her more than anything she could remember.

She had had little social life in Weyville in the past year, apart from learning to play golf with Cousin Alice and sitting round making small talk with older women after the Saturday afternoon games. She had been out with one or two young men, remainders of the old boarding school dances, who were still single. She herself was almost the only single woman left from those times.

She found to her surprise around the middle of the year that she was legally single. A letter arrived from Denny's lawyer. She didn't know he had one until then, though she was aware that her parents had got one on her behalf and that he was trying to organise a legal separation. She gathered that she would be legally married for years to come. It didn't seem to matter much, but the lawyer had been very irritated by the difficulty of his dealings with Mr Rei, who had not seemed co-operative, or even interested. Harriet had pressed no claims for maintenance, which had apparently annoyed the lawyer too. He didn't seem to understand that so totally was she trying to exorcise the past, for Denny as well as herself, that to haggle over money had been the last thing she wanted.

Still, a large legal letter was waiting for her one day when she arrived home from work. Cousin Alice didn't ask her what was in it, as she didn't ask questions like that any more, but Harriet gave her the letter to read anyway. She handed it back in silence.

Denny wanted to remarry, and as he was aware that evidence for a divorce on the grounds of his adultery had been obtained, he was anxious to know whether it was going to be used or not. The tone of the letter suggested that he hoped it would be. As well as general distaste for proceeding with such a divorce, Harriet felt that perhaps she should protect Gloria from the ignominy that being named in court would bring. She knew that if she were to voice such an objection to anyone in the family, they would be horrified — Gloria was a scarlet woman. But Harriet wondered if she was any worse or any sillier than she had been at times. She had a feeling that Gloria might have started having an affair with Denny without even knowing about her at the outset. Denny certainly hadn't been in any mood to broadcast her existence when he went to work at that office. Of course Gloria must have known fairly soon, as Denny couldn't hide a wife forever, but perhaps by that time she had slipped too far down the precarious path towards loving Denny. After all, Harriet had loved him once; why should she not expect another person to feel as she had done. She thought her feelings towards Gloria must be odd or unnatural, but she

A BREED OF WOMEN

continued to think that she would protect her, until the letter from Denny arrived.

For a few nights after that she lay awake, hot-eyed, weeping from time to time, remembering the tiny boy and her loneliness and fear. For the first time she began to hate Gloria, with a bitterness that surprised and exhausted her. She even considered withholding the divorce to punish them.

A week or so later, worn out, she wrote to the lawyer who had been acting for her, saying that as far as she was concerned the divorce could proceed as quickly as possible. Shortly before Christmas she was advised that she was free. Free. The word had a mocking ring about it. There were things she would never be free of, but try telling a lawyer that.

When she was putting the rubbish out one evening, she was surprised to see that Cousin Alice had wrapped it up in *Truth,* a paper that her relative didn't usually deign to read. Harriet asked her lightly what had brought about her change in reading habits. Because of the way that Cousin Alice coloured up and stammered, Harriet immediately knew the answer — she was afraid that the divorce had been publicised. Harriet started to worry about it too, and got back copies of the paper, and watched the ones that came out each week, but before many weeks had passed it became obvious that there were bigger and more salacious divorces than theirs to report.

She was told, long after, that it was not Gloria whom Denny wanted to marry, but some girl from up north. Whether she was from Kaikohe or not Harriet never found out, nor did she try. With the divorce, her relationship with Denny was over.

These events made her long for a total change of scenery more than ever. There had been no trip to Ohaka this year, now that the Wallaces had left the farm. Instead, her parents came down and spent Christmas with Cousin Alice and Harriet, their first break away since they had gone to the farm when Harriet was thirteen. Gerald was grouchy and lame because of his back, which still hadn't healed; Mary was worrying about their new place and whether Gerald would have to be permanently on sickness benefits, or whether he would eventually be able to do a light job. It was clear to Harriet that Mary didn't relish the thought of being at home all day with Gerald, and she talked somewhat fearfully of getting a job herself, 'if anybody would have her'. Through it all Cousin Alice was an excellent hostess, and if her guests proved trying at times, she didn't show it. At least, as she remarked quite frankly to Harriet afterwards, it was better than sitting round staring at the wall on Christmas Day.

Still, Harriet had badly missed the break that Ohaka had provided before. Wellington began to seem like the Promised Land. She hoped it wouldn't be as hot as Weyville, which was locked in a blistering heat wave day after day, the sun reflected off iron roofs, the tar bleeding in the streets, the lake almost drying up.

When she finally arrived in Wellington to complete her library course, she was delighted to find it refreshing, with pleasant sea breezes cooling even the hottest days to a bearable level. She boarded at an unobtrusive but adequate guest house on Oriental Bay Parade, and her bedroom faced the ocean. In the morning she woke to the bluest, crispest sea she could imagine; in the evenings she walked beside it and sometimes waded in it. The city enchanted her, with its houses seeming to cling to the hills in a primitive effort to survive. It wasn't lush like Auckland, or as sprawling or crowded. There was a vigour in the air, a purpose to the place. Others on the course asked her whether the public service atmosphere of the city irritated her, and she could only look at them. To her, it was the loveliest place she had ever seen.

One Sunday afternoon she decided to climb the hill behind the bay, and an hour or so later she found herself at the top of Mount Victoria. The impact was devastating — the sea seemed to stream away from the land as far as she could see. In one direction she could see far away across Cook Strait, and she imagined she could glimpse the distant Kaikouras of the South Island. The opposite way, she could see up into the industrial Hutt Valley area, snaking away into the hills. The Orongarongo Range across the harbour appeared so close she felt as if she could lean over and touch it. It is as if all the world is opened up, she thought, and realised at the same time that it was the first time she had ever been truly alone in all her life, the first time she had ever been accountable to no-one else in the world but herself. This was the beginning of the world.

There were films to go to, and a play at the Opera House. The crowd at library school were pleasant enough company too, and on the last weekend she was invited to a party with them all. There she met Max Taylor, a shy and pleasant young man who was the brother of one of the girls on the course. He was pleasant to look at, though Harriet thought his crinkly sandy hair and fair skin that burned too easily in the sun would not have made him stand out in a crowd. She enjoyed his company and they sat on the floor in a corner while the others played loud music. She and Max were among the oldest there, and acknowledged it in quiet conversation apart from everyone else in the room.

Afterwards he walked her home along the sea front. The tide was full in and slapping gently on the seawall as they balanced their way along the top of it, laughing and mildly drunk. She took him up to her room, and they made love, the first time she had been with a man since Denny. Their lovemaking was timid to be sure, and tentative at best, but she was glad to have him against her, nestling into the small of her back afterwards, his sex still fluttering like a small trapped bird against her buttocks, his hands cupped around her breasts.

She saw him once again before she left Wellington. Over lunch, he asked what work was like up Weyville way. He was a draughtsman with a government department, and the Forestry Service were always calling for people in that area; maybe he could get a transfer. Anxious not to commit herself too far with him, she gently discouraged him. He asked her why, and she told him that she'd been married and didn't want to get involved. He said he understood, thanked her for her honesty and the time they had spent together, and kissed her cheek when they finally parted on Lambton Quay.

The morning she left there was a wild storm blowing. She had seen some less awesome indications of the sort of weather Wellington could turn on, but this was what the locals termed 'a

southerly buster'. As the northbound train pulled out of
Wellington she felt she could love the place in its fury. A stormy
petrel among the doves, she thought. And then, I'll come back
here, yes I will.

Weyville was a challenge now. She joined its small theatre
group, got Miss Mullins to agree to special projects for children in
the library, arranged that a writer visiting the country from abroad
should make a special trip down from Auckland to give a lecture.
A mad project, Miss Mullins said, but Harriet approached the
English departments at the local high schools, and to everyone's
amazement, four hundred people filled a school assembly hall to
hear him. The local paper said it was, 'a red-letter day for Weyville
when its young people started to play such a leading and inspiring
role in community affairs.'

Her bank balance was growing, and the idea of going abroad
was beginning to take definite shape. The thought of going on her
own was daunting, but she told herself that she was an adult
woman now who was capable of handling whatever she tackled.

In the middle of the year, Miss Mullins became ill, and,
querulous and sad, she had to go on extended leave. Harriet was
appointed acting librarian in her absence. She had become a force
to be reckoned with in Weyville, her salary was stepped up, and her
bank balance continued to grow.

Came the end of winter, and with it Max Taylor. He walked into
the library one day, saying that he'd come to look the town over. It
was obvious he liked what he saw, even if he went no further than
the library to inspect the view.

Harriet supposed she loved him. He certainly loved her and they
talked idly about travel over the next few weeks. The possibility
that they could travel together was raised. Certainly it would solve
the difficulties that Harriet had envisaged about travelling alone.

She married Max in the Weyville Registry Office a few months
later. Some of the elderly regulars at the library thought it was a
funny thing, her getting married in a registry office, a lovely girl
like her, but they brought her wedding presents of crochet work
and hand-stitched linen wrapped up in tissue paper and wished her

all the luck in the world. This time her parents and Max's were there, as well as his sister from library school, Cousin Alice and a couple of her friends with whom Harriet had played golf. Cousin Alice gave the wedding breakfast back at the house afterwards.

A sort of churching, thought Harriet. Take, eat, this is the making of a respectable woman.

Genevieve was born towards the end of 1963, the same year that Kennedy was shot. There were no complications and the baby was perfect in every way. Harriet could only look at her and Max with gratitude that other needs, if they existed, had simply melted away.

10

Genevieve was four when Harriet began to feel restless. The whole nature of Weyville was changing. In place of the old shops faced with plate glass, two-and three-storeyed concrete buildings had started to create new facades of their own. Suburbs were springing up at random round the outskirts of Weyville and the right and the wrong sides of the tracks had been defined more positively than before.

When Max and Harriet built their modest but attractive little ranch-style house, designed by Max, Cousin Alice indicated the areas were she thought the best buys could be found, a section in an area which would hold its value. They never had cause to doubt her advice for as long as they remained in Weyville. When the subdivision had first been opened in 1960, the city fathers had dubbed it Camelot. It was where the brightest and nicest people of Weyville made their homes. Max and Harriet qualified for a five per cent loan, Max let the building of the house on a labour-only contract and was able to save enough money for ranch sliders and a patio immediately. They planted silver birches and silver dollar gum trees round the section in the very first year, and before long they were flourishing and seemed to be taking over. The ice-pink glimmer of their sesanqua camellias shone from corners of the garden, and they drank wine as well as beer with their barbecues when the neighbours dropped over on Saturday nights.

There never seemed to be a quiet moment. From the beginning of her residence in suburbia, Harriet was keenly sought for committees. Genevieve was a Plunket baby, and it followed that Harriet would be invited to go on the Plunket Committee. Peter followed a year later, so she was asked to become president. During her year as president, the first rift developed between her and the women in her community. The occasion was the annual money-raising effort, which was traditionally a jumble sale held in a local Maori pa on Family Benefit Day. The theory was that Maoris never had any money except when the welfare handed it out, and if you could catch them before they went to the pub and blew it all, they would spend it on cast-offs for their children.

Harriet objected and said she felt that this was an insult to the Maoris. A committee member raised the point, quite reasonably, that the jumble sales had always been a success in the past and that they had raised a great deal of money. This was a fact, and Harriet could look at the records and see for herself. In that case, said Harriet, they should either hold the jumble sale in their own community where the locals could have equal access to the bargains, or they should go to the pa on a non-Family Benefit Day. As long as she was president of the local committee, there would not be a jumble sale on Family Benefit Day. The committee was of course entitled to take a vote on the matter, and she assured them that she would not interfere with the outcome. When asked to vote for or against, those in favour raised their hands, tentatively at first, but seeing that they had friends, one by one the whole committee voted in favour, with Harriet's being the only dissenting vote.

Harriet did not tell Max about this, knowing that she was supposed to have put her past behind her. For all she knew, he might have agreed with her — after all, he appeared to agree with most things that she did or said, so why not this? It was just that she knew that he could only relate it to her past, something so dead and buried between them that she could not resurrect it.

Harriet only partly attributed her attitude to Denny, supposing in a confused kind of way, that he had made her think about issues that she might otherwise have ignored. But if she'd been a different sort of person, she might never have noticed. Yet the thought of

208

Denny and his family being expected to hunt through other people's castoff clothes haunted her.

At any rate, she kept away from the jumble sale, which was as usual, an outstanding success. One woman, who thought Harriet was totally in the wrong but who nevertheless liked her style, told her that she had got into just about as much hot water as Harriet herself. It seemed that she had given away her husband's rugby blazer, which had been collecting mildew in the wardrobe. Unfortunately, it was covered with sew-on badges of past triumphs. Her husband hadn't known about it going to the jumble sale until he was driving through the Maori area, and suddenly looming on his horizon was a big fat Maori with his blazer on; it was too short in the arms and he could only do up one button across his great beer-filled belly. His wife was in big trouble, and she said she wished that she'd gone along with Harriet and boycotted the jumble sale altogether. If she was looking for sympathy from Harriet she didn't get it, so she retreated to her other friends and took comfort in the hilarity her story generated. It appeared that Harriet didn't have a sense of humour.

She resigned as president, but Genevieve was due to go to kindergarten and she was asked to go on that committee.

So it went on. Harriet supposed she was happy enough in the suburbs. She was known to be a woman with a mind of her own, and she took a secret pride in that. There was also a slight element of mystery surrounding her. One or two people appeared from the old football club, and vague rumours circulated about her from time to time when the coffee cups were rattling. She had a past, it was said, though substantiating it proved difficult; the gossip simply died a natural death, without anything positive to feed on. Harriet avoided the women who were married to members of the old crowd, cultivating a formidable aloofness.

Sometimes when the children had been tucked up for the night, she would see Max looking at her reflectively. She would wonder what he was thinking and then decide against asking him. She had nothing to hide from him, he knew her, she had never lied to him. He seemed to her a plain man in his needs, and she tried to provide

209

for them. One night, however, he asked her, 'Harriet, are you happy here?'

She had been folding nappies; Peter, her second child, acted as if he was going to wear them for the rest of her life. Surprised, she put down the pile she had been about to take to the airing cupboard.

'I don't know, I haven't really thought about it. Do I seem unhappy?'

'No,' said Max, thinking as he went along. 'But I remember you in Wellington, when I first met you. You've changed since then.'

'Of course I've changed, silly,' said Harriet, laughing at him. 'I didn't have you and the children then.'

'But you were going to do so many things with your life then. You were very excited. And you haven't done any of them.'

'I opted for something different.'

'Not quite,' said Max. 'Most of it's just happened. I think you thought I'd share some of the things you wanted to do.'

'And did you mean to?' Harriet sat watching him. Something was happening between them, but she didn't know what it was.

He shook his head. 'I don't think so. I thought all of this would just follow the way it has, and that it'd be what you wanted anyway.'

'Well then, are you trying to tell me it's not what I want? What are you trying to talk me into, Max?'

'I don't know.'

The moment had passed and they were both backing away from it. However, Harriet never forgot what Max had said. He deceived me, and he knows it, she thought. He was trying to be honest now, but perhaps it was a little late for honesty. He was a perpetrator of some great lie, like all the other men who lived in the suburbs of Weyville. True, he was vaguely aware of it without recognising exactly what he had done — but then, neither did Harriet. She told herself that she was happy; she was, she knew it. Then she began to have flashes of anger against Max, who had tried to provoke her into thinking she was behaving badly because she didn't fit exactly into the mould that all the other women did.

This led her to believe that Max observed her more closely than

she realised. Had he wanted a totally conventional woman? She
supposed that he must have done. Maybe he hadn't known what he
wanted at that time any more than she had. She decided to ask
him.

'Do I seem different to other women round here?' she said.

'Yes and no,' he replied defensively.

'What do you mean, yes and no? What sort of an answer is that?
Do I embarrass you? Aren't you comfortable with me? Don't I
preserve enough fruit? Aren't the children clean enough?'

'Of course they are, sweetheart. You know they are.'

'The children are clean enough, we've established that, but what
about the other things? You haven't answered any of them.'

'Well, that was the last thing you asked me. Logically it was the
first one to answer.'

'Logic,' she said bitterly, 'You're fencing. You started all this.'

'I did?'

'Asking me if I was happy. You know you did.'

'What in God's name is wrong with asking your wife if she's
happy? If you love her, of course you want to know that she's
happy.'

'Some men don't.'

'All right then, you want me to be like some men. I'll try harder.'

'Max, you're twisting what I say.'

'Why don't we just leave it?'

So she did. She felt as if she was walking through cobwebs. It
must be her fault, turning that brief moment of his self-revelation
and doubts into a crusade, worrying over it, blowing it out of
proportion. She must try harder, do better, not rouse such strong
feelings in people. Because she did. She'd split the kindergarten
committee down the middle on what, looking back had been a
fairly minor issue. There had been no need for it and she could
have avoided taking it so far, but she hadn't.

It was the same when they went out to dinner. Harriet was lively
and more widely read than many of the people in Weyville, so they
came to be included in the dinner parties given by the town's
intellectual set, or those who saw themselves as such. They were

schoolteachers, a few scientists who were gathering round the milling complex, lawyers and doctors. But whereas the rest of the company were content to follow well-laid conversational tracks, Harriet was unpredictable. Often she would seize like a terrier on any issue that interested her shaking it and everyone present, and refusing to give up till an opponent was routed.

One night she took issue with a middle-aged lawyer who had been defending a rape case.

'Of course, my dears,' he said, looking round conspiratorially at them all, in the candlelight, 'You know she asked for it. Women nearly always do.'

'That's an absurd generalisation,' said Harriet sharply.

There was a quickness in the air around the table. Max moved uneasily, for the lawyer was considered the best in town, and as sharp as a flick knife. If Harriet was about to take him on on his own ground, she was obviously due for her comeuppance. The women sat back to enjoy the sight of blood, though only half believing that Harriet would pursue such dangerous quarry. The lawyer, Nick Thomas, waited; it was clear he expected the battle to be brief.

'Come, come my dear girl, a woman like this one sets up her charms to attract men. If she succeeds, then she can hardly complain, can she?'

'Presumably most women set out to charm men at some stage of their lives. Haven't we all? said Harriet, looking round the women. 'Or did all the men here simply come and take you off a shelf marked available for marriage?'

The women smiled tentatively. 'I suppose we must have,' one of them said.

'The point is, we had the right to choose who we slept with, didn't we?' She knew she had reached the point where Max would like her to stop.

'Of course you did,' said Nick, 'But then you must realise that this — lady, if you like to call her that, had chosen to sleep with many men.'

'I can't see what difference that makes,' said Harriet.

'It makes a great deal of difference in the eyes of the law,' said Nick.

'Then the law is an even greater ass than some people already suppose,' said Harriet. 'She didn't choose to sleep with this particular man, did she?'

'We don't know that. We don't know whether in fact she's simply paying him back for a tiff they had afterwards.'

'But you said she was covered in bruises.'

'Possibly self-inflicted.'

'Do you honestly believe that?'

Nick shrugged. 'My client denies it, and although he was foolish to become involved, I consider him of better character than the witness.'

'Because he's a man. Look, Nick, what d'you think about uninvited guests in your home? Would you let them stay?'

'Of course not. I'd throw them out.'

'Because you've got the right in law to choose who enters your home?'

'Obviously.'

'But you do, do you not, invite many people into your home?'

Nick, still not taking her seriously, walked into the trap before he was aware she had made one. He smiled assent.

'Then don't you think that whether a woman has one man or many enter her body, the choice is even more important than who should enter your house? Or do you place respect for possessions ahead of respect for a woman's body?'

Nick flushed angrily. The anticipatory fidgeting had stopped and there was a fixed stillness in the room.

'I see. I see,' he said sighing heavily. 'Well, as we've established a philosophical principle, do I have the permission of counsel for the prosecution to make one or two practical points?'

'Please do,' said Harriet.

'Very well then. This — lady, open, one might say to many men, claimed that she was attacked in her home, on the other side of Weyville. She screamed, she struggled, she fought and she bit, but in the end despite all her protests, she was overpowered and ...' his

213

voice sank, 'ravished. What sort of a town is Weyville, I ask you, where a young woman could scream her lungs out and not be heard and helped by her neighbours? If any one of you people here were to hear a woman screaming in her house, would you not immediately rush to her assistance?'

They reflected. Elaine Mawson said tentatively that perhaps some of them might think twice about interfering in a domestic dispute. After all, people did get mad at each other on occasions.

Nick fixed her with a stern eye. 'Would you be prepared to take that chance if you heard another woman in distress? Would you not at least approach the house and try to determine the nature of the crisis? Especially if that woman was shouting for help? As this person claimed she was doing?'

Everyone agreed that they certainly would but Harriet did not answer. 'Don't you agree, Harriet?' asked Nick, leaning eagerly over the table.

'No,' she said. 'You're simply trying to turn aside an ethical dilemma you can't answer with courtroom tricks that make you appear to be reasonable and make people afraid of challenging you in case they make fools of themselves.'

'Dear Harriet, forgive my saying so, but I'm starting to find this tedious.'

'Then let's simply finish the topic by proving whether or not it's possible to cry for help and go unheard in Weyville. Why don't we all, on the count of five, scream help as loudly as we can, and see how quickly help arrives? As there are eight of us here, then it should test the validity of your theory eight times more effectively.'

The hostess said nervously, 'But then we might have the police around.'

Max said, 'Shouldn't we be ringing and checking the babysitter, Harriet?'

She looked around at them, all flushed, all more than a little embarrassed, unable to cope. She was enjoying herself very much at that moment. Suddenly Elaine Mawson, giggling palely, said, 'It can't hurt can it? After all, Nick could say he was testing a theory. They wouldn't arrest us, would they?'

Nick, piqued, but unwilling to prolong the scene further, suggested tersely that he give the count. On five, Camelot resounded with a crescendo of shrieks. For fully two or three minutes, they continued to shout and scream, then, one by one they fell silent, astonished. The silence continued, somebody laughed nervously. 'Nobody's coming,' they started to say to each other. And it was true. Nobody did come.

Harriet and Max left early. In the car Max was quiet and cold. As they parked the car in the garage he said, 'If you can't control your drinking, I'd prefer we stayed home at the weekends.'

'I wasn't drunk,' said Harriet calmly. 'I simply wanted to wipe the smug look off Nick Thomas's face.'

'And mine too?' he asked bitterly.

'Did you think I did that to make a fool of you?' Harriet said, in real surprise.

'You know I wanted you to stop. Surely that was enough?'

Harriet started to cry softly, her face streaming with tears in the dark. 'Max, Max,' she said, 'Hold me, I'm sorry, I'm so sorry. Please forgive me.'

After he'd paid the babysitter, he led her to bed and made her hot cocoa. When he joined her, he held her against him for a long time, stroking her hair. She drifted off to sleep, and woke towards morning, aware that he was still lying awake, holding her in the same position as when she had gone to sleep. Why, she wondered to herself. Where am I taking us? Or is it me, it must be me, because I cried and said I was sorry. I always cry though, that's my weakness, once I cry I'm lost. Thank you, father, You gave me that. That, and always saying I'm sorry. Thank you for nothing.

'You must be uncomfortable lying like that,' she said to Max.

'I didn't want to disturb you,' said Max, removing his arm with relief.

'What are you thinking?'

'Oh ... this and that. Would you like us to have another baby?'

'Would you?'

'It could be a nice idea,' he said.

'Of course,' she said gratefully. It seemed to make perfect sense.

The next time Harriet visited her, Cousin Alice looked at her shrewdly. 'You're becoming quite a celebrity my dear.'

'What have I done this time? No don't tell me, I don't want to be reminded.'

Cousin Alice shook her head. 'I wish I'd been you,' she said.

Harriet looked at her in astonishment. 'You don't mean that.'

'I don't know,' said Cousin Alice lightly, 'I must say you seem to make life extraordinarily difficult for yourself ... I don't know whether I'd have had the constitution for that. But at least you're living.'

'Hmm, nappies and squashed crayons, that's about all there is to it.'

'They'll grow up, and then, a person like you, there'll be the world at your feet, you're still so young. You've got spirit, girl. I could see it at the beginning. Why do you think I put up with you?'

'You were hard on me at times.'

'Hard or wrong? Eh? No, you don't want to answer me that any more than I want to myself. But you learnt from it, didn't you? Some people never learn from any experiences, good or bad. You have.'

'You credit me with too much,' said Harriet. 'Anyway, Max wants us to have another baby, so it looks as if I'm not going to be quite as young as you think when they're grown up.'

'Do you want it?' asked Cousin Alice.

'Why not?'

'Don't have it,' said Cousin Alice. 'You've got enough. You're a good mother now, you'll end up hating the lot of them.'

'Probably too late,' said Harriet. 'I threw my pills away last week.' She said more or less the same thing to Nick Thomas when he rang her a few days later and suggested they have an affair.

'It's unethical,' she said, laughing it off.

'Not at all,' he replied. 'Neither of you is my client.'

'Then you're touting for business. You want to handle my divorce.'

'I want to handle you, my dear,' he said.

She burst out laughing. 'Oh Nick, you're so subtle,' she said.

'Listen to me,' he said fiercely into the telephone, 'I haven't stopped thinking about you, damn you, since you made an idiot of me. I'll tame you — you'll like that!'

Thinking about his grey-shot hair, the soft velour of his folded face and his immaculate energetic hands, she thought that, yes, she just might too.

'No good,' she said, 'I'm off the pill. Max thinks a baby might keep me quiet in public places.'

'Damn Max, you're not going to have a baby.'

'Give me a chance, the idea's quite new.'

'You're not pregnant. Get back on that pill, and we'll wait till you're safe again.'

She laughed again and hung up. Odd how she'd felt towards the man. She really disliked him. When he won the case they had been discussing, her dislike deepened, though she supposed she was unreasonable to the point of irrationality over the whole matter. She felt for the woman whose character he had so soundly assassinated in court. It emerged finally that she was Nance, now Noddy's ex-wife, from the days of the milk bar. Old Nance, she wouldn't have stood a chance Harriet thought. Come to think of it, she wouldn't have had the brain to invent a story like that in the first place. Poor bitch, poor cow.

Nick was right, as it turned out. She wasn't pregnant then; it took a couple of months of trying. Really, having a child seemed the safest and most sensible course of action.

She was drinking wine one Saturday afternoon with Don Everett, who had called to borrow their lawn mower. Later, she couldn't remember where Max had been, though she thought he might have been helping a friend to build a fence. Things like that appealed to Max on a Saturday afternoon, and she thought that he must have taken Genevieve with him, because the house was very quiet. Peter she could account for; he would be sleeping, for he only needed to be shown his bed to fall asleep on it. An excellent being, young Peter. She could forgive him a few scatalogical deviations. From time to time he would defecate in a corner of the house, and stand calmly unmoved while she cleaned it up. He had learnt early that cleaning up shit was women's work. It seemed a small price to pay for peace.

Don and Miriam were older than the Taylors, but Miriam, remembering Harriet from her library days, had seen her as a welcome addition to the Camelot circle. It was to Miriam that Harriet turned when things became rough; Miriam had once even lent her money when the grocery account had skyrocketed and Harriet had been afraid to tell Max. She didn't know why she had been afraid to tell Max, who rarely criticised anything she did, but in recent years she had had a strange feeling that he was watching her and waiting for something to break inside her. When she behaved as she had done with Nick Thomas at the dinner party, Harriet felt, rightly or wrongly, that Max saw this as a manifestation of what he most feared in her; for her part, hiding extravagance or having a baby were the price she paid for peace.

Miriam was a willing listener, sometimes acid in her reactions, behaving as Harriet imagined a strong-minded middle-aged schoolmarm would. The couple had two teenage boys, who seemed happy, affable children. Miriam was a schoolteacher, and was teaching one of them, who seemed not to have any resentment towards her on this account. If anything, the Everetts had a better relationship than most teenagers and their parents. It was a pleasant well-run home, and Miriam, brisk and efficient, appeared to accomplish miracles of housework in the shortest possible time, as well as doing her job. Harriet was impressed and envious, for Miriam could do effortlessly what it took her all day to do, and keep her hair set and her clothes well-pressed at the same time. She didn't yearn to be like Miriam, sensing, despite their friendship, some gaping chasm in their personalities, but she did wish she could do certain things as well as she did. There was no doubt that Miriam was the dominant partner in the marriage; one hardly noticed Don when she was around.

To be sure, he turned a barbecue as slickly as anyone in the suburb, he tramped with the boys and organised holidays for them all, from which they would return brown and ebullient each year.

Holidays were a luxury for the Taylors, despite their pleasant house and a degree of style. It took them a long time to pay off their house and, like many other people, they had to endure the long summers by the small, brackish lake of Weyville. There was, of course, the occasional pilgrimage to the Wallaces, but in those years, when the children were little, the Wallaces more often came to stay with Max and Harriet.

So Don had his uses, as Miriam would say, and when Miriam was caught up in conversation with other people, he proved to be good company, too. He was an industrial scientist at the mill, though it was hard to fit him into any context of mill life. Yet he loved it. It was the wood, he'd told Harriet once, he loved wood, and had learned to carve it into beautiful shapes. Once he showed her some of the carvings he had done. They were beautiful, curving with a silky sheen where he had tried to capture light, erupting with rugged force in those pieces where he had set the elements against matter.

Harriet had once asked him for one, and he had asked her what she would do with it. 'Put it on a shelf, I'll find a place,' she had said. 'Somewhere where I can look at it regularly, every day.'

'We'll see,' he'd said, and it had then occurred to her that none was on display in the Everett household. He never gave her one.

But the times that they talked to each other were rare. Details of that Saturday afternoon were hard to remember, because one didn't recall details with Don. However, it seemed important to remember the afternoon because she saw it as a turning point.

They talked about poetry. She told him that the men who talked to her about poetry were always banished from her life. It was just a coincidence that they were men, and there'd only been two of them anyway, but still they had been sent on their way, so he'd better be careful. Again she didn't recall how the conversation had started exactly, but she thought that she had made some chance remark and he'd replied with a quotation that she had recognised. He'd been excited by that and said he had known all along that she was a kindred spirit. The thought that Don should be warned off was a bit ludicrous, she mused later, but suddenly she had felt it was necessary, she did not know why.

He said she should write poetry. It would be good for her. 'Why should I do something that would do me good?' she asked him.

'I don't know,' he said, shrugging and smiling. 'Try it. New life.' He indicated her stomach. 'It might be the time to try.'

Just then the phone rang; Miriam wanted to know where Don was. 'Drinking wine and talking about poetry,' said Harriet gaily. 'I'll send him home with the lawn mower.'

She wrote her first poem that night in secret. Over the next months poems came to her, emerging unbidden when her hands were full, when the children needed her, when Max was expecting a meal. Some poems she caught, others seemed to be lost forever. She fretted and raged with herself and with whatever had stood between her and the poem. Often though, when she was sitting down, weary as the birth drew closer, the lost poem would come back, and, grateful, she would commit it to paper.

She told no one about this, and though she sometimes wished that Don would appear again so that she could talk to him, she didn't pursue him. When the poems were done, she put them away at the bottom of the mending cupboard, one place that Max probably wouldn't find them. She supposed that eventually she would show them to him, but she thought they weren't particularly good; did it really matter whether he saw them or not?

For the time being, they were a part of her, like this baby, kicking fretfully away in her womb. She'd never known a child carry on the way this one did. She was sure it knew when she was desperate to write a poem down, and was frustrated. She could have sworn it cowered and put its hands over its head to keep out the noise when she shouted at the other children, but when she was quite exhausted she knew that it was crouching down, trying to keep very still and quiet so she could get some rest. She more than half resented its presence, but when it did things like that for her, she felt inordinately tender, and would place her hand, on her stomach, and say, 'There, there little one, it's all right now.'

However the poems, like the baby, were not ready for independent life. Unlike the baby, they could be forgotten if they became unmanageable, and so she put them away.

Emma's birth was the only difficult one she experienced with any of the three children. Struggling and exhausted, she kept remembering the first baby she had had.

'It's going to die,' she shrieked at the doctor.

'Don't be so silly,' said the doctor. 'Really, a grown woman like you.'

The scenario hadn't changed much. She had been praised for being a good girl with Genevieve and Peter, but then they hadn't hurt. Being good meant not hurting, not causing trouble.

'Fuck you, I tell you it's going to die,' she shouted.

'Language' said a nurse reprovingly.

Emma emerged to a torrent of abuse, reproaches and weeping. No wonder she was such a shy nervous little girl, Harriet thought later. At least she had the stamina to stay alive, she refused to die, though her life hung in the balance for two days. Harriet knew she had no right to have a favourite child, but Emma had demanded a larger space in the scheme of things than the others.

While she was still in hospital, Max broke his leg, a ridiculous classic accident in the home, standing on one of the children's toys, with wheels on it. One foot had shot out in front of him, the other had buckled underneath. When Harriet heard, she felt a certain smugness that she had been tucked up safely in her hospital bed when it happened. She knew she would have been blamed if she'd been around.

Don broke the news to her, calling in to see her on the way to work. She was in the mood for dire news, with Emma still a fragile little bundle when she fed her. Don shambled in, looking awkward, as if suddenly wondering what on earth had prompted him into such an unlikely errand of mercy.

She sat up, feeling starry-eyed and alarmed.

'Hey,' he said, 'Don't look like that, it's only a broken leg. Max.' He was trying to give her as much reassuring information in one breath as possible.

She fell back on the harsh hospital linen pillows. 'You're sure it's nothing worse than that?'

221

'I promise. I called into casualty on the way up here and they said it wasn't a very bad break. They were just putting him in plaster.'

'I'll have to get out of here,' she said looking frantically round the ward.

'No, you don't. Come on, relax, old girl, you're as jittery as they make them.'

Harriet started to snuffle. 'Oh, bloody hell. Get me a tissue, will you Don? Somebody should have told you I'm a weepy bird. Don't worry, look the other way if you want to, it's just the baby being such a sickly little thing. They tell me she's going to be all right, though.'

The nurse marched over, ready to take charge. 'Come on, Mrs Taylor, your friend here said it was nothing serious.'

'Would you pull the curtains, please?' said Harriet. 'Go on,' she ordered as the nurse hesitated. 'We're not getting up to anything, you can just imagine how much fun we'd have with the condition I'm in.'

'You are a one,' said the nurse, whisking the curtains round the bed with a steely clatter.

'You are a one,' mimicked Harriet, half under her breath.

Don looked anxiously around at the enclosure they were sitting in. 'You're cruel to her,' he said, watching her malicious look.

'Nurses ought to have babies as compulsory military training for their jobs. They've got no heart.'

'And you're all heart,' he said, attempting cynicism. He looked at her wan face, and relented. 'What is it, Harriet?'

'I don't know, Don,' she said, continuing to snuffle into her handkerchief. 'I'm tired, and things are going wrong, and I was so damn scared over the baby, I still am, and my milk's not coming properly, and now Max, and everyone keeps saying, everything'll be all right and expecting me to believe them.'

'Why don't you try?' said Don gently.

'Because things do go wrong. You see, I know. Did you know I had a baby that died before I married Max?'

She was astonished to hear herself say this.

222

He was silent for a time. 'Are you sure you want to tell me this?'

She shook her head. 'No,' she whispered. 'I don't know why I said that to you.'

He took her hand and started to stroke it distractedly. 'Your milk, is it clogged up?' She nodded. 'Has it happened before?'

'No, that's why it's making me so miserable. Besides, this baby needs it more than the others.'

'You should get them to give you hot flannels and express it very gently. You know how to express?'

'Of course. I fed the others. Anyway, how do you know?'

'Oh, it happened to Miriam,' he said, surprised that she should ask. 'Oh, and get them to give you some cream to rub on your nipples, they'll get cracked if the baby suckles and there's nothing there.' He blushed, dull crimson seeming to seep even up to his high forehead, as they realised how closely they were studying her breasts, pushing blue-veined and swollen above her nightdress. He let go of her hand and got to his feet.

'It took us a long time to find out what the trouble was,' he mumbled. 'They don't always tell you in these places, but it's simple, really, if you know what to do. I'd better go.'

'Thanks for coming, Don. Really.'

With his back to her, he asked, 'Would you like me to come again? If there's anything you want, now with Max laid up?'

'Yes, that would be very kind.' She stared at him, helpless. 'There's nothing I want ... I mean, need.'

Suddenly he smiled. 'I'll see if I can think of anything you might need,' he said and disappeared.

'He won't come back,' she thought all that day and the next. It was just as well, perhaps, because in the afternoons nearly everyone in Weyville seemed to turn up to see her. Amazing how a disaster drew them, even a minor one. She tried to reject the uncharitable thought. Kind, that's what they were.

The second evening, Don arrived. It was raining outside, a bleak, sleet-filled Weyville night. The summer should have come, but spring had lingered on, retreating back into winter every week or so. His old brown mackintosh was dripping soggily.

'I got in as a representative for your husband,' he said glancing at the other fathers in the ward, for only fathers were admitted at night. 'They weren't going to let me in.'

'It should make a good item for the town crier.'

'D'you mind?'

'Do *you* mind?' she repeated, inviting him to sit beside her.

He half-shrugged, and extracted a pot of jam from his pocket. 'Japonica jelly, left over from last year. Miriam said it's better for you than the jam they give you here, too sweet. She said you should keep off chocolate and stuff. For your — you know, your chest.'

'Miriam knows I don't eat chocolate,' said Harriet indignantly.

'I expect she means just in case. You could get a craving, couldn't you?'

'That's before the baby, not after,' she said crossly, beginning to wish he hadn't come.

They sat saying nothing while he pushed a non-existent piece of dust round the floor with the toe of his galosh.

'It was nice of Miriam to think of something you could bring.'

'It was, wasn't it?,' he said, brightening. 'Actually I was so pleased she suggested I come up. It was at tea time, and I was just thinking, "How on earth shall I tell Miriam that I'm going up to the hospital?" because if I say you need anything she'll probably offer to come herself. She had some marking to do, and she said one of us should come and see you, so I said I'd come. She said if I was sure it wasn't too much trouble, because I'd been in to see Max earlier. Did you see him before he went home?'

'No. He rang me and said he'd come up if I wanted him to, but it seemed silly, that wing's so far away. By the time he'd thumped through here on crutches he'd have woken every baby in the hospital. So you were going to come up?'

'Oh yes. I had this for you,' He fished through another coat pocket, and produced the *Oxford Anthology of Modern Verse*.

They pored over the book. Don had marked poems he thought she should read with pieces of paper.

'You don't know what trouble you're inviting,' she said.

'It's a calculated risk,' he said.

'Do you always have to tell Miriam where you're going when you go out?' she said curiously.

'There's never any reason not to tell her,' he said. 'Habit, I suppose. Don't you and Max tell each other where you're going?'

'Ye-es. Only I've just decided we'll stop. It's unnecessary, really, if you think about it.'

'Much safer if you do.'

'Safe? In case of accidents? You don't have to worry. Miriam always makes sure you have clean underwear, just in case. She's told me.'

The next evening she had a present for him. It was a poem about Emma's birth. 'Women's trash,' she said, averting her face.

She had never shown anyone a poem before.

'It's good,' he said quietly.

'Rubbish,' she said. 'You're just saying that because you see yourself as my mentor.'

'Had you rehearsed that? What if I'd said it was bad?'

'I'm sorry. I — it did take an effort, you know ... to show you.'

'Yes. I should know that. All right, it's not perfect, but I think it's very good. I'm probably biased, you're right of course, but for what it's worth I think it's good. Why don't you get it published?'

'You're serious, aren't you?' she asked curiously. When he nodded, she added, 'I'll think about it'.

'That's not good enough. Look, I'll get it typed up at work, and you could send it away. I'll bring you a list of addresses you could try. What d'you say?'

'I'd say, do you seriously think you could get your typist to type up something like that? She'd think you were round the twist.'

'Well,' he said, avoiding her eye, 'I'm not a bad hand on the typewriter myself. I thought maybe in my lunch hour ...'

'You've convinced me,' said Harriet. 'I must be mad.'

As he was leaving he said, 'That's not the first poem you've written, is it?'

'No. I took your advice.'

'Thank you,' he said.

225

'Before you go,' she called him back once more, 'If you type it up, when you come to my name ... could you put Harriet Wallace on it?'

When he brought it to her the next evening, she hardly recognised it as her own work. 'Did I write that?' she said, in wonder.

'I told you it was good.'

'I didn't mean that, though it's better than I expected, somehow. But disembodied. It doesn't seem to belong to me any more.'

'It won't if I send it away for you,' he said seriously. 'Are you certain it's all right?'

'It was your idea.'

'I'm bad at taking responsibility. Ask anyone, ask Miriam.'

'I'd rather not. Does she know where you are tonight?'

'No. Nor last night, either. You won't tell her, will you?' he said unhappily.

'She'll know,' said Harriet.

'I find it difficult, telling her I'm working late, you know.'

'Never mind, you'll be relieved of the terrible strain of being my surrogate husband as from the time you leave tonight. I'm going home tomorrow.'

She detected a note of disappointment in his voice as he said, 'I was getting used to it.'

'That's as bad a habit as the one you've just broken. Go on, go home and take my poem with you. Don't forget to post it ... husband.' She enjoyed watching him colour.

'Take care of your tits,' he said, boldly paying her back for his discomfiture. As all the other husbands were kissing their wives goodnight, he pecked her on the cheek.

She didn't speak to him alone for a long time after that. Her poem was accepted by the magazine he had sent it to, and she rang and told him. He said he was pleased and looked forward to seeing 'their baby' in print.

They saw each other as a fact of their everyday lives, practically day in and day out. He would be passing her house or she would be passing his, or they would have drinks together on Saturday afternoon, a beer after all the lawns were done, or lunch on Sunday. Harriet would wheel the baby down to Miriam's in the afternoon when her friend arrived home from school. Miriam would throw the washing on, talking as she went, lighting cigarettes, leaving them to burn on the bench and catching them just as they were about to scorch the formica, throwing Don's grimy underclothes into the machine. Then Harriet could see him, sweat, grubby crotch, the lot, or their striped flannel sheets lying on the floor. Miriam and Don. An unlikely combination.

The poem's publication had a strange effect on Harriet. Nobody in Weyville appeared to notice it, so she went through some of the other verses she had stored in the mending cupboard, and now some of them seemed better than they had before. She asked Max if she could have a second-hand typewriter for her birthday. She felt compelled to show him the poem that had been published. He looked at it for a long time, and said at last, 'Why didn't you tell me before?'

'Thought you might laugh at me,' said Harriet, carefully arranging chrysanthemums.

'When have I ever laughed at you?' he said angrily.

'Never, but I thought there might be a time to begin.' She inserted the fifth flower into the arrangement and added greenery at the back.

'You don't trust me much, do you?'

'Do you like it then? The poem?'

'I don't understand it. But that doesn't matter. It's the showing that matters.'

'Have you tried to understand it?'

'I don't know. It's like asking me to understand you.'

'And that's hard?'

'I don't know ... can't explain ...' his voice faded away into the distance. Realisation through flowers, something she had been taught, an acquired skill, nearer my God to thee. Max, where are we going?

227

1978

11

Michael came to her when he said he would. On the evening appointed in late February, she had met him at the same hotel where they had first introduced themselves to each other. Harriet, who worked on contract and was not required to report daily, had spent much of the day in a state veering between lethargy and frantic activity to ensure that she would be prepared for the evening's encounter. She bathed in the morning, shaving her brown legs and afterwards rubbing oil into them till the skin shone like silk. A man had once told her her skin was like silk. That man. Yes, well he was better forgotten about, he belonged in yet another place again, somewhere in the gap between Denny Rei and Michael Young. That was a big country to cross. It didn't bear too much thinking about, not on a day like today.

Then she lay in the sun again, knowing that in a way it was the last day of the summer as he had created it for her that year. From that evening on, they would enter a new phase of this relationship. Yet these past months had been so beautiful that now at the last moment she didn't really want to give them up. After she had lain in the sun, she decided to shower, then decided against that and bathed again, this time pouring lavish amounts of scented bath oil into the water. She'd washed her hair in the morning. Was it right? She wondered now, standing in front of the mirror. Surely this was how teenagers went on. Genevieve came to the door of her bedroom and irritably demanded what had happened to all the hot water. She'd had physical education at school, and on a day like

231

this was she expected to go without a shower? The girl flounced to her room, and Harriet felt guilt-ridden and anxious.

Would they be all right tonight, the children and Max? It was a ludicrous thought from someone who came and went as she was in the habit of doing. And yet, during one of the active frenzies of the day she had prepared a handsome meal, made special things that all of them particularly liked.

Now, her daughter made her angry. She had no right to make her feel guilty. She must have noticed something about her mother, something that made her insolent. She knew how to get under Harriet's skin, did Genevieve.

She walked through to the sitting room. Emma was trying to do her sums. Her small face was frowning with effort and unhappiness. 'Oh God,' thought Harriet, 'don't tell me I'm going to have to sort this one out. I can't, I don't have the patience.' Yet, despite herself, she tenderly looked down at this most vulnerable and most gentle of her children. 'Don't let me make her a target,' Harriet begged of herself.

The child looked up. 'You look pretty tonight, Mum.'

Harriet dropped on her knees beside Emma, persevering with the sums that neither of them could do. But it was a help. Emma stopped frowning and seemed to care less whether they were right or wrong.

'What a thing to feel grateful for,' Harriet's inner voice nagged at her.

But at last she was away from them all, her conscience as clear as possible. With luck, she would relinquish it altogether by the time she got to the hotel.

As she parked, she gathered together her armoury of small talk. Much as she had waited for Michael, now she was in a state of acute nervous tension. They were to meet in the bar, and she assumed that they would have a drink, then make their way to a slow and leisurely meal, and then? Well, she'd thought so much about that, now she wondered how she could go through with it.

Books, politics, plenty to talk about there. The summer had been rank with discontent on the political scene; the country's sour mood was continuing. Her cocoon of the past few months hadn't excluded the influences which had started to colour people's thinking. And reading, she'd done plenty of that. Indeed, she kept finding things in books that had made her think 'I must tell him about this', or 'I wish he were here now, so that I could tell him that'. She had thought out whole conversations dealing with his imagined responses — he'd disagree here, concede ground there. It had all been very interesting.

Now she supposed they would talk, but was it to be a carefully charted course which would lead to the bedroom? If that was the sort of conversation it was going to be, she was sure she didn't want to have it. For a moment she thought of not going in. In panic, she decided that he wouldn't be there, that he might have missed his plane and not been able to get in touch with her, been ill, or never really meant to see her at all. His presence in the bar was, after all, something of a shock. She walked in looking for him, and somehow he was behind her and she hadn't seen him.

'Hullo.'

He wore the air of someone vaguely exasperated, as if she were late, perhaps. 'Am I late?' she asked uncertainly, sure that she wasn't, but needing to have it confirmed that there had been no mistake.

'Of course not. I'm just very hot and tired. I really didn't think Wellington could be such a miserable hole in the summer, it's usually so bloody cold. I need a shower.'

'Are you going to sit here and have a drink, or come up to the room?' he asked abruptly.

As she hesitated he said, 'Good. I've got a pile of manuscripts, for the magazine, you know. I wouldn't mind you looking at them.'

In the bedroom, he threw her a bundle of papers and said, 'There you are, amuse yourself with those.' His tone was downright rude.

'What do you expect me to do with them?' she called as the shower began to run in the bathroom a moment later.

'Tell me what you think of them,' he called.

She flicked through them. Perhaps she had imagined the summer and their meeting the time before. He could be just a rude,

233

rather arrogant young man trying to leech a bit of her time and energy into something she had no desire to do.

'They're junk,' she called.

The shower was turned off. 'If you say so.'

'When are you going to get this magazine off the ground, anyway?'

'Possibly never. As you say, that's a pile of junk. About the standard of the average New Zealand manuscript. If there's no talent here, how the hell am I supposed to put together a New Zealand-orientated periodical?'

'That's arrant nonsense,' she retorted. 'You simply haven't approached the right people.'

'Well, maybe the right people aren't very co-operative. Too damn scared of their own skins, from what I've noticed.' His mouth was apparently full of toothpaste.

He emerged, bare to the waist and barefooted, and started scrummaging around in a suitcase, apparently for a clean shirt and socks, not looking at her.

'D'you feel better?' she asked coolly, wondering how soon she could leave.

He swung round. 'Don't go away. Please.'

'How did you know I was thinking that?'

'I'm sorry, I'm sorry, I didn't mean to put you through that. Nerves, I suppose.'

Somehow she found herself flat on her back with him between her legs. Most extraordinary. He was such a very large man that she found him quite discomfiting physically. Her legs wouldn't encompass him, and waved feebly in the air like those of a praying mantis. She saw, to her dismay, that the heel of one of her best summer shoes was coming adrift. It really looked quite tatty. She tried to shift, but it was impossible under his weight. 'I wonder if I'll be able to iron my skirt,' she thought. 'I can't possibly go out to eat looking like this.' And then, 'How appalling if this is merely going to turn out funny.'

'Would you mind if I took off my shoes, please?' she asked him aloud.

234

'Do you mind about all this?' he said. There didn't seem to be anything much to mind so far, so she said that she did not.

'Before dinner or after?' he asked politely, in his creamy English voice.

'Can't we do both?' she said, and that was the first moment that it stopped being ludicrous.

So the summer began to make some sense, as their voices and their touch turned to tenderness. He undressed her, and she, loving him, helped him, taking off her bracelets and watch so that they would not catch on his beautiful skin, standing still for him so that she could reveal her breasts with pride, lying down and opening out her arms to him, and lying there, looking up into his face, seeing for a moment his blue eyes receding into a skull which seemed to be covered with translucent parchment, as if some terrible storm was taking place within.

'God, I need this,' he said.

Only long afterwards did she remember that he had said 'this' and not 'you'.

Later that night, when they returned to the hotel room after dinner he lay waiting for her, and she, astride, came, calling on him to join her. So they had entered the lovely and treacherous sea, and she was abandoned to it, her blood singing Michael, Michael, Michael, in all the cadences that water or blood might sing.

'You're so beautiful,' she whispered to him.

'So are you,' he replied, not challenging his own grace.

Let the tide stay high, we have such a short time, Michael, my golden eagle. You are only a passing visitor to these shores. I will say goodbye when the time comes without weeping.

'I love,' and his voice faltered, 'I love to watch you come.'

'I love you. I just love you.'

'Do you?' he had asked alarmed.

'Don't be afraid.'

'How will you cope, then?'

'I don't understand.'

'Emotionally? Will you be hurt?'

Harriet had rolled over onto her stomach, her arms pushed up under the hotel pillow. 'He has a right to ask me,' she thought, and remembered how long it had been since she had surrendered herself without reservation like this, feeling a part of her slipping out of her control. Oh, she'd loved, yes, but she'd been the dominant one. Nobody owned Harriet Wallace. They might have thought to, but there was always a reserve, a part that stood back, and said well, well, well, Harriet Wallace, so here you are and there you are.

'You've nothing to fear from me,' she said fiercely.

'I'm not afraid of you,' he said.

'Yes, you are,' she said. 'Listen, I tell you, there's nothing to worry about in me. I wouldn't try to possess you. I won't ask anything of you, I don't want my life changed, my patterns are made, do you understand that? Nothing changes anything, only death, and I ask nothing, there are no demands to be made or met. I only want you to come to me for as long as you can.

'Can you be like that?'

'Can't you?' she said.

'I'll try, if you can.'

'I don't want to hurt anyone'. I don't want to know about your family, I don't want to tell you about mine. I only want to exist in the time we make together.'

'Why this?'

'You came to me, remember?'

'Yes. I remember.'

'Then why you, any more than me?'

'Oh God, then what sort of an animal does this make me?'

'You mean that?' said Harriet, frightened for him again.

'I don't know. I don't know.'

As they rose to shower together, she glanced at the initials on his suitcase, M.S.Y.

'What does the S stand for?' she asked while he was finding a spare towel for her.

'Seamus.'

'Michael Seamus Young.' She fitted them together. 'You're Irish, then.'

236

'You could say so, colleen,' he said, trying to make light of it. 'A distant ancestry.'

'You don't sound it.'

'I've never lived there.'

'Which side do you belong on?'

'You ask a lot of questions.'

'My interviewing technique.'

'Interview me under the shower, then — or, better still, let me interview you. What would you like to do next week?'

'You're coming next week?'

'Mm-hmm, and the one after that.'

'Make love,' she said, the water splashing over her face. The top of her head was level with his shoulder.

In the following weeks they continued to see each other, as he had said they would. When they were together they lived in a private world of great pleasure and intensity, tempered from time to time with anxiety about his work. At first she let his concern flow round her, happy to listen and talk, but not to suffer it.

It assumed a greater importance however, as the implications of what was happening to him began to sink in. It was starting to look as if the market was wrong for the magazine. The financial situation was tightening, potential advertisers were not as enthusiastic as they had been when the idea of the magazine was first mooted, and with the prospect of increasing inflation it appeared unlikely that many prospective buyers would be prepared to spend money on a quality magazine. He talked anxiously about cutting production costs. He was visiting Wellington to pursue possible leads with different printers, but lower pricing invariably indicated an inferior product. It was becoming more and more evident that the magazine simply might not eventuate. Bleakly Harriet faced the prospect that this might involve his early return to England. He would feel that he had failed.

They talked for hours over this point at dinner on his third visit. It was not, she insisted, a personal failure. He couldn't have foreseen the decline in the economy and it hadn't been his idea to come out here in the first place. His bosses might at least have realised that New Zealand, behind the rest of the world in most things, had been behind other Western countries in its economic recession, and must now be hit at a time when the rest of the world was starting to recover. Michael accepted this at a rational level but rejected it at a personal one. 'He's so young,' Harriet thought. 'I forget how young he really is, the difference in our ages is more than years. He has the smell of success on him. He doesn't understand what it is to accept defeat and start again.'

She sensed that he was rich. Whether or not he had always been rich it was hard to say. He had told her more about his background in their earlier meetings the previous year. She inclined towards the idea that he had been brought up in a comfortable middle-class atmosphere, where strong ambition prevailed. He had accepted the patterns of hope, and there had been enough money for him to receive a sound classical education. Nothing had been really difficult. The right doors had opened for him, and marriage to a very rich young woman had followed.

That was what Harriet understood, indirectly. She tried not to let the rich and beautiful young wife prey unduly on her mind. If she did, she was afraid that she might even begin to feel guilt. She ought to know about betrayal. But I want nothing of him, she would tell herself, nothing — except of course she wanted everything. She found out bits of information about him by asking people elaborately casual questions. She had asked one day round the studio whether anyone had met Michael Young, the man who wanted to start up this magazine. A producer had said yes, of course, they were the crowd that threw the big party up in Auckland when they opened up their offices there. A wonder she hadn't been invited to it. Yes, sure he remembered the guy. And his missus. What a smasher. What knockers. The sort of bird you didn't cross — not that it mattered, she looked down her straight little nose at you all the time anyway. Poms, bloody Poms. You wondered what a crowd like that really wanted out of the country. They weren't here to put anything into it, whatever they said.

Harriet, although inclined to agree in principle, didn't comment, beyond saying that she thought there was a programme in it somewhere. 'Not likely now,' said the producer. 'Sounds as if the outfit's about to go broke.'

'Then perhaps I should document its decline and fall,' Harriet had said, changing the subject, but nonetheless feeding greedily on the information.

Waiting for Michael between his visits to the city had become an agony of suspense. She would wait for the telephone to ring, to hear his voice, to be ready to go to him again.

She was sure that people around her must notice. Her family seemed to present problems, but she knew they were only in her mind. Only when they threatened to stand in her way did her calm falter in front of them.

Oh, how the mighty had fallen. She was careful and guarded with some of her more forthright friends who had forceful views about men in general. She was in love, helplessly, day by day, hour by hour, even minute by minute, it seemed. She was grateful for the drives backwards and forwards to the studio. They gave her time in the car alone. The music she chose to put into her car cassette had become sentimental. Gliding, driving, dreaming music she called it, and felt she ought to be ashamed of herself. To be so helpless was certainly to be on a perilous edge.

She wondered how much of her feelings he guessed. After her admission that she loved him, she had tried by implication, to steer a middle course, though it had nothing to do with the abandon of their nights together. But she was sure he knew. At times he let his natural arrogance take its course. Deliberately? It was hard to tell. They would be dining somewhere and she would have her hand resting on his knee under the cloth, amazed at their daring, being in public together, so obviously together. People would look at her and look away, or sometimes say with apologetic half-greetings, 'Oh excuse me, but you are Harriet Wallace aren't you? Sure I'd seen you on the telly,' and she would incline her head and withdraw to safety.

The way in which she was known presented both a threat and a source of pride to him. He couldn't always cope with it, and he would sometimes put her down — ever so gently so that at first she

239

wouldn't know it was happening. He did it superbly, by means of little things, such as testing her New Zealand schoolgirl French which had been brushed up in recent years so that she could acquit herself well in restaurants. She would stumble, humiliated, and everything would falter — the cutlery in her hands, the way she ate her food. She hated him when he did that to her, and herself for caring. Then he would seek her forgiveness and order a fresh bowl of strawberries, one of his favourite foods, urging her to have some too. For some reason she had refused them on the first evening they had been together, and he had urged her to try one from his spoon, and another and another, so that amidst the low lights and the silver and the flowers he had fed her delicately piece by piece, a bird feeding its young, sharing the fruit with him. Now they finished their meal like that, and it was his apology. He was a moderate drinker and they would leave soon after the strawberry ritual, provoked by it, rather than by the wine, to return to his room. Then they would forget his business worries, his edgy pride, the small hurts he could inflict on her.

The room was always as good as you could buy for his night in town. If the company was in a precarious state, it certainly didn't show in his personal finances, reinforcing her opinion that he was wealthy and that his pride was being affected by this business reverse rather than his pocket. She felt like Cinderella in more ways than one as she scurried off home to the children, and Max, ever patient with her 'business commitments' that kept her out till long past the time that he had given up and gone to bed.

Shortly after Michael's return to Auckland on the last of these trips, he rang, buoyant again. The newly-established Auckland office was not closing, the magazine was on. The company had elected to gamble on a return to stability in the economy. The only thing was timing, and the launching, it had been decided, should be held over till later in 1978, maybe even early 1979. By that time, they prophesied, going on the performance of other countries, there should be an upswing. Harriet suspected that the company had already invested a considerable amount of money in the venture, but dismantling the operation at this stage would probably also be highly expensive. In the meantime, the magazine and a number of subsidiaries were to be consolidated on the local market and Michael would be briefed on this when he returned to England.

'You're going back to England, then?' Her voice sounded rigid with fear.

'For a little while, just a couple of months,' he said cheerfully. 'And not yet, not till winter. The London office is going to be short of an editor for a couple of months, and I'm replacing him, that's all. There's a lot of things to sort out on this scene, the two tie in together, all right?'

'Is your family going?' she heard herself ask, and wanted to tear her tongue out for breaking the rules.

'No, they'll stay behind. It's not really sensible for that length of time. Not when we'll be going home maybe six months afterwards, anyway.'

At least that much was a reprieve. If he was leaving them in New Zealand, then it really did mean he was coming back. Harriet felt she could breathe again. She had news of her own for him too.

'I have to come to Auckland soon,' she said. 'In about a fortnight's time, to make some programmes. Will I stay in a motel or with friends?'

He hesitated on the other end of the phone. 'When will you be up, Harriet?'

She gave him the dates in late April.

'I'm going to be pretty frantic round then, with going away,' he said.

'You won't be able to see me?' she said sharply.

'Of course I will, but maybe not very much. Well . . . you'd better stay in a motel then. He laughed uneasily. 'Sounds a bit like some low-grade novels or a B-grade movie, doesn't it?'

'Why?' she wondered as he hung up, 'Why, now he has to visit a motel instead of me having to run backwards and forwards to hotel bedrooms?' She tried to push the thought to the back of her mind, and by the time she arrived in Auckland a week or so later it had gone away.

241

She arrived at the motel when it was still quite early, having caught the first morning plane. The studio had sent her to interview a number of people for background in a new series of programmes they were doing, and the morning involved checking that all her subjects would be available at the right times, going over her research material, and gearing herself for the next few days. It was always difficult fitting oneself into a totally new situation with technicians and crew that you didn't know, a strange studio, and so on. You had to be on your mettle just that little bit extra.

Before she set down to work she called Michael. She was put through a switchboard, and then to his secretary, who sounded totally cool and protective. 'Is it urgent?' asked the girl. 'Mr Young is rather tied up at the moment.'

'Well,' Harriet hesitated, and then thought, why shouldn't I? What's to stop me giving my name? 'Could you just ask him if he has a moment to speak to Harriet Wallace, please? If he hasn't, I'll leave a number for him to call.'

After a minute or so, Michael's voice came on, cooler, more careful than usual. 'Nice to hear from you, Harriet,' he said, as if it were a surprise.

'When will I see you?' she asked frantically, after she had told him where she was staying.

'I'll have to give you a ring back on that. Can you leave a phone number?'

She hung up, feeling numb. He must have had someone there, maybe even his wife. Perhaps the secretary was really untrustworthy and listened in on his calls, maybe he was in the middle of negotiating something important.

Trying hard to concentrate, she sat down to work. The bits of paper in front of her kept floating away from her range of vision. The white concrete walls of the motel seemed cold and unwelcoming and she was stuck here on her own for days. None of the friends she would usually see had been contacted, she had wanted to keep each day whole and perfect for him, outside working hours. She had even dreamed extravagantly that he might drive her up to Ohaka one day, and that she would be able to show him something of the countryside that she knew so well; it was something she could teach him about.

It was eighteen years since she had been back to Ohaka. To have returned with Michael would have been to share with him something so private, so increasingly necessary to her, that it would have singled him out forever in her life. She and Max had never gone there together, for by the time they had met, the Wallaces had left the farm. They often talked of going together and, as the children grew up, they asked her about going there, but somehow they never did. It would have been a small detour on one of their trips to Whangarei, but on the trip north the children were always tired and anxious to complete the journey. On the way back after the anxious visits to the Wallaces, when the children would be too noisy for Gerald, and Mary was valiantly trying to keep everyone happy, but getting frailer and vaguer in her attempts, there would be a feeling of relief about getting on the road again. Faced with an 800-kilometre journey home, it would be a case of putting as much time on the road as they could before the day was too far advanced and the traffic got heavy. She and Max would share the driving all day to save the expense of an overnight stop, and there was really no time for side trips.

She harboured a suspicion that these were all excuses. They could have made a day trip from Whangarei, but they hadn't. That was because they were, in theory, preserving their energies for the trip further up north which, in fact, they usually made. The real reason, Harriet believed, was that once there, she didn't know what there would be to show them. All that way for a paddock or two, a tree perhaps? Where would one start? They might be disappointed in Ohaka. She had talked to them about it, but what, after all, would it mean to them? Perhaps it was better just to leave it in limbo, the place where Mum had come from.

Yet, more and more, she had formed a private desire to go there. Perhaps Michael would take her. Since she had met him, it had become an obsession, so that she almost believed it would happen, like his coming to her after the long wait.

She had brought a bottle of gin with her, on impulse. That in itself was an admission that something might go wrong. Tucked conveniently in the back of her mind was the thought that naturally he wouldn't be able to come every single night she was in Auckland, and a couple of drinks would help to put her off to sleep if she was lying there thinking about him; better than having to hover round some bar by herself. She had never liked that much. Didn't know why she thought she'd be short of company. That never happened much either, there was sure to be someone around, or if she really needed to, there were the friends who hadn't been warned of her coming. What a surprise Harriet is, they would say, pleased to see her.

So why had she brought a bottle of gin? Because of that hesitancy on the phone when she had told him she was coming to Auckland?

She poured some gin into a thick motel glass, and sloshed some water over it. It steadied her slightly, and she had a second drink. God, how easy it would be to wipe herself out now. She remembered the interviews she had set up for the afternoon, and turned as resolutely as she could back to her papers. As she did so, there was a knock at the door.

'Harriet?' His voice held a note of question in it.

She started to tremble violently. It was him, and here she was, smelling of gin, scratchy with worry about him.

'Just a minute,' she called. In the bathroom, she flushed the toilet to cover her rinsing her mouth and squirting it full of breath freshener. She undid the door a moment later to let him in.

He was coatless, tieless. It was still like high summer here in Auckland, the day hot and still. Having left Wellington in a cold southerly that had had her panicking that the plane might not take off, she was overdressed and sweltering. He burst into the room looking like summer itself.

'You came. You came,' she said, collapsing against him, weak with relief. His arms closed around her as she reached up, dabbing at him with kisses, the wide column of his neck, the side of his face, wherever they might land, until he bent his head to kiss her properly. Did she imagine it, or was he straining away from her? Was there ice in the blue chips of his eyes? She backed away from him a little.

'I'm so glad you came,' she said faintly, at the same time desperately flicking her eyes around the room to make sure that she had put away the gin botle. She had.

'I can see that,' he said, with a semblance of the tolerant amused look he produced for her when she was volubly grateful for his presence in Wellington.

'What shall we do? Where shall we go?' she said, taking his hand and leading him to the bed to sit down. 'By the way, welcome to my place for a change.'

'It's a bit grotty, isn't it?' he said, looking round.

She was stung. In fact she had paid extra to come to such an expensive place, more than the television corporation's standard accommodation allowance, so that he wouldn't feel out of place. 'It's no worse than the places I come to you in,' she retorted. 'Come on, you'll get used to it.'

'Not this time, I'm afraid.'

'What do you mean?' she said, although she knew already.

'I'm really flat out, love ... I had to make time this morning. And the evenings are difficult for me.'

'Why didn't you tell me before, then?' she said. 'I could have made other arrangements. Didn't you know that I'd have made every moment free for you?'

He looked despairing, touchingly so, and she started stroking his face trying to translate her love into comfort. She wanted to hold him like a child. he looked so unhappy.

'When could I have told you? I didn't know till you told me on the phone, and I haven't seen you since.'

'You could have rung me before I came up, so I wouldn't have built on it so much.'

'It seemed better to tell you to your face.' Tell her to her face. Really, what did he mean?

'Hadn't you better get to the point?' she said.

'I don't think I can go on with this,' he said miserably.

245

'Why? Why not?' Her voice was a tiny whimper.

'I'm no good at it. I'm hurting you too much.'

'You're not. Please, Michael, you're not, you've never hurt me until now. Only the thought of not being with you hurts me.'

'Then don't you see? It's no good, because we can't be together.'

'Didn't you believe me,' she said slowly, 'When I told you that I didn't want to possess you? That I only wanted to be with you for as long as it's possible? Do you think I want to take you away from your wife and children? That I want to — to marry you or something?'

'I'm not that arrogant,' he said.

'Aren't you? I don't think you believe that it's possible that I might want to give you something without asking for a tangible asset in return.'

'That's not true.' He got to his feet, walking round the motel room in long agitated strides, bumping his huge frame into them as he went. 'You said you wanted to be with me while it was possible.'

'Yes?'

'Well, I feel it's impossible, that's all.'

She shook her head. 'I don't understand.'

'Because I'm no good at coping emotionally, that's why.' And his eyes seemed to retract into his skull again as they had done the moment before he had entered her the first time.

Her heart lifted. This then, meant that he loved her. It must. 'Come to bed,' she said, starting to tremble again. 'Please, darling, it'll be all right.'

He looked like a man drowning.

She said again, 'It'll be all right.' She started to slip out of her clothes. Wanting her and showing it, he followed her. She lifted back the covers on the bed so that they might lie on the cool sheets. With sudden violence he turned to her, insisting that they make love dog fashion, as if to humiliate them both. Afterwards he lay staring at the ceiling with unshed tears behind his eyes.

It was nearly midday, and Harriet realised that she was due in the city in less than an hour for her first appointment. She would have to dress and find a taxi.

Michael said that she need not worry, he would take her into town. They dressed, hardly speaking to each other, he seemingly irritable. He felt a migraine coming, he said. He found the place claustrophobic.

The car was a handsome new BMW.

She wondered if it was the company's, and decided that they surely couldn't be out to make that big a splash on the New Zealand scene. She wished she was better at wearing riches. If he had to pick her as his woman, that was all very well, but surely he could have found someone to go with his image better. Mug shots on television every week hardly added up to the beautiful people, however much they, the performers, might sometimes like to project themselves as such. If she hadn't been competent, she would have lost her job by now. Even so, a few pointed remarks had been made about her weight from time to time, and if she hadn't been looking so well in recent months she would probably have been due for a general tidy-up. Her image had been due to slip sideways around the time she met Michael. She had been revamped by him, but it was an illusion. When he went, she would slide into middle age. For a little while he held her in aspic.

She didn't want to keep him forever and had never anticipated doing so; she could wear his youth and his wealth for a certain amount of time, and then the affair would be over. The short time that they had together, its prospects, this was what she could cope with; something that would last for a specified time, never to be given too much time to disintegrate, to sour, for them to see through each other.

She remembered a conversation they had had in a restaurant some weeks before. She had been reading a contemporary English woman novelist, and told him about her. To her surprise, the next time he saw her he said that he had read a couple of the woman's books.

'They're fun,' Harriet had said, 'But so unreal. All the women are rescued from their predicaments by money. They have inheritances or their mother's jewels to flog off when the going gets rough. They

247

cheat; they create honest situations and then find dishonest escape routes. Real life isn't like that.'

'Oh, I don't know,' he'd replied, quite seriously. 'I read one in which the girl was very poor all the way through. It was very good I thought.' He named the book.

'But don't you realise, on the last page, someone rich walks in and promises to rescue her, so she can get away from the disgrace of being poor? The whole book's a diatribe against people who aren't rich.'

'Well, being poor is rather boring, isn't it?' he'd said. 'Why do you have to be so bloody virtuous about it?'

Perhaps that was how he saw himself in relationship to her; maybe that was what made him afraid. Of course she complained about money and the fact that it was getting harder and harder to live. She was afraid they were going to have to stop being a two-car family in spite of her job, and it was going to make things awfully difficult. He must have deduced by now that she and Max just made ends meet like most of the other people they knew. Maybe he saw in her someone who really was waiting to be rescued, and that as she didn't seem to have found anyone else to do it for her, the price of his love would be to extract her from the depths. It was an awful idea, and, looking at him, not one that she cared to pursue now. There had been enough drama for one morning.

As they drove, he seemed calmer, as if he had settled something within himself.

'I understand if you can't see me.' she said, as they drifted through the suburb and out onto the sea road. Her mind was already moving ahead to plan how she would spend her time in Auckland. She knew she wouldn't see him again on this trip. It didn't seem to matter, because now he had told her that he loved her. For the moment she believed she could live with anything, even his absence, if he loved her as she loved him. He took her hand, holding it in his lap as they drove.

'There's only one thing that I could ever ask of you,' she said, 'and it's nothing that could hurt you.'

'What is it?' he asked.

'Of course,' she said, 'I told you I'd never ask anything, only this is different. And it's easy. But it's the most important thing I could ask, I want you to understand how important it is, because if this is the most frightful demand I can make, you'll see how easy I am on you.'

'Try me,' he said.

'I want you to promise me that if it should be over, really over, before it's time for you to leave New Zealand, you'll tell me. That's all. I'm too old to start making a fool of myself, making phone calls when you don't want to hear from me, making arrangements like this that might never come off. Please save me from making an idiot of myself, Michael.'

'Yes,' he said, 'I'd do that.'

'You promise?'

He nodded, and in a few minutes they were in the city. 'I'll be down soon. Don't worry about anything,' he said, assuming the role of comforter.

And she was left in the street, watching the big shining red car draw away into the traffic.

But he didn't come to Wellington again before he left New Zealand, nor did he get in touch with her. As the weeks passed, the silence was broken only by her calls to him. The secretary was always cool and polite, but occasionally firm.

'Mr Young really does have wall-to-wall appointments today,' she had said on one occasion. Harriet on the other end of the phone had spluttered with anger.

'Do tell, when does Mr Young manage to roll up the carpet and have a little space to himself?'

'Perhaps if you called him in the morning?' suggested the secretary.

'Kindly tell him I rang, and will be available to accept his call at nine o'clock tomorrow morning.'

At nine o'clock on the dot, the phone rang. 'Hey,' he said, 'what's this I hear? My secretary tells me you sound like a subscriber who's missed three copies of the magazine in a row.'

'Tell her she sounds like a pain in the arse,' said Harriet.

249

. 'I don't think I'm going to see you before I go, Harriet,' he said. 'I mean, it's only a fortnight, and I've got so many people to see.'

'Yes. I understand,' Harriet replied dully. Two and a half months, you might as well say three, before she saw him again. The winter stretched in front of her forever. She was doodling on the telephone pad in front of her. She had drawn his initials in a squirly motif. M.S.Y. Michael Seamus Young. 'Are you a Catholic?' she asked.

There was a pause on the other end of the line. Then he said sharply, 'I think my religion's my own business.'

It was extraordinary to her that the question had never seriously occurred to her before. 'I apologise,' she said. 'Politics and religion, taboo. Only we've talked about politics, how was I to know that it was a discriminatory process?'

'Harriet, I'm in my office,' he said. 'Please.'

She hung up. Catholic guilt? It made sense, the sudden turn-around when she had arrived in Auckland. If it was simply sexual guilt, then he would never have become involved with her in the first place. But whatever strange torments he had put himself through on her account, he had come to her, away from home. From the way he had joked during their first meetings, she had thought that he was in the habit of taking women to his bed. Certainly he gave every indication that he had done so before his marriage, and nothing had changed her opinion on that point. But it had occurred to her after they became lovers that extramarital affairs were not his forte. He wanted her so desperately, or wanted someone, anyone maybe, that he'd been prepared to risk his conscience. What had he said? 'God, I need this.'

So that was it. A frustrated playboy, hung up on religion. For which, measure for measure, she reflected, you could buy the cheap cynicism of a lapsing non-believer if you liked.

She wept hideously in private, over the next two weeks, stricken with grief and loss. In public, she saw friends again, went to the parties on the literary circuit, gossiped about men with Lynley and Joan, was more talkative about her lover, dropped reckless hints about him. Appraising her gaunt face they absorbed her back into the fold, guessing that she had now really joined the clan.

Their barely disguised sympathy made her angry with herself for ever having confided in them. She resolved to fight back with Michael. He had said — or seemed to say — that he loved her. He had promised her that when their affair was over, he would tell her. She had trusted him from the beginning, so why was she like this now? She was too analytical, which she had been told before, too unaccepting, so questioning that she spoiled things. She would not spoil this with doubts. Nothing had changed her love for him.

Before long, her anger began to dissolve and give way to compassion for him. She chose to call it compassion, not pity. She had been told somewhere that pity was the most disgusting of all emotions, that nothing more degraded the relationship of two people than if it were built on pity. She tried to relate into Michael's situation, how he must see the world if what she now believed of his religious background was in fact true. Did he see eels sliding over rocks? Were there black holes in the mattress at night?

Did Michael lie in the dark at nights awaiting the arrival of the devil? Did his bed crawl with snakes, and was she one of them? We all have our darknesses, perhaps I have become his, she thought. She mourned for him, and for herself as well. She could not absolve him but at least she could persist in asking him to trust her. But it seemed unlikely that he would.

251

12

Harriet started to come apart at the seams the year after Emma was born. It was a long period of disintegration, caused by several things. The baby had been fractious ever since she brought her home and Gerald Wallace had stayed with them several times while a back specialist in Weyville was treating him. When Mary was in the house to keep a tether on him, Harriet could cope, but Mary had kept away, thinking that two women in the house would be too much trouble. Gerald had shared a room with Peter, and moaned and grumbled about his uncomfortable narrow bed. Max complained too, about having his father-in-law in the house. His attitude seemed unreasonable, particularly as his parents came to stay for an annual fortnight, up from Christchurch. There seemed to be months of simply having various grandparents to stay, with a camp stretcher put up in the main bedroom and no sex because there a restless wakeful child lay wide-eyed in the dark each night. Max would become tight-lipped, pale and tense, no matter whose parents were visiting. When the Wallaces came, Harriet felt inordinately guilty, as though she had perpetrated some cardinal sin against him and their marriage bed. There was nothing wrong with their marriage bed when life was running normally; it was amazing how comfortably and satisfactorily they accommodated each other. They were so well suited that there seemed little to ask of each other. But denied that bed for any length of time, Max became very difficult.

And three children were harder to manage than two, even if

Emma hadn't been such a cross baby. Harriet would start the washing soon after seven each morning, and continue with it in between feeding them all, until ten or eleven, till she got the last of the nappies out. They would lie dankly in the still soggy air of Weyville, sometimes drying enough to finish off in the airing cupboard, other times having to be strung around the kitchen.

Max had succeeded in one thing, certainly, they kept off the dinner party circuit now. Harriet was too tired even to think what to wear if she went out, let alone to put something on and try and make herself look presentable. Max took a job three nights a week at a local petrol station so that this year they might have a proper holiday, seeing that she was so tired and rundown. She would often contrive to be asleep when he came home.

When he got some unexpected back pay, she said she guessed that would do for the holiday, and suggested he leave his part-time job. It seemed, however, that he had other ideas, and suddenly eager to bestow gifts on her, he said that he'd decided they should get a television set. It would give her something to look forward to in the evenings, and he'd stick with the job. Harriet said that it hardly seemed worth all the effort. She'd like the television set, but would probably feel better if he put some of his surplus energy into helping her fold nappies and tidy up the place in the evenings. He appeared to listen, but stayed at the petrol station all the same.

On one of his nights off there was an office party. Harriet said, 'For God's sake, Max, you know I don't feel like going out at night lately. I'll be happy in front of the television, it's fine by me if you go'.

'You're getting too dependent on television,' he said, and she thought, 'Christ, isn't he ever satisfied? He got me the bloody television set, let me get on and enjoy it.'

And indeed on many evenings, he came home to find her slumped in front of the set, a glass of sherry in her hand. It was proving a bad winter.

'I want you to come to the party with me,' he insisted. 'It wouldn't look right if I went without you.'

'Make up your mind, Max,' she said voicing her frustration over

253

the television in a different way. 'Either you want me to come with you, or it wouldn't look right if I didn't come. Which is it?'

'Why do you have to split hairs all the time? Please. Just come with me.'

So she went while Miriam babysat. By the time they left, Harriet was beginning to feel that the outing might have possibilities. She'd managed to lose a considerable amount of weight without even trying, she was back to the shape she had been when she married Max, her legs were all right, they suited the shorter skirts. During the day she'd had two good letters, one from a girl she was in library school with, forwarded from a magazine which had published a number of her poems the previous month, asking if it was really the same Harriet Wallace, and how good her work was. The girl, whose name was Helen still had a flat in Wellington — if Harriet was ever passing through, she was welcome to a bed. The other letter was an acceptance slip from still another magazine. These secret things kept her going.

Armed with these private thoughts and a couple of gins thrown down while she was putting the children to bed, she began to think that she might even enjoy herself.

The evening was a fiasco. The car had a flat tyre, and by the time Max had changed it, Harriet could feel herself getting flushed round the neck as she always did after a few drinks, and irritable at being kept waiting. It was cold in the car, and what with a hot face and cool feet, she felt decidedly uncomfortable.

The party was a smaller gathering than Harriet had expected; she had hoped that it would be a large group in which she could comfortably lose herself. Instead, Max's boss was there, and the pecking order was clearly defined. Harriet was expected to take her place in the line. She would have given such a dinner party herself a year or so before, but she had slipped so far out of the Weyville social scene that she simply hadn't bothered recently. Still, she could feel Max's resentment that his junior, as their host was, should be entertaining their mutual boss.

The evening wore on. Harriet was careful and diligent in conversation to Mrs Pegler, the wife of Max's boss, listening to her

talk of travels abroad and grandchildren. Max watched Harriet
carefully out of the corner of his eye. 'Blast him,' she fumed,
'Doesn't he know that I won't do anything? He's safe. I'm not going
to make any trouble, I wouldn't dream of answering anyone back,
even if they spat on me.'

She forced her attention back to Mrs Pegler. 'I beg your
pardon?' she asked.

'I said,' repeated Mrs Pegler, 'Aren't you the little girl who writes
poetry under the name of Harriet Wallace?'

'How did you know?' said Harriet flatly.

'Someone must have told me,' said Mrs Pegler. 'Yes, of course,
Mrs Everett, Mirian ... you do know her, don't you?'

Miriam. The bitch. She had never once mentioned the poetry to
Harriet. Had Don told her? But much did Don know? She hadn't
told him about any other poems since the first one. She supposed
he might have followed them up. But telling Miriam wasn't fair,
nor was it right that Miriam had said nothing to her. Of course
Miriam might have found them at school — she did teach English,
after all.

'Yes, I know her,' said Harriet.

'How quaint,' said the chief engineer's wife, who was standing
next to them. 'Did you hear that? Harriet publishes poetry.'

'So we've got a real writer in our midst,' said Mr Pegler.

Their hostess, a nervous twittery girl, anxious to say the right
things, said, 'Really, you're so modest, Harriet. Is it terribly hard to
be clever?'

'Must read a bit of it, eh? Let the cat out of the bag there. How
does it feel having all the family secrets down on paper, Max?' her
husband contributed.

'Of course, I took the trouble to look them up in the library. A
trifle gauche, shall we say, but readable. It's nice to see the young
trying. You could be quite good some day if you persevere,' said
Mrs Pegler.

To the best of Harriet's knowledge Mrs Pegler had never
exhibited the slightest literary qualification in her life. Still, she
supposed the same could be said of herself. Soon she told Max that

255

she thought they should be getting along; she was very tired.

Their journey home was silent. They put away the car, and Harriet thought, 'Not a fight, please not a fight tonight. I haven't done anything, I behaved, I was on my best behaviour all evening. I tried for you, Max, please.'

Miriam was watching the late news when they got in.

'Good time?' she asked brightly.

'All right, thanks,' said Harriet. Max was checking the children in their rooms. 'Mrs Pegler was there. She said you'd shown her some of my poetry.'

'Did she? I hope she told you how much we both enjoyed it.'

'Did you?'

'Yes, we were both in the library having a chat a couple of days ago, and I picked some up. Good heavens, I said, Harriet Wallace, isn't that what our Harriet's name used to be when she worked here? We both read it. Well, I haven't seen you since, I was going to mention it of course.'

Miriam was always so matter-of-fact that it was impossible to fault her. 'Thanks ever so much for looking after the kids,' said Harriet.

'Fine, any time. I've always got something to do. Got a pile of marking done tonight before I sat down in front of your goggle-box. We will get one, I suppose, Don's always on about it, but you know me, so much to do, I simply couldn't allow myself to get hooked on it. I can see how easy it is. Ah well, I'll be off then.'

She stretched herself, tidy and sensible in her twinset and tweeds. 'Come and see me one afternoon and we can have a proper talk. I see so little of you these days, I miss out on the important things.' You couldn't really doubt Miriam. She was a good friend.

When she'd gone, Max came through. 'How much of this stuff is there, then?' he said. His voice was hard.

'What stuff?'

'You know. Poetry.'

'What do you mean stuff? Are you ashamed of it? What's wrong with writing poetry? It's quite respectable.'

'Only you don't tell *me* about it.'

256

'Do you tell me everything you do?'

'That's not the point. You choose to make a public issue of the matter, which is all right as far as I'm concerned. It would just be nice if I didn't have to find out about it at my friends' dinner parties and in front of the people I work for.'

'You know,' said Harriet, 'that's a side of you I never considered when I married you. Who would ever have thought that you had so much side? You seemed quite a mild unambitious person then, though I suppose following me up here was quite an ambitious move on your part. I think you did well enough out of the bargain.'

'I didn't ask for a bargain,' said Max, in a strangled voice, 'I asked for a wife.'

'And all that that implies in the conventional sense of the word?'

'Why is your poetry a secret? That's what I want to know.'

'I don't know,' said Harriet. 'It's something I can't explain. I suppose it's to do with keeping a part of myself intact. There are things I want to say aloud which are unsuitable, so I put them down on paper instead.'

'So these things that you write ...' He turned away. She knew he'd been going to say that he supposed they were unsuitable, and equally that he knew how stupid it would sound to them both. 'I'm trying, Harriet,' he said. 'I try to give you what I can, to make things easier. I don't like seeing you like this. What are we going to do about you? Think you should see the doctor, old thing?'

'What for? So I won't write poetry? So I'll be a better Mrs Ordinary Housewife?' Her voice was rising.

'Yes, if you like,' Max shouted.

The bowl of marigolds that had stood on the mantelpiece landed slightly to the right of his ear, hitting the lampshade. It smashed in a shower of fragments, splattered water and bruised flowers.

'Was that difficult?' asked Max.

'Don't stand there trying to be God,' screamed Harriet. 'No, it wasn't hard. I'll show you how easy it was.'

She ran through to the kitchen and tore open a cupboard door. Her hands lit on a pile of cups, which she scooped up and hurled at the floor. She started to laugh, with tears running down her face, as

257

they splintered upwards, the chips rebounding high. Max caught her arm as she hurled dinner plates through the glass panel of the back door. 'Stop it!' he shouted.

'Not likely. I'm enjoying myself.' She seized a bottle of tomato sauce and watched it explode on a wall, the contents splattering round the room like blood.

She suddenly found herself pinned against the far wall, both her hands held behind her back. Max was deliberately hitting her face.

Shocked, she stood still. He didn't seem to notice, but continued to hit her. She could distinguish him saying, 'I've got to do it to you, Harriet, I've got to do it.'

'No, you don't, you're enjoying it,' she heard herself crying, in a voice coming out of some alien part of her.

They both stopped, panting and out of breath. Harriet reached up and touched her face as he freed her hands. 'I must be crying,' she thought, feeling the wetness. But it was Max who was crying — she was bleeding.

'I'll put you to bed,' said Max.

'Yes, please.'

'And I'll get the doctor in the morning.'

'If you like.'

'If I've marked you, I'll tell him what happened. No lies.'

'I won't tell anyone, though.'

'It'll be all right, then. We'll keep looking after each other,' he said, leading her, limp and bedraggled, to the bedroom Her head was thumping and splitting.

It was still aching in the morning, as if she had a hangover. Perhaps that's what it was, she thought. Maybe I was simply pissed out of my mind. But she hadn't been, she was sure. She'd slowed down after those two drinks. Scared silly she'd do the wrong thing. No, it wasn't alcohol. She went out to the bathroom.

'What are you doing up?' Max said, from the kitchen.

'Just going to the loo.' She put her head round the door. The kitchen was immaculate.

'I'll bring you your breakfast in when I've fixed the children's. You'll have to have your tea out of one of the best cups.'

'Did I break all the breakfast cups?' she inquired.

'Don't worry, I'll get some more today.'

'You'll be late for work.'

'I'm having a day off.'

The doctor examined her briefly, wrote out a prescription and went away to talk to Max. When he'd gone Max came in and sat on the bed.

'What did he say?' she asked.

'He's given you a prescription for some sedatives.'

'I don't want sedatives. I'm not going to be a walking pillbox for the rest of my life.'

'Steady on. He doesn't want you to be, he just wants you to take something for a week or so. Then he thinks you should have a holiday.'

'We can't afford a holiday, and who'd look after the kids?'

'I would. I'll take my annual leave, and you can have the money I'd saved for all of us to go away.'

'But that's not fair.'

'It is fair. I'd thought it out before the doctor came. It's what I thought you needed, too. You're probably right, I think it would be a disaster to take all the kids away at this stage. It'd be far better if we got out of this mess. What about going to Whangarei?'

She shook her head. 'I think father and I have seen enough of each other to be going on with.'

'Your mother would enjoy making a fuss of you.'

She shook her head again, determined.

'Then will you go to my parents?'

'No.'

'My sister?'

Harriet was quiet for a moment, thinking. 'I'll tell you what,' she said, 'I'll go down to your parents if you don't mind my stopping over in Wellington on the way. I've always wanted to go back.'

'Where would you stay?'

'There's a girl there. Your sister would remember her, she wrote to me the other day, we were all at library school together. Helen, you met her.'

259

She explained the letter she had had from Helen with her invitation to stay. There was no knowing what Helen would be like now, but if it was all right to stay on with her a day or two, why not? If they didn't like each other, then she could go on to Christchurch. It was as simple as that. Provided his parents knew it was a flexible arrangement, she didn't see that there was any problem.

Max finally had to agree with her. Wellington was the place where they had met and if it seemed to be important to her, then maybe her visit there would be best for them all.

'You won't have had a holiday at all, though,' said Harriet, when it had been decided. She was fighting guilt, hoping that he would reassure her.

'Oh, it doesn't matter,' Max said. 'Perhaps I could take a couple of days fishing over Taupo way a bit later on. I haven't done anything like that for a long time. Give me a good excuse.'

'Promise?'

'Yes, promise.'

The following week, Harriet caught a bus bound for Wellington, and was met by Helen Burnett, who hardly seemed to have changed at all. She was slightly younger than Harriet, and had red hair and quick pale-blue eyes. She was waiting at the bus station, as slim as when they had last seen each other, dressed in a long flowery frock down to her ankles.

'You haven't changed a bit,' exclaimed Harriet.

'You have, but not all that much.'

'Oh me, yes, three kids later, what d'you expect?'

They stood uncertainly on the kerb while Harriet's suitcase was unloaded. 'Are we going to like each other?' said Helen.

'I think so. You must think I'm awfully idiotic or pushy, turning up like this so soon after you wrote to me.'

'No. I thought it was a good sign.'

'I've been a bit low. I just wanted a complete change of scene, but I'll try not to get in the way.'

'Don't be an idiot. I can tell it's going to be all right. I'm glad you've come to us.'

260

'Us?'

'There's a crowd of us live together. You'll have to share a room with me, d'you mind?'

Harriet felt stricken. The very thing she'd come for was to get away from people and making conversation, small talk, exchanges. What sort of people were they, and what sort of an effort would she have to make?

The place was an old house on The Terrace. The two women walked, taking turns to carry Harriet's suitcase, as Helen said it didn't seem worth getting a taxi. She pointed the house out ahead of them as they rounded out of Bowen Street. 'D'you like it?' she said.

'It's a bit far away to tell,' said Harriet.

Helen glanced at her. 'Hey, you're all in. Are you really ill?'

'No it's all right,' said Harriet, 'Don't worry about me.'

'But I will, can't you tell me?'

'I don't know how I can face your friends, that's all. I thought it was just you. It was silly of me to come, I just needed to get away so desperately. I can't describe the feeling. I don't know, I suppose it's a breakdown of some sort, only you're not supposed to have those where I come from, you're supposed to be all of a piece.'

'And you're not?' said Helen thoughtfully.

'I guess I'm not.'

'Hey, look,' said Helen. 'Why don't you just put yourself in our hands. I reckon it'll be a change for you. Why don't you go along with us, see how you like what we're doing, and if it doesn't work, well take off. Will you try?'

Harriet decided she had nothing much to lose. She wondered what Helen and her friends were involved in, and how profound a change was implied in Helen's words.

It turned out that only two young men were at home, whom Helen introduced as Rex and Stephen. Harriet gathered that there was another girl called Wanda who came and went. The house was a high-ceilinged place full of white light, with bars of red and gold striped across it where the evening sun shone through high stained-glass windows. It was furnished simply but pleasantly, and Harriet

261

felt her spirits lifting. Rex and Stephen were both bearded, and Stephen wore his hair long enough to tie back with a leather thong. He had a meal waiting for them, a big pot of fresh sweet corn, picked that morning at Otaki, he said. They had cold ham and slices of bread, with red wine to wash it down. They suggested she should sit on the floor with them on the big plaited mat in the front room, it was pleasanter than the kitchen and they could play some music.

As she began to eat, holding the corn in her fingers as they used to on the farm at Ohaka, Bob Dylan sounds filled the room. She felt herself melting into these people.

'I like your poetry,' said Rex, 'Helen showed it to us.'

'Thank you,' said Harriet. She felt vulnerable again. The last time people had talked to her about her writing, she'd cracked up. Was this to be another attack?

'I can't say you look like the sort of person who'd have written things like that,' said Rex.

'What do I look like?'

'A suburban matron. Very proper.'

So it was an attack. 'Do you always put people in categories?' said Harriet.

'You don't need to, mostly they put themselves into them. I guess there's exceptions. Who knows,' he said shrugging, 'Maybe you're one of them. What d'you think about the war?'

'The war? You mean Vietnam?'

Rex looked long-suffering. 'You really are an ostrich, aren't you? I thought as much.'

Helen looked at him warningly. 'Quit it, Rex,' she said. 'Harriet's been having a rough time.'

'Yeah, I'll bet. Provincial smugness — don't see a thing, don't let it bug you, she'll be right.'

'How can you be so sure you know so much about me?'

'Because I've been there, that's why. God, take Hamilton, where I come from, you wouldn't read about it. I was brought up there, my mother *my mother,* for God's sake, wears twinsets like yours. And she says what war, too.'

Stephen had been sitting quiet while this exchange took place. Harriet's eyes were full of tears that she was fighting to hold back. She wondered where she could go tonight. Why was nothing ever easy?

'Come on Rex, stop it,' Stephen said. 'Why don't we help Harriet relax a little. So you left your scene behind, so she's left hers, maybe for just a little while, but your only contribution is to force her into defending her position.'

'I wasn't even going to do that,' said Harriet in a small voice. She was searching through her mental pictures. Were Weyville and Camelot, really as bad as they made out? She hated Rex for making her so defenceless. She was in poor enough shape to start with.

'I'm sorry,' she said, 'Nobody briefed me that where I lived or what I looked like was a condition of your liking me.'

'I don't like or dislike you,' said Rex. 'I simply don't care about you.'

'That's a lie. You're very hostile.'

'Oh I am, am I?' said Rex, sitting up a bit straighter.

'You're a very hostile personality. Oedipus complex. Mother hatred. You only get on with women who aren't like your mother. Helen, do you have a dress like yours I can put on, so we can calm your friend?'

Rex flushed. 'Okay, okay, so you've got a tongue. Truce?'

'Was there a war?' said Harriet. 'What war?'

'Aaa-h. Funny lady.'

'Tell me what you're doing,' Harriet said. 'I know I'm ignorant, but I don't have to stay that way. You could try telling me.'

'Virgin soil,' said Rex.

'I don't know about that. I kind of forget what that was like, just a few bare patches.'

Stephen then started to tell her about the war in Vietnam, about kids who went off and got killed because people had persuaded them it was a good thing to do. They were being hoodwinked because the West's prosperity depended on keeping the war going, and the Yanks were backing a corrupt government. New Zealand was feeding living people into a war machine.

Rex interrupted and told her about the villagers and how innocent people were suffering, and how the guys who went over there lost their sense of humanity.

Harriet knew vaguely that what they were talking about made sense. She had read newspapers, she'd seen these things on television, but had felt detached. It was like Kennedy's assassination, when she'd been carrying Genevieve. They heard about it on the eight o'clock news, and it was a shock, kind of scary, but it didn't mean anything. At first she had thought that it meant *something*, that the assassination would change the world, and that the people who lived in Camelot — either the Kennedy Camelot or her own — would never be the same again. But it wasn't like that. She went out into the garden and called out to her neighbours and asked if they had heard the news. They had said yes, that chap Kennedy was shot, wasn't he? Funny business that, and then they asked her how she was. All day she'd wandered round, saying to people, 'Did you hear about Kennedy?' and most of them had. 'Never liked him much,' one of them had said, 'showed too much of the whites of his eyes.' And gradually, even as the shocking pictures had started to fill the newspapers, she realised that her world hadn't changed at all. Newspapers changed nothing.

She tried to tell Helen and her friends something of this, to communicate what it was like in the vacuum, how her life was full, and yet empty of reality. They listened; what she was saying made sense.

Did she want to commit herself? Did she want to stay empty, would she be too frightened to fill the blanks a little? She told them no, no, she would like to know more. What should she do?

There was to be a demonstration the following day. They expected two or three thousand people to march through the city to the American Embassy. It could be violent, and there were sure to be a lot of arrests. The arrests could be indiscriminate if there was a scuffle, and if she got in the way it could just as easily be her — was she prepared to take that risk?

An urgency was being generated among them all. More people

drifted in; some had been posting bills around the city, then a crowd turned up to complete some banners. She was afraid in one sense, but it didn't seem to be a deterrent. The fear was a strange emotion and it stayed with her for days — an emotion she could neither isolate nor recognise. She supposed at first that it must be fear of the consequences if Max found out she was doing these things, but on closer examination she knew that this was not so.

Whatever it was, she pushed it deep down inside her. She was talking again. They had released the springs inside her that had slowly been drying up in Weyville. The shutters were off and she could say things that nobody had wanted to hear for a long, long time. Some of them listened, others had private conversations of their own. Now she could tell people about things that were important to her, how she'd made herself stop caring and hidden her poetry and the story of her marriage to Denny — shameful secrets, yet they were so much a part of her that they made her what she was. She had been hiding them because people were afraid of being told things that might disturb the image of where they lived, of what they were building for themselves. Talking was healing.

Stephen said to her at last, 'Don't go too far too soon.'

'What d'you mean?' she said.

'You think you're healing yourself, don't you?'

'I am, I am,' she said vehemently.

'But before you heal you have to open up the old wounds and clean them out. That's what you're doing now. You mustn't open up too many all at once, because you'll go away from here with some of them still open and we won't be able to help.'

She nodded, an eager disciple, ready to listen to whatever he said.

'I think you should go to bed now,' he said. 'There'll be tomorrow. You can explore further tomorrow.'

The day dawned, bright, sharp, crystal clear, the way Harriet remembered Wellington at its best. She woke expecting to feel hung over, but she was not — it was as if some energy source had been trapped in her body, urging her on. Helen was already up, and came through with a cup of coffee for her as she was dressing.

'You okay?' she said.

'Feel marvellous,' said Harriet. 'I wasn't too idiotic last night, was I?'

'You were great. We all felt very close to you.'

Nobody had ever said that to her after she'd talked too much at a party. If only this nameless dread would lift. She did feel fine, but then it would surge up. She had to resist it and part of her energy must be diverted into suppressing it.

Helen asked her what she was going to do until eleven-thirty, which was the rallying time for the demonstration. She herself had to go to work, but she was taking the rest of the day off. Harriet had wondered how they lived. Helen said she was still doing library work, she was in a government department, and she had leave owing to her. It seemed that she tried to avoid taking long stretches of holidays, and instead kept time up her sleeve, so she could apply for leave when there was something on. She'd meant to take the whole day off, and maybe the following day too, but she'd promised to finish a cataloguing job so that some urgent material could be released. This responsible public servant aspect of her hadn't appeared the night before. It made what they were about seem all the more reasonable.

The others did various odd jobs. Rex was still a part-time student and several of the people who'd been in the night before were students. Stephen was one of the leaders of the protest movement, and had given up a promising career in law to devote all his time to it. He worked when he had to, but a lot of his time was spent looking after people who were suffering because of their political beliefs. People stayed with them if they got the sack, for instance, and there could be a big crowd through tonight. Stephen had been up north the day before and got in large supplies of cheap food, using a borrowed truck. This was the practical side of the movement. It wasn't all ideology and preaching and demonstrating.

Harriet decided to wander round the city, as she hadn't been there for so long that she felt like getting the feel of the place back again. Helen left her with instructions about meeting them in Tory Street soon after eleven, and Harriet set off.

Lambton Quay was quiet and almost deserted. She felt disorientated, wondering where to start, and not quite knowing what she wanted to do. She had very little money to spare. And what did she want to shop for? Unless ... the idea took hold of her. It was the most irresponsible thing she could think of doing and it wasn't very difficult to persuade herself, once she started. She hurried over to the post office on the far side of the street and wrote out a telegram at one of the booths. At the counter she very nearly turned and ran, but the woman was holding out her hand impatiently and calling, 'Next, please', so Harriet handed over the telegram to Max's parents saying that she had decided to stay a few days in Wellington and then return home.

Her next mission was to the airlines office to cash in her ticket to Christchurch. She was to have flown from Wellington and then, on her return, right through back to Weyville, which had just recently opened its new airport. She turned the money over in her hand with delight. It had been so easy. It was after ten and she didn't have a lot of time before meeting the others, so she found a toyshop and bought some presents for the children. She supposed that was silly if she was going to stay a few days, but it seemed necessary to justify the wad of money she had in her hand. Immediately she had bought them she remembered that she would have to carry her parcels all the way through town on the march.

On her way up Manners Street she spotted a canvas carry-all bag in a craft shop window. It was the sort you slung over your back if you were a very casual person, and was ideal for the things she was clutching in her hands now. The only trouble was, she wasn't a casual-looking person. But ideas seemed to be flowing thick and fast. She look round and saw what she was looking for, a tiny shop, wedged in amongst the larger shopfronts, that sold modern gear.

Ten minutes later she emerged in a long embroidered cheesecloth garment with a sleeveless suede jerkin over the top of it. The clothes she had been wearing had been done up in a neat parcel for her by the sales assistant, a fey-looking teenager with blonde hair down to her waist. The parcel was tucked up in the canvas bag with the others. She felt comfortable and daring at the same time, then downright scared when she saw someone walking towards her whom she thought she knew, and it was herself reflected in a shop mirror. If that's me, I don't know whether I can get on with me, she thought. I hope that woman I just saw is an okay person. She told herself sternly that it was merely a token gesture, though she knew it wasn't.

Helen had difficulty recognising her when she got to Tory Street, Harriet had run frantically the last part of the way, afraid she was late because she had stopped to buy some sandals. High heels looked ridiculous with her caftan and her feet were sore already, so she guessed she would have had trouble marching all the way back with the demonstration.

'We don't need any more revolutionary activity today,' Helen said when they'd found each other. 'You've done it all.'

'Like it?'

'You look terrific. You're still feeling good, then?'

Harriet assured her that she was. She saw what she thought was a flicker of concern cross Helen's face, but the crowd was building up and there was no time for chat.

The air was charged with urgency. People were starting to converge from all points, pouring up the side streets in swarms like ants. Stephen and Rex made their way over to Helen and Harriet with Wanda in tow, a vivid eccentric looking Maori girl, with a shock of wild black hair across her shoulders; her hair was decorated with a single white feather. A sort of procession was forming, straggly and uneven round the edges, but still a recognisable column. At its head young men were using loud hailers to instruct the crowd and Stephen broke away and joined them. Then Wanda threw her head back, and in a voice usually reserved for chants she cried 'Let my people free'. The crowd answered back with one voice.

The march was on the move. Wanda began to sing 'We Shall Overcome,' and again the huge procession responded, singing along with her. So they passed down through the streets, singing and chanting, surging like one great moving, weaving serpent. Harriet raised her voice with the others, emotion sometimes drowning her voice in her own ears. 'I am one with them, this is how I am meant to be', an inner voice was saying to her.

In Lambton Quay, a counter group was waiting for the marchers. Their mood was ugly. 'Get back to work' they screamed. 'Bloody commies! Stirrers! Troublemakers!' they howled as the procession kept on down the street. A bottle landed among some of the marchers up near the front, splintering on the road, Stephen called out on his megaphone, 'Keep on marching, don't respond, just keep moving.' Lambton Quay was no longer deserted, but a great seething mass, from one side through to the other and right down its whole length.

Outside Parliament Buildings, the police stood in a solid phalanx. 'Don't antagonise them,' Stephen bellowed at members of the march who had started to shout 'Pigs'!

Outside Parliament the crowd swelled with lunch hour workers who hadn't been able to take part in the march. There must have been another two or three thousand waiting there. It was impossible to tell how many people there were altogether, but news reports later in the day estimated eight thousand. 'One, two, three, four, we don't want your bloody war!' The chant swelled, erupting in a great chorus out of the crowd.

A man broke away, running for Parliament steps. A policeman hurled himself at him and brought him down with a flying rugby tackle; a minute later he was dragged bodily off to one of the nearby police vans. The demonstrators' mood changed, and the dense mass started pushing towards the police. Chaos broke out all around Harriet, who found herself being buffeted from side to side. Someone hit her on the side of the head, and she screamed at whoever it was. The police were in among the crowd. One policeman was hitting Rex, or Rex was hitting him, it was hard to tell, but he had blood streaming down his face. Harriet made her way across to him and started pulling at the policeman's arm. Rex saw her, and shouted 'Fuck off, you stupid bitch! Go on, piss off, Harriet — you don't have to be a bloody martyr.'

Another policeman closed on her from behind, locking her arms behind her. She collapsed passively to her knees and waited for the handcuffs to encircle her wrists, but miraculously he let her go, diverted by a new fracas close by. As she was trying to get to her feet, panic-stricken lest she be trampled, someone grabbed her by the arm, and she was pulled up and away to clear space outside the crowd. It was Stephen.

'Come on, let's move it, this crowd's turned nasty.' His face was white. 'Can you run?'

She shouted yes, above the noise, and they ran down towards the junction of Molesworth Street and Lambton Quay. At the corner he allowed her to rest a moment and then forced her on, turning up Bowen Street, past the Turnbull Library, and turning up onto The Terrace. She could feel a stitch developing in her side. 'I can't run any further,' she panted. 'Please, you go on up to the house without me, I'll be all right.'

He didn't leave her but instead guided her up Bolton Street, where they slowed down to a trot. They pushed their way into the old Bolton Street cemetery, a wild overgrown place, full of pioneer graves and gnarled trees. Only then would Stephen let her rest, as they collapsed onto a grave.

She huddled there, her breath coming in rasping sobs. At last she said, 'Did you start that diversion when the policeman had me?'

'Yes, I had to get you out of it, or they'd have come back and nabbed you.'

'Thank you,' she said, 'I don't know what I'd have done.'

He appeared not to be listening. 'Silly bastards,' he stormed, 'They shouldn't have fought, it doesn't help. Non-violent demonstration, they'll close us down, we won't be allowed to demonstrate if they do this. I told them, I told them.'

'Are you going back?' she asked him.

'What's the use?' he asked wearily. 'They'll have to sort it out for themselves now.'

The sun soaked into them, and for a while it was good just to sit there peacefully, away from the noise. Stephen was lost in his own thoughts and Harriet was trying to come to terms with the sort of person she had been that day. She'd changed her appearance, she'd thrown out careful family plans as of no importance whatsoever, she'd marched in a radical protest movement, she'd nearly been arrested. The whole thing was bizarre. Her elation grew.

Finally a small cold wind sneaked up on them. They both shivered, and Stephen, holding out his hand to help her up, said, 'Come on, we'd better go and find out what's happening to that lot.'

Harriet offered to buy some food, and he didn't refuse. She noticed that her money was dwindling. She'd have to watch that she had enough for the bus fare home.

He took her hand absently as they ambled up The Terrace, their flight no longer urgent.

Up at the house, there seemed to be general confusion. People were milling round aimlessly from room to room. Wanda had been taken into custody, and people were looking for Stephen to get some money out of their funds so they could post bail for her. Helen and Rex were nowhere to be seen, but it was said that Rex was at the hospital and Helen was with him. Everyone was hungry and dejected.

Stephen told Harriet that he'd have to go and do what he could for Wanda, and asked her if she'd be all right till he could come back and arrange some food. Harriet asked him if she could start feeding people, and he said that would be marvellous.

It was nine o'clock that night before she finished ladling out mountains of stew and mashed potatoes to the army of people who were going through the house. Stephen didn't appear for hours; there seemed to be more people in trouble at the police station, and he was trying to help as many as he could. Wanda turned up, but didn't stay for long, nor did she say whether she would be back or not. Helen brought Rex in, his head bandaged. He was frantic with anxiety because he hadn't been able to see out of one eye, but no-one at the hospital would listen when he tried to tell them. None of

271

the injured demonstrators had been given much sympathy; several officials had told them they were a pack of troublemakers who'd brought it all on themselves, and keeping them busy when more deserving cases needed their help. Rex had nearly been thrown out of the hospital when he'd started to tell a doctor that it would be a jolly sight worse for him if he had to go and look after the wounded in Vietnam, and he ought to be grateful that people were trying to protect him.

A few people wandered into the kitchen and started helping Harriet to clean up, and at last Stephen arrived. She'd saved him a meal which was going hard around the edges in the oven. He didn't seem to notice that, and sat at the kitchen table wolfing the food, before helping her to finish off the cleaning. Helen came through and said she'd put Rex to bed in her room, as he was feeling so bloody. Because Wanda's room was full, she asked whether Harriet would mind bunking down in Stephen's room. From the look on her face, Harriet guessed that she probably loved Rex.

There was an unmade bed in Stephen's room and a camp stretcher with a sleeping bag on it. Harriet asked Stephen if Rex had moved out of Helen's room the night before to make way for her. When he said yes, she asked why on earth Helen had invited her if it was going to be so inconvenient. Stephen simply said that they were always making accommodations like that for each other — it was the way things were there. She believed him.

As he prepared to get into the sleeping bag, she said, 'That looks awfully uncomfortable.' D'you want to get in with me?'

He climbed in beside her without comment, and put out the light. He had let down his hair, and as he turned beside her it swung across her face and she felt immersed into the fur springing from his body. He seemed to be dressed in a great coat of hair, his beard softer than she had expected against her shoulder. She lay tense as he put his hand across her.

'Cuddle me,' he said, against her ear.

She rolled towards him, putting her arm round him.

'I won't do anything, you know,' he said.

'I don't mind if you want to,' she said, quite truthfully, for it had been she who had invited him.

'It's all right love, I can't, I'm hopeless at screwing,' he said.

'Is there anything I can do?'she asked, committed now to the bed.

'Just holding me would be nice,' he murmured.

In the night she woke to find him masturbating against her thigh. She pretended to be still asleep, and, contented, he rolled back away from her and fell asleep again, leaving her wet and dismayed.

They sat around much of the following day in a desultory anticlimatic way. Nobody had much energy, and there was talk in the air of the government clamping down on demonstrations. It was a case of back to the drawing board, putting forward ideas for better crowd control, and so forth. Rex seemed better. He'd slept solidly till nearly midday, and when he woke up his vision was normal.

In the middle of the afternoon, someone caught a news bulletin. Lyndon Johnson had decided not to run for a second term as president of the United States, in view of the growing opposition to the Vietnam war. There was a stunned silent disbelief amongst them all, then joy. Somewhere, the protest movement was becoming effective, it wasn't all in vain. The mood of the place changed, the talk livened up. Stephen wanted to tell Harriet about the whole scope of the liberal movement throughout the world; these were things she must know.

Later in the afternoon she decided she should go and see about arranging to get home. She had a growing feeling that if she stayed here much longer she might never leave. It was hard to recall that she had three little children and a husband and a quarter acre section in Weyville.

Halfway down the street, the nameless, shapeless dread descended on her again, but this time there was no resisting it. It was so overwhelming that she had to lean against a lamp post, she felt so weak. And at last she could see it for what it was.

These people had irrevocably changed her life. She was not like the other people of Weyville, or she would have run a mile, a hundred miles, from her new friends. She could never go back and be exactly as she had been before, because now she knew she was different. The fabric of her life had been stripped bare. In a desperate attempt to hold on to the Harriet she had been, she found herself running down the street. She ran all the way to the railway station, and instead of arranging a seat on the bus for later in the week, she bought a ticket for that night's train. With the last of her money, she got a taxi back to the house on The Terrace and kept it waiting while she threw her things together, then had it drive her back to the station, after a round of hurried goodbyes. Stephen said, 'Too much, too soon?' and when she nodded, he added, 'Take care, you're one of us.' Then she left them all behind.

She got into Weyville in the early hours of the morning, and sat huddled in the station waiting room until morning broke, then she rang Max, and asked him to come and take her home.

It was nearly ten years since Mr Whitwell had offered her the less travelled road. At last, she had set foot on its narrow and dangerous way.

13

For nearly a month after her return, Harriet lived in a state of profound shock. For days at a time she sat, listless and withdrawn.

Max clearly resented the money spent on her adventure, whatever it was. She had told him little about what had happened in Wellington. She had said that at Helen's place she had simply felt homesick and decided not to go on to Christchurch, that she had wanted to come back to him and the children. In a sense, it was the truth, and it was also unarguable. Her new clothes had been put away in a drawer, and she moved from day to day, doing what had to be done for the children, like a sleepwalker. Max would enquire if she was still ill, and she had said that she supposed so, but that it would go away.

And she did feel as if she had some sort of sickness. There must be something wrong for her to reject her surroundings so completely. She had helped to make this home, she had borne these children, chosen to marry this man. What aberration was she suffering, that she now felt out of place? Some days she would shout at the children, as she had never done, and afterwards she would sit rocking backwards and forwards with one of them in her lap, particularly Emma, who was too small to resist and the most amiable about her mother's strange behaviour.

Slowly she began to feel better, to accept that she was a changed person and must face who she really was. She took out her new clothes, started to wear them, and, as winter was coming on, she made herself a couple of warmer garments, fashioned like the one

275

she had bought in Wellington. She took up the skirts she already had, for women were now wearing either long dresses or minis. Genevieve and Peter were both going to morning kindergarten, and Emma slept well during the day, so that she began to organise her time better. The first day that the house was quiet she got out her typewriter and laboriously typed out some new work, the first she had tried for a long time. A neighbour rang while she was working to see how she was — she had heard, she said, that Harriet wasn't quite herself these days. Harriet told her that she was very well indeed, thank you, and that she was working at the moment. The woman at the other end sounded mystified, and said how dreary it must be. Housework did get to you, and she'd pop down and have coffee with her to give her a break. Harriet had replied firmly that she was working at her writing, and that it really needed absolute quiet. Though she was grateful for the offer of company, she said, she would rather be on her own. As her caller was quite unaware that Harriet had this 'little interest' as she later called it, she hung up somewhat offended. Harriet had been amazed at how easy it was.

This became the pattern of her days. From time to time she emerged in what the locals of Weyville described as her 'weird gear'. Harriet Taylor had always been difficult, they agreed, but now she was eccentric.

Max's behaviour in the face of these changes was strangely ambivalent. He made no comment, even appearing not to notice particularly. He took his trip to Rotorua, and came back as edgy and difficult as Harriet had been when she returned from Wellington. She supposed they had grown apart.

One morning she was sitting at her typewriter, picking away, and trying to recall what little she had learnt at the Weyville College's night classes, when the phone rang. She cursed it, even though it rang little these days, for the word had gone out that she was not very approachable. It was Don Everett. She gave a guilty start, knowing that she had been very neglectful of Miriam recently, who had been nothing if not kind to her through many trials.

She could hear herself being over-effusive. 'I've been meaning to ring Miriam for ages,' she said. 'She must have written me off. You must call in and have a drink with us some evening, both of you. I don't know, Max and I seem to have been a bit preoccupied lately.'

'That's all right,' he said. 'I've been thinking about you a lot, that's all. I'm very proud of all the work you've been publishing.'

'And so you should be, it was you that gave me a push in the right direction. I was beginning to think you'd forgotten that. Anyway, where are you ringing from?'

'Home, actually,' he said, after a short pause. 'I had a couple of days' leave that I had to use up or I'd lose them, so here I am. Why don't you come round and see me? Have a cup of coffee?'

'I can't do that, Emma's asleep.'

'Oh yes. Emma. I shouldn't forget her, should I?'

'Why don't you come round and see me then?'

'Would you mind?'

'Of course not. I'd love to see you.'

When she hung up she thought wryly, 'Now there is a turnup for the books, asking Don Everett round to have coffee in mid-morning, for all the women of Camelot to see. And why the hell shouldn't I?'

It was almost as if Don had been waiting in the wings, she reflected later. As if there was a point at which he had said to himself, ah, yes, now she's ripe for the picking.

She felt that Don's arrival demanded some special effort on her part. After the last time they had been alone together something was surely required. God, sitting up in bed in the hospital looking lumpy and tearful, with her great swollen boobs. There didn't seem to be a lot to do besides taking her apron off and putting some lipstick on. She wondered if he would prefer her crouched over the typewriter or looking domestic. A bit of both, perhaps. She left the typewriter out on the table, and started grinding the coffee.

She let him in a few minutes later, wearing the same battered mac that he had worn to the hospital. 'I'll take your coat,' she said, assuming that he'd stay a long time.

As she hung it on the hall rack he said, 'And how is Emma?'

'All right. She's different to my other babies. Would you like to see her?'

'We won't wake her?'

'Not a show, she keeps her waking up bits for the middle of the night. You don't really want to see her though, do you? You were just being polite.'

'I think I would like to, actually. After all, I stood in as her dad.'

'Oh ... you're not going to let me forget that, are you?'

'How could I? It's something I can't forget.'

He followed her into the child's toy-strewn bedroom. No wonder Max broke his leg, she thought. And I bet Don thinks so too. Miriam would never leave a room littered like that. Emma lay peacefully, sucking the edge of the grubby blanket that she always kept with her.

'Is she walking?'

'Just.'

'She's lovely,' he said. 'I'd have liked a daughter.'

'Well,' said Harriet as they closed the door, 'What a pity we don't give our children godparents, you could have been hers. Max would like it if I suddenly started bestowing godmothers and godfathers on all our children. It would make them more respectable.'

'But you're not, are you, Harriet?'

'Respectable? Probably not. Though I tried it for a while.'

'And didn't like it?'

'I did it badly. I suppose you know I had a ... crack-up, I think Max calls it.'

'Well, I did hear something.'

'I'll bet you did. What are they saying about me out there in the wasteland?'

'You're hard on them. They do like you, you know.'

'Oh I know,' she replied impatiently. 'I like them, too. I just don't want to do the same things that they want to do.'

'You've changed,' he said.

'Yes, I've changed. But don't tell me that's a brand new discovery.' She poured coffee into pottery mugs.

'Why do you say that?' he asked.

'You know perfectly well you wouldn't have come round here in the middle of the day like this to sit and have coffee with me if I was just the same as before.'

'Am I that transparent?'

'I don't know, Don. All right, I've changed. I can't gauge how much, except through other people's reactions to me. I suppose I watch them a bit harder now. Narcissism. I expect to see a reflection of my own behaviour.'

She shifted a pile of yesterday's unfolded washing so that he could sit down. 'I'm a slack housewife,' she observed. 'Miriam's a much better doer than I am.'

'It's not the be-all and end-all.' He stirred his coffee more than was necessary. She saw that his hand was shaking. 'There was something I wanted to ask you,' he said miserably.

'If it's about going to bed with me, don't sound so unhappy about it. The worst may never happen. I might say no.'

He shook his head. 'I really don't understand you.'

'No. Well, that can't be helped. The point is, you want to, don't you? All right, I can see the answer's yes, but you feel really bad about it, and terrible about Miriam and Max. If I said no, you'd be awfully relieved and you could go on lusting innocently after me, if there is such a thing as innocent lust. I suppose not, what's the Bible say? He who commits adultery in his heart is just as guilty . . .' she broke off.

'Then how do you feel about Max?'

'Oh, all right. We're just not — very together at the moment.'

'I wouldn't help that then, would I?' he said.

'I don't know, do I? I don't know what you're like.'

'Where would we . . .?' he searched round desperately, seeking an escape. Serves you right, she thought, serves you darn well right if I do go to bed with you.

As she helped him undress, she reflected that so far she was making a fairly conventional mess of being different. There wasn't much she could do about it, though — she had to start somewhere. He got his zip caught in the corner of his singlet, and they had to perform a delicate operation to get it undone without breaking it completely. She knelt on the floor so that she could get a better grip on it, and thought she might lose an eye in the process. They were in Peter and Genevieve's bedroom and a rubber toy squealed as they collapsed on a bed.

'You're so maternal,' Don panted as they began their exertions.

It turned out to be much more successful than either of them had anticipated. The difference between herself and Miriam turned out to be quite simply that Harriet enjoyed making love and Miriam didn't, according to Don. Judging by the initial urgency of their encounter, it was probably true that Don had a fair bit of lost time to make up.

Being a scarlet woman in Weyville proved easier than Harriet had imagined, at least for a while. Don would take an early lunch, park his car down the road and walk up to Harriet's. She kept the curtains closed in the children's bedroom until he came so that the neighbours wouldn't see them being drawn after his arrival. Not that she had any illusions that they didn't notice him mooching towards her place at regular intervals.

They tried to devise different ways for him to come; some days he parked his car in the opposite direction so that he had to pass a different set of neighbours, then they thought of the back way, but that was more obvious than subtle. The people at the back certainly had food for thought when they saw Don Everett climbing the Taylors' back fence.

There was always the terrifying thought that Max might slip home for some reason or other. He was not in the habit of doing so, and yet there was always the nasty thought in the back of her mind that he might forget his wallet, or spill coffee over his trousers and have to come back and change them. There were endless variations on this theme, but Max never appeared, and as the affair continued and prospered, these thoughts receded and were finally shelved.

Difficulties arose when Emma decided to take her nap in the afternoons. Harriet had been afraid of this, and was surprised that she had taken so long to conform to the others' pattern in this respect. This meant that there was nearly always a child awake in the house somewhere. The first few times that Emma woke up from her morning sleep, if they were still in bed, Harriet would say that she'd be all right in her cot. She started to get nasty suspicions that there might be a God lurking around somewhere, despite her attempts to exorcise Him (or Her, a recent notion). Surely there must be some just being who would strike down such a wanton woman as herself, fornicating in the house where her child was. Don found it difficult to resist Emma's urgent pleas for Mum-mum to come and rescue her, and Harriet, too, would begin to imagine that she might have her fingers jammed or be choking to death with her head through the bars. With sighs and embraces they would extricate themselves, and Harriet would go through to rescue her child. Then they would sit around the kitchen table like any good family, and Harriet would make coffee while Don fed the child pieces of biscuit and baby-talked to Emma. There were times when she thought he really did believe he was Emma's father.

Harriet had alienated herself from the neighbourhood to the point where asking people to have the children was difficult except in emergencies, and she didn't think it would be clever to draw more attention to her activities by inviting any of the women round about to look after her children at the same time that Don was beating a track to her door.

The whole matter demanded an unexpected amount of ingenuity and resourcefulness. On the weeks that it was her turn to do the kindergarten run, for she did still have that link with a few nearby families, she took to spending quite large parts of the morning helping out at kindergarten and chatting amiably to other mothers. People were generally surprised. Harriet was coming right again, they said, she's making an effort. In the rush to be supportive, a number of them responded to Harriet's rediscovered warmth. Some of them had children who were friendly with the two older Taylor children. It took only a week or two for Harriet to come up with the idea that what they all needed was a proper break from the children every now and then. A whole day would be wonderful. Absolute heaven, agreed the other mothers. Then why, Harriet suggested, with a low cunning which astounded even her, did they not arrange a day or so a week when she took someone else's child, or children, home in the afternoon, and they could do the same for her on other days? As they said, only Harriet could have thought of an idea like that.

It meant of course that Don couldn't come quite so often, but it worked. Instead of having an early lunch hour, he took a late one on the afternoons that Harriet's children were playing in another part of Weyville, and Emma had been put down to sleep.

Harriet also rejoined the theatre group that she had belonged to before her marriage. This meant that she could leave the theatre early and Don could meet her for an hour on the way home.

His problems about telling Miriam where he was going seemed to have vanished. After all, with the effort she was putting into their affair, it was only right that he should try to be as inventive as she was. Though, to be sure, in the back seat of his car down at the Weyville lake front, she found that she needed to be a little more inventive than in the old days of her escapades on that same spot. 'Ah,' Don would sigh, 'You make me feel very young again.' She wondered if he realised just how young. Some might have called it juvenile, but she didn't think she really cared.

That was possibly because she thought that she might be in love with him. They often said that they loved one another, and late in 1968, Harriet began to think that it might be true.

It had been a strange year. She and Max were ambling along more amiably than they had done in a long time. The fact that she had to be generally expansive to people in order to get her way and her freedom, (the two were not necessarily synonymous, but that was how she saw them) seemed to spill over into their relationship. Before her trip away, Max had seemed to have a hunted look but now he seemed more assured, less jumpy. Harriet congratulated herself in having managed to live so comfortably with two men, though she felt twinges of guilt about having deceived Max. There seemed little point in labouring this point, though; it seemed far better for everyone concerned to leave things the way they were. Even Miriam looked happier when she saw her. Harriet imagined that she and Don must be more contented, now that Don was not putting pressure on Miriam.

When the two couples met from time to time, as they still did, Harriet would catch herself out every now and then, taking up some point that she and Don had been discussing the day before, forgetting that the others didn't know the background to the conversation. Don would flush and catch Miriam's eye, as Harriet broke off in mid-sentence, but Miriam would smile tolerantly and say, 'You two are simpatico, you can read each other's minds,' and pour everyone another sherry.

Yes, it seemed cosy, here inside Camelot. The world outside had been thundering with disasters, and Harriet followed them with keen interest. Don professed himself a closet radical, and seemed glad to have someone to talk to when the second Kennedy murder took place and then the assassination of Martin Luther King. Talking to him made Harriet feel less isolated. He also continued to take an interest in her poetry, and by and large, people in Weyville were beginning to be rather proud of their strange prodigy, even if Harriet's nearest neighbours did shake their heads darkly as if they knew of dark deeds that they were not prepared to discuss. Whatever the rumours, Harriet, being a little different, must have allowances made for her, the more enlightened souls of Weyville thought. At the theatre group she was very much favoured, despite the fact that she confined her talents to play readings and refused parts in major productions because of the children. She had been tempted, to be sure, but as the theatre was a means to an end, she felt that such a wholesale commitment might hinder rather than help her efforts on behalf of Don.

She and Max agreed that each would have one night out a week. He had taken up with the local gun club, and seemed to derive a great deal of pleasure from it. His evenings out were idyllic for Harriet. When the children were down to sleep she would put her feet up, turn the television off, unless Julie Felix happened to be on, and read till her eyes were dropping out of her head, or else she would get on with some of her work. Since the children had changed their routines, Max's evenings out were the only times she had the house to herself, unless one counted the time she made for Don's visits. She was content with this bit of borrowed time, for now she was beginning to see that things would improve, that she would not always be tied to the same timetables. Genevieve was due to start school at the beginning of the next school year, and that fact opened up new prospects. A year after that Peter would be at school, and then Emma would be at kindergarten. Of course things became easier, even if it was sometimes hard to keep on believing that.

Sometimes, just occasionally, she looked at herself, and wavered.

The theatre group held a demonstration of mime all one Saturday. The artist and instructor, was a Frenchman visiting New Zealand, and by a rare stroke of cultural good fortune, he included Weyville on his itinerary. The theatre was blacked out, the stage bare, he was lit only by a single spotlight, yet he created magic. He walked for miles, an old man getting tired towards the end of some journey which had started with meaning and lost its point by the end, without ever leaving the place where his feet thlip-thlopped out the rhythm of the old man's footsteps. He made them cry, he made them laugh, without so much as a sound from his lips. He was a trapped man in a cage, his hands flat and frantic on the invisible walls until he found the exit. Harriet watched, spellbound.

In the afternoon, he invited the group to learn some basic principles of his art. They followed him with enthusiasm, engrossed in the emotions he drew from them, revealing more of themselves and to each other than they knew was there to tell. As the session was closing, he suggested that they escape from a cage as he had done. Utterly outside of herself, Harriet knelt on the floor, her hands in her armpits, beating her elbows against her body. The man came over, and stood watching her.

'You are a bird then, not a person, yes?'

'I am a bird,' she replied.

'Why can you not get out of the cage then, little one?'

She looked up at him in real anguish. 'Because I have fallen out of the sky. I never learnt to fly properly, don't you see?'

'Ah, poor, poor bird,' he said turning away.

She sat on the floor weeping, her arms wrapped around her legs. Why had she done that? In the recesses of her mind, a cloud of sparrows appeared, falling away from a great soaring bird. She knew she had seen them before.

So the year slid away, with Don and Harriet unresolved in their feelings towards each other. In August Miriam was away on a ten-day course and the boys went off on holiday. This period had greatly enhanced Don's and Harriet's activities, for it meant that Harriet was able to get away to his house once or twice. 'There's nothing like a change of environment,' she said, and he laughed, looking at his all too familiar striped flannel sheets and the pictures on the wall that he saw every morning when he awoke.

At Christmas there was a break of six weeks or more because of school holidays, but it was not intolerable, they agreed. The Everetts went away on a family expedition to the South Island, and the Taylors went north to Whangarei to see the Wallaces for the first time since Emma's birth. Mary and Gerald were pleased to see their daughter looking so contented and Gerald went so far as to take his son-in-law aside and compliment him on taming his daughter, 'after all the trouble we had with her, you know.'

After their return, towards the end of January, something upset Max. He suddenly became profoundly irritable and morose. Harriet treated it as of no consequence at first, but after a few days she began to panic. Had he found out about her? she wondered. Had someone talked? She had come to take her luck for granted. She was unfair and she should be made to pay. It didn't matter how one might toy with the concept of emancipation; she was a cheat and the penalties were bound to be extracted.

She tackled him one evening in early February. They had been gathering plums from one of the first trees they had planted on the section, and in the gold, still evening, life looked peaceful enough on the surface. Had she done something, she asked him? Why was he so unhappy?

He turned on her with a look of what she read as pure hatred. 'For Christ's sake, leave me alone,' he said.

285

She heard the car backing out of the garage a few minutes later, and he didn't return till late that night. She had gone to bed but was lying awake, tensed and waiting for him to come back.

'Are you awake?' he said, as he came into the room.

'Yes.'

He switched the light on. His face was wan and he looked old. 'Harriet, it's nothing to do with you. Please believe me, I can't say anything more than that.'

'Are you in some sort of trouble?'

He hesitated briefly. 'No,' he said. 'Let's just say that I've got a few of my ideas mixed up.'

'Like I did last year?'

'Something like that.'

The next morning he behaved as if nothing had happened, although he still looked pale. The matter wasn't mentioned again, and he made what she believed to be a deliberate attempt to be pleasant to her. His expression in the garden that evening continued to trouble her. That was not her only problem. Don hadn't been in touch with her since the Everetts' family holiday.

She was in the butcher's shop one day, and just as she was buying her weekend roast, she glanced sideways and saw Miriam and Don sitting in the car outside, watching her. They waved when she turned around, but had driven off by the time she paid for her meat. It was disturbing and she decided to ring Don at work the following week, now that Miriam was back at school.

But it was Miriam who rang her first, on Monday after school. 'You haven't been down for such a long time,' she said. 'Why don't you pop over and tell me how Genevieve's getting on at school?'

Genevieve was, in fact, tired, and Harriet wasn't enthusiastic about trundling everybody over to Miriam's, but on the whole it seemed to be a good idea to go. Miriam appeared delighted to see her. She talked with great enthusiasm about what they had done on their holidays. It all sounded terribly energetic. Harriet thought that if she were married to Don it would be a terrible effort to keep up with him on holiday. Marry Don? What on earth was she on

286

about? 'I beg your pardon?' she said to Miriam, having missed entirely what she had been saying.

'I said, we saw you in the butcher's shop on Friday.'

'Yes, I saw you too, you'd gone when I came out.'

'Such a pretty outfit you had on. You're getting quite daring, taking your skirts up as high as that, aren't you?'

'They do seem to be the fashion.'

'You've got the legs for it, but my dear, if I may say so, I think you may be going a little far. Your suspender was showing underneath the hem, you can get those panty hose now. If you're going to wear them quite as short as that, I really think you should see what you can do about it.'

'Is that what you were looking at?' She had nearly said 'staring'.

'Well, yes, actually it was. Don noticed first, he said she can't get away with that, someone should tell her. So I thought, well, for your own good Harriet, better for me to tell you.'

Harriet rang Don the next day in a bitter fury. 'How dare you discuss me with your wife like that?' she shouted into the phone.

'Hush, I can't talk to you now.'

'Don't you want to talk to me at all?' He hung up. A few minutes later as she was preparing another onslaught, he rang her back.

'Look,' he said, 'I'm in someone else's office now. I couldn't talk to you before. Don't take any notice of Miriam, she was putting words in my mouth and she repeated them back to you to be a bit spiteful.'

'Why should she be? Does she suspect us?'

'Well ... she did say one or two things on holiday.'

'I see,' she whispered. 'Can't you come over and see me? I need to see you terribly. I could make a bit of free time tomorrow.'

'I'll see what I can do,' he promised as he hung up. She rang Cousin Alice and asked her if she could bring the children over. She rarely did this, for it seemed as if she was imposing on her ageing relative. Cousin Alice said she loved to see the children, but Harriet knew she couldn't cope with them for long. She had given up golf the previous year, and her step was much slower than Harriet remembered it from the days when she lived with her.

However, on this occasion Harriet was desperate enough to ask her to have Emma for an hour or so in the morning. Just one child didn't seem too great an imposition.

After she had left Emma with Cousin Alice, she rang Don and told him that she was free. He appeared furtively at the back door twenty minutes later.

'What did Miriam say?' Harriet asked almost immediately.

'Nothing much. She just threw out a few hints that she had her eye on us. I thought I'd let the dust settle a bit before I came back.'

'You could have told me.'

'I was going to, but it sounded cold over the phone, so I thought when it was safe I'd come and tell you.'

'Everything's safe now,' she said.

In bed, she said, 'Would you like to be married to me?'

'Is that a proposal?' he asked, trying to turn away the question.

'Would you like to be?' she persisted.

'Well of course, I would,' he said 'but you don't want an oldie like me.'

'I do, I do,' she said. It all seemed so sane, so reasonable; she didn't know why she hadn't been able to see it before. She and Don had lovely times together. Max didn't love her any more, he might even hate her, and she gave Don a better time than Miriam did. Obviously they should be married to each other.

'I'm serious, Don,' she said, 'Please, the children would love you.'

'Yours might at their age, but mine wouldn't. They're too old.'

'You've thought about it, then?'

'Dreams are free.'

'You dream about being married to me? Then we could, don't you see?'

Don shook his head. 'It wouldn't work. You'd get tired of me, we'd get pulled apart by our children.'

'We could have some more. I could have a baby with you.'

'Is that your answer to everything, Harriet? Just have another baby?'

She sat up, as hurt as if he'd slapped her. 'I thought you liked my babies.'

'I do,' he said. 'But sooner or later you'd have to stop having them when things went wrong, and I'm sure there could be plenty to go wrong with us.'

'Are you breaking it off, then?'

'Not exactly.'

'You mean you want to have your cake and eat it too? We just go on and on sneaking a bit of afternoon here, a bit of morning there, a quickie in the back seat of your car? God, what sort of a life is that?'

'It was all right before.'

'But it's stopped being all right, don't you see? What are you afraid of, the scandal?'

'I wouldn't like to hurt Miriam,' he said.

'Miriam! I thought you liked being with me better.'

'I do. But Miriam's my wife.'

They seemed to have reached a stalemate. Don asked if he could come back next week if she could make some time.

Through the weeks that followed, Harriet continued to fight internal battles. She wanted him, she wanted to possess him, she seemed to have always lived half a life, and Don would give her a whole one. She and Max were barely speaking to each other. He came and went, and was gone more often than he was home. She was too wrapped in her own misery to notice properly. It was the silence of mutual self-absorption rather than of open hostility.

They were into April when Miriam rang one afternoon and said that she and Don would like them to come over that evening. They had something to talk over with Harriet and Max. They would send one of their boys over to babysit for a while.

Harriet smelt so much danger in the air that she was, once again, going to say no, but she said yes because it appeared a safer decision. She told Max, who said he was too busy to go. It was only when she pointed out that they hadn't been anywhere together for a long time and she didn't often ask him to go places with her that he finally agreed. Besides, on second thoughts, he seemed to be interested in what the Everetts wanted to talk to them about.

By the time dark fell and the children were asleep, it was raining. The Everetts' elder son John turned up to babysit about eight o'clock, and even though they were only half a block away, Max suggested that they take the car. There seemed no point in getting drenched, and he could run John home if it was still raining later.

The lights were all on in the verandah of the Everetts' brick bungalow. There was an air of permanence and solidity about the place, as if it was an impregnable part of the landscape, an enduring symbol of suburban Weyville. Like a fort, Harriet thought foolishly as they splashed across the concrete drive, water running in a steady stream as the rain pelted down.

At the door Miriam greeted them too brightly, or so it seemed to Harriet. Yet everything looked the same; the pictures hadn't shifted, the bright scatter rugs on the polished floor were all in the same place, the comfortable big linen-covered armchairs hadn't been shifted. Only Don looked out of place in his own home. He was sunk on one of the chairs, all angles, hands and feet not knowing where they should be. He looked at Harriet abjectly when she came in.

It was too late to run. There was nowhere to run to. But before she had come, there had been nowhere to go. The feeling had communicated itself to Max. He looked edgily at the door, and resigned himself. Whatever was to be could not be stopped. Nice for him, thought Harriet — what does he have to worry about? Except knowledge. Yes, Max was going to have to wear knowledge.

The rituals were beginning. Miriam poured them all sherries, rather large ones. Harriet didn't like Miriam's taste in sherry, which was too sweet for her, but still it was a drink and there was no denying that she needed one.

The opening gambits were performed by Miriam too, once she'd settled herself in an armchair. They were all seated now, Miriam contriving to look relaxed, with a cigarette, blowing fine blue smoke out of her nose, cradling her sherry in her hands.

'Don and I think it's time we had a little talk to you two,' said

Miriam, finally having arranged the scene to her satisfaction, or perhaps as far as was possible without prolonging things any further.

Max said stiffly, 'If it's about our personal lives, don't you think that's between Harriet and myself?'

'I wish it was,' said Miriam. 'But life is never as simple as that, is it, Max?'

Harriet was looking at Max in surprise. It was almost as if Miriam and he were sharing knowledge from which she, Harriet, were excluded. That was impossible. Whatever secrets there were in the room were between her and Don, or should have been.

'You've got yourself in quite a mess, haven't you, Max?' Miriam was saying.

'Your grapevine seems to be working efficiently,' said Max. 'Is that what you brought us over here for? So you could tell my wife what your rotten little network's come up with? I suppose this is what you call coming out with things in the open. Not talking behind my back.'

Miriam was starting to unwind now. She was getting the bit between her teeth.

'You young people,' she said, 'So self-centred. It affects us.'

Harriet looked from one to the other of them, bewildered.

'That's nonsense,' said Max, starting to get to his feet. 'What goes on in our household has nothing to do with yours.'

'Just a minute, we'll come to that,' said Miriam, mysteriously. She was taking on the appearance of a soothsayer, sitting under the lamplight. She appeared to have inhabited her chair forever.

'What does Max know?' said Harriet sharply. 'If you don't say what you have to, I'm leaving. Don't think I don't mean it, because I do. Don't under-estimate me, Miriam.'

'Nor you me,' said the other woman. Then, 'All right, Max, about the suit Roy Mawson's filing against you. What are you going to do about it?' It was out, or part of it. Max looked at Harriet.

'I was going to tell you,' he said.

'Suit, what suit?' said Harriet.

291

'There you are, are you satisfied with what you've done to her?' Max said to Miriam. 'Go on, tell her the rest.'

'Like you said, that's for you to tell Harriet,' Miriam responded. It was like some crazy game.

Max cupped one hand and squeezed the other into a ball, banging them together. 'Elaine Mawson's husband is petitioning for a divorce. Roy's named me as corespondent. We spent a weekend in Taupo last year ... he found the receipts.'

'The fishing weekend?' Harriet asked. He nodded. 'And the gun club nights?' He didn't need to reply.

She sat, stunned. Twice in a lifetime? Surely not. What sort of woman was she? Not one that kept her man, that was for sure. She looked towards Don, hunched in his chair. Perhaps she was to be allowed this one. She wanted him. Loved him? Perhaps. They could be all right together. If he'd let them be. But would he? He looked away from her.

'I don't know why you had to interfere,' Max was saying to Miriam.

'Because I don't want to lose my husband,' said Miriam, rising from her chair and pouring more sherry, for herself first, and for the others by way of token. 'We have a good life, Don and I. We've got two sons, we've a good home, we have a good compromise. I saw him restless, and I let it go. It'll pass, I told myself. The girl's unhappy too, and who's to blame her, always a fish out of water in this neighbourhood. There was a time when I was a bit like her myself, all past now, I've felt — sorry for her? Yes, I suppose I have. If he has to choose someone, I should be glad it's her. So I let it go.'

Neither of their names had been spoken, yet everyone in the room knew that it was Harriet and Don of whom she was speaking. Don said, 'Miriam, you have no right,' and broke away.

Max looked at Harriet with disbelief and scorn. 'You wanted him? You've had him?'

'And I said to myself,' continued Miriam's relentless voice, 'Her husband's playing the field, not that one could altogether blame him either, so why shouldn't I let it go a bit? But Max was silly and got caught. So he's going to have to make some decisions. So I wanted to tell you Harriet, that if you're on your own, I'm sorry, but you don't get my husband.' She polished a fingernail delicately with the hem of her dress. 'He's had his bit on the side.'

'She knew all the time?' said Harriet, appealing to Don, asking him to tell her that it wasn't true. He nodded.

'Pretty well,' he said.

'You told her things about us?'

Don continued to sit, his head bowed now, seeming to shake, as if he was weeping.

'You're sick,' Harriet said to Miriam.

Miriam raised a pencilled eyebrow. 'Possibly, though, some people enjoy bad health,' she said.

'That's disgusting,' Harriet stood up. 'I am leaving.' At the door she stopped and turned, 'What made you think he was so safe with me? He might have left you for me.'

'It was always a risk,' said Miriam. 'I considered it. Oh yes, I thought about it a lot. But you see, Harriet, it seemed to me that he had less to concern himself about making a respectable woman of you.'

'You bitch. Oh you bitch,' said Harriet softly.

'Whereas Max has a different problem. The opposite, one might say. I must admit, Harriet, I couldn't risk your availability.'

Harriet ran out into the driveway. The rain was still teaming down. Don caught her up at the edge of the verandah, as she backed away from the downpour. She didn't have the car keys, and the only escape route was through the rain.

'I'm sorry,' he mumbled.

'Oh for Christ's sake, piss off,' she shouted. The Everetts' milk bottles were standing on the side of the porch waiting to be put out for the night. Harriet stooped, swiftly taking one by the neck, and, as she straightened, she smashed it on the side of the house. Glass broke around them, rain, explosions. She half crouched in the rain, ready to pounce on Don with the bottle.

'The other answer, Harriet?' said Don, his eyes a mixture of sorrow and fear.

293

A hand like a steel band gripped her wrist, squeezing it until her fingers opened in spite of herself. The broken milk bottle fell out of her hand, tumbling away into the begonias.

It was Max. 'I'll open the car door for you,' he said. He frog-marched her to the car without speaking to Don, holding onto her arm until he had thrown her into the car and shut the door on her.

He backed jerkily and very fast down the driveway, forgetting to put his lights on until they were some distance up the road. Then he accelerated away past the turn-off to their house, at the end of the block. Harriet lay back in her seat, dazed. They were heading away from the town in the direction of the mill. The car ran along a road bordered by the brooding spikes of pine trees. The windscreen wipers didn't seem to be working properly so that the water bucketed across onto her side and she could hardly see where they were going, just moving into the great menacing dark outside with no relief, no holes in the black. He is going to take me into the forest and kill me, she thought. She wondered if she should jump out of the racing car, but she felt too tired. She might live, and then they might expect her to cope with pain. More pain. It might, conceivably, be worse than this.

After what seemed a long time, but what was probably no more than ten minutes or so, Max pulled the car over to the side of the road, under a clump of pines which grew close to the road. They formed a shelter, easing away the rain, and Harriet could see that the car was on a rise overlooking Weyville. She supposed that he was going to be angry with her. It occurred to her that she could as easily be angry with him. Elaine Mawson, for God's sake. That mousy permed little blonde. Still, she had spoken up for her at a dinner party on the night she and Nick Thomas had done battle. It seemed like a different lifetime.

'I'm sorry,' she said.

'Isn't everybody?' he replied.

'Are you going to go with her?'

'I wanted to.'

'I won't stop you.'

'Past tense. I stopped, oh, a long time ago. It seemed to have gone too far. Meant to break it off after Christmas. After we'd been away.'

'It seems everyone meant to. The great summer reunion. What happened?.

'I got caught. Very conventional — angry husband. When I was getting round to finishing it.'

'Funny how they never cotton on until the fun's over, isn't it?' Harriet said.

He grimaced. 'I thought you'd appreciate that. Even before I knew about Don. Don!' he repeated in amazement. 'For God's sake, Harriet. You can't want *him*.'

'Probably not. It would mean more babies. He's right. I don't really want them.'

'Babies. You and Don. Christ.' They sat in silence for a while.

'They won't do anything, he said. 'The Everetts. But I'm in trouble. I'll go away if you want the house.'

'D'you really want to go away?'

'I don't want to stay here.'

'Neither do I,' said Harriet.

They looked at each other, the lights from the dashboard throwing them into profile. Harriet thought, you wouldn't stand out in a crowd. But we noticed each other. Somehow we noticed each other. He spoke first.

'Shall we leave Weyville?' he said.

She looked out across the flat plain below them. The lights were like smudges on the horizon. Somewhere down there her children were sleeping. She'd had the full toll extracted from her in that town.

'It wouldn't be the same,' she said. 'Things can't be the same between us. There would have to be change.'

'I could say the same.'

'I can survive without you. I have been by myself before.'

'What's the price?' he said.

'Your life and mine.'

'You strike a hard bargain.'

'Yes,' she said, 'but we don't have much choice, do we? You no

295

more than I. You can change the order, but in the end it's much the same.'

Max organised a transfer to Wellington; one presented itself as if by magic within days of their decision to leave Weyville. They lost heavily on the house. A tavern had been built nearby when they sold up and for the time being it had depressed values in Camelot. The buyers of their house were in a position to beat them low, and they had no idea what they would be able to purchase in Wellington. There was no other place that Harriet could conceive of going, once the proposition had been put to her. It was the right place for them; somehow they would contrive to begin again.

Miriam and Don offered to have a farewell party for them, but after effusive thanks, they turned the proposal down. Cousin Alice was Harriet's main concern in leaving the town. Very early on the morning that they left, she drove over by herself, to say goodbye. Her cousin, on sticks now, was wearing her dressing gown. The monkey puzzle trees, a little ragged these days, glimmered in one of the winter's first frosts. Max and the children had been in for a meal the night before and they had all said their farewells then. The old woman clung to her, dropping her sticks. Harriet had been more than a daughter to her, she said.

'And you've been more than a mother,' Harriet said. 'Better and worse.'

'You'll come back?' Cousin Alice said.

'Someday, to see you,' Harriet said, 'but not for a long time. Weyville seems to have got a bit small for me.'

'No,' said Cousin Alice. 'You've got too big for it. You're like a lizard, you couldn't go on splitting and shedding your skins forever.' Strange how age changed one, Harriet thought. Who would ever have believed that this was the voice of the Cousin Alice she first knew?

The two older children were strapped firmly into the back seat of the car and Emma was sitting on Harriet's knee when they finally drove away from the stripped house. The moving vans had gone before them. They drove away past the houses of the people they had known. Past Nick Thomas's place. 'You're an idiot,' he had said to Harriet, meeting her in the main street of Weyville a few days before their departure. 'I could have done much better for you.' It was impossible to tell by his ambiguous smile what he had meant. She understood that he was acting for Roy Mawson in his divorce against Elaine. Nick added she was bad for business. Mawson would probably drop his suit, if he knew anything, since Harriet was whipping his victim out from under his nose. 'You must love that streak of tap water you're married to,' he said sardonically. 'Well, good luck to you. At least you must know by now that marriages aren't made in heaven.'

They drove on, past the library, past the sleeping morning houses of Julie and Dick, and of wicked Nance, past the lake, clad in vapour, the ugly little lake, thick with the steaming shapes of ducks, and the bristled rushes. On, on to the far side of Weyville, past all the other places they knew. They had left the Everetts' house behind too, almost the first place they had passed but the hardest one to put behind. Miriam and Don were survivors in suburban warfare. They might have land mines planted round the house, they might have dug trenches in which to hide from each other, but in the end they'd come over the hill, brandishing their hats and calling for more, laughing at the game. Survival of the fittest.

But Harriet and Max were not done yet. That was something to think about. Like the rest of Weyville, the Everetts were already dropping into the past, as the road opened up before them. This time Harriet knew she would not return, except as a voyager on her way to other places. They were heading for Wellington and the 1970s. Their life was about to begin again.

1978

1978

14

Harriet described to Leonie the long slow haul of years after she and Max and the children had migrated to Wellington, the struggles with money, which had been tolerable in Weyville, but were sometimes almost impossible in a larger city; the realisation that if she was going to follow a path which had any meaning for her, it had to be lived through herself, and not vicariously through men; the understanding that she had made a commitment to her marriage which had not been present before, and which demanded hard work and courage. Courage to express hurt and resentment in terms which they could mutually understand, not through violence and destruction. They must heal the wounds they had inflicted on their children through their apartness.

Harriet's work had become high on her list of priorities, this seemed essential from many points of view. A job would relieve some of their immediate financial anxieties, it would channel the energies which she had used to create havoc in the past into some sort of meaningful form, it would stop her relying too heavily on Max for emotional support. Starting life over, yet again, didn't mean using each other as crutches. Both of them were in no condition for it, anyway. If each had leaned a little too heavily on the other, either was likely to fall over in those first years.

At first Harriet had looked for library work, but it was not easy to get in the capital. Many of the library graduates who had trained in Wellington liked to stay on in the city, and they got first pick of the jobs. One or two vacancies had come up, but they looked

301

dreary when she had gone to look at them. She decided to take a straight clerical job until something turned up, and ended up as a receptionist in television. She fitted in, got on with the people there, and after a year or so, people noticed that she could be good at other things besides answering telephones.

The publication of her first book drew attention to her. At morning tea one day a producer had asked if anyone knew the Harriet Wallace who had just had a book of verse published. She had admitted her identity, been interviewed that day for the evening's *Town and Around* programme, and, a few days later she was invited to audition as an interviewer. It had fallen together so easily, that Harriet often wondered at first when it would start to fall apart. But it didn't. She wasn't always in front of the camera. Thanks to her library training, she was a competent background researcher and she put together good workmanlike documentary scripts. They often let her work at home, and if one of the children was sick she could simply take a pile of stuff home. Life was so much easier than it had been in the first year when she'd had to take a day's sick leave to stay with a sick child, and then when that time had been used up, she'd eaten into her annual leave. There were school holidays when she had to pay to have someone look after the children, and that was her salary gone for three months of the year. So when she did get her break, there was no stopping her.

She became caught up in the feminist movement, marched for Germaine Greer and joined radical groups, without displaying obvious party affiliations. She came to believe in her own lifestyle. She continued to be known as Harriet Wallace, and her way of life didn't conflict with Max's. Only their small inner circle of friends, mainly the parents of their children's friends, knew the connection. Harriet emerged as an entity in her own right. Max asked for, and was given, a quiet life. Harriet's work took her away from home quite often, but now she was better organised and managed her absences with a minimum of fuss for all concerned.

She was thrown into the company of many men, and cajoled her way among them without giving away anything of herself. A number of men became her friends, and she came to treasure the knowledge that real friendship could exist between men and women without their having to go to bed to prove it.

She was happy, and it showed. One morning Max woke up and said to her, with quiet wonder. 'Harriet, I love you' and she had been able to respond in kind. He told her that he had come to accept her difference as the quality which had first drawn him to her, and not a symbol of her failure to conform. The person she was now was a new, better and more whole human being than she had been before. She loved this person with whom she had fought such desperate battles. They were united in a common aim. The question of mutual trust didn't need to be raised, for it was a mutual assumption. Besides, their meeting ground was home territory, and what worked there was important. If Max strayed she didn't want to know about it, though she doubted that he did. He was an excellent sounding-board for her when she had new ideas, or if things went wrong, which of course they did from time to time.

Harriet's new life still created problems; she was slighted by academics who considered her an imposter (a few became her friends, but it took a long time), she had had her fingers burnt on occasion by courting too enthusiastically the people she admired, thinking at first that some people were godlike, and finding them merely mortal. Wanting to try everything, she would overextend herself in fruitless pursuits and have trouble extricating herself. Only now, the problems had solutions.

Two things became apparent to Leonie, over the months which followed her first lunch with Harriet. One was Harriet's belief that work solved all. The work ethic had transformed her life — she was sure it could change Leonie's. At times Leonie thought Harriet resented her because she didn't have to work. It would be nice, Harriet said, if one were in a position to choose, but if she had to choose between a life of working or not working, then she would choose to work. Leonie had the benefit of choice, and quite clearly she would be happier if she worked. When she had heard Leonie voice her dissatisfactions, her loneliness, her rootlessness, and her love for Todd Davis in Toronto, Harriet had said briskly that the best thing for her would be to get off her backside and find herself a job.

She tended to be impatient when Leonie raised objections. Her husband Hamish would not tolerate the idea of a working wife. It would discredit him in the eyes of the oil company executives who were his colleagues. Besides that, the Coglans had a position to maintain, and Leonie was the domestic caretaker of that position. All the more reason to demonstrate her identity, Harriet had maintained.

The arguments were circular and resolved nothing. However, Leonie was beginning to think that Harriet might have something. And, if she was ever going to work or express any kind of independence, New Zealand could be the place to do it, known territory; the people, even if unreal from this distance in years, were recognisable; the society, at least on the surface, was sufficiently egalitarian to absorb her without raising too many eyebrows among the oil community.

The second thing that Leonie divined about Harriet was more an intuition rather than a spoken thing between them. Harriet, she thought, was terrified of any romantic attachments that might shake the foundations of the world she and Max had built. Leonie believed in Harriet's commitment to her marriage; it was profound in a way that hers was not. Harriet and her marriage had gone to the fire too often; now she needed to hold on and to believe. She suspected that Harriet was afraid of her attachment to Michael Young, that perhaps, even, she had chosen him more deliberately than she realised. In finding someone who seemed to offer a finite relationship, she had been prepared to enter into it, longing, impulsive, a romantic, despite her liberal labels, believing that she could survive it and come through with her world intact at the end, simply because there was an end. A beginning, a middle and an end. Like a good storybook. And Harriet, being the person that she was, would demand that it was very good. Only the story seemed to have stopped in the middle.

Through the winter, Harriet waited for Michael to come back to her. She believed that he would. She cocooned herself in a world where his existence was as real as if she had seen him yesterday. It was easy to believe that he would return, knowing that he was 'abroad'. One didn't have to wait for the phone, wondering if it would be him, or for business trips which might take either of them north or south. One had only to wait for the date of his return.

During those months of his absence she built up a fantasy world about him. She had to build the magic for herself. At nights when the fierce southerly winds lashed the house and woke her, she would lie thinking of him, surrounding him with the aura of her belief, invoking his body in her imagination, stealing her hand between her legs, then holding at bay the breaking wave, holding his face above hers, sliding quietly away into safe waters, before she turned to stretch herself against her husband's back. And he, tender, would turn in his sleep, and hold her. How many people dwell inside me, she would wonder, that I need, must live this double life?

A little magic. A passing miracle, that is all, she would tell herself. But the longing started to grow different dimensions. When asleep again, she would dream of pleasant lands, far away, places she had never been to, only to wake once more, as morning broke, and lie, dry, gritty-eyed and resentful. There were gaps in her life, things she had never done. She had allowed herself to drift along. From time to time, over the years, she had tried to take her destiny into her own hands. Some might say she had succeeded, that she was a successful modern woman. Yet she asked for more, and the things she had asked for, looking back, did not seem unreasonable. If only, somewhere, she had had the courage to say yes, that will happen, and no, that will not happen. Only it hadn't been like that. When events had crowded in on her, she had let them, and she had let other people take her along with them. She wanted distance and space, she needed a place to look at herself, rather than to have people looking at her.

For so long now, she had said confidently, believing the lie, I don't mind staying here, not going abroad, not seeing the rest of the world. There are some who must go and there are others who must stay and record what is here. But how much did she really do?

305

Mediocrity, small jealousies were too often the scope of the world she had to record, and , hemmed in, she began to fear that they were claiming her.

Now the world had come to her, in the shape of Michael. A stray eagle on a far-flung Antipodean outcrop. Already the bird was preparing his flight, and who could blame him? When he came back from England, she knew that he would have already made the arrangements for the family's return, that he would have found them a new house, that soon there would be nothing to keep him here in New Zealand. And she had had so little of him. Ideas began to take shape in her mind. She would go away for awhile. She would flee these shores too. Other people went all the time, why not her?

At first the idea was a tantalising nonsense, but gradually it began to assume possibilities. Perhaps not this year; the children, particularly Emma, were too young to leave, but in another year's time. She would take extra work and save. Perhaps while she was overseas Michael would give her work. The idea wasn't too absurd, after all, he had asked her to work for him before. Maybe she expected him to rescue her — but no, she was rescuing herself.

How pleased he would be with her, breaking out of the confines of her life, being prepared to take her fate so firmly in her hands. She would go and live on the edge of the Mediterranean somewhere, as she had always imagined she would do, and he would come and join her in Italy, or Greece, and they would have a month in the sun. She would write, and he would help her.

The idea was becoming a reality. To her friends, she began to say, with mysterious little smiles, I am thinking of going overseas for a few months, oh not right away, but within the next year or so. It seemed quite a reasonable proposition and no one seemed surprised. After all, most of them had been overseas long ago, or were still going every few months or so — there was nothing sensational about the idea of going abroad. They were surprised she hadn't done it long ago, a person like her. It would be good for her, they said.

She even told Max she was giving the matter some thought. 'Your time'll come,' he said.

The date for Michael's return came and went. The weeks rolled by. Then slowly she began to understand that she was not going to hear from him again. Perhaps he had never returned to New Zealand, she had no way of knowing.

She was assailed by anger. He had promised, he had said that he would let her know if things changed between them. But perhaps that was all he had tried to do at the end of the summer, that day in Auckland, and she simple hadn't listened. Then why had he agreed to her promise? Had it simply been to get her out of his hair? Her dreams of flight began to fade, evaporating as easily as they had appeared. The treachery of her imagination dismayed her. And having created a reality out of those dreams, she was now landed with them. Friends would ask her about her plans, and she would say, yes, yes, of course they were going ahead. But her heart was no longer in them.

When she calculated he would have been back a month, or maybe a little longer, her producer called the weekly programme conference to discuss ideas and plan content. There seemed to be a programme gap. These gaps usually gave Harriet her opportunities to promote her special interests, to throw in an item about the arts or books, rather than to accept assignments developed by the whole team. Did she have anything in mind? Terry asked her, pushing his little blue denim cap back on his head.

She tried frantically to think of one of her bandwagons but there was an awful blank in front of her.

What about that story she'd brought up months ago about the man who wanted to start up a New Zealand edition of that magazine? Was there still something to be had there?

She explained that she thought the company might not have found the market particularly propitious, and, as no magazine had resulted, she assumed that they were not going ahead.

One of her colleagues reminded her of the enormous splash that the company had started with in Auckland, nearly eighteen months ago. Surely there must be some sort of story there, even if it was to illustrate how financially hostile New Zealand was at present.

Harriet said that she thought they had covered that fairly thoroughly and fairly regularly, and everyone must know that. They only had to go to the supermarket and, good God, her groceries had cost her over sixty dollars that week. Did they want to do a week in the life of Harriet Wallace? That should cover the economic climate pretty thoroughly.

But Terry the producer was not to be put off now he had the bit between his teeth. It was easy to change the subject but this was a different angle, the big guys with the money losing out, getting thrown to the wolves like everyone else. The perfect story of the baby being thrown out with the bath water. Harriet groaned suitably, and everyone else laughed. He was ordering her to do the story. She was to go and get on to it right away.

Harriet sat down at her desk wondering what to do. She could always say that she had tried and that the victims were not interested in doing a story. But she knew better than that. On reflection, she'd only get sent off to find out why they were stalling, in case there was a story in that alone. Besides, she had often thought of ringing him, but the whole cycle of ringing and mentally reversing the calls was too bad to contemplate again.

He might be unpleasant to her. She thought that he could be unpleasant if he chose. He might simply tell her what she had been refusing to admit to herself for so long, that he didn't intend seeing her again.

To have a watertight excuse to ring him was the answer. Then, if he had been ill, or afraid that she had deserted him after all this time, she could reassure him. Yes, whatever his reaction, she was covered. And she would know.

'It's Harriet Wallace,' she said, 'Is Mr Young in?' Such a simple request, so fraught with danger.

She was sure the girl's voice held the slightest trace of amusement, as she said, 'Oh, Ms Wallace. The one from Wellington?'

'That's right. I want to discuss a television programme with Mr Young. It's quite urgent.'

'Really,' drawled the girl. 'Mr Young is in conference now. I don't think I can disturb him.'

So he was back. That answered that. 'Very well, when will he be free?' asked Harriet. After all, damn him, he'd been keen enough for the publicity, said her television mind taking over. He could jump to her tune. 'Mr Young was rather keen on having an item done on television about his magazine and he'll have to make up his mind whether he wants it or not.'

The girl hesitated. 'I could discuss it with him and call you back.'

'Are you running his business now?' said Harriet icily.

'Of course not. But Mr Young is under a lot of pressure at the moment, as I'm sure you'll be aware.'

Bitch.

'I haven't the faintest idea what Mr Young's business commitments are,' said Harriet. 'I simply want to know where he stands on this programme, and my producer wants an answer within an hour. I'll expect a call from Mr Young within an hour.' She left her number at work and hung up.

An hour later the phone had not rung. 'I am justifiably angry now,' she decided. She put the number through again. 'Is Mr Young still if conference?' she snapped at the secretary.

'I'm afraid he is.'

'Then would you place a written note in front of him, advising that if I don't hear from him within half an hour we shall run our own story surmising why his magazine has not appeared in a New Zealand format.'

'Can you hold on a minute?' said the girl.

'Not unless he intends coming straight to the phone,' said Harriet.

'Just hold,' she said. A series of clicks and buzzes ensued, and then his voice came through on the line. For a long time afterwards she would think that that was the really sad moment in their relationship, how she had waited for month after patient month for the sound of his voice, and when it had finally come, she had been so angry she could hardly speak civilly to him.

'Michael, it's Harriet here,' she said.

309

'So I gathered. For God's sake, what are you playing at? I'd have rung you back later in the day when I wasn't so tied up.'

'Because I do have to provide an answer about this programme.'

'What programme?'

The one you wanted me to do about the magazine. Didn't that bloody bitch tell you?'

'Harriet, please. I've got people in the room.'

'I don't give a stuff who's in the room,' she shouted. 'If you really think I was just ringing to come crawling to offer you a bare bum again, you're mistaken. I've had it laid on the line, since you put me up to the story in the first place, that we'll do our own investigation on the magazine if you won't play ball with us.'

'Oh, God,' he said wearily. 'Harriet I'm sorry.'

'Did you tell that sodding little cow that she wasn't to put me through if I rang again?'

'Harriet,' he said, 'No, truly, it wasn't like that. Please understand, I can't talk to you now. But about the programme, I'll be in Wellington at the beginning of next week. Can we have a drink and talk about it?'

'What do I tell my producer then?'

'Can you stall him? Please. I need the time. I'll tell you about it all when I see you.'

She felt the usual cave-in. 'All right,' she said.

'I'll ring you when I hit town,' he said. 'Next Monday, okay?'

Okay. He'd better watch it, he'll end up sounding like a Kiwi.

The week ahead stretched interminably. The winter that had passed seemed to have gone in a trice, compared with what she was now asked to endure.

There were times when she drank too much. She had been aware for a long time now that she relied on alcohol when she was under stress, and aware that Max knew it too. He had never been given to excessive drinking, though for a time in Weyville when things had been bad between them he had come home a bit the worse for wear. Since their move to Wellington he drank little, more to keep her company over a couple of drinks in the evening than anything else. After he finished his drink with her, she would return to the kitchen and continue to drink while she prepared the evening meal. She was not an alcoholic, she would tell herself anxiously, and poured over quizzes which diagnosed in forty easy yes-no questions whether she was or not. She was good at these quizzes and where she thought a situation was half true of herself, she gave herself a half mark, so that with a little careful manipulating of the halves, her score always came out on the side of the angels. Well it was true, anyway. She could go without a drink for a week (Alcoholics Anonymous said if you couldn't go a month you were a goner, but obviously they were committed to extreme points of view, and who could blame them?) It was just that once she started, there were times when a little trigger would be released inside her head, which made it pointless to stop.

In the summer she had hardly drunk at all, but despite the web of fantasies she had spun around herself in the winter, she had had more to drink than she could remember. At parties she found herself rambling on boringly, or, worse, when Max came home from work, she would be there already sitting in the kitchen crying. Drink made her cry, but then so did a lot of things. Over the years she had tried to subdue that dreadful weeping, and she would think she had succeeded, and then it would all begin again. Booze was no help, she should have known that by now.

She was afraid that she might drink the whole week uselessly away if she were not careful. A week-long binge was hardly her style. Too much drinking was still an accident for her, both in its perpetration and its aftermath, and one that she always regretted. There was hope for her, she supposed; she was no better and no worse than the majority of women she knew, in the kitchen sink brigade. To be on the safe side she shied away from drink all week.

She was too fat, her hair hadn't been cut properly for months and she had allowed the winter to take its usual toll. Soon she would be getting a rocket from the studio to tidy herself up again. Now she had the perfect incentive to put herself to rights, though what one could do with four kilos of extra weight in a week she couldn't imagine. She rifled through one of the numerous diet sheets that were tucked away in her cookery books, looking for the one which would be the most painless, hoping that she could find one which suggested she eat an enormous number of goodies and promising her an instant transformation in a week. In the end she settled for the only one that offered any hope, namely eating nothing at all.

By the weekend she was pale and irritable and possibly a kilo lighter in weight. The children wanted to involve her in numerous projects which she wished to resist. In the end she decided that it was better to give in; at least they passed the time, but finding her poor company the children withdrew into themselves, complaining that she kept forgetting to answer them.

On Monday morning Max didn't have a shirt ironed, and they were out of milk for his cup of tea. In an unusual burst of anger he berated her and said he could understand her not getting round to things during the week, but she'd had the whole weekend, for Chrissake. It blew up into a major shouting match, and he stormed out of the house, running late. The children slunk off to school, armed with money for their lunches.

At ten o'clock Max rang to apologise while she was in the bath. She had thrown herself, dripping and naked, at the telephone, expecting to hear Michael's voice. Quietly and soberly she and Max expressed their regret to each other. She had been in the wrong, she was sorry, she seemed to be a bit under the weather at the moment. Max asked her if she shouldn't take a break, she seemed to be going at things at such a pace these days. Harriet assured him that she wasn't going to the studio that day, seeing that she was going out to work tonight. He sighed. That was what he meant, she never really had a rest. She should try and get a proper break and when did she have leave owing to her? She said she would look into it and not to worry about her. Had he remembered that they really couldn't get out of going to the Coglans for dinner the following night? Leonie was in quite a state about it, and anyway, she did want Max to meet her because she was different from her other friends. Would he mind too much going out with her? They finished the conversation on a note of mutual goodwill.

Lying in the bath again, she remembered the first time she had gone to Michael, and the way she had prepared herself for him. It would be like that again, she would be as ready for him, as lovely as she had been then. She wished she was still brown, he had liked that. Mentally she ticked off the days since her last period, and calculated that she still had three days to go before the next one was due. Sailing close to the wind. A few days more and the reunion might have been a bit of an anticlimax. Oh dear, how unsuitable the most useful words were at times.

By noon she had not heard from him. It was more than she could bear, the waiting. She drank a glass of wine with her lunch, she had decided she should have something to eat. Her stomach had rumbled all morning. So much for dieting — a rattly stomach in the bedroom was all one needed to deter the most ardent of lovers. Assuming that he was still an ardent lover. Thank God Leonie's invitation had been for the following day. Leonie had gone to such pains to arrange this meeting — the poor girl was frightened out of her mind by that husband of hers. She hoped to God she wouldn't have to be rude to him. He sounded like a prize prick, and it was a pity Leonie didn't have the gumption to put him straight herself, but she supposed she had to make a start somewhere, and if Harriet could help her do it, she thought she would. She still owed Leonie that. It was hard to define exactly what she did owe her, for neither of them really seemed to know what they expected of each other. They veered backwards and forwards. Someday, she supposed, they would talk about it all. She poured another glass of wine and felt herself relaxing.

By the time she had finished her drink, she felt angry again. How dare Michael leave her stranded like this? She hadn't rung him to chase him. It was business, he had suggested the meeting, did he expect her to wait around all day for his call? Not that she would have been likely to do anything else. Of course he'd know that. It wasn't good enough. The weather was sulky, but the planes would be getting in and out, no problem there.

She dialled the number of the hotel where he usually stayed and asked the board to put her through without bothering to ask if he was there. He answered immediately.

'So you are there?'

'Of course I'm here. I said I'd be here.'

'Then why didn't you ring me? Or had you changed your mind?'

He gave a rather dramatic sigh. 'I was going to ring you, but I've been —'

'Been busy' she said, over the top of his voice.

'Exactly. And now I've got meetings this afternoon, and dinner with a crowd of people I have to talk to afterwards. I thought we could fit a drink in, if you've got the time. Say around six o'clock.'

'Fit a drink in?' She heard her voice falter.

'Well of course, if it's not convenient, I could discuss the matter now.'

'The matter?'

'You wanted to talk about the programme. I'm afraid it's not on, but that's what I wanted to explain to you. Are you too busy to come in?'

'No,' she said faintly. 'But I ...'

'What?'

'I don't like being fitted in between meetings, that's all.'

'I'm not fitting you in between meetings. I want to see you, or I wouldn't have made time at all,' he said. 'Are you coming, or not?'

'Yes,' she said, knowing she sounded waspish. 'I'll come all right.'

She contrived to leave as Max was coming home. She had avoided the children all afternoon, as well as her housekeeper. She was tired, she told them, and needed a rest. The children were hardly surprised, after her antics of the morning. The problem was that by four o'clock, she had had to sleep off the amount of wine she had drunk. When she got up, she fumbled with her makeup and dropped it, and she dressed later about five. She had meant to change her underwear, but obviously it hardly mattered.

The fresh air revived her a little. By the time she walked into the hotel she felt that she was beginning to function again.

She saw him in the bar among a group of men. The sight of him made her catch her breath. She had almost forgotten what he looked like, it was amazing how one carried an image in one's mind, but when the reality was seen it was hard to merge one into the other and make a whole. The number of people surrounding him dismayed her. It seemed that he was taking no chances on being alone with her.

She saw him first. He had always been easy to pick out in a crowd because of his height, but as she approached, he turned and saw her. He appeared pleased to see her, but he had the sort of manners that would make him appear pleased to see a rat on the dinner table, she thought sourly. He'd probably offer it a piece of cheese.

'Have a drink,' he was saying.

'Oh yes, thank you, the usual,' she said. Christ, she was starting to behave badly already. He flinched ever so slightly, and gave her order. The men who were with him were advertising men with whom he was winding up business agreements. A few of them were prepared to keep their advertising on, even though the company was pulling out of its New Zealand operations, but they were the ones who had international products to offer and might attract overseas business. She really couldn't follow the complicated manoeuvres that were taking place among them. As a good researcher she should be, she supposed — after all, that's what it was all about, in theory. But her head was aching, and she felt ill. He was going, she had always known he would go, but for him to leave like this was unbearable. The story must have a proper ending.

'I should like to speak to you alone,' she said loudly, too loudly. Michael looked pained.

'Excuse me a moment,' he said to one of the men. They were looking at her, faintly embarrassed at being involved in some obviously personal crisis, but intrigued none the less.

Michael drew her over to one side. 'What is it, Harriet? I thought you wanted to hear about the arrangements to wind the company's operations up.'

'You know perfectly well I want to see you. I don't give a damn about the company,' said Harriet. 'Why are you pretending like

315

this? How can you try to behave exactly as if there's never been anything between us except a business arrangement? Or perhaps that's all it was, eh? While you wanted a little publicity, was that it?'

'Please keep your voice down,' hissed Michael, his careful charm starting to disintegrate. 'Look, I'm sorry, these people stayed longer than I expected, but I thought you'd like to meet them.'

'I think they're revolting,' she said. A few of the men looked over.

'They heard that,' Michael said.

'Good. Shall I betray my origins a bit more? You were really slumming it with me. Your bit on the side down under. Like the missionaries, Bibles and balls and shouldn't we be grateful.'

She knew he would have liked to shout at her to be quiet or hit her, or both. Instead he said quietly, 'If you don't keep your voice down I'll ask the management to have you leave. If you choose to go and sit through in the other bar I'll join you in a few minutes.' His face was scarlet under the sickly lights in the hotel, as she turned without speaking again, and went through to the bar he had indicated. She found a chair by herself, and collapsed into it, her drink slopping over her dress. Oh, she'd blown it now, she really had.

After about five minutes he sat down opposite her. 'Was that necessary?' he said.

'Something was. It seemed appropriate.' She felt crumpled and dejected. She caught a glimpse of herself in the mirror behind the bar; she looked quite ghastly, even if one made allowances for the fact that they were sitting under a large pot plant lit by green lights.

'I want to go to your room,' she said standing up.

'No you don't,' he said, violently.

'But I do, I know what I want,' she said. He sat, refusing to budge. 'Look', she said, exasperated, 'For God's sake, I feel rotten, I'm half boozed, I suppose that's obvious, I look revolting, and I'm going to cry. I can't help that, you don't owe me a thing, but at least couldn't you offer me some privacy to talk to you for a few minutes. I won't tear my clothes off or make a scene, if that's what you're afraid of.'

He looked doubtful about that as he followed her to the lifts. And well he might, she reflected, having just been part of the scene she had made. She wasn't at all sure that she had told the truth herself. She didn't know what she was going to say to him when she got to the room.

She didn't think she had anything left to say, but when they were in the room, she heard her voice, whining at first, rising to a torrent of abuse. She swore at him, and shouted feeling a tide of anger of which she didn't know she was capable, as if he was every man who had ever betrayed her. And he was. Why should he look for devils? He was the devil himself, the one she'd waited for, to turn up through her bedroom floor when she was a child, the eel that crept through the dark pools, all the things she had ever been afraid of. He stood stunned, and at last, so was she. Her voice trailed away, and broke off.

They stood staring at each other. 'Why me?' he said at last. 'Why did you have to choose me to love?'

'I don't know,' she said, tiredly. 'I don't even like you very much.' It was her last reserve of unpleasantness. She was totally drained.

'Neither you should. I'm a horrible man.'

She glanced at him quickly. 'If I didn't know better, I'd say you believed that.'

'I don't know what I believe,' he said. 'You don't know what it was like for me.'

'You could have let me try. If I'd understood ...'

'I tried, but you didn't want to know. Besides,' and he was accusing her a little now, 'You told me you'd be all right. That you had nothing to ask.'

'Except being with you. I wanted that.' She put her hands out to touch him, wrapping her arms about his neck. She felt him go rigid, as if he was disgusted. Her arms fell, and she gathered her handbag and handkerchief together. 'I'm sorry,' she said. She opened the door and walked down the passage towards the lifts.

They seemed to take forever to arrive. 'Harriet,' she heard him calling after her. He ran down the passage towards her, the lift stopped, and he put his finger on the button to send it on.

'Don't do that,' she said, 'I've waited long enough for the bloody thing.'

'I can't let you go like this,' he said.

'You should have thought about that sooner,' said Harriet, coldly. The scene was over, Michael was over, she wanted him to go away.

'Look, I've got a man coming up soon, we're going to have dinner together. But we could talk this over sensibly. I can't have you going off through the hotel looking like that.'

'I don't think my appearance should worry you particularly. I promise I'm not going to go and tell all to your mates down there.'

'I didn't think you were. I just don't want to stand here in a hotel lobby quarrelling with you.'

'Appearances. You keep them up so well, don't you? Well you have nothing to quarrel about. There's nothing. Simply nothing.'

He took her elbow. The lifts opened and a man got out, recognising and greeting Michael as he did so. Michael dropped her elbow.

'For Christ's sake, piss off,' she said to him. He looked at her as a man might look at a woman who had just dropped her sanitary pad at an Embassy reception.

And serves him bloody well right, she thought as she walked out onto The Terrace. To appear to be molesting unescorted females in hotel lobbies was poetic justice for the likes of him. Though who was to blame him for being revolted by a loud-mouthed abusive drunk middle-ageing-woman slobbering over him?

Somehow, she felt she could.

After she left the hotel, she drove up The Terrace and headed away from the direction of home, not quite knowing where she was going. When she headed out of the Mount Victoria road tunnel, she guessed that she must be making for the sea. She followed the road out towards the airport, and at the turnoff from Cobham Drive, veered left towards Shelley Bay. She had known where she was going all the time, she guessed, as she parked the car on the sea front. It was the place where she and Michael had sat, nearly a year

before. It could have been ten years, so much of her life seemed to
have been expended in him.

She got out of the car, and climbed down to the beach and sat
down. It was a harsh little strip of coast, and sharp stones bit into
her as she sat. Why, she wondered, had she been willing to fall so
helplessly before this irritable, rather arrogant, but decidedly
beautiful young man? Looking back, she supposed that there were
a great many things about him that she really didn't like
particularly. But surely it had been more than his physical
attraction. She thought it was, but it was hard to define. She would
never know now, not even in retrospect, because she would never
truly know him. He had killed that possibility in that one act of
rejecting her. However shocked he might have been by his
handiwork a moment later, the act had still been performed. He
had killed any feeling between them.

And he was right to have done it. Through all the people that she
had been, she had never learned to stand alone. Even with Max,
with whom she had defined so many terms, she still tended to stand
against him, rather than with him. They would go on, they had
become indestructible it seemed, but if she was wrong and he were
to go away, or to die, what then happened to her emotional
dependence? From Michael, she might at least have learnt a
measure of independence. It should be like that, she would have to
work to make it so, as one always did in any new situation. She
would like to think that she had taken one thing of value from it
all.

There was so much to learn. She wondered if there would ever be
enough time for her to learn all the lessons that were required of
her.

When she was calm, and the cold sea air whipping in the wind at
her face had restored her to some sort of order, she made her way
home. She must have sat by the water for longer than she had
realised, for it was past nine, and the family had turned in for an
early night. She went to the bathroom, and washed her face and
cleaned her teeth. In the mirror she looked passable now, her face
bleached of colour, but otherwise composed. There would still be

319

some bad times to come out of this, but for the moment she would present the familiar face that carried her through from day to day.

Max was still awake and reading. She told him briefly that it had been a hard session with a recalcitrant businessman who'd wanted to make life difficult for her. The best thing she could do would be to get some sleep, especially as they had to go out the next evening. Max groaned, and switched the light off, saying 'Couldn't we possibly get out of it?'

'I wish we could,' she said, rolling over to him, 'But I can't see how.'

In the meantime, Hamish, Leonie's husband, was raising objections to friendship between Harriet and Leonie. He had watched Harriet's performance on television a few times, and suspected her line of questioning. He felt that he and Leonie would be better off if they were not mixed up in her politics. Leonie protested that broadcasting people were required to demonstrate political impartiality, to which Hamish replied that that did not stop them belonging to organisations which had leftist and radical inclinations. Take organised women's groups, for instance. They invariably had a bias towards the left, whatever their apparent motivations. Leonie wondered about the Country Women's Institute but didn't like to say so as one didn't argue with Hamish. She wondered how Hamish knew what groups Harriet might be associated with, as she hadn't told him, but it wasn't too difficult to deduce when he told her one night after watching a television programme featuring Harriet, that 'a friend' had told him that Harriet Wallace had been involved in anti-Vietnam demonstrations in the late 1960s. There were photographs in existence to prove it, he'd been told. There was a subversive side to Harriet's nature, which it would be well for people like themselves to avoid.

When Leonie told Hamish that she had invited Max and Harriet to dinner, his face darkened in anger. 'Why have you done this to me?' he said. 'I give you a good life, don't I? What hold has this woman got over you?'

'No hold,' Leonie said. 'I simply want to choose a friend of my own for once.'

'What about the husband? He might turn out to be frightful,' said Hamish.

'I would have thought that you would have found out about that,' said Leonie.

He hesitated for only a moment. 'I believe he's all right,' said Hamish smoothly. 'A pleasant enough chap from what I've heard, puts up with his wife's exhibitionism. Not much to him, I would imagine.'

'That's something we'll just have to find out then, won't we?' Leonie replied.

'Very well,' said Hamish. 'If you're quite determined to go through with this, I'd like to ask a couple of friends around too.'

'Why?' said Leonie, startled.

'Why not? If these people are coming, I'm certainly not going to be a poor host to them. Make it a party. Do the thing properly. We'll invite the Smythes. Would you ring Liz tomorrow, please?' And he buried his head in the paper.

The Smythes. Good reliable, up themselves Liz and Neil. Close enough to Hamish to keep their mouths shut if things got out of hand, and to form a front. Oh, Hamish was a clever bastard. It was a masterly stroke, giving himself party lines on which to do battle. And of course, he would expect her, in the final analysis, to join ranks with him — hadn't she always? Not to do so would be treachery beyond his worst expectations. She was curious to know just why he saw Harriet and Max as such an explicit threat, though. Was he really afraid of them, and if so, why? Or did he really consider himself so superior that he was going to rout them once and for all?

Maybe he read more into her than she believed. Women are always doing that, she mused, hiding things and feeling guilty, and analysing how much men read into their actions. Really, it was nothing, Hamish was just so used to the same kind of people, that he did not enjoy the prospect of meeting others without back-up. Such a conservative. Well, they would see.

As the hour for their arrival drew closer, Leonie decided that if the Smythes were coming it would be unsuitable for Harriet to bring up the subject of working wives. But getting to the phone was virtually impossible because Hamish had come home early. It was clear that he was going to spare no effort in entertaining his guests. When, finally, she was able to snatch a moment, it was too late. Genevieve Taylor answered the phone and said that her parents had already gone out.

The Smythes arrived first. Liz, amiable and placid, had earned her good service medal years ago and was comfortably installed in her seat of power. If she had an overbearing manner, at least she was not competitive. She had no need to be. Leonie felt reasonably at ease with her, though she knew well enough that Liz could cut the ground out from under her feet at a moment's notice if it ever proved necessary. Neil was the suntanned, iron-grey-haired type who looked as if he spent his life in swimming pools or on a Bermudan beach, and who kept a deceptive veneer over his vast knowledge of the industry he served. The couple were, in short, the kind of people Hamish would most like the Coglans themselves to be in another ten years.

By the time Harriet and Max arrived, they were into their first drinks. Leonie took Harriet through to the bedroom to take off her coat. She was about to ask Harriet not to discuss anything controversial, when Harriet turned to her and said, 'I saw Michael Young yesterday. Last night.' Leonie looked at her face. It was pale and strained.

'It's over,' said Harriet flatly.

'Why didn't you ring me today? How long have you known you were going to see him?' said Leonie.

'I was busy today. I've known ... a week or so.'

'I see.' Only Leonie didn't quite see. She had thought she and Harriet had become closer, but perhaps that had been an assumption on her part. Maybe Harriet had regretted her early confidences.

'I'll talk to you about it tomorrow,' said Harriet. 'I couldn't before.'

The two women went through to join the others. Leonie noticed that Harriet had made a special effort to be conventional. She and

Max looked exactly like anyone else they might have been entertaining, and Leonie silently thanked them for that. Though she was getting as bad as Hamish — had she expected them to come wearing love beads and jeans? she wondered. She accepted her drink from Hamish, her fourth already. It was easier to drink in private than to make phone calls.

Hamish seemed slightly nonplussed. He and Max were talking about the past rugby season in an amicable fashion and Max was giving sound advice on which clubs their son Brent might consider joining. Max had played for a couple of seasons in Wellington before meeting Harriet and going to live in Weyville.

It was sound advice too, Neil told Hamish. He didn't know why they'd never talked about it before — after all, his boys played football. Harriet asked for a sherry; Leonie noticed that she sipped it very slowly. It was barely touched when Leonie asked Hamish to refill her glass. She glanced in the direction of Harriet's drink and Max, following her look, smiled, and said affectionately, 'I think it was a heavy night last night, wasn't it, old girl? Business got a bit rough.'

Harriet turned her head towards him, a gesture of complicity. My God, thought Leonie, and she talks about other people as survivors. She's a survivor from way back. Something I always knew, I suppose. Long ago I thought that I was the stronger one, but she has come through, not I. After what Harriet had said in the bedroom to her, the look she had cast at her husband was quite incredible. Perhaps she thought she was on television; surely she didn't always feel as convincing as she looked on the screen.

The meal was almost dull — not in its presentation, for Leonie was a superb cook and hadn't spared herself, but in its orderliness. She glanced at Hamish from time to time to see how he was taking his guests. Harriet was talking about television, describing the shooting of a particular documentary, discussing the logic of putting a certain emphasis on it as seen by the producer, agreeing politely with Neil that it showed a bias in some particular direction, but offering the alternative that was to follow and give it balance the following week. The Smythes were obviously fascinated by this

323

inside glimpse into the studios. Equally clear to Leonie was the fact that Harriet was feeding them exactly enough to hook them without giving away her hand. She had been through this a score of times; this was far from the first time that she had been set up. Hamish and Neil were enchanted, and Leonie knew that Liz would repeat the information she had been given, like a seer, over coffee.

Leonie had underestimated the Taylors as a couple. If anything, she, Hamish and the Smythes were being set up. The whole thing was a clever game, and they were losing. For once, she was glad to be a loser.

About ten o'clock, they took coffee through to the lounge, where a small television set had been brought in. Hamish suggested that it be switched on, not that they usually watched it of course, but it was Harriet's night on, wasn't it? It would be nice to get the double image.

When the pre-recorded programme was over they sat discussing it idly for awhile. Harriet's had been a straightforward small item amongst a number of other meatier topics, a lightweight assignment that week.

'How do you two cope with Harriet's public life?' said Hamish.

Leonie's heart sank. The warning lights had just come on. Once they got into dangerous personal waters, there was no knowing what turn the conversation might take. She looked over at Harriet for the umpteenth time that night, but Harriet was looking steadfastly ahead. She knows, Leonie suddenly saw, she knows that I do not want her to persist with this exercise in front of Neil and Liz, and she's going through with it.

'We cope with it very well,' said Harriet, 'because we both believe in it.'

'You have children, though. Who looks after them when you're not around?' asked Liz.

'I have regular home help,' said Harriet.

Liz looked faintly disapproving and said she didn't agree with that.

'I can't see that there's anything wrong with it,' said Harriet. 'After all, you've all lived in different parts of the world, from what

Leonie's told me, where you had native help with your children.'

'But this is New Zealand,' Liz pointed out.

'I had noticed,' said Harriet, drily. 'I suppose you could say that one difference in New Zealand is that I have to pay the person I employ a wage in proportion to what I earn. I assure you it makes quite a hole in the forty-hour week, paying someone else at the same rate as myself for ten hours of that time.'

'Our servants always enjoyed a very high standard of living,' said Neil stiffly.

'As high as yours?'

Neil was silent.

'Anyway,' said Liz, with an air of finality, as if her pronouncement would settle the argument, 'We weren't working, we women. There is a difference, you know.'

'I'm sure you weren't,' said Harriet. 'A shame for you.'

Hamish said, 'It might suit Max, but some of us like our wives to be supportive to us at home'.

'Oh, she's most supportive,' said Max, with a bit of a grin. 'Her salary's quite good, even when she has knocked off a few bob for the home help.' Now he and Harriet really were conspirators.

'It's not what I'd want of my wife,' said Hamish, applying the acid test.

'Possibly not,' Harriet replied, 'but have you ever asked your wife what she would like of herself.'

'Harriet, stop,' said Leonie.

'Well I'm sure my wife will tell you what she wants herself, won't you dear?' Hamish was saying.

She was silent. The others waited.

'I want to go back to Toronto,' said a voice Leonie recognised from afar off as her own. 'I want — Todd!

She got up and left the room. At least she thought she had, but maybe it was later on. She must have done some time, because when she woke up it was morning, and she was in her room in bed, with her negligee on, and everyone had gone.

Leonie stared around at the carnage in her kitchen. Waking had been a particularly dreadful experience for her this morning. Her hangover had been very bad — they seemed to be getting worse. The feeling of disorientation was acute to the point of being nearer to disembodiment. The old terrors crowded in, in a new and frightening dimension. When she had reached out to find whether Hamish was there or not, the bed was empty. Her relief lasted for only a fraction of a second. He should have been there and he was not. The night before closed over her.

The house was very still when she got up. There were signs of Hamish and the boys having got their own breakfasts, amongst the chaos of last night's leftovers and undone dishes. Hamish must have got the boys up. She looked round for a note, but there was nothing.

She got a couple of disprin from the cupboard and dropped them into a glass of water, watching them shoot to the surface and dissolve into white clumps. Not knowing quite where to start, she picked up a pile of dishes covered in the tiny fragile bones of chickens, the remains of the coq au vin. She was usually meticulous about tidying up from dinner parties before she went to bed, but she had been half drunk before this one even started. By the end of it, even the rituals of tidiness had deserted her.

The bones looked pathetic, so small. When the children were little they had saved the wishbones of chickens when the family had them, placing them on a sunny windowsill, in whatever house they happened to be living in at the time, till they were ready to be pulled apart between them and one of them could make a wish. Brittle bleached little witch doctor's fingers they would be reduced to. Leonie wished that she could find a bone amongst the debris now, instantly dry it, and wish her troubles away.

Instead, she wandered out onto the flagstone terrace. It was spring, there was clematis growing thick around the pillars, the branches of a tree scraping against the side of the house were shot through with a pale cloud of green satin shoots, the scent of jasmine lay heavy on the air. Only a slight breeze ruffled the calm morning. Away to her left the sea shone in its many shades of blue. She might have called this place home, given the chance. But then, had there ever been a home for her anywhere? Or would it be possible to find one still? She thought of her sons. What price, her leaving?

She tore a piece of jasmine to shreds in her fingers, and the lemony perfume struck sharply in her nostrils. Inside, the phone began to ring. Perhaps if she let it ring it would go away. It stopped and she sighed with relief, but a moment later it began again.

She gave in to its insistent clamour, knowing that the caller would be either Hamish or Harriet. She didn't want to speak to either of them yet — it was too soon. She was filled with hatred towards them both.

Hamish spoke when she answered the phone. He was off to Dunedin on a later flight that morning, he said. He had had an early call from the office. She'd been too heavily asleep for him to bother trying to wake her, so he'd collected up his things in a suitcase. He'd be back the following evening.

'Do you think it's a particularly good time to be going away?' she said.

'I don't know what you're talking about,' he said.

'We have ... some things to talk about.'

'Why don't you talk to your friend about them? You seem to have done quite a lot of talking to her in the past few months.'

'What did she say to you?' said Leonie.

'Very little, to her credit. It was you who did the talking. She told you to be quiet several times before she left, but you weren't content with a little bombshell, you were quite prepared to go on all night.'

'I don't remember,' whispered Leonie.

'I'll bet you don't.'

'Please, can't you come home and sort things out with me? Talk to me, I need so much to talk to you. Things aren't impossible. I need you with me right now. Please.'

'It's impossible. I've got to leave for the airport in twenty minutes.'

'Can't someone else go, just this once?'

'For God's sake, we've got a strike on our hands if I don't go.'

'Is that more important than us sorting things out?'

'Leonie,' he said, 'I have nothing to sort out, except the messes you've made. You sort yourself out. As far as I'm concerned, the only sorting out I've got to do is whether the Smythes are going to keep their mouths shut or not. Unless you felt it was worth the trouble to do something about it.'

'In other words, whether my — my indiscretions are going to ruin your career or not?'

His tone was deliberate. 'Oh, they won't do that, Leonie. I promise you that. I won't let them.' He hung up, and she put the phone down slowly, thinking of the other wives who had been quietly dumped. He wouldn't want that, he would make sure that that didn't happen. But if the worst came to the worst she supposed it was possible, though unlikely. What would he expect her to do now? She should make her peace with Liz, perhaps. He had as good as suggested that. If Liz and Neil were allowed to adopt the role of counsellors and conciliators, they would stand behind them. A vicarious pleasure. Unless she felt it was worth the trouble. That was what he had meant. Good heavens, they'd adopted that posture themselves with a young couple once, out in the Middle East. Kept in the family. It had been touch and go, that old scandal, but the Coglans had seen them through it. They still got Christmas cards from them.

She would have to ring Liz. That was what was expected of her.

And Harriet? Why had Harriet done that to her? She must have been able to see. Was it because she was so wrapped up in her own unhappiness? Spite seemed low on her list of motives. She had no reason to be spiteful towards Leonie. They had been friends, hadn't they? Yes, friends. For longer than she cared to remember.

That seemed closer to the heart of the matter. Could Harriet see what she could not see, or refused to see? Their beginnings. I do not want to see my beginnings, I sought her out with the past as a reference only, not as a map. But she remembers, she wants me to face who I am. The yellow roses. The old room. The orphanage. Weyville. Her and me.

Tomorrow she would ring Liz. She would sort something out tomorrow. For now, she would think about Harriet.

328

She cleaned the kitchen. It seemed to take hours. It was nearly midday when she put the last glasses back in their places. Her head had cleared by then, and she bathed and showered. Once she had talked to Harriet, things would start to take shape again.

There was no reply to Harriet's phone. She tried several times during the afternoon, until she knew that even if she did get Harriet, the rest of the family would be in by then too, and the conversation she wanted with Harriet was not a family one. She tried her at work too, but the girl in the office said that Ms Wallace wouldn't be in that day. No, she didn't know when she would be in, and yes, she supposed she was on an assignment of some kind. Perhaps she would like to try her at home if it was urgent. Would she like the phone number? Leonie thanked her and hung up.

The boys came in, and she wondered if they knew anything of the events of the night before. It was hard to tell. Laurence's face was totally non-committal. She would never read that boy. Brent seemed gentle and distracted.

She got steaks out and started to prepare one of their favourite meals. They would sit and eat together, in front of television.

'Will I get you a drink, Mum?' Brent said.

'Not tonight, son,' she said.

The boys laughed uproariously at the comedy programmes, and shushed each other through the news so that their mother could hear it properly. It all seemed very normal. Afterwards they took the plates out and stacked them in the dishwasher. Laurence went to his room to do his homework, but Brent came out and sat with her on the sofa. She put her hand on his and he returned her grip.

'Everything all right, son?' she asked.

'I've decided what I want to do when I leave school,' he said.

'That won't be for a long time yet.'

'I'll be fifteen next year,' he reminded her.

'That still doesn't mean you'll be leaving school.'

'Not for a year or so. But I had a talk to the careers advisor today. About getting a farm cadetship. I want to go onto a farm."

She was startled. 'A farm? Here in New Zealand?'

'Yes.'

329

'Dad won't like that much.'

'No, I know, but it doesn't matter. I can cope.' Looking at him, she felt that he could. She loved him, but he was breaking the cord. He was telling her that he no longer needed her.

In the morning she tried to ring Harriet again, but the phone continued to ring unanswered. It was becoming strange. By mid-afternoon, she had still received no response, and she still hadn't rung Liz. She wanted to talk to Harriet before she spoke to Liz. But why? It was all some strange nightmare. Hamish would be home in a few hours, and she had done nothing. It was no nightmare, it was reality, she couldn't turn the clock back, everything that had been said, and done, had still to be dealt with. What did she want to say to Harriet? How crazy to have delayed ringing Liz in favour of some nebulous conversation about the past. If this was facing up to things she must be crazy.

She would try one more time. A woman answered when she dialled Harriet's number. Mrs Taylor had gone away up north that morning, she told her. Away? For how long? She didn't say, said the woman, she came in to help. Gone to some place called Ohaka, she thought, right away up the island.

So Harriet had gone. Gone without even ringing to find out how she was. Wrought all that havoc, and gone away. She was on her own again. Fear nearly choked her.

She lifted the phone once more, and called Toronto.

After the dinner at Leonie's, Harriet was upset. It had ended so badly. Max had tried to comfort her, but coming so close to her own disaster, she felt as if her world was falling apart. It was impossible, of course, to explain this to Max. Nor did she care to tell him how she had thought it was just like the old days in suburbia. These people couldn't see themselves like that, but that's what they were. When you break the pattern, no one can pick up the pieces. These people are no better at holding on to the pattern than anyone else. And Leonie, poor bewildered Leonie, had seen her sadness and thought that she was pitying her. She had read it in her face. In fact, Harriet pitied them both, they were more sisters under the skin than either of them could possibly have realised.

330

'We're instruments of our own destruction,' Max was saying. 'I've heard you say that. She did it to herself.'

'I stood by and helped her make a good job of it, then,' said Harriet.

She was a destructive force in Leonie's life. Leonie had been right in accusing her of that, she had been playing games in a far more complex situation than she had known. She would ring her, wish her well, and leave her to work out her own destiny. There might have been a time when they could have helped each other, but that moment seemed to be past. Fleetingly, she wished that she could simply confide in Max all that had happened to her in the past year, that he would relieve her of thinking of the causes and effects of her behaviour in other people's lives, as well as her own. But by doing this, she would add to the destruction. Max was, after all, a human being. As was Michael. And Leonie. As she was herself. There was a point at which one could ask too much, and she kept silence.

She intended to ring Leonie briefly and casually from work the next day.

On her way to the office, she stopped in town. She had remembered that it was Mary's birthday soon, and she would have to get her present away that day if it was to arrive in time. Her mother depended more and more on her contact with her daughter. Harriet often felt guilty that she could not see her more often, especially as Mary wrote to her that Gerald's health was failing and he was becoming more cantankerous. It was becoming more difficult to buy a present for her, but she expected she would find something. She settled for a pair of fluffy slippers, and made her way to the greeting card section. She stood, hovering undecided in front of the section labelled 'Mother's Birthday,' remembering that Mary and Gerald actually read the words inside the cards she sent them.

A voice behind her said, 'Harriet Wallace? It is, isn't it?'

She turned round, expecting to see someone who had watched her on television. She was quite sure she had never seen the man before in her life and, expecting to have her assumption confirmed, she composed a polite but firm dismissal. He was tall with a dark beard shot with grey, and his slender nervous hands reached out to take hers.

'I've always hoped I might meet you again somewhere,' he was saying as she avoided his hands. 'I've heard you're quite famous now. Who would have thought it? But of course I should have known. You don't remember me do you? Francis Dixon.'

It took seconds for the name to register, then it came flooding back. Francis. Beautiful remote Francis, Wendy's brother, who had walked, stooped and withdrawn, round Ohaka School. It was almost unbelievable. Francis of the dark secrets, the one who had gone away.

'I can't believe it's you,' she said, accepting his hands now. They stood like that in the shop, transfixed, trying to roll back the years and find points in each other's features with which they could identify.

'Come on, we can't stand here all day,' he said. 'Let's go some place and have coffee.' He had a slight drawl in his voice.

'Please. But first,' she indicated her mother's parcel, 'I have to send a birthday present to my mother.'

'Your mother? How is she?'

After all these years, here was someone she could tell about her mother, here in a Wellington department store. All the people she had met, who had passed through her orbit, and not one of them had ever been able to say, 'How is your mother?' knowing her as a real person.

She started to tell him, and at the same time he was agreeing that of course the parcel must be sent. He chose wrapping paper and said that she held the nicest card in her hand. She always chose things well. In the same breath he demanded of the shop assistant all the requirements for wrapping the parcel, and he did the job right there on the counter, as beautifully as if wrapping parcels was the special task for which his long well-manicured fingers had been designed.

There was news to exchange as they made their way along the street. Wendy was married and lived in England, though she had been back to New Zealand a couple of times. That's how he knew about Harriet; Wendy had seen her on television, and had thought of getting in touch but supposed Harriet got besieged by people like her and hadn't liked to bother her. 'I'd love to have seen her,' Harriet cried, and found that she meant it.

'I'll write and tell her that, she'll be pleased,' said Francis as they settled themselves in a coffee bar.

'You've been out of the country, then?' said Harriet.

'Almost forever,' he said. 'Australia. I fiddle for a living.'

'A musician?'

'Not a very illustrious one. Symphony orchestra, second violin. I thought I was going to be great, I was quite promising, you know, but I'd left it too late to be a prodigy. My parents never approved of me.'

'I remember that. I remember so much about you now. Mind you, I'm surprised you remembered me,' said Harriet. 'You never let on that you even knew I was alive when I was a kid.'

'Oh, don't worry, I was most aware of your existence, Harriet. I admired you intensely.'

'Good heavens, did you really? I wish you'd told me. It might have changed my life.'

'I doubt it. And anyway, would you have had it changed?'

She reflected. 'Funnily enough, no. Though lots of things have gone wrong in it.'

'I'd heard that. Wendy told me about your first marriage. I take it you're married again?' he said, looking at her hand.

'Oh, yes. I'll regale you with all the domestic details. But tell me, why didn't you ever speak to me if you didn't mind me too much?'

'I was terrified of you.'

'Why?'

'Hard to explain, really.' He thought back over the years. 'I think it was perhaps because I felt trapped. I could see all the other people around me at school going straight into the cowsheds, marriage, or off to training college —'

'Like Wendy?'

'Exactly. You do understand that, then? That's right, I

remember she told me years afterwards how cross you'd been with her over that, and quite right too. Whatever she did, Wendy said to me, Harriet had a capacity for living. And that's what I was afraid of. You had that energy, that restless seeking vitality, that made all the other girls in Ohaka look pale beside you, and I was sure that if I stayed I'd drift into marrying you, especially as you seemed to rather like me, and that we'd destroy each other.'

'Plenty of people have tried to do that. I seem to attract disaster,' Harriet said.

'I'd have been a bigger disaster to you than most,' Francis said. 'I was clear-sighted enough to know that it would have been a frightful mistake, but in those days I didn't know myself well enough to ask why.'

Harriet, looking at him and meeting his eye, guessed that he was homosexual. He smiled gently in assent, without the question being asked aloud.

'I miss not having had children,' he said. 'That's all, really. So tell me about yours.'

Later, she said, 'It's wonderful sitting here talking to you. I just had this strange feeling that I'd known you all my life, and of course, then I realised, it's true, I really have, well most of it, anyway. All of it that seems to matter. You know there aren't many people I can say that about.'

'Roots, we all need them,' he said. 'How does Ohaka look these days?'

'I haven't been there for a good eighteen years. Strange isn't it, we pass the turnoff on our way north every year, but we never go there. Introducing one's past to the people in one's present seems to get harder every year.'

'I'm going up there tonight. I haven't seen my parents for about three years.'

'They still live there, then?'

'Oh heavens, yes. They've had share milkers on the farm for years, but they'll never leave there now. Why don't you come with me?'

'To Ohaka?'

'Why not?'

And indeed, she thought, why not. 'We could take my car,' she offered, 'It's a bit beat-up but it'll get us there, or I could take Max's, I guess.'

'Marvellous. I was going to fly, but that would be nicer.'

'Then I could go on up while you're staying at the farm and deliver mother's birthday present to her. It's a splendid idea. And I've got leave owing, and Max thinks I need a holiday.'

Late that afternoon the road unwound beneath them, stretching far away to the north. With Francis, it was like exploring a new country, one which she knew so well that she could name every strait, every range of hills, and yet one which she had only begun to explore. They talked as they drove, and Harriet found in Francis a willing and uncritical listener. She left nothing out in recollecting her days since their childhood in Ohaka, and that too was like looking for the first time at a chart which mapped out the progression of her life.

They swept on past the little towns, stopping at Taihape and eating stale pies and drinking fizzy orange, all that they could find at that hour, and pushed on up towards Hamilton. The lights of Weyville, lying in the hills away to their right floated past them, and Harriet thought of Cousin Alice, and was glad that they had decided to circumnavigate the town. For all that she cared for the old lady, Cousin Alice was for another time, another journey, living out her life as she was, a frail little ghost in a Weyville old people's home, calling for her children to return.

They had taken turns with the driving, and were able to make good time without feeling the effects of the journey. It was nearly midnight when they made Hamilton.

'We must be mad,' said Harriet. 'We should have stopped at Taupo instead of coming up round the back of the lake, and got a bed there. We're never going to find a place to sleep.'

But night staff in one of the large hotels rather grudgingly said they could have two rooms, looking at them as if to say who's fooling who, and ostentatiously put them in adjacent rooms. Francis noticed too, and amused, advised her to lock the door.

They were on the road again before nine, Ohaka only a few hours journey away. Through Auckland, spread in a giant pincer movement across the land, across the harbour bridge, peeling away the cities, only remembering that Michael lived in Auckland when they were off the motorway and miles beyond the city.

Freedom, on the road at last. Set free. The day blue, the sea dazed with light, flashing beside them, Whangaparaoa stretching in the far distance, and then through the farmland, and the sea coming to meet them again as they spilled over the top rim of the Brynderwyns, and away down the other side, Bream Tail and the Hen and Chickens lying nestled on the blue floor of the world. Along through Waipu, and then the turnoff, the one she had passed and avoided for so many years. The road was sealed all the way in. How things had changed. Perhaps the local bus wouldn't be such a boneshaker now, but then on the last strip up to the Dixons' farm the tar seal gave way to gravel, so that coming onto it they almost skidded off the road.

It had been agreed that Harriet would go with Francis to the Dixons for lunch and leave him there while she went up to explore the old farm and the little town. She would be welcome to stay the night, he told her. The Dixons had always had a soft spot for her, but if she wanted to go on up to Whangarei that night she should do so. This journey should have no constraints on her, he told her; she must take it at her own pace. When she had seen her parents for a day or so she would come back to Ohaka and pick Francis up, to take him back as far as Auckland so he could fly to Australia.

Harriet spent a pleasant hour or so with the Dixons. They really were pleased to see her, and would have held her there all day if Francis hadn't intervened. She pored over photographs of Wendy's children, far away in England. The grandparents sighed wistfully over them — they'd seen the children once, of course, but it wasn't the same. Perhaps they would go over some day, but they were getting old, they told Harriet. They felt they hadn't had much luck with grandchildren, what with Francis never having married and Wendy over there all that way. Still, there was another daughter who had done all right by them; a couple of nice kiddies and her husband a good chap, settled on a farm down Kaiwaka way.

At last they let her go asking whether she intended to see the Colliers. Harriet had almost forgotten that they existed. Surely they were not all alive up there still? No, the old man had been gone a good few years back, but old Doris was still up there and the boy was too, though very poorly, they'd heard. They were sure they'd be pleased to see her.

She drove slowly towards Ohaka township. Ohaka. A hard place to describe, though there was little enough left of it. There had been three main stores, and the stock and station agency and the bank and two churches and the school, standing in the middle of the paddocks with the road threading away through them. But what was it, really? A place where she had lived. It was a special place that only those who had lived in it could understand. She was coming home.

The three general stores were closed now with boards across their gaping fronts, unpainted and collapsing. Now there was a big building trying to imitate a city supermarket, brightly lit and vulgar, and alongside that a chemist's shop. Apart from that nothing seemed much changed. Children were starting to dawdle from school. They could have been the same children of twenty-five years ago; she could have been one of them. Something was missing, though, and at first she could not place it.

Then she realised that the church wasn't there any more. She stopped the car, and walked over to where it had been. The trees were still there, the same old apple trees, and they showered petals on her as they had done in the spring of her confirmation. Where the church had been was now just a pile of rubble and charred foundations. It had been burnt down, and that shook her. The devil must have had his way. Amazing how he kept rearing his ugly head. There must be some sort of symbolism in the destruction of the church. Perhaps she just wished God might have His way once in a while. But then, with friends like Father Dittmer, who needed enemies? She recalled that moment when the Bishop had spoken of heaven being home and home being heaven, and how she had felt

337

excluded. There were no magic keys and possibly she would always be locked out.

Along at the end of the road was an old barn close to the road, one she remembered passing regularly. It appeared to be opened up to the road now with a gateway leading in, and a sign up outside. She wandered along to it, curious. The sign read 'Crafts'. How odd, she thought, crafts in Ohaka, forgetting the many tiny pottery shops which she and Max visited when they holidayed in the north. That was one thing, but crafts in Ohaka, that was something else. She went in, the barn had had a floor put down in it, and three trestles were suspended around the room, displaying indifferent artefacts, second-rate pottery and homemade knitted garments. A pasty young woman with her hair pulled back greasily into a rubber band was sitting in charge, knitting. A toddler whimpered round her feet, and she pulled it off the wares, with irritable exclamations from time to time. The room was buzzing with flies. Harriet found it dispiriting. The mother had a strangely familiar look.

'Are you from round these parts?' Harriet asked.

'Yep. All me life.'

It was hardly possible, yet she had to ask her. 'Are you related to Ailsa Wilson that was, by any chance?'

'My mother. Know her?'

'Oh, long ago. I lived here when she was a girl. I haven't seen her in a long time.' Harriet told the girl who she was, and asked to be remembered to her mother. For a moment she entertained the thought of going to see her, but she guessed she knew the story of Ailsa's life without being told. A grandmother already. The girl said laconically that she'd pass the message on. She didn't seem particularly interested, though she did say, 'Not been back in awhile then?'

'Eighteen years.'

'Long time. You'll see a few changes, then.' The girl was perfectly serious.

She drove on up through the valley, to the old house where she had lived with her parents. But it too had gone. A new place stood on the old site, a shiny solid modern brick farmhouse. This was something she hadn't bargained for. The woman was right after all, there were some changes. It made it more difficult to approach the occupants of the place than she had imagined. It was one thing to walk up to a door she had entered thousands of times, but she felt intimidated and out of place, confronted by this new house. The occupants might think she was idiotic wanting to go sauntering round their paddocks.

She decided she would go up to the Colliers to break the ice. She drove carefully up through the paddocks to the old house, glad to see that it at least was unchanged. Across at the shed a man was bringing in the cows for milking. She waved, expecting it to be Jim, and the man responded, uncertainly, not knowing who she was. From this distance it was impossible to decide whether it was Jim or not.

Doris Collier met her at the door, a big thick old woman, her legs swollen purple and folding over the edge of her slippers. She looked at Harriet without comprehension. 'I'm Harriet, from across the road,' Harriet said at last.

The old woman put her arms out and folded her against her spotty apron. 'Of course it is, of course it's Harriet. You've come to see him, then?'

She led her inside, closing the door behind her. The smell of must and decay impregnated the air and something else again, sickly sweet, which she could not define. The wallpaper was curling off the walls, the floral carpet, once the envy of Ohaka, was worn thin, with great brown threads actually showing through near the doorways.

'It's not been the same since Dad died,' said Doris, seeing her looking around. 'We miss him, Jim and me, you know.'

'I'm sure you do. He was a very ...' Harriet sought for a word, 'a very kind man.'

'Aye, he was that,' agreed Doris. 'You don't get the heart to do things the way you did, girl. That's the truth of it, and nursing Jim day 'n' night I don't get much time to look to things beside him. Come along then, you'd best see the boy.'

The boy, whom Harriet now took to mean Jim, was propped up

on a great pile of white pillows. The room was very neat, and clean, in contrast to the rest of the house, as if all of Doris' energies centred round this one spot.

Some of the smell was explained in this room, too. It was the smell of sickness, of cancer and of approaching death. The burly Jim she had known was a tiny bundle of a man now, only a huge distended stomach showing any size at all. His eyes were sunken deep in a luminous waxy face.

'You've got a visitor, Jim. The lass has come to see you,' said Doris, as if they had been expecting her.

'Might have known,' said Jim. 'She was a good 'un, eh? Always was.'

'And to think I didn't know her on the doorstep! I should have, seen you often enough gawping out of that box at nights.' She indicated the television set in the corner of the bedroom. 'There's one that made good in spite of herself, I say to Jim at nights, don't I, Jim?'

'Aye, Ma, you do too.'

'It was the shock of seeing you on the doorstep instead of in the corner, I reckon,' said Doris. 'Well, girl you'd better have a cuppa. You sit here and have a natter to the boy while I put the kettle on.'

The boy was nearly fifty, if Harriet's calculations were right. He was always the boy, she supposed, when a mother saw her own flesh and blood dying before her eyes.

'I'll not get better, you know,' said Jim.

Harriet had nothing to say.

'You were a good bit of a kid to me. We got on all right, you and me, didn't we?'

'Yes we did, Jim. And you were good to me. Looked after me. I'm grateful for that.'

'Grateful, eh? Well I dunno about that. You needed looking after. You get that Maori joker off your back all right, then?'

Strange how one is caught, Harriet thought. If anyone, anywhere else had said that, I'd have bitten his head off. Yet what can I say to this man, locked far away from the rest of the world in a diseased body and his old prejudices, the prejudices of Ohaka?

340

And yet, hadn't Jim once defended Maoris to her father? A strange mixture, these people of the land, a blend of practical tolerance and intellectual reaction. She wondered what Jim would say to that comment, and smiled.

'What you smiling about then? It's not funny,' he said crossly.

'Just that it's good to see you.'

'Aye, and you. Got kids?'

She spread photos of the children out across the bed, and he plucked feebly at them, admiring them.

'You done right to get away from here,' he remarked. 'There's no way outa Ohaka, 'cept by flying young, or dying here.'

'Maybe,' said Harriet, 'The trap is if you try to fly too high, and don't quite make it. I've got a long way to go yet. I've no way of knowing that I ever will.'

'You got outa here,' he said stubbornly. 'I died here long ago, long before this lot hit me, girl.'

It was getting on for evening when Doris rang the people across the road and asked them if Harriet could go down to the river. She wanted to give her a meal, but Harriet said that she was expected in Whangarei. This was not quite the truth, but she'd decided to push on to her parents' place, rather than sit round at the Dixons'. Francis would understand how she felt, but the Dixons themselves would want to lay claims on her, and ask her what she thought of this and that that she'd seen, and she felt she could cope better with Gerald tonight.

She wished she had something to give Jim, something that said thank you for being a good man, having led as good a life as you knew how to, but there was nothing. His and Doris's eyes seemed to say that her coming was enough. She wished that she had been as good as they believed.

Doris's phone call had eliminated the need for her to see the people on the old farm; they were quite happy for her to wander round as suited her. With a rare and surprising tact, Doris had simply said she was a girl who used to live across the road, without saying it was the girl on telly, or anything that would make them offended if she didn't go and say hullo.

The spring growth was coming away nicely and she wondered if they'd make hay this year. The trees were alive with buds and the breaking hawthorn. A living landscape and a dying people.

She didn't stay as long as she had expected. the air was full of ghosts; her own ghost was strung between earth and sky on a fallen poplar branch, full of hope and dreams. She wasn't that girl any more, but someone different, a stranger in a foreign land. The channel of the river had been cleared of willows and it flowed cleanly between the banks. A dark flash flicked through the shadows on the water. The eels, always the eels.

At least she still recognised the perils beneath calm surfaces.

She walked thoughtfully away, back up to the car. Perhaps some day she would bring Emma here. She might know what to make of it. The others would make their way here of their own accord, if they wanted to. It was hard to know what it all meant. Now she would go to her parents, to their old age, and their pride, and their loneliness, to their talk of 'home' and 'the old Dart' which had become a dream that went the way of most dreams.

Harriet rang Leonie Coglan on her return, but Laurence, the younger of her sons, told her that Leonie had left for Toronto the previous week. He would give her a forwarding address if she liked, and she listened while he read out an address. It was care of someone who she recognised from the name as being Leonie's lover. So he was real after all.

'When will she be coming back?' she asked, and was not surprised to hear that she wouldn't be back at all.

This time, Harriet knew she would not see Leonie again, unless through some fateful accident. She thought that in the back of her mind she had always expected to see Leonie again, after returning to Weyville and finding her gone. This time it was final.

In part, she supposed that she must be responsible, and was sad, but really thought that there was little that she could have done. She and Leonie had tried to resurrect some common bond, and it had failed. Someone was bound to be hurt. She was sorry that it must be Leonie's children, and presumably, through her parting with them, Leonie herself. She hoped the compensations of flight

342

warranted what she felt she must do.

Harriet believed she might have loved Leonie once, and again, twice. But it was too late. As she might love Max. Leonie had been right to suspect them of complicity. Harriet had seen the flash of suspicion in Leonie's eyes. And it was true, she and Max were in some kind of collusion, but now Max had become a watcher and a waiter. He waited for her when he might have gone away. He saw her when she thought he did not. He waited for her to see him, through the eyes of other men, as if they were the field of discovery, and he the object of her exploration. Leonie had been wise to go away; perhaps Max was wise to stay. But that was his business. Harriet had come to a point where what she most wanted was to see herself.

To be sure, there were times when she would wonder how Leonie was, and if her going had been worthwhile, but it didn't do to dwell on the subject too much. One thing she believed she had learnt was that she and Leonie belonged to a breed of women who were indestructible. They were survivors. As Wendy was. Or Julie. (Remember Julie?) Or her daughter Genevieve, or her mother. Mary might prove her triumph only by outliving Gerald, but Harriet knew she would do it.

Some days she would watch Emma with a special quiet anxiety. She was not so sure about her. Looking round at the brittle fragile lives of her friends and colleagues, she could see that some of their children were watching them all, and deciding that the price of survival was too high. Then they would quietly fold their lives away, leaving gaping wounds and unanswered questions. In those moments, she would wish with a fearsome intensity that might even have been prayer, that Emma too, would survive, that she would be not only of her, but like her.

There was also a note for her at work from Michael Young when she came back from the north. 'I came back to town looking for you. I couldn't leave things the way they were,' he had written. 'Will I see you again before I leave?'

She scrawled 'No' across it, initialled it and sent it back to him. Let his secretary deal with that.

Not that she wished Michael any harm. She even admired him in a distant detached kind of way. Now it was difficult to understand the unrelenting passion with which she had surrounded him in the past year. It was a manufactured magic, but there had been moments of reality too. She was glad about that. He was her golden eagle still, and he would soar back across the seas, maybe a little wiser, a little more compassionate, she hoped a little more careful about middle-ageing ladies. Even French mistresses should be approached with care, she suspected.

Cousin Alice died soon afterwards and left her a considerable amount of money. Don Everett turned up at the funeral in Weyville. He seemed pleased to see her and offered her a ride back to the house, as she had flown up and was without a car. He'd joined the National Party, he said. It had taken him a long time to see the light but that was what growing old did to you, you turned to the right when you saw how the Polynesians were taking over the country. She said there was no harm in being right-wing, that was his business, but did he have to be quite so reactionary? He asked her if she'd like to go down to the lake and have a bang for old time's sake. She gathered he was asking her to have sex, remembered, as she refused, that she had rather liked Miriam once, and might still do, but the effort of finding out seemed too great. Interesting to think about Miriam after all these years. Another survivor.

Cousin Alice's children materialised like vultures. They advised Harriet through legal channels that they considered her a pretender to the money she had inherited and knew she'd always been after their mother's money. They were going to contest the will; Harriet negotiated a settlement through her lawyers which reduced her share to a few thousand dollars. Apparently it was acceptable in view of the amount of money that it would have cost them to take her to court, and they let her have it.

She could have spent it on a trip away. Only a few months before, she certainly would have done. But there was the mortgage, and her car was on the point of breaking down for good. They would put some of the money aside and let it gather some interest, and maybe, next year, someday, they would go to Fiji, or Australia, something like that.

You really did have to learn young if you were going to be a high flier. But then again, the meaning of her commitment was becoming clearer.

One other thing changed. She got too fat to front her programme. At least, that's what they said. She promised to go on a diet. She'd done that before, Terry said. It never worked for long. She argued that she was good at her job; men got fat and didn't get demoted. That was different, said Terry. Men understood other men getting fat and women forgave them. They didn't forgive women. That was letting the side down. She could have made more of a fuss, but eventually she decided against it. She still had time on her side, and something would always turn up. In fact, her new season ticket had only just begun.

For fat, she read middle-aged. She had reached a watershed, the middle-aged New Zealand woman. But it was a timely break for her.

Time to start fighting free of labels. Time to be herself, rather than an image. Time, if you like, just to be a woman. And some time, too, to write down what it had all been like and how she had arrived at the present, as a preparation for the future. Come to think of it, she had always had time on her side.

MORE ABOUT PENGUINS

For further information about books available from Penguin please write to the following:

In New Zealand: For a complete list of books available from Penguin in New Zealand write to the Marketing Department, Penguin Books (N.Z.) Ltd, Private Bag, Takapuna, Auckland.

In Australia: For a complete list of books available from Penguin in Australia write to the Marketing Department, Penguin Books Australia Ltd, P.O. Box 257, Ringwood, Victoria 3134.

In Britain: For a complete list of books available from Penguin in Britain write to Dept EP, Penguin Books Ltd, Harmondsworth, Middlesex UB7 0DA.

In the U.S.A.: For a complete list of books available from Penguin in the United States write to Dept DG, Penguin Books, 299 Murray Hill Parkway, East Rutherford, New Jersey 07073.

In Canada: For a complete list of books available from Penguin in Canada write to Penguin Books Canada Ltd, 2801 John Street, Markham, Ontario L3R 1B4.

The Woman Who Never Went Home
and other stories
Shonagh Koea

An often startling first collection of short stories, by a New Zealand writer of unusual ability. The women at the heart of this book take themselves off to French Polynesia, to the great sub-continent of India and to the teeming cities of the East. Buffeted by the swirl of humanity, they stand aloof on behalf of visions of what might have been.

The fourteen stories in *The Woman Who Never Went Home* range widely and with a wicked indulgence of their characters' powers to deceive themselves along with everybody else.

Merciless in focus and disconcertingly funny, the stories reveal a major talent of unsettling perception.

Electric City
and other stories
Patricia Grace

Thirteen new stories by Patricia Grace, in which the joys of discovery are tempered by the knowledge of a harder, colder world. Sunlight, childhood and nature set against conflict and misunderstanding, in the ever-present shadows of the spirit of the land.

After the major success of her novel *Potiki*, Patricia Grace returns to the short story. Haunting, delicate, deceptively simple, these are the work of Grace at her very best.

Oracles and Miracles
Stevan Eldred-Grigg

Ginnie and Fag are twin sisters growing up in the Christchurch of the thirties and forties, a city of peeling paint, flaking iron, cracked linoleum, dusty yards, lean-tos and asphalts, dunnies and textile mills.

Soon their lives will change. But in the meantime let's join them on their treadmill of dreams, a fantasy world where dreams do come true and where like Ginnie and Fag we find 'love, love which conquers all, love which takes goose maidens and factory girls and school kids and Cinderellas and carries them off . . .'.

Rarely has New Zealand working-class life been captured with such power and precision as in this rich, unusual novel.

'Oracles and Miracles is marvellous and stylish and lovely.'

Fiona Kidman